Cities of Glass

Roger Collins

ALL THINGS
THAT MATTER
PRESS

To Bob
Thanks for
your support!
Roger

I dedicate this book to my parents, Mrs. Eda Collins and Mr. Vincent Collins. They and their love were the source.

Acknowledgment

My journey from writing nonfiction to writing fiction was surprisingly and enjoyably challenging! The surprise arose from my naiveté and the joy from the support I received along the way. And so, I'd like to thank Ursula DeYoung, founder and editor of Embark Literary Journal, who published the first two chapters of my novel in Issue 10, October 2019. I believe the journal's mission to bring attention to emerging authors nudged me toward publication. I'd also like to thank the numerous leaders of writers' workshops in which I was one of the dozens of hopeful novelists awaiting your words of wisdom. I like to think I've heeded at least some of your advice. And most importantly, I'd like to thank the steadfast writers of two mutually assisting support groups in Cincinnati, ISG and Inktank, with whom I shared countless drafts on my journey. Thank you so much for your help along the way!

Our plane dropped below the rainclouds and a steel gray sky replaced the impenetrable mist that was now visible only above us. Below, the rain-dappled sea rose quickly, roiling blue, green, and gray, and I squeezed the armrest, bracing myself against the sensation of free-fall.

The speakers hummed, barely audible.

"Ladies and gentlemen," our flight attendant announced. "We've been cleared to land and will begin our final descent. Your seat harness will be fastened shortly, so please make any final preparations you require at this time."

Her faint West Indian accent couldn't have been more soothing, and I loosened my grip on the armrest. The sweet scent of tea-tree oil diffused a calming aroma throughout the cabin.

We swooped downward toward Piarco Jetport as though on a magic carpet, the capital's skyscrapers, visible through the transparent fuselage, twinkling like crushed glass in the burnt-orange sky.

"On behalf of United Caribbean Airlines and our entire crew," our stewardess continued, "I'd like to thank you for joining us on this trip and we are looking forward to seeing you on board again in the near future. Please enjoy your stay in Trinidad and Tobago."

***

I'd scanned my fellow passengers before departing LaGuardia, wondering who were tourists, natives, and who were like me, a little of both. Returning home after a long absence had always filled me with an uneasy mix of emotions: the excitement of a tourist and the self-assurance of a native.

The jetport's concourse hummed with scores of scooters, cars, and bubble-cabs whisking travelers to their homes or hotels, like blood cells carrying nutrients to vital organs.

"Commerce, the lifeblood of our nation," as Mother would say.

And I wondered what she would say about her daughter quitting her job. About her daughter returning home unemployed. At thirty-three, my very dependence on her support was maddening, reliance on a crutch I couldn't wait to be free of. And then I thought of her, eagerly awaiting my arrival, and I cringed at my analogy.

I hopped onto a conveyor which took me to the cabstand on the outskirts of the terminal where actual drivers waited for arriving passengers. The robotics of the Northern sphere had yet to replace the human labor of the developing South and there was something quaint and romantic about hiring a carbon-based chauffer.

"The Plaza Hotel, please," I told my driver, who was an East Indian woman watching a football match on the cab's monitor.

"Business or pleasure, ma'am?" she asked, guiding the cab toward the automated highway.

"Both," I said. Please, please, I thought—don't ask me to elaborate. I didn't want to spend my ride describing the job-hunting that awaited me.

"Well, welcome to Trinidad."

I sighed with relief as we transferred onto the new St. Ann Extension and glided past patches of brilliant wildflowers and manicured gardens, their leaves and petals vibrant in the darkening twilight. Roadside merchants were closing down their food wagons even as the scent of curry and ginger still lingered in the air, making my mouth water.

"Who's king of calypso this year?" I asked.

She told me. And the name of his band and queen of calypso, too. "I can play the road march winner." The screen on the backseat glowed for a moment.

"No, thanks," I said. "Just curious. I'd rather look outside."

She shifted our cab to manual-drive on St. Ann's and steered through several blocks of opaque buildings—brick, wood, and stone—a portion of town that would have been called "Old" in the North, like "Old Manhattan" and "Old Detroit," but too common in Port-of-Spain for a quaint moniker.

Then we turned a corner and the Plaza Hotel loomed ahead of us, a giant glass tower, two-score stories tall, radiating light and life from within. It had been six years since I'd seen it in person, and then only the skeleton of what it would become. Seeing it now, the newest construction downtown, shining on its surroundings like a colossal lantern, a shiver of pride passed through me. It looked like a magnificent shrine, a sign of my homeland's bright and prosperous future. As if in affirmation, our cab jerked onto roadway automation and delivered me up to the hotel's dazzling entrance.

When I reached the registration desk, I glanced up at the camera to be identified. The clerk, a young, brown-skinned man, casually walked over and scanned the readout above the desk.

"Good evening, Ma'am Anueche," he said, returning to me. I nodded. "Welcome home."

I smiled at my second welcome within the hour. But unlike my cab driver's, the clerk's came with a glimpse of my abridged bio.

"Your bags have been delivered to your room," he said. "One night's stay, I see. Please let us know if we can assist you in your travels tomorrow."

On my way to the lift, I passed the lobby, intrigued by the large crowd gathered there and the thrum of their conversations, punctuated by laughter, and clinking glasses and tableware. If not too tired, perhaps I'd return, I thought, mostly to look and listen—to see and be seen— given I doubted I'd know anyone.

I arrived outside my third-floor room, had my retina scanned, and entered. Four strides forward or sideways defined my living quarters, but the furnishings were immaculate, comfortable, and well beyond the budget of an unemployed scientist. Besides, the suitcase and knapsack on the bed fit easily under it, and I needed only room enough to accommodate a few toiletries and traveling clothes. Plus, the small size of the room prompted me to leave it and explore the lobby below.

On street level, the hum of the spacious reception area drew me like a magnet—the laughter, the banter, the ambient jazz so compelling I found myself meandering among the guests, soaking up their good cheer. These were mostly the beautiful people who traveled the world, but who found themselves in Port of Spain that evening, speaking of other locales like Havana, Miami, London and of far-flung friends and relatives. Their fashionable dress accessorized the lobby's décor, their outfits of see-through silk, chiffon, and translucent leather complementing the glint of glass all around us. I glanced at myself, a ghostlike reflection on an interior wall, and felt more than a little under-dressed in my coarse, cotton travel-wear.

My passage through the lobby brought me to the entrance of a tapas restaurant where the clock above the door read 9:30—too late to eat and too early for bed. I stepped outside onto the portico and squinted under the glow of the arc lamps. A Flying-Eye descended from the scaffolding and hovered above me, watching and recording, before returning to its perch. I looked past it, at the black sky, now clear of clouds and speckled with starlight, and decided to head east and window-shop along the boulevard.

I felt less conspicuous outside the hotel, my opaque attire more forgivable on the street. The air was fresh, the night breeze gentle, and the lampposts' fixed-focus cameras blinked their obligatory attention to everyone's comings and goings.

It took several blocks for the hotels, banks, and office buildings to give way to the boutiques and storefronts I was eager to browse— Chantilly Chateau, Crystal Bliss Gemstones, and Sea Aster Skin Bar. And following them came more modest shops, Ali's Roti and Roxy's Pizza, and Ricardo's Bake and Shark—a montage of displays that conjured memories from my youth and long dormant nostalgia. As I continued, the signage appeared darker, more difficult to read, as the lampposts became fewer and farther apart. And the fixed-focus cameras were no longer blinking.

I stood still as a thin layer of sweat chilled my forehead. It had been several years since I'd felt this unease, this sense of being alone, of having no one watching over me, of being completely invisible. I glanced at the stores and houses around me, at their impenetrable walls, feeling suddenly lost, disoriented, as though I'd been misplaced.

I turned to backtrack toward downtown; my footsteps echoing as though amplified, the sound sapping the strength in my legs, as though I were walking uphill. But the glow of the business district ahead of me grew brighter and my breathing easier. I thought of Mother's crazy saying, her reprimand for my wandering too far from home as a child: "Tie-goat don't see what loose-goat see." I'd always wondered if her warnings and overprotection contributed to driving me away from home as an adult. It was a theory anyway. A theory without a test.

Then, in the distance, I heard another's footsteps, asynchronous with my own, but with a longer stride, a heavier step. A man's, I guessed. Walking in my direction, catching up to me as I stood, waiting.

I breathed a sigh of relief. Company. Safety.

The other's footsteps slowed and then stopped. For too long, I thought. When they started again, they sounded softer, as though the person were walking on tiptoes. The apparent caution surprised me. For one odd moment, I thought he might be afraid of me.

I was about to call out reassurance, when a man's silhouette emerged out of the dim lamplight, stepping slowly, watchfully it seemed, toward the brick wall of a home on the opposite side of the street. He reached into a jacket pocket and pulled something out.

Instinctively, I glanced up at the naked lamppost, with only its globe to illuminate the scene. I hadn't yet reached the capital's zone of surveillance.

The man walked to the wall and began moving as though writing on the brick. I watched, transfixed, like a child watching someone light a fuse to fireworks, eager and anxious at once.

He stepped back and then turned to me as if to show off his handiwork:

ONLY THE GUILTY HAVE REASON TO FEAR

My gaze shifted between the man and the words he'd written, a phrase I recalled from history classes: one of those iconic quotes every schoolchild studied. His phrase was a rallying cry during the birth of the Age of Transparency. Only the guilty have reason to fear. Supporters of transparency explained that innocent citizens had no reason to fear universal surveillance.

The guilty, however, the terrorists, embezzlers, rapists, insider traders, and nuclear cheats were the ones who had reason to oppose close scrutiny. But that battle was fought and won decades before I was born. Why would this man commit a criminal act to advocate a truism that contradicted his own behavior?

He stared at me, motionless, as though giving me time to recognize the phrase and wonder at his intention. Then he walked back to the wall, turned to write more, and, finally, showed me his revision.

NOT ONLY THE GUILTY HAVE REASON TO FEAR

The revision turned his original statement into a word-puzzle I couldn't solve. Who *else* would have reason to fear Transparency other than the guilty?

He took a step forward and gestured to his face with a childish innocence seemingly designed to reassure me. In the dim light of the lamppost, I could see his face wasn't the flesh I'd assumed but was covered in white latex—a mask that couldn't disguise, revealing, as it did, the bone structure beneath it, sufficient enough for any face-recognition program to identify him. If there'd been a camera nearby.

A sick, sinking feeling filled my gut and I stumbled away from him and began to run toward the lights downtown. I wasn't sure what I was running from. I wasn't sure what I'd just witnessed. It felt assaultive. But was it hateful? Rebellious? Simply fantastic? The answer didn't matter, of course. The man, his act, was something to run from as fast and as far as I could manage.

The next morning, I awoke in the half-light of dawn, eager to start the day. There was no return message from the authorities who took my statement on the incident of the previous night. That was fine with me. I'd done my duty and now they would do theirs. I had other duties to attend to. Besides, I wanted to distance myself from that offense as soon as possible.

I checked my suitcase and knapsack, packed mostly with the gear I'd need for the interior: hiking boots, micromesh jumpsuits, raingear, and a safety helmet I couldn't imagine any use for. I ran a hand over the clothing and reminded myself that the rainforest may be lovely, dark, and deep, but the protective armor required was utterly vulgar in its opacity.

The room's glass interior wall began to glow, surprising me, as it glazed pearly white—an incoming transmission. It took only a moment to recognize the brown face of the older man who resolved into view.

"Welcome home, Fitima," he said.

"My third welcome since I arrived," I said, greeting Lloyd, my pollster, the man who'd been surveying my opinions since I was old enough to have any.

"The third time's the charm," he said, smiling. "Speaking of which, is this a good time?" I glanced at the time stamp below his image. "I booked a cab. I'm heading to Mother's camp."

"I assumed so," Lloyd said. "Do you have time to talk?"

"A few minutes," I said, propping myself on the edge of the bed.

"Well, first off, your flight. Departure, arrival, transfer. Separately or together."

"Together: ten out of ten. One awful surprise ... which I'd just as soon forget."

"We have our obligations though, don't we? So please, do tell."

I gave Lloyd the description of the incident I'd given the authorities, swallowing my disgust, but feeling satisfied at having fulfilled my responsibility to appraise the experience, objecting only to not being able to assign it a negative number.

"Thank you," Lloyd said. "I know re-visiting that bit of nastiness wasn't pleasant." He stroked his chin, assessing my expression. "A few more questions?"

I nodded.

"I see you haven't had any contact with your colleagues since you—"

"*Former* colleagues," I interrupted.

"Correct. You've had no contact with any of them since you left."

"Since I quit. No, I haven't."

"Do you feel the same way about quitting?"

"It's only been two weeks since you asked that. Do you think I'd change my mind in two weeks? Of course, I still feel the same way. I wish I didn't have to quit, but I'm fine with quitting given the circumstances."

"Okay, okay," Lloyd said. "You know I have to ask. Stability of attitude, and all that. We have to sample your attitudes over time."

"Well, my attitude hasn't changed. I'm fine with quitting."

"And by *fine,* you mean what exactly?"

"Eight point four. Same as last time."

"I'm sorry, Fitima, I know the topic is still raw."

"The wound, you mean." I stood and buckled my knapsack, then glanced back at him. "I haven't told Mother yet. About the job."

"I'm not surprised," Lloyd said. "You're an old fashioned kinda girl. I'm guessing you want to tell her in the flesh."

Yes, Lloyd did know me, but after all, that was his job. He'd had his finger on the pulse of my opinions for as long as I could remember.

"I think we should stop here," Lloyd said. "I'm threatening reliability, aren't I? You deserve a chance to get settled."

"Thank you."

"I'll be in touch," he said. "Tell your mother I said hello."

She would appreciate that. She'd always been fond of Lloyd. Some parents requested and usually received permission to change their child's pollster, but Mother did more than approve of Lloyd. She actually liked him. Of course, she had more interaction with my pollster than I had with hers, so I could only hope, for her sake, she held her own in such high regard.

I ate a quick breakfast at the hotel and waited outside for my ride inland. A bubble-cab rolled up to the entrance and the driver stepped out, leaving a passenger seated in the rear. I'd booked a private cab, so I didn't pay them much attention.

"Ma'am Anueche?" the driver said, surprising me.

I nodded.

"I'm your driver."

I glanced again at his passenger, who didn't appear to be leaving. "I reserved a private cab."

Now the driver, too, looked at his passenger. "Sir?" he called out.

The rear window rolled down and the face of a young man filled the frame. "Your mother sent me," he said matter-of-factly.

I stood speechless for a moment. This was the price of dependency, I thought. I hadn't paid that price for half a dozen years, but it was now coming back to me.

"Of course," I said, not to either man in particular. To the heavens perhaps. "I reserve a private cab and Mother sends an escort."

The passenger shrugged and the driver took my knapsack and suitcase as I slid into the backseat.

"Nelson Woon-Sam," my escort said, nodding politely.

"Pleased to meet you." And I might have been pleased to meet him at Mother's camp, but I'd been looking forward to a quiet, introspective drive there.

The cab rolled down the ramp and onto the automated roadway. "May I call you Fitima?"

"Why, yes," I said.

Several silent minutes passed while I regained my composure, readjusted my expectations. "What's your role with the project?" I asked.

"Civil engineer."

That surprised me. His calloused, sunbaked hands and mud-spattered jumpsuit made him appear more like a laborer than a technician. I looked at him more closely. Nelson Woon-Sam, African-Chinese, I assumed, even if his eyes were more striking for their grayish tint than their almond shape. A handsome man, I concluded.

I nodded toward the driver. "A couple round trips for our cabbie, eh?"

"Hey, it's a federal project," Nelson said. "Besides, you wouldn't want me to pick you up in any of our excavation vehicles."

"How long have you been with the project?" I asked.

"From the beginning. Six months."

"How's it going? The project, I mean."

"Well. Very well."

"How close to completion?" I pressed.

"Close."

"Let me guess. Very close."

He smiled at me. "Exactly."

"Well, I hate to be pushy, but could you be more specific?"

His smile smoothed into a serious expression. "I don't mean to be difficult. Your mother said she wanted to fill you in. Insisted," he added.

I understood that operative word. "Okay."

"I'm sorry, but—"

"No, really. It's fine."

I turned and looked out the window. I was more disappointed than angry. Reconciled. Outside, the palm trees on the hillside edged closer to the road as we continued, eventually darkening the roadway in their shadows. I caught a glimpse of Nelson's reflection on the window, and I could see him watching me, and I found myself enjoying the attention. The road broke into a pasture and his image faded with the sunlight.

"How'd you like the States?" he asked.

"Great place to make a living," I said, spying a lone white egret strutting in the field.

"Especially for a mathematician," he said.

I turned and glanced at him, wondering if he'd learned this from Mother or if he looked me up in the Repository.

"Will you be staying long?" he asked. "I mean at the compound?"

"It's hard to say," I shrugged, realizing we'd exchanged roles. He now the eager questioner and me the reluctant responder.

"Well, you better come up with an answer," he said. "That's the second question your mother will ask after how are you."

Now I smiled. "You're right. The problem is I've got a hundred possible answers."

The cab stopped to allow a shepherd boy to lead three scrawny Brahman cattle across the road and I recognized we'd long since left the automated highway.

"What's it like at the site?" I asked.

The sound of cowbells clanged through the cab's closed window as the cattle ambled across the road.

"The locals say everything living there is armed with thorns, claws, or venom."

"Locals?" I said. "In the forest?"

The cab jerked forward, moving into a tract of rolling hills.

"Poachers," he said. "They come to steal fledgling macaws from their nests. I think that thorns-claws-venom business is what they tell newcomers to scare them off. Of course, that didn't work with us. We cleared them out."

Our cab continued south along the coastal highway, passing intermittently through palm groves and stretches of seacoast on our left. When I was a child, Mother told me if you flew due East, you'd hit Africa's west coast, the slave coast, she called it, then had me look it up in the Repository.

We took a sharp right onto a road that cut through a dark mangrove wood. We'd entered the rainforest.

"Vehicular guidance," Nelson said, pointing at the newly laid road, an amalgam of dirt, clay, and quartz.

"Out here?"

"We're bringing tourists to the forest," he said. "Commerce, the lifeblood of our nation."

I smiled inside, recognizing one of Mother's maxims. I glanced up at the treetops, catching glints of glass and steel.

"Cameras, too?"

"Out here, yes. Further in, no."

"Further in, like Mother's compound?"

"Correct. We've got cameras inside the trailers, of course. Standard issue. But none around the campsite as yet. We've laid the infrastructure, though. Surveillance will be up and running soon."

Very soon, I thought.

"For the tourists," he continued. "They'd expect nothing less."

Along the way, he pointed out the progress they'd made: the visitors' centers, the viewing platforms mounted high in the canopy, the zip lines and eco-trails, the footbridges, and transportation hubs. His pride in these accomplishments were unmistakable.

I wished I could feel as upbeat about their work. I had taken great exception to Mother's move from her office into the forest. She was an architectural planner, after all, not a field hand. But I couldn't blame her superiors—she'd volunteered for the assignment. As usual, our argument over this change in workplace didn't last very long. We just added this difference of opinion to our list of let's agree to disagree.

Our cab continued through stretches of dry grassland, marsh, and inky ponds, accompanied by the intermittent shrieks of parrots and howler monkeys and the oscillating hum of countless cicadas. In the distance, the hiss of laser-saws grew louder, along with the crack and rustle of falling trees. A faint smell of ozone and burnt wood seeped inside the cab. Then, quite suddenly, we emerged from a tree-lined tunnel into the sunlight, a grassy clearing ringed with bright yellow construction trailers and mud-crusted excavation vehicles.

"Welcome to the end of the road," Nelson said.

The door of the trailer opposite us sprang open and Mother stood in the doorway, her arms outstretched. "Fitima!"

We ran to each other and met in the middle of the clearing. She felt soft yet strong in my arms, and my heart swelled in the warmth of her embrace.

"Let me look at you," she said, holding me at arm's length. "You look wonderful."

"It's great to see you. It's great to be home."

We stood several moments gathering each other up through our senses, our first in-the- flesh meeting in six years, filling in the blanks of the digital images we'd exchanged during that time. I inhaled her shower-fresh mango scent and brushed my cheek against hers, her mahogany skin as smooth as most women's my age. At sixty-five, she still carried herself with amazing youthful grace. She'd combed her white hair into a kinky bun on top of her head, leaving a few thin braids to fall on the sides and tickle my neck.

She took my hand and led me toward her trailer while calling to Nelson over her shoulder to take my knapsack and suitcase to the trailer next to hers.

"An escort, Mother?" I muttered. "Please."

"He's a good man, but—I don't know. Maybe not your type."

I tightened my grip on her hand. "And now, reverse psychology? You're a bit transparent."

She shrugged. "Shouldn't we all be? Besides, it's my job to find prospects."

Playfully, she pulled her hand back as we stepped into the trailer. The front room felt shrunken. Its ceiling lower than I expected, its walls a bit too close, the furniture scaled down. I sat snuggly on a floral sofa flanked by two mini-armchairs of clashing plaid, one greenish and the other orange. A small bare bones communications desk sat in one corner of the room. An oak-paneled wall divided the trailer lengthwise and a low-slung doorway at the far end led to a parallel room in the rear.

Mother closed the front door and the room dimmed, lit by the peephole in the door and the frosted globe on the ceiling. The muted light, the opaque walls, the very compactness of the place drove me deeper into the sofa.

"Six months out here in the woods," I said, resisting the urge to disapprove. "And so much accomplished."

"We've worked hard, and we've worked smart," she said, sitting on the greenish armchair.

"But there's been a delay, yes?"

"That's another story," she said. "But I want to hear about you. The job troubles? Resolved?"

Back in high school, I'd worked for a store clerk I hated, the feeling being mutual, and I asked Mother what she thought about my quitting, and she said it would be fine—assuming I secured a job to replace the one I left.

"I quit."

"Quit?" she said.

I looked at the communication desk in the corner. "Do I have one of those in my trailer?"

"You just quit?" she said.

"With no backup plan," I confessed. "Do I have one of those?" I repeated.

"Yes, yes … of course."

"Then I can begin my job search here."

She stared off for a moment and then seemed to remember.

"Are you thinking about that job at that grocery store?"

"Oh, Fitima. That was advice when you were young. It was my duty. Life lessons. You never listened, anyway. I'm just sorry things got that bad at the Institute."

"Well, they did. My director refused to post our findings."

"Ramsey?" Mother said.

"Yes. And I gave him many chances."

"What about your mentor? Jim?"

"I complained to him, too. I guess I got a little obsessive. I tried to post data on my own. They deleted it. Ramsey, with Jim's approval. Can you believe it? Scientists deleting data? Hiding data?"

She shook her head. "I don't see how." She pointed to the mini-cam above the communication desk. "I mean, even *we* can't hide out here. Not that we'd want to. Surely *your* work at the Institute was being monitored."

"I know. I can't explain it. Even trying to explain it scares me. How could they circumvent surveillance? And Ramsey claimed that was exactly his intention. But how? Bribery? A breakdown in the system?"

"With the money we spend on surveillance?" she said. "And why? What could justify trying to keep data secret?"

I hesitated to answer, not to keep anything from her, but because the explanation was so complex.

"Ramsey claimed some secrets are justified," I said. "He said secrecy can prevent the misuse of dangerous knowledge."

"Dangerous knowledge?" Mother said. "Your black hole project? Dangerous?"

Ramsey was correct about our results being potentially dangerous, but dangerous or not, there was no precedent for keeping findings secret. At least not in the modern world.

"You'll have to explain your project to me. Yes, yes, I know. I mean explain it *again*. Especially this supposedly dangerous part." She glanced again at the mini-cam in the corner and then trained her gaze on me.

"You have to admit," she said, "it's amazing he told you. Frankly, I'm amazed he *allowed* you to leave."

It was the way she said it, her inflection on *allowed*. Of course, I too was suspicious of Ramsey letting me leave. He had to assume I'd report his transgressions. But Mother's tone darkened my doubts further. Did I have reason to fear Ramsey? Was Mother attempting to warn me? Another life lesson?

She sat back in her seat. "I'm very sorry to hear it."

I sighed, relieved to have finally shared the problem. "I reported it, of course."

"I understand. Necessary. But difficult."

A lump rose in my throat, and I thought I might cry. I'd been too angry to realize how hurt I'd been by the whole affair.

"You haven't heard back?" she asked.

I shook my head, and then remembered the incident in the capital, the graffitist who'd frightened me, who I also reported to the authorities. But I didn't expect to hear back about that.

I told myself I had to separate these two episodes, one an ongoing affair that could possibly affect my career, the other a random, fleeting occurrence. And yet they were both deeply disturbing—violations of the way the world was supposed to work.

"I'm not sure what to expect," I said, "how long before I hear from them." Of course, I'd never submitted a complaint to the International Science Commission. I didn't know anyone who had. "They know I'm out here, of course. They know how to reach me." Which reminded me. "Lloyd says hello."

She beamed. "Well, take some time for yourself, dear. Relax. I'm not sure how much longer we'll be here, but it's peaceful. A well-deserved breather."

I smiled, thinking of Nelson's prediction and how wrong he'd been. Mother never did ask me how long I'd be staying.

Mother walked me to my trailer where I unpacked my gear, and together we walked to the largest trailer in the encampment—wider, longer, and the only one equipped with a refrigeration unit. It was the dining trailer. The crew had already gathered there, a lively bunch of three men, including Nelson, three women, and one male cook. Mother made a point of noting that they represented every continent except Antarctica.

"And we've worked all around the world, too," Nelson said. "Except Antarctica."

We took our seats around a rectangular wooden table which the cook circled, ladling generous portions of curried codfish over our plates of brown rice. As we ate, the crew's spirited chatter grew louder and their tales taller, as each of their former projects was declared largest, or most dangerous, or most important job imaginable. My face flashed at their shamelessness, like watching someone slather on too much makeup before going out in public. Yet their brazenness became more tolerable the bolder their stories, as if the wildness of our surroundings welcomed their immodesty.

After lunch, they left to resume the tree planting, cutting, and trimming—the forest management phase of the project—which they were engaged in when Nelson and I arrived. Nelson lagged behind and chatted with Mother, and I prepared myself to hear their undoubtedly prearranged plan.

Nelson spoke first, clearing his throat. "Would you like to go for a stroll in the forest?"

"Please," I smirked.

"I was hoping you'd appreciate the humor," he said.

"Not that funny," I said.

"But I was serious about the forest," he said. "I mean, about taking you there."

I looked between him and Mother, wondering if they were up to something.

She shrugged. "I'm tied up right now. Administrative work."

"No hidden agenda," Nelson said. "Just thought you'd like to take a look."

I thought about my job search, but I knew that could wait. "Okay," I said, but pointedly turned to Mother. "I intend to hear about that *another story* you mentioned."

"Sure," she said. "It'll keep."

After Mother retired to her trailer, I met Nelson in front of his, directly across from mine. He'd wanted to go back for gear he was now wearing around his waist: a woodland utility belt with a gunmetal gray machete hanging from it.

I pointed to the machete. "Thorns, horns, and fangs, was it?"

"Close. Thorns, claws, *or* venom. And that mantra was *meant* to scare you."

"It does. So does the machete."

He lifted the blade and ran a finger along its edge. "For dangling vines. Maybe some pesky undergrowth. My machete's strictly vegetarian."

"Comforting," I said.

We left the sunlit clearing and headed down a narrow trail into the shadows of the forest. The ground was spongy underfoot and the air smelled of wet leaves, wood, and mud. Our grass-trampled path twisted and turned, and the renewed whine of the crew's laser-saws grew fainter and was eventually drowned out by the drone of cicadas. Tall palms closed in around us, intermittently blocking the sun. Nelson took the lead, of course, and as he'd said, he had to hack overhanging vines in our path from time to time, while I kept close watch on the underbrush, alert for any suspicious movement.

"This path will be a lot easier for tourists," Nelson said. "They'll get to walk on raised composite planks designed to discourage," he winked and glanced down, where I'd been looking, "critters."

"Lucky them," I said, returning to my vigil.

In my youth, Mother and I had visited Trinidad's rainforests and swamps, tar lake, and bird sanctuaries, but I'd been raised a city girl by a metropolitan mother, and our ventures to these remote sites were clearly that, ventures—rare forays into unfamiliar territory. It was one reason I was so annoyed with Mother volunteering to work in the field. The nature of the work and its locale didn't correspond with the experiences of the woman I knew. And, of course, the locale didn't correspond with my experiences either.

As we continued, however, I found myself breathing easier and more able to appreciate the wildflowers unfurling in full glory on the spot lit patches of the forest floor, the bristling life skittering over the rotten stubble of a dead palm stump, and the rippling of a stream somewhere in the distance to our right.

"What did you end up telling her?" Nelson asked.

"Excuse me?"

"How long did you say you were staying?"

I laughed. "Never did get to say. I've been invited for the duration."

"So, she told you about the delay?"

We were crossing a shallow stream, perhaps the one I'd heard earlier, stepping cautiously on the haphazardly spaced flat stones, trying to maintain our balance. My pause seemed natural, an expected concentration on the task at hand, and not an unnatural meditation on lying. Later, I'd wonder if I'd been infected by Ramsey's secrecy. Or I'd suffered a side effect of the graffitist's lawlessness. Perhaps the crew's fabrications or the absence of cameras in the forest had tilted me toward deception. Regardless of the reasons, I found myself considering lying to Nelson.

He stepped on solid ground and extended a hand to pull me alongside him. "Having fun yet?" he said.

I quickly nodded, distracted.

"Well," he continued. "She told you about it."

"The delay?" I said. "Yes, she did."

I knew it was a lie. I understood his question and I answered freely with a false statement I knew he'd interpret to be true. Mother had only admitted to the delay I'd mentioned to her. She had not told me about it. That was another *story* she'd promised to tell me.

As children, we'd laugh at accounts in the Repository describing how grownups once fooled themselves and each other with such notions as white lies. We'd learned truth-telling before we could talk. Every child recalls at least one time in the swimming pool, watching dark blue dye stream from between their legs as they urinated in the pool's telltale waters.

Repeat after me, children, our caretakers would lead the choral refrain: *Truth and lies: All will be revealed.*

"So now you know," Nelson said, startling me. "We wait while the archeologists fight it out with the Ministry of Tourism."

I let go of his hand. I knew lying had its consequences. Guilt and shame. But now I could feel them burning my skin, prodding me to bury my face in my hands.

"Are you okay?" Nelson asked.

"Yes ... it's just that—"

"I know, but I can assure you, we're nowhere near the grave sites. We've walked in the opposite direction."

I felt as though I'd been pushed into that training pool, drowning in a vortex of blue telltale water.

"I-I ..."

A loud echoing grunt broke my stammer. The ghostly sound came from somewhere above us, but from a direction I couldn't determine. And then another.

Nelson looked up into the canopy. "Howlers."

I caught my breath and regained my composure. "Like this morning? But they sound different."

"They're closer," he said. "And right now, they're greeting us. This morning they were greeting each other. They'll pipe down as soon as we pass. But they'll start up again tonight."

I had no answer for that prospect, at how such an unearthly sound could carry a certain kind of splendor.

"But about our delay," Nelson continued.

"I'd rather not talk about it," I interrupted. "Not now, anyway. Later, okay?"

He looked at me as though something might be wrong.

"I just got here, remember? Give me a little time."

He nodded as though his question had been answered. "Sure. Sure."

I wished I knew nothing rather than the snippets about gravesites, archeologists, and conflict with the Bureau of Tourism. But I'd heard too many proverbs against lying to think I could escape punishment for my transgression. I would just have to endure the suffering I deserved.

We stepped out of the shadows of trees into a circular sunlit clearing of flaxen grass that looked as though it had been carved out of the forest.

"This field looks almost artificial," I said.

"A fire-meadow," Nelson said.

"But the perfect shape."

"A lightning strike, a fire, a sudden downpour, and voilà—a ring from Mother Nature."

I stared across the field, about four hundred meters wide, and spotted the outline of a structure that also appeared man-made.

"What could *that* be?" I said.

"Looks like a hut."

"*Looks* like," I said. "Haven't you been here before?"

He shook his head. "Not to this particular spot." He spread out his arms, referring to our surroundings. "There are thousands of hectares out here, you know."

"Fine, but I'd prefer one you've explored already." I squinted into the distance, recognizing the structure was indeed a hut. "You did clear everyone out, though—right?"

"Yes, as far as I know."

"As far as you—"

"Listen," he interrupted. "Poachers aren't dangerous. They're more afraid of us than we should be of them."

He started off toward the hut.

"You're going over there?" I said, afraid to follow, but afraid to stay behind. Nelson cupped his hands to his mouth and shouted, "Hello."

His call was greeted by a brief burst of birdsong. I stared at him, incredulous.

"No one home," he said.

He continued walking toward the hut while I trailed behind, allowing the distance between us to increase.

The door of the hut swung open, and we both stopped. Then it banged shut again in the shifting breeze.

Nelson started again and I fumed, too afraid to shout my protest and draw unwanted attention.

When he reached the hut, he pushed the door open and stuck his head in. I glanced around the perimeter of the field. Nothing stirred.

"Someone's been living here, all right," he said from inside. "Recently."

I ran my hand along the outside wall, a rock-hard blend of dried mud, grass, and twigs. Tightly woven palm leaves formed the hut's conical roof. Fighting back fear, I stepped inside and caught a whiff of musky dampness. The strip of sunlight seeping past the door shone on a small solar stove on the floor in the middle of a patch of trampled grass. Several dirty rags and a few shrink-wrapped food-packs lay at the edge of a gray blanket covering a small mound.

"Poacher, I'd guess," Nelson said, lifting the blanket, disclosing a bed of dried grass and a strong sour scent. "Planning to stay awhile."

A deep moaning sound came from outside the hut and my heart froze.

Nelson stepped out of the hut, and I joined him, both of us scanning the field for the source of the moan. I jumped at the click of Nelson unlatching the machete from his utility belt.

"What are *you* doing?" I said.

"Preparing," he said. "Not planning. Just preparing."

Before I could object to his word play or his action, the moan sounded again, now clearly a man's. And louder. It didn't sound like someone injured or in pain, but I couldn't determine more than that. Except it didn't sound harmless.

A tall, thin, bearded man stepped from the trees, only forty meters to our right. He looked old, disheveled; I couldn't possibly guess his age. He wore a soiled khaki shirt draped over his shoulders, unbuttoned to his waist, with sleeves cut off at the elbows and large blotches of sweat staining the fabric. Two cords of rope crisscrossed his exposed chest, and another belted his muddy pants. He was barefoot.

"Are you all right?" Nelson called to him.

The man didn't answer.

"Is this yours?" Nelson said, nodding toward the hut.

"Eh, eh—it was." The man narrowed his eyes. "Is it yours now?"

His voice sounded gruff yet melodic. At that point, I judged him to be in his seventies by his salt-and-pepper beard and hair receding high on his forehead.

Nelson pressed the machete behind his right leg, trying hard, it seemed, to appear non- threatening.

"No, it's not ours, sir," Nelson said. "We were just wondering who it belonged to."

The man lifted his arms and spread his legs, reminding me of Da Vinci's Vitruvian Man, but with no reason to strike such a pose. That's when I noticed the machete dangling from his wrist,hanging by a strip of rawhide.

"Looking inside someone else's home," the man said. "Wondering who it belongs to?"

"My apologies," Nelson said. "Curiosity got the better of me."

The man took a step forward and I instinctively looked up for a camera, before remembering where we were.

"Stop right there," Nelson said in voice deeper and more commanding than I'd heard before.

The man stopped.

"I want to be polite," Nelson said. "I'm sorry if I wasn't. But I expect politeness in return."

"Looks like you're prepared to fight for it," the man said, motioning toward Nelson's machete which he'd exposed, voluntarily or not, I couldn't say.

"I'm prepared to defend myself," Nelson said.

"No need for that," the man said, untying the machete from his wrist and lowering it to the ground with exaggerated slowness.

"I'm Nelson Woon-Sam." Nelson turned to me.

My first attempt to speak produced only a dry rasp. "Fitima Anueche," I said finally, hoarsely.

The man grunted.

"And you?" Nelson asked.

The man hesitated, as if the question required thought. "King Juba," he said.

"The calypso singer?" Nelson asked.

"Former calypso singer," he said.

I'd never heard the name, but that wasn't surprising. I'd always felt several steps behind the trends of pop culture.

"What are you doing out here?" Nelson asked.

"What are *you* doing here?" King Juba said.

"We're with the construction project," Nelson said.

"Ah, yes," King Juba said. "Bringing civ-i-li-za-tion to Olokun's land."

I heard the contempt in his voice and glanced at Nelson, assuming he'd heard it, too, and I waited for him to begin our leave-taking from this King Juba. There had to be others, professionals, who dealt with poachers.

King Juba closed his eyes and began to rub them harder than seemed normal, as if he were trying to scratch a deep, burning itch, with such force that a clearly audible squishing sound came from his eye sockets.

"I've seen evil," he said, his eyes closed, "and I can't say it hasn't touched me." He moaned the way he had before we saw him. "Olokun! I call on you to protect this land, to watch over it with your all-seeing eyes—their eyes, be damned."

He opened his eyes, bent to pick up his machete, and lurched toward us. Nelson grabbed my hand and yanked me sideways and we stumbled past the hut and through a wall of thorny scrub behind it. I tried to ignore the thorns scratching and piercing my skin and focused on remaining upright. Don't fall, I thought. This was no time to trip or stumble or become otherwise helpless. I followed closely behind Nelson as we pushed hard against the thicket, progressing, but almost in slow motion. My face burned from cuts and sweat, and I fought against giving in to the pushback of the vines. Nelson stopped and glanced back at me, his grip tightening around my wrist, and he jerked me toward him.

Suddenly, the ground gave way and the world turned upside down and I was slamming against ground, trees, and bush, dazed by the tumbling and the collisions. I drew myself into a ball and rolled wildly down the slope until I landed beside Nelson on a foot-beaten patch of grass. We stood unsteadily and glanced around our surroundings. Nelson pointed left and we headed in that direction, buoyed, or so I felt, by the possibility of escape. I listened for sounds of pursuit behind us, too afraid to turn around, but I heard nothing but our own footfalls and a soft high-pitched whine ahead of us that grew louder as we continued. The crew's laser-saws.

We finally broke into the clearing at Mother's camp, surprisingly close to where we'd left. I bent over and grabbed my knees, trying to catch my breath.

Nelson leaned next to me. "I'm sorry about that," he whispered.

I stood up and winced when I saw his face, crisscrossed with bloody scratches. "You, too," he said, examining my face. "Let's get some treatment for those cuts."

"He wouldn't follow us, would he?" I said.

Nelson shook his head. "Poachers steer clear of us. Don't worry. We'll get him moved out of there by nightfall."

The door of Mother's trailer opened, and she stepped out, staring at us, her expression turning from delight to distress, paralleling my realization that Nelson and I must have been quite a shocking sight.

I need a break from this breather is what I wanted to tell Mother the next morning in the dining trailer. But my empathy for her feelings proved stronger than my impulse to be transparent. She was still upset over the Juba incident. The previous evening, she'd sent several of the crew out to search the area, but Juba had fled. But I could tell she was still upset as she picked over her breakfast.

After breakfast, the crew departed for the forest, and Mother and I walked back to her trailer. We hadn't spoken of our intentions, but we knew we had our own and that an uninterrupted conversation was long overdue. I sat on the sofa and expected her to sit in the chair opposite me, but she sat on the floor in front of me and scooted backward between my knees.

"What's this?" I said.

"Braid my hair?" she asked.

I hesitated, thrown off by the request. Yes, of course. She was still upset. When I was a child, I'd braided her hair from time to time, and it was usually a sign that she'd had an especially difficult day. And I was happy to do so. Braiding Mother's hair was my child's way of showing her my love. But that was decades ago.

"I haven't had much practice," I said.

She nestled her shoulders between my knees.

"I don't have a comb," I said.

She pulled a comb and small jar of pomade from her pocket and held them up to me. I laughed.

"I thought of it this morning," she said. "For old time's sake."

"For present's sake," I said, taking the comb and jar. "But we have to talk."

"Of course," she said, tilting her head back.

I worked the comb through her hair, combing out her bun and squaring off several sections. I dipped my fingers into the jar of pomade, releasing a faint scent of coconut, and began greasing her scalp between the sections.

"I want to hear about your project," I said, determined to learn about the gravesite Nelson had disclosed. My shame about lying to him had been replaced by uneasy curiosity.

"You said ending the project was *another* story," I continued.

"Brace yourself," she said.

My fingers froze around a handful of hair. "We came across several graves," she said.

I held my breath, still shocked to hear what I knew. "Graves?"

"Incredible, no?" She craned her neck to look at me.

"Very. Incredible. In the forest?"

She relaxed and leaned back. "We had to stop the project, of course."

"Of course."

"At least near the graves," she continued. "A team of archaeologists came out here last week." She again turned to look up at me. "Brace yourself."

"Mother, please!"

"Runaway slaves!"

"Whose graves they were?"

She nodded and faced forward.

Of course, I thought … the archeologists. Until then, I'd set that detail aside, a piece of the puzzle that didn't fit. But now and then I considered the time between this year and the official end of slavery in Trinidad, 1834. Almost 300 years?

"Amazing, no?" Mother said.

"Amazing, yes."

Fragments of information popped into mind. Lessons from grade school. My classmates and I learning that actual freedom wasn't granted Trinidadian slaves until 1838, the minimum of four years they were required to serve as apprentices to their former masters. *Beginnings and Endings* never meant the same to me after that.

"Of course, you need to protect the gravesites," I said. "But when will you know how?" Mother shook her head.

I stopped combing. "I assume they cordoned off the gravesites. The archeologists. So, how close can you get?"

"Not very," she said. "But you can see them with field glasses." I'd been combing her hair aimlessly, wondering, imagining.

"What braids would you like?" I asked.

She ran a finger along the part in the center. "Remember the hexagons?"

"Of course. How large?"

"Five centimeters across?"

My fingers started slowly, deliberately, seeking the old rhythm, the warp and woof of that pattern, parting six-sided sections of hair, braiding three strands in the middle of each section, one hexagon after another.

Mother reached up and held my wrist. "Did I ever tell you I thought braiding hair gave you your feel for mathematics?"

I stopped braiding, trying to recall.

"That's my theory anyway," she continued.

I didn't recall her telling me. I examined the honeycomb mosaic taking shape on her head and wondered if that were possible.

"A reasonable theory," I said. "I guess we could rummage through the Repository and look for confirming evidence."

"Or you could simply take my word for it, and we could get on with our lives." We laughed.

"I never got to tell you," I said, "about my adventure in the capital."

"Adventure?"

"Outside the central district. A man defacing a wall. Writing graffiti. Right in front of me."

"But beyond the cameras," she said.

"I know, I know."

"Not that surveillance is the deterrent it used to be," she said.

"What do you mean?"

"Well, the hooliganism, for one," she said.

I remembered that word from the Repository. And its definition: *The flagrant violation of public order expressed by a clear disrespect for society.*

"It got so bad at football stadiums," she continued, "they had to suspend games."

And then I remembered another definition of hooliganism: *the unruly behavior of overzealous fans at football matches.* I'd stopped watching the illustrative film as soon as I saw the ugly violence depicting this definition. "How could that happen?" I said.

"All you need is enough misbehavior in the stands that more fans are watching hooligans than the match. At least that's what I heard."

"But my cabbie was watching a match on my ride from the jetport. I remember it distinctly. I wanted to ask her which teams were playing."

"Recorded," Mother said. "A previous game. Some people can't get enough football, I guess."

"But to suspend matches?"

"A few bad apples. Or just enough, anyway. And they were all under surveillance."

For a moment, I wondered if this problem was peculiar to Trinidad. Then I thought about Ramsey, about how he'd violated protocol while under surveillance. And at a national laboratory right outside New York City.

"So ... what about this dangerous knowledge?" Mother asked.

"You scare me, you know."

"As a mother should."

"I was just thinking about Ramsey," I said.

"Well, please think out loud."

"He said our work would make the discovery of atomic weaponry look like child's play."

"*Your* work?" Mother said. "Sorry. No offense intended."

I tugged gently on a braid. "None taken."

"I said sorry."

"But you're right, to a degree. Our work is all simulation. Computer modeling. Theoretical. Imaginary, you might say. But a good theory can turn out to predict reality."

"Or be wrong," Mother added. She raised her hands in surrender. "Please, no more hair pulling."

"Or be wrong," I agreed.

"So how can your theories be dangerous?"

"Let's drop that whole idea of dangerous. It's a phony excuse. There's no such thing as dangerous knowledge. There may be dangerous people who behave badly with knowledge. And even if some knowledge is more startling or even scary compared to other knowledge, the best defense against danger is more knowledge. It's not *hiding* what you've discovered."

"You're yanking again, dear."

"Sorry."

"Maybe we should continue this discussion after you've finished braiding."

"I said sorry. It's just that ..." and I stopped, realizing the complexity of the explanation she wanted. And recalling the fear that had begun to hover over our work.

7

When I began my graduate studies, Mother asked about my area of specialization. I could have told her simply, astrophysics. I could have even added mathematical astrophysics.

But I felt she deserved more. And I believed she could handle more, but I wasn't sure how much more. So, I began rather simply, knowing it probably wouldn't end that way.

Imagine an everyday apple, I began my explanation, and a worm is crawling on its surface. If the worm wanted to get to the opposite side of the apple, it could crawl along the surface where it would have to travel half the circumference of the apple. But if the worm tunneled through the apple, it would have to crawl one-third less distance in one-third the time to reach the other side.

I study worms crawling through apples, except instead of worms, I study probes, and instead of apples, I study black holes. This is where my analogy departs from reality. A major difference between our apple wormhole and a black hole is that with the black hole, we're tunneling through space and time. When tracking our worm, time isn't a relevant variable.

When it comes to everyday apple-crawling, we can assume time is constant. But in the cosmos, time is not constant. Time slows at velocities approaching the speed of light. Time is also slowed by gravity. Gravity also bends and curves physical space. I'm not talking about the earth's puny gravity. I'm talking huge gravitational forces – like those inside and around black holes. In thinking about black holes, we need to think about its structure in terms of space and time. We need to consider time as a variable in addition to the three dimensions of space which may, in fact, be bent and curved. We need, therefore, to represent location inside a black hole in geo-temporal coordinates, along axes of space and time.

My job, metaphorically speaking, is to follow the worm into the apple and figure out where and when it might end up. In actuality, I calculate the effects of make-believe probes entering make-believe black holes. Oh, black holes are real enough; we've identified scores scattered across the universe. But the ones I study are computer models. That allows us to manipulate variables in our simulations. We can vary the size of their openings—their event horizons. We can vary their electrical charge, the angular momentum of their rotation.

Of course, we can't conduct these experiments in real life because nothing has been invented that could enter a black hole and survive its gravitational forces. But by following make-believe probes through make-believe black holes, we can determine, theoretically at least, where and when they might end up in space-time. In particular, my team wants to know if there's a past the probe can enter. Or whether, as many believe, the present, this very moment, is the only reality in space-time.

I'd decided to pause to read Mother's mood.

She looked at me skeptically. "It sounds to me like you're trying to find a needle in a haystack. Not only where it might be, but when it might be. Or when it was."

Before I could comment, she gushed, "I love it! It seems like you're as much a prophet as a scientist. Of course, I won't tell my colleagues that. I'll just tell them you're an astrophysicist. That should suffice."

I smiled at that memory, interrupted by the shrill caw of a bird that sounded just outside the trailer. Returning to Mother's braids, I gathered the last tuft of hair between my fingers and began weaving a final strand above its hexagonal border.

"The problem is," I said, "sending anything back in time — a quantum of light, a subatomic particle, anything — can be problematic if it were to actually happen. Of course, none of us believe it can happen."

"The impossibility of changing the past and all that," Mother said.

"But then came the secrecy. And Ramsey's rationale for it."

"And he admitted to secrecy."

"In his office. On the record."

"Well ..."

"And getting away with it," I said.

"So far," Mother added. "Getting away with secrecy *so far*."

That would be my next task, even before initiating my job search: exploring the Repository for our results.

"But if I had to think conspiratorially about this," Mother said, "I mean, if I were forced to, I could come up with a couple ideas."

I wanted to see her face, read her expression. Was she serious? Was she playing?

"You have to ask yourself," she continued, "what information might someone send back in time that others, others with clout, would want to keep secret? Information that would bring about political dominance maybe? Financial dominance? Military dominance? Just brainstorming, mind you. But you hear the key word, no?"

I could never tell if Mother's flights of fancy were intended to annoy me or if that was merely their unforeseen effect. Her references to dominance unsettled the temporary peace I'd made with my doubts. Now I had to get back to my trailer to search once again for our research results.

I smoothed my hands gently over her spikey hair. "Finished."

"Thank you, thank you, thank you," she said, clambering up from the floor. She turned to me, and we hugged. "How do I look?"

Her braids and their hexagon frames gave her a wilder appearance than her demure bun.

But I liked her new look. "Beautiful," I said.

"I hope the braids are tight enough to stay braided a while."

"Maybe I should've yanked a little harder," I said with a smile. "I have to get back. Check on loose ends."

We laughed at my unintended pun. She rested her hand on my shoulder. "Don't worry, dear. Really, don't worry. Your job search will go just fine. When one door is closed, another door is opened."

***

Back in my trailer, it took only a moment to determine that our research results had not been posted. I had to decide if I would allow that mystery to haunt me or if I could move on to searching for my next job. I concluded the two were not mutually exclusive, and so, for the next several days, I made myself scarce around camp and turned uneasy attention to contacting prospective employers.

I was familiar with the most productive and respected research institutes in astrophysics. I needed to review their current projects, their recently hired personnel, and their latest budgets. Similarly, my background could be easily accessed by any interested employer. If we did our homework with due diligence, my interviews would consist mostly of social pleasantries and determining the potential synergy among mutually respected colleagues.

The one question that concerned me was the one omitted in my profile: Why I had left Ramsey's project.

Of course, I could refer them to my report and its allegations, but that report had yet to become official, and my personal copies were clearly unofficial. Besides, accusing Ramsey of impropriety in the course of finding a new job was one thing – implicating all of my former colleagues and mentor was quite another.

I could tell them Ramsey's project had lost its appeal. I could say I was looking for a new challenge. Neither would be a lie. But neither was the whole truth, either. Deceit made me feel dirty. Even worse, deceit made me guilty of the same offense I was accusing Ramsey of.

Rather than deceive, I'd have to maintain attention on my agenda: the contributions I could make to their upcoming projects. What do they say? *The past is prologue. The future is now.*

The initial interviews I scheduled went well. Intense and tiring, naturally. Matchmaking of this kind was difficult work. Success didn't rest on a formula. Intuition was involved. Hard data, too, of course. But maximal complementarity depended on matching the transcendent perspectives each scientist applied, individually and collectively, to the physical phenomena under study. And this took a great deal of energy. And a great deal of time.

But my interviews also had unintended outcomes. I couldn't spend much time with Mother or Nelson for several consecutive days. They each had their own responsibilities to attend to and my interviews seemed to always conflict with the times they were available. Nelson wanted to take me to view the gravesites and I was eager to see the discovery, especially after he convinced me we were unlikely to run into another poacher. So, we were pleasantly surprised the afternoon we were both free to finally take that tour together.

As Nelson had promised, we left camp in the opposite direction of the path that led us to King Juba. The hot midday sun blazed only intermittently, in gaps between the palms high above us, spotlighting our way into the woods.

Nelson filled me in on what he'd been doing. Like myself, and the rest of the crew, he was exploring future employment opportunities. No one knew if the Ministers would permit Mother's project to resume or for how long. It seemed only Mother was focusing exclusively on continuing the project.

"It must be difficult," I said. "I mean, the uncertainty of these projects. Trying to plan."

"Have vita, will travel," he said. "That's been my motto. Become a civil engineer and see the world."

"Any home base?"

"Here. Where I grew up."

We stopped at a stairway of logs and flattened earth which led up to and disappeared into a thicket of foliage above us.

"You can see quite a distance from up there," Nelson said, gesturing upward.

The ululating cicadas completed several cycles of rhythmic din before I made up my mind to continue. Then we climbed the steps, past the foliage, reaching a wooden platform circling half-way up the trunk of a broad cypress tree that had been hidden from view. A bridge of wood and rope stretched out before us over a deep verdant valley, disappearing into a similar thicket of foliage on the other side. Nelson stepped onto the bridge which swayed slightly.

"You're kidding," I managed.

"Rather sturdy, I'd say."

"No safety belt?" I said.

"Please. This is a walkway, not a zip line."

I looked down into the valley, scores of meters below.

"We'll only go far enough to get a good view of the gravesite."

I still didn't move.

He pulled field glasses from a cargo pocket and brandished them as inducement. I stepped gingerly onto the wood-and-rope bridge which was surprisingly sturdy.

Nelson's backward glance flaunted an "I-told-you-so" smugness. But it was conjuring the valley below—its depth and its denizens—that fueled the fluttering of my heart, even when, as Nelson advised, I didn't look down. We continued slowly and steadily three-quarters of the way across the bridge, where I could finally see our platform terminus at another old cypress, as well as a high, narrow waterfall and two other canopy walkways in the distance. Nelson stopped and began scanning the eastern side of the valley with the field glasses.

"There," he said, pointing.

He handed me the glasses and oriented my line of sight past a small pond, around a stand of giant fern with roots drooping from their branches, beyond a grassy hillock to a flat parcel marked with five dark rectangles.

"Those patches?" I said.

"Gravestones."

I'd expected vertical headstones.

"The archeologists will survey the extent of the cemetery," he continued. "You can't assume those five are the only ones buried there."

"Are there markings?"

"Faint," Nelson said. "Crude etchings and the stone is overgrown with moss and lichen. But with imaginative reading, you can make out the basics. Names. Dates of births. Deaths. Years, anyway. The oldest death I remember was 1798."

I wished we could get closer, of course, to stand beside the graves. But I understood that precautions had to be taken.

"Were you there?" I asked. "When they made the discovery?"

"No. Wish I was. The crew took photos, though, once they realized what they'd found. Shots of the markings and artifacts. Rusted nails, a couple knives, shards of pottery. A few strings of beads. Red and blue. Maybe meaning to the colors."

Meaning, I thought. Yes, there was meaning, all right, to the entire site. And I wondered what the plans would be to decipher, display, and disseminate that meaning.

"So, you're waiting to hear from the Ministers," I said.

"That and a little more."

"More?"

"You've talked about this with your mother, right?"

"Listen. Let's commit to a free exchange of info, okay? This, *did-you-check-with-your-mother* routine is getting old."

"I'm only cautious out of respect, that's all. There's nothing clandestine going on."

"Great. I'm listening."

"Your mother wants to memorialize the site."

"Memorialize? How?"

"I don't know how. I don't think she knows. But she wants to develop the site as a memorial—add it to the project."

"Add to the *cost*," I said. "I assume that's a part of the debate: can they afford to go over budget."

"Probably. But that's as much as I know. I'm not privy to your mother's negotiations with the Ministers."

Negotiations with the Ministers, I thought. I knew what that meant. It meant Mother was no longer issuing instructions. She was now engaged in a no-holds-barred fight among her most powerful rivals.

8

It didn't surprise me to find Mother at her desk early the next morning. She'd been secluded in her trailer for the last day and a half, which Nelson had explained to me the previous evening. At noon, Mother was scheduled to participate in a video conference to negotiate her proposal to memorialize the recently discovered grave site.

All the heavy hitters from federal would weigh in: The Acting Minister of Tourism, of course, Community Planning and Development. Commerce, The Remember When Institute, Forest and Environment, Animal Husbandry & Fisheries, Rural Development, Information and Public Relations.

After I'd heard the roll call, I was of two opposing minds: their diversity would offer Mother at least a few allies. Or their collective opposition would prove formidable indeed. But not insurmountable.

Preparedness was the key, of course. Intellectual. Emotional. Physical. So I expected Mother to be preparing herself for battle or, at worst, trying to reschedule to give herself more time for eventual victory. What I found instead was Mother sitting at her com-desk admiring a static hologram of a city street scene.

"O-k-a-y," I said, singing my surprise. "What's going on here?"

Mother closed her eyes and pointed to the hologram on her desk, the stationary image of a dozen or more scanty-dressed children standing in a semi-circle, staring at an elderly woman seated on a box.

"It's dusk" Mother said, her eyes still closed. "Scarlet Ibis are flying south to roost in the mangrove swamp behind our village."

I squinted at the still image, but saw no birds, no swamp.

"Children are playing games in the street," she continued. "Hand games, ball games, jump-rope games."

The children I did see, but the image was still. They were simply standing around an elderly woman. Waiting, it seemed.

"Gramma arrives," Mother continued. "She sits on a wooden box under the streetlight. The children are quiet. Then the stories begin."

"Who is she?" I said, examining the old woman's face.

Mother opened her eyes. "You see, Fitima, you must pay attention. If you don't, friends and relatives lose their features. You're left with only thoughts about them."

"But who is she?" I repeated.

"You have only a few trace memories here and there," she continued. "Gnarled fingers. A welcoming smile. And that might be it. That could be all. All that's left of people we once knew."

I sat on the sofa and wondered what to say. I could ask again about the old woman. I could ask why Mother hadn't shown me images of her before. I could have asked why now. Or, more basically, I could have simply asked, why?

"I need these images," she continued. "I prefer the static ones. For reminiscing, I mean. I troll through the Repository and when an image catches my eye, I just say, 'Stop and capture,' and see which moment in time I've caught. Family gatherings are best. Well, they're earmarked so it's easy to retrieve them. Birthdays. Anniversaries. Graduations. Weddings."

She stopped and refocused her attention on me. Although she'd been looking at me, it felt more like she was looking through me.

"Funerals," she continued. "Or gatherings like this one. Storytelling."

"Please send me the image," I said. "Okay?"

She nodded, but absently.

"Don't forget," I said. Gramma, I thought. Maybe I hadn't been paying attention. But I could correct that. I wanted to correct that.

"But why now, Mother? Why this," I asked, pointing to the hologram, "only a few moments before the conference?"

"Why aren't I preparing? I am, sort of."

I muttered my disbelief.

"I'm thinking about history, dear. Personal history. Social history. How far past is the past? Does it depend on how far back you look? Where you look? How often you look?"

I sighed finally figuring the connection—the link between her exploring the Repository and her upcoming conference.

"The graves," I said. "Nelson showed me the site yesterday. An amazing find, really. And now a conference?"

"And now a conference."

"Nelson mentioned … disagreements," I said.

"Could discussions of policy be otherwise?"

"Well, there was consensus about this project before the graves."

"Key word: *was*."

"Disagreements over…?"

"They want to reinter the remains," she said.

"And you?"

"I want the site declared a World Heritage Site."

"We can move the artifacts. A museum, maybe. But we should not relocate the remains."

I recognized her tone, that line in the sand. Except with Mother, it was more a stone wall than a line.

"I agree," I said, for what it was worth. I never knew, exactly. "How's it look? Any straw polls?"

"No actual votes. But I've read memoranda between the lines."

"And their objections?" I asked. Disagreement over project costs, my default assumption, wasn't obvious in this case.

"Revenue. Revenue projections. They assume tourists will buy beauty. Orchids. Butterflies. Waterfalls. Scarlet Ibis roosting at dusk. Not gravesites. Not history. Especially not disturbing history."

"Can you help them re-vision the project?" I asked.

"I hope so. I intend to. Too much beauty can be dangerous."

I'd been following her logic till then. "Excuse me."

"Beauty can be deceptive," she explained. I shrugged, still confused.

"I want tourists to see things that challenge them," she continued. "To see things that might even upset them."

"I was thinking along the lines of history buffs," I said, trying to regain my footing.

"But these officials don't understand the paradox of repulsion. They don't see how something repulsive can offer something of value. They don't believe that feeling the full range of human emotion can deepen one's life."

I maintained my composure despite my growing concern. I agreed with Mother, yet I couldn't follow her logic. I doubted the Ministers would be even willing to try.

"But will repulsion deepen the treasury?" I said. "That's what the Ministers are concerned about. Listen, I agree with you about the graves. But you can't ignore their concerns. You can argue the attraction of history. Cite the numbers who scan the Repository's Age of Memorials. Remind them of those who watch recordings of smoking rubble where buildings once stood—where people once lived. And what about tourists who travel to the actual sites to see the remnants and read inscriptions like *Never a Next Time!*"

"I'll tell them these choices are not mutually exclusive."

"I know. I know," I said. "Listen, your ideals are all well and good, but your project was funded for practical purposes. The Ministers speak revenue. I don't think they're interested in ideals. They want to generate capital. Create jobs. And the competition is relentless. These days, tourists can fly to the moon and climb lunar craters. They holiday at undersea resorts. They don't need our island. Heck, many have islands of their own!"

But I'd finally come to the crux of the matter for me: Mother's reputation. Her legacy. "You're going to scare them to death with your talk of the paradox of repulsion and upsetting tourists."

She laughed. "It sounds like I'm scaring you."

"You are," I said.

She slapped her hands hard against her thighs, startling me. "Then I'll stop." She pointed to the communication desk. "It'll all unfold soon enough. In the meantime, we both have business to attend to, no?"

I was too shaken to understand what she meant.

"That job search?" she reminded.

***

Later that morning, the rain sounded like gravel pinging against the roof and sides of my trailer, the gusts of wind changing the strength and direction of rainfall with hypnotic effect. I struggled to keep my eyes on the holographs of charts and reports floating above my desk as I considered which laboratories to contact.

It took a few seconds for me to recognize the unfamiliar audio signal coming from my com-desk. An incoming communication. I hurried to sort and store the images above the desk, and I opened a channel to receive the new hologram. It was Lloyd.

"Has it been a week already?" I said.

"You must be having fun," he said.

That's not how I would've described it, but I assumed we'd get to that shortly.

"I must admit, though," Lloyd continued, "my poll feels sort of pointless this week. You haven't purchased any merchandise, consumed any restaurant fare, or been exposed to any newscasts."

"None of the above," I confirmed.

"We don't have Q-of-L questions for assessing life in the jungle."

"Really? Too bad. That's all I'm prepared to talk about. Except …"

"Listening …"

"Do you ever offer your opinions?" I asked.

"A pollster offering opinions?"

"What about off the record?"

"We both know there's no such thing."

"Aren't you curious?" I teased.

"Actually, I am. Which means I'll initiate a qualitative line of inquiry where I serve as both interviewee and interviewer. I'll respond to your questions, you'll respond to my responses, and I'll submit our transactions to content analysis. In the end, you'll still be the focus."

"Fine."

"You may begin."

"Well, we never got to debrief an incident back in the capital."

"I apologize," Lloyd said. "I cut our last interview short; omitted the open-ended."

"My question goes beyond that one incident. It was a case of vandalism, plain and simple. But Mother tells me they've suspended football matches here due to hosts of these ... hooligans. That's my term."

"Hooligans?"

"No, hosts. Hooligans is defined in the Repository. But it seems there are hosts of them."

"Go on."

"Well, I'm not sure if this is the same thing, but I ran into a poacher in the forest. And I've been told there've been others. I don't know, but to me it feels like too much law-breaking. Do others feel this way? More importantly, do the authorities feel this way?"

"Well, too much law-breaking is too vague a descriptor for the authorities. But law-breaking, any law-breaking, is always a concern."

"Of course it is," I said. "I'm talking about an increase. And the nature of it. The purposelessness of it."

"Troubling," Lloyd said.

"Yes. Nine-point-five on a ten-point scale! Now, are you going to tell me what you think about this or not?"

"I'll share a few thoughts. Then you tell me what you think. Okay, for starters, a few analysts claim these incidents can be traced back to a few anarchists. These people ... well, let's just say they're special. They crave privacy. Secrecy, even. Their acts of vandalism are protests against full disclosure."

"But who are these people? Where do they come from? It's like civilization stopped evolving for them."

"They say it's random, these analysts. An affliction among some individuals. A need. An obsession, really. And some of them, hooligans, as you call them, act out of frustration of that need." He stopped, observing me closely. "Your thoughts?"

"Interesting. Hard to believe, but interesting." I shook my head, still puzzled. "But why an increase? Are there more of these people now? Or have the few of them been acting up more often?"

Lloyd shrugged. "Or maybe surveillance is detecting more perpetrators. Or maybe all of the above."

"You pollsters track trends. Which is most likely?"

"Can't say. Insufficient data."

"With all we spend on data collection?"

"Well, you're right. It's not so much insufficient data. We've got tons of data. I should've said insufficient analysis. The public wants answers. Insufficient analyses only raise more questions."

"So, if the analyses are insufficient, you don't release anything? Sounds like another case of *dangerous knowledge* to me."

"Don't be so dramatic," Lloyd chided. "When we get answers, we'll disseminate them."

He pinched the bridge of his nose as if annoyed. Or maybe just fatigued. Or perhaps worried.

"What's the matter?" I asked.

He looked me in the eyes. "I need to ask one question, however. A speculative question. Your best guess about a future opinion."

This was new. I had no idea what he was talking about.

He took a breath. "Do you believe you'll ever be as happy in another job as you were at the Institute? I'm not talking about the way things ended. I'm asking you to compare what lies ahead for you compared with how things started at the Institute."

For a few moments, I simply sat there stunned, staring at him.

"What kind of question is that?" I said finally. "You're asking me to predict the future. How can I know the answer?"

"Is your answer that you can't answer?"

I shook my head. "My answer is, I hope to be as happy in my next job. That's my expectation."

"Even though you understand no job is perfect."

"Of course I understand that."

"And given that you and Jim were so—"

"Wait a minute! What are you doing here?"

"I'm establishing a context, a perspective from which you can select an opinion about your prospective new job."

"It doesn't feel that way. It feels like you're trying to influence me."

"Influence, no. Clarify, yes."

"Well, let me make this as clear as I can. I want no part of Ramsey. Or his team. And that includes Jim. It was wonderful when I started there, but that was then, and this is now."

"Okay, okay," Lloyd said. "I need reliable opinions. Emotional outbursts like this reduce reliability. *No* data is better than bad data."

He paused, providing time for my concession, but I only stared back at him, relishing the silence.

"Okay, then," he said finally. "Until later."

The image of his face crumbled into a cloud of pixels which faded and finally disappeared.

The space above my desk seemed more deserted than simply empty. Lloyd and I had never ended on such a sour note. But I couldn't shake the feeling he was trying to encourage me to value my time at the Institute. That he was trying to persuade me to return. Or was this what it felt like to be paranoid—to be emotionally disturbed enough to believe a trusted confidant could join the enemy and turn against you?

9

At noon, I set out for the dining trailer to meet Nelson to take my mind off Mother's conference, but the trailer was empty. The cook told me the crew had packed fry-fish an hour ago and left to mark time on a few make-work tasks while waiting for the final decision about the project.

After a quick bite, I returned to my trailer and looked for the hologram Mother had promised to send, but she apparently hadn't gotten around to forwarding it. I had all the symptoms of acute work-avoidance, hoping to lose myself chasing images linked in the Repository. But without that distraction, I was left to continue my job search. The rain had stopped, but new causes for drowsiness cropped up: the inevitable post-lunch fatigue, the heat and humidity stalemating the trailer's air-conditioning, my own ambivalence about finding a new job. Drowsiness turned into resting my eyes which turned into a mid-afternoon nap.

The knock at my door startled me into realizing I was not at my former lab fuming with colleagues over something or other—only the anger remained. I rubbed my eyes and shambled to the door. Only when I saw it was Nelson did I realize I'd been hoping it was Mother.

He didn't speak, but simply pointed.

Mother was standing in the clearing between our trailers, but there was something not quite right about her appearance. Sunlight and shadow dappled her body and gave her an unusual appearance, but as I walked toward her, I realized it wasn't only the play of sun and shade that made her look different, it was her crooked posture and the uneven braids rising from her head. I glanced at her hands, clenching the coiled strands of hair.

"What happened?" I said.

She straightened herself and stared at me defiantly.

"What did you do to your hair?" I insisted.

"It's not your fault," she said. "The braids were lovely. It's just that ... they just weren't me. They weren't me anymore. Don't be angry. I feel better now."

"What do you mean?"

"I feel better. More myself."

"What does that mean? I don't understand."

"I wasn't feeling quite myself. I was feeling out of sorts?"

"Sick?"

"No, out of sorts! Don't question me if you're not going to listen to my answers."

I stood there speechless, silenced not by her reprimand but by the sight of the braids in her hands and the remnants on her head, frayed and wildly uneven. The shabbiness of her appearance made me want to cry. It was only hair, but it was if she'd mutilated herself. Yet what upset me even more was that she acted as though her behavior were normal.

I took her in my arms. "I'm worried about you," I whispered.

"Because you don't understand," she whispered back. "But I do. And that's what matters." She pulled back to look at me. "To me, at least."

I hugged her again and took her arm to walk back to her trailer. That's when I remembered the video conference.

"The conference," I whispered, half-question, half-answer. Could it be connected to her feeling out of sorts?

"Ah, the conference," she sighed. "It didn't go well. They have no vision," she said.

Still, I saw no connection between a failed meeting and Mother cutting her hair. A tantrum? Out of frustration? But that wasn't Mother. Tantrums served no purpose. Then I wondered if she had a Plan B. Her Plan A's seldom required one.

Nelson opened Mother's trailer door and I was glad he'd accompanied us. I thought of him as offering the kind of support Mother could use. And support for me as well.

We entered the trailer and Mother and I sat on the sofa while Nelson went to the communication desk and activated the console. The trailer's light tinted to indigo, and the coolness of the hue calmed me, and I hoped it calmed Mother. I nodded my appreciation to Nelson as he sat beside the desk.

"They cluck-clucked false flattery," Mother said. "You've taken us where we are today, Zola. You've helped us reach our destination. We'll find a final resting place for those poor souls. Outside the attraction. But that forest is where the runaways escaped. It's where they hid. Where they cared for each other. Where they buried each other. That site is holy ground. I want to draw strength from it. I want others to draw strength from it. I want to strengthen ties between the living and the dead."

Once again, I was struck by how I could follow Mother to a point. But then she would lose me. I wanted to support her unconditionally, but it seemed she would add a thought that left me behind. And I guessed, and worried, the Ministers would feel the same way.

"Where do things stand now?" I asked.

"They claim to be deliberating," she said. "My proposal's under advisement. Come on, it's all about money—whether the grave site will promote or hurt tourism."

She glanced at the camera above the communication desk. "Anyway, that'll give me time to review the meeting. Conduct a thorough analysis. Identify potential allies. Look for cracks in their alliances, their arguments." She sighed and noticed the coils of hair in her hand as though for the first time.

"Would you like any help?" Nelson offered.

Mother seemed less surprised by his offer than I was.

"Thank you, but no," she said. "If you'd participated, yes, I could trust your interpretations. It wouldn't be fair to you. You had to have been there."

That's when I knew I had to share my concern about Mother with Nelson. Their relationship was deeper than I'd guessed.

***

After retiring to our trailers, I gave Nelson time to get settled before visiting. When he opened the door, I had the feeling he was expecting me. He held a green coconut in one hand and a bottle of clear liquor in the other as he greeted me.

"You drink gin in the afternoon?" he asked.

"On a regular basis, no. You?"

He shook his head. "Only as needed."

"Like this afternoon?"

He nodded and walked down the steps. He set the bottle and coconut on the bottom step, reentered the trailer, and returned with his machete. With one swift sidelong stroke, he split the top third of the coconut clean through and it rolled onto the ground. He poured the liquor into the mouth of the coconut, swirled the contents, and motioned for me to join him inside. He retrieved two plain jelly glasses and poured milky liquor into each.

"A toast," he said, raising his glass. "A Chinese proverb: *Strong hearts scare away bad luck*. To you and your mother"

We clinked our glasses, sipped our drinks, and sat in the trailer's two armchairs. The pale concoction bit my tongue but went down smooth and warm and settled pleasantly in my stomach.

"Not bad," I said.

"The milk masks the gin," he said.

I took another sip and nodded. "Funny, I don't think of you as Chinese."

"Neither do I. Sometimes I surprise myself."

I smiled at him. "So, you've been with this project six months. Time enough to get to know my mother."

He nodded, ever reserved.

"Actually, I'm not interested in the project. I'm worried about her."

"I understand. I understand why."

"Can you say more?"

"It struck me when she said she wasn't feeling herself. Outside her trailer. I'd been thinking, she really *hasn't* been herself. Not lately."

"She mentioned feeling out of sorts, whatever that means."

"I'd say she has good days and bad days."

"No mystery as to this day," I said.

"It's not like her to misread the opposition."

"It's not like her to cut off her hair! Am I the only one who sees this as extreme?"

He shook his head, affirming my concern.

"Personally, I think she needs a break," I continued. "A break from this project. From all the infighting. A timeout. Does that ever happen? A recess?"

"No. A pause, maybe. Like now. Born of necessity. But not a deliberate break."

"Well, I can still hope for a quick resolution to this gravesite business. I think the whole idea of it is weighing on her mind. It's enough to weigh on anyone's. There's not much uplifting about discovering long-forgotten graves of runaway slaves."

"Except," he added warily, "she seems to think so."

We sipped our drinks. I wasn't ready yet to explore with him the oddities of some of Mother's thoughts.

"Where will you go next?" I asked. "When the project's over."

"To the capital. R & R, urban style. Spend some of my earnings. Then look around for what's next. Like you."

Don't remind me, I thought. But his mention of R & R sparked an idea. "Take a holiday together," I mused out loud. "Mother and me. Some place relaxing. Now that's a search I could throw myself into."

I was amazed at how quickly and deeply the idea took hold of me. Why hadn't I thought of it sooner? Despite Mother's absence at dinner, the prospect of the two of us taking a joint holiday lifted my spirits. My redirected explorations in the Repository only added to my euphoria. I spent most of the night identifying enough options that Mother would have to find at least one of them attractive. To me, they all looked wonderful, even if they all were outside Trinidad—perhaps especially because they were all abroad. Why shouldn't getaway mean getting away? I remember drifting off to sleep, thinking how glorious it felt to look forward to the coming day.

10

The next morning, I sent Mother a collage of the vacation options I'd found and an invitation for her to add others for us to discuss over lunch. My second task that morning was to check on my job queries. I'd directed prospective employers to contact me via my trailer's com-desk and I wanted to see if I'd received any. Given my commitment to vacation with Mother, any reply might turn out to be, well, inconvenient.

When I heard a knock on the door, I again expected Mother but was, once more, greeting Nelson. His somber expression soured my smile.

"What?" I said.

"Come with me," he said.

"Mother?" I said, jumping down the steps into the damp morning air. We rushed to her trailer, and I overtook him as we reached the door. He grabbed my arm. "You've got to keep your head."

I yanked free of his hold and ran into the trailer. "Mother?"

"In the bathroom," he said.

I found Mother hunched over the washbowl, her palms pressed down onto shards of broken glass in a pool of blood. I tried to pull her hands off the glass, but she resisted, and her palms slid on the bloody porcelain.

"Coax her," he said. "I tried but couldn't."

"Mother, please!" I said, still pulling her arm, but managing only to glide her hands though the bloody glass.

She only stared at herself in the mirror's fractured remnants.

"I recognize my voice," she whispered, lifting her hand from the washbowl, and tracing a bloody finger across her cheek. "But I don't recognize myself."

"I sent for bandages," Nelson said.

"We need a doctor," I said.

"We'll have to get her to the capital."

I tugged her gently not knowing what to expect, but she allowed me to walk her to the bedroom and sit her on the bed. She looked at her blood-splattered arms and hands as though they were not her own.

"I'm sorry, Fitima."

"It's all right," I said, sitting beside her. I slipped my arm around her shoulder and stroked her head, running my fingers through her snaggled braids. I tried to quell the trembling I thought for sure she would feel.

"Forgetting is sinful," she said.

"I think the Ministers contacted—" Nelson began.

"I don't want to hear about the Ministers!" I said, holding Mother tighter.

"It's an insult to the past," she said. "Forgetting is indecent. I'm ashamed."

I didn't know if she was talking about not recognizing her face in the mirror or the removal of the slaves' remains. Regardless, I needed her to stop.

"Hush," I whispered, stretching the word like she did with me many years ago. I swallowed hard against my queasiness. "Everything will be all right."

Light footsteps creaked inside the trailer and the cook appeared and handed Nelson a roll of thick-skins and just as stealthily backed out of the room. Nelson handed the roll to me. I picked out several slivers of mirrored glass and loosely bandaged Mothers hands.

"I'll call the hospital," Nelson said. "We'll need transportation."

I remembered there were no suitable vehicles at the camp.

"She'll need laser-seals for these cuts," I shouted as he left the room, the opacity of its walls bearing down on me, my mouth welling with nausea at the primitiveness of the place.

I bandaged Mother's hands, but I couldn't shake the clawing thought that her cuts would heal, but what about her mind? Her injury was self-inflicted, after all. And her talk about forgetting and not recognizing herself? Her thoughts weren't adding up and they hadn't been for a while.

I heard Nelson's voice at the communication desk, and I wanted to shout one further instruction, but I couldn't voice the words. Not in front of Mother. I could hardly admit them to myself. *Psychiatric*, also!

Nelson had requested a hovercraft to take us to the hospital and the wait seemed endless. And perhaps, too, holding onto Mother, so familiar yet strange in my arms, distressed me even further. I shut my eyes against the sight of her bandages and her ragged braids, but I couldn't shut out her whispers: "I know my name ... Zola Anueche. I know my age and where I'm from. But that face, so round it looked like a doll's. Those eyes ... so weary. So tired. So defeated."

Again and again, over and over until finally, thank the Lord, the hum of the hovercraft came from a distance, growing louder and landed outside Mother's trailer. Nelson and I walked her into the clearing where the crew had gathered at the edge of the downdraft. They exchanged furtive looks but averted their eyes from the three of us. None of them spoke a word. I was thankful for that.

The hovercraft settled down gently and cut off its engine. The vehicle looked smaller than I expected, with two turbo fans in the rear and on either side of a vehicle only twice as large as a bubble cab.

I secured Mother in the rear seat and sat beside her while Nelson took a seat up front.

The pilot appeared only as silhouette, a man in a ball cap.

"I'm reminded," Mother whispered.

"Shhh," I said, hoping to calm her.

"I'm reminded of a saying," she continued.

"Shhh, please," I said, desperate for her to be quiet—for her sake and my own. "*Every day carry water from the well*," she recited, "*one day the bucket-bottom must drop out.*"

I touched my finger to her lips. "Please."

She nodded, hearing my desperation. Or so I believed.

The engine revved full throttle and we lurched upward, leaving a cloud of dust shrouding the crew, standing motionless, like statues, which was my last view of them.

As we sped toward the capital, the hovercraft whipped up scents from below, marking our progress—the musk of the wetlands, the sunbaked straw of the grasslands, and finally, the industrial exhalations of the city. Above the drone of the engine, I heard Nelson and the pilot arguing.

Nelson turned around to me. "He can't get clearance to land at the hospital."

"What does that mean?" I asked.

"We'll have to drive in," Nelson said.

Up the hospital entryway, I assumed.

We descended and merged into street-level traffic, but not the hospital entryway. "Where are we?" I asked. "How far away?"

"We're in line," he said.

In line, I thought, peering outside. There were more vehicles on the road than I expected and several seemed to be moving independently of the automated navigation. Suddenly, our hovercraft swerved to avoid sideswiping a cab, and I craned to see if our pilot-turned-driver was steering manually. He was.

"The road guidance system down?" I asked.

The wail of a siren erupted around us, and I realized it was coming from our hovercraft. "The system's fine, ma'am," our driver said. "We got a few rogues out here."

Rogues. It reminded me of hooligans. "They're driving manually?"

"Yes," he said.

"As are you," I pointed out.

"Yes, Ma'am. Got no choice. Gotta protect myself. Gotta protect *you*."

That threw me, the idea of our needing protection. A sudden stop pressed me hard against my harness and I glanced outside the window. "Are we there?"

"Traffic jam," our driver said.

Nelson turned to us; his jaw clenched.

"You'll find traffic jam in the Repository near traffic congestion along with other quaint terms like road rage and rubbernecking."

I had no idea what he meant. "But where's the hospital?"

Now I heard several other sirens, our distinct ululations frighteningly out of sync. "I thought we were in line," I said.

The hovercraft lifted above the street-bound vehicles and began to weave its way among the few other flying craft.

"Now we're rogues, too," Nelson said.

"Only out of necessity," our driver apologized. "But we still won't be able to land on the helipad."

We turned a corner and Carlyle Hospital came into view on the north end of San Rafael Boulevard, a broad and busy thoroughfare. From a distance, the glass high-rise appeared pockmarked, as though its transparent skin were diseased. As we got closer, however, the pockmarks turned out to be black casings covering several of the balconies. Closer still, elegant etchings of ocean waves and seashells gave the glass facade the paradoxical appearance of being both stylishly decorated and curiously blemished.

The hovercraft lowered onto the hospital's street-level entry ramp, the entrance I had expected to see a while ago. A variety of vehicles blocked our path while others streamed past us—hovercraft, ambulances, patrol cars. I drowned out the noisy chaos and focused on the attendant pushing a wheelchair toward us. Nelson had jumped out and was soon helping Mother into the wheelchair.

I climbed out of the craft and startled as a hand cupped my elbow from behind. "Ma'am Anueche?" the man asked.

I nodded.

"I'm Dr. Hooks," he said. "Lawrence Hooks. I was sent to meet you."

He was a handsome, brown-skinned man about Mother's age, with hair so white, rounded, and fluffy it reminded me of a dandelion seed-head. He was dressed in a business suit of pearl grey translucent fabric which hung from his slender frame like water pouring down rugged rock.

"Someone needs to see to her hands," I said.

"And we will," he said. "I've got a room prepared."

Dr. Hooks pointed the attendant to the entryway, and we followed them inside, leaving the clamor behind.

"I apologize for the backup at the helipad," Dr. Hooks said. "I know street-level traffic couldn't have been pleasant."

Nelson shot him a sidelong glance, but those troubles were behind us now. Getting Mother proper care was all that mattered.

We hurried through a maze of glass walls, each hallway awash in soft blue light. The smell of the place made me queasy, a sickeningly sweet combination of disinfectant, body lotion, and freshly washed linen—not horrible, but not an aura of healing one might hope for.

We followed a trail of blinking yellow lights along the floor which led to a room identified as CONSULTATION. Dr. Hooks pointed the attendant to an adjacent EXAMINATION room and the attendant wheeled Mother inside. I watched as he helped her into one of the room's two chairs, the soft voice of his encouragement making its way to our room.

Dr. Hooks took a seat behind a frosted glass desk containing several multi-functional screens and consoles, all dormant. He motioned for Nelson and me to sit in the chairs facing him.

"Can you tell me," he asked, "when you first noticed any sign of distress?" I glanced at Nelson and then turned to Dr. Hooks.

"Distress?"

"Anything out of the ordinary."

"Excuse me, but—"

"Dr. Hooks is a psychiatrist," Nelson said.

"Oh my," Dr. Hooks said. "I thought you knew."

Nelson looked at me sheepishly. "Sorry. We didn't have time to discuss it. I mean, you and me."

"Your call from the trailer?" I asked Nelson.

He nodded.

I was surprised by our agreement that a psychiatrist was appropriate.

"I hope that's okay, Ma'am Anueche," Dr. Hooks said.

I gave a quick nod.

"I'll consult with her family physician, of course," Dr. Hooks said.

"Dr. Locklear," I said. "Robert—"

His expression told me I need not continue. He'd accessed her file. He leaned back in his chair. "First signs of distress?"

"She cut off her braids?" I said tentatively. I glanced at Nelson, wondering if he would agree. "That was only yesterday."

"Why do you say that was a sign of distress?" Dr. Hooks asked.

The skeptical arch of his eyebrow unnerved me.

"It's ... it's just not like her."

"I see. Any provocation? I mean, was there any discernible cause for her unusual behavior?"

"I'm not sure," I said. "I mean ..." I had to shake off my unease. "She was working on a proposal. To present to the authorities. Ministers. Management. They turned her down. I'm sure that upset her. I know it did. She took it hard. But I can't say it definitely caused her to cut off her braids. We never got to talk about it."

Whether out of habit, courtesy, or for confirmation, Hooks looked to Nelson who nodded his agreement.

"Any unusual behavior since then?" Dr. Hooks asked. "I mean, before … this incident?"

I looked at Mother sitting in the examination room, staring back at us through the wall. I tried to think quickly so Dr. Hooks could go to her, help her, but my urgency only muddled my thoughts.

"I'm not sure," I said. "She talked about the graves they found in the forest."

As soon as I'd spoken those words, I wanted to take them back. But Hooks' furrowed brow made me say more.

"They discovered several graves of fugitive slaves," I said. "But it wasn't so much that she … it was the *way* she talked about them."

Dr. Hooks still looked confused.

"We were in the process of determining what to do next," Nelson explained. "Given that discovery. Should the graves be removed? Should they remain?"

"And your mother was involved in that debate," Dr. Hooks said.

I nooded.

"I see," he said. "Can you recall anything specific? Anything unusual. About the way she talked about the graves."

I hesitated, questioning my judgment about what was normal and what was abnormal.

"She spoke about strengthening ties between the living and the dead," I said. "Maybe it's me. I thought that was unusual."

"The living and the dead," Hooks repeated without emotion. "And this morning?"

"Do you have access to the tapes?" I asked, suddenly remembering them.

Dr. Hooks shook his head. "Not for the rear of the trailer."

That damn trailer, I thought. The damn forest.

"She spoke of not recognizing herself," Nelson said.

"In the mirror," I added. "She didn't recognize herself in the mirror."

"The day before she said she wasn't feeling like herself," Nelson said. "Before she cut off her braids."

"Anything else?" Hooks asked, staring at me, as though he sensed I was holding back.

"I'm not sure what she meant," I said.

"Yes?" Hooks said.

"She said losing memory was a sin. That forgetfulness was sinful."

"But?" Hooks persisted.

"I'm not sure what she meant. I'm not sure if she was referring to herself."

"Or?" Dr. Hooks asked.

"Or the graves," I said.

I looked back at Mother, afraid for her.

"Well," Hooks said, rising from his chair, "let's see what Madame Anueche has to say."

11

Nelson and I watched Dr. Hooks enter the EXAMINATION ROOM and introduce himself to Mother. Her hands were wrapped in fresh white bandages, the laser-seals apparently worthy of covering up. The attendant left and Hooks took a seat across from Mother and the muffled sounds of their voices mingled with ambient noise from the corridor.

"Did you see any earlier signs?" I asked Nelson. "I mean, before I arrived."

"It's hard to say. Or maybe I just hate to say."

I swallowed hard. "Like what?"

"They were so subtle. And it could just as easily be me."

"Like what?"

"More irritable maybe. Quicker to criticize. Your mother's a moderate person. Stubborn, but moderate. Seems like she was becoming a little more extreme. But like I said, I found her exploring an old holograph in her trailer. Right before the video conference."

"Odd, no? And she was projecting onto the image, things that weren't there. Associations, kind of. Did you notice that—her spending time with images from the Repository?"

Nelson shook his head. "No, just what I said. More intense from time to time? But it was so subtle it's hard to say for sure."

For an instant, I thought of Lloyd and his caution against incomplete answers.

As a scientist, I'd learned to live with incomplete answers as a given. As a citizen, and as a daughter, incompleteness was nearly unbearable.

"I'm sorry," Nelson said.

"No need. Neither of us is a psychiatrist."

"I mean for your time with us," he said. "It's been one thing after another."

I looked at him and nodded, recognizing the kindness in his eyes.

"All while looking for a new job," he continued.

"The least of my worries," I said.

"Not to mention King Juba."

"Wish you hadn't. Nor the anarchist in the capital. Nor my pollster trying to persuade me to return to my old job. It's been one wild ride."

"I missed a couple of those unmentionables."

"Regardless, they're all the least of my worries right now."

"But worries nevertheless."

"I guess so. But still the least."

"Well, if you ever want to talk about them," Nelson said. "Any of them. From least to most. I'm here."

I thanked him. Twice. And meant it doubly, too.

"One day the bucket bottom must drop out," I whispered absently.

"Excuse me," Nelson said.

"You know it? *Every day carry water from the well* ..."

"Of course. *One day the bucket bottom must drop out.*" He closed his eyes. "*Things fall apart,*" he recited. "*The center cannot hold. Anarchy is loosed upon the world.*"

I shrugged.

"Poetry," he said. "And lyrics. Of a darkening kind. Believe better."

"That's all? Believe better?"

He nodded. "That's all I've got." He sounded apologetic. But sincere.

Believe better. The bromide tumbled around in my mind as I watched the murmured pantomime between Mother and Hooks in the adjacent room. Finally, Hooks stood and called an attendant to stay with Mother and entered our CONSULTATION room with the inscrutable expression of a seasoned veteran. He took his seat behind his desk and leaned forward.

"She needs to remain under observation," he said.

I glared at him. "What does that mean?"

"I think she needs to be admitted."

I was too stunned to speak. My worst-case scenario was Mother being sent back to the camp with prescribed pharmaceuticals. But I was actually hoping Hooks would recommend a long rest at her home, or better, a vacation with her daughter. It never occurred to me he'd recommend she be admitted.

"Under observation?" I said.

"And treatment, of course," Hooks said. "But we need to make sure she doesn't harm herself. Further. That's a priority we can ensure."

"You believe that's a possibility?" I said. "Her harming herself?"

"I can't rule it out" he said.

I looked at Nelson, more for relief from Hooks than for rescue.

"We were hoping a break from work would do the trick," Nelson said.

"Very reasonable," Hooks said.

"Even some time at her cottage," I said softly.

"That's not impossible," Hooks said.

I turned to Hooks, unable to read his expression. "So, she wouldn't stay here long."

"I mean during her stay," Hooks said.

"I don't understand."

"We can convert her room's balcony," Hooks said. "Use a scene generator. Holograph verité."

"The black casings!" Nelson said. "On the hospital's façade."

"Yes," Hooks said. "The backs of the scene generators. We can retrieve specs of her cottage from the Repository, select a view and project those, details on her balcony. If you think that would help her recuperate, I can prescribe it. All I need is justification."

"And she approved?"

"She left it up to you."

"To me?" I said, looking to Nelson. "She left this decision to me?"

Hooks nodded.

I tried not to think how unlike Mother that was. "Have you contacted her physician?"

"I've left messages. Locklear's on holiday. Apparently off the grid. I'd be your mother's attending physician, but I'd step aside when Locklear became available. I'll send him updates, of course. In the meantime, I owe you and your mother my professional opinion."

I wasn't convinced, but my resistance was beginning to feel more stubborn than sensible. And at least Mother would get rest away from that camp.

Dr. Hooks ran his fingers through his downy white hair, his avuncular expression consoling. "I understand how you feel," he said. "We choose our physicians like we choose our friends. We don't rely on coincidence. But in this case ..."

I again glanced at Nelson, although I wasn't sure why. It was my decision to make. Alone.

"Okay," I said. "Admit her. And keep trying to reach Locklear."

"Of course," Hooks said.

"And in the meantime?" Nelson said. "What about us?"

"You can stay next door," Hooks said.

"Next door?" I said.

"At our partner hotel," Hooks said.

"We can arrange a room for you there." He glanced at our hands. "Or rooms."

Hooks hadn't had time to examine our profiles so instead he examined our ring fingers.

"Rooms," Nelson and I said simultaneously.

"Hospital admin can handle the details," Hooks said.

"I have to ask," I said. I assumed a noncommittal reply, but I needed to ask regardless. "What's your prognosis? I mean, how long do you think ..."

"Let's get her situated," Hooks said. "A few days rest wouldn't hurt, right? Install the scene generator. Allow me a few sessions with her.

Twice a day. I'll be in touch with you after each. You can visit her, of course. As long and as often as you'd like. Give us several days and we can take it from there."

I'd latched onto the prospect of visiting Mother as long and as often as I'd like. For only a few days. And after that, a vacation together. A tolerable future after an intolerable week.

12

The Carlyle Hospital and Hotel admitted Mother and registered me and Nelson in only a few minutes. Dr. Hooks had said he'd meet us shortly at Mother's room on the fifth floor. His delay, he'd said, would give us time to orient ourselves and settled into the new surroundings.

After Nelson and I left the hotel and proceeded to Mother's floor of the hospital, the monitor above the hallway entrance greeted us: NEURO-MEDICAL SERVICES. Several hospital personnel strolled past us as we got our bearings and headed down the corridor toward Mother's room. The first few rooms were occupied by single patients who gave us little notice. Others were occupied by patients and their visitors. Most amazing, however, were the interior spectacles displayed in several of the rooms. We passed one room where the dull roar of a waterfall seeped into the hallway, its cascading torrents splitting and spilling around extruding rock, spewing waterless mist into the room.

"Holograph verité," Nelson said.

In another room, a dirt footpath lined with trees with flaming red foliage, disappeared into the balcony's horizon. In yet another, a quiet pond extended far beyond the balcony, where a small flock of ducks paddled or dipped their beaks, rippling the water.

"And the view from your mother's cottage?" Nelson asked.

"The ocean," I said. "A westerly view of the ocean."

"Good. No holograph verité envy."

I appreciated his effort at humor, the effort more amusing than his remark. We stopped outside Mother's room; her name already affixed to the glass door.

"That was fast," I said.

We entered and found Mother reposed on the hospital bed, perking up upon seeing us, rising, and pointing out the amenities: the club chairs, the communication desk, ceiling cameras, chest of drawers, a basket of fruit, the washroom area. It seemed a classic case of avoidance.

"How are you feeling?" I asked.

"Dr. Hooks ordered the fruit," she said.

"Nice," I said, absently fingering the cellophane. "But you're feeling okay?"

She extended her arms, signaling her surroundings. "I can't complain. Except for the com-desk. It's not connected."

Her gaze darted between Nelson and me, but we had nothing to offer. She sighed.

I opened the top dresser drawer and was greeted by the scent of ozone-bleached fabric. The drawer was stocked with a half dozen gauzy hospital gowns in one-size-fits-most proportions.

"Think you'll be needing anything?" I asked.

"Besides a com-link?" Mother replied.

"Yes, besides com-link."

She shrugged. "I'm eager to see this holograph whatsit." She pointed to the empty balcony. "Sounds impressive."

"I think it'll add a nice touch," Nelson said.

I wondered if the facsimile might even help me feel more comfortable there.

***

It took only a day for the technicians to install and program the scene generator on Mother's balcony. I stepped back when I first saw it—unexpected and so lifelike—the blue sky matching the color of the rippling sea except for the thin dark horizon and patches of white clouds floating by. Wavelets rolled gently onto the sugar-white sand which advanced up to the wooden railing of the wraparound porch. And the porch: furnished with that blue padded lounge and matching striped pillows, and the card table and chairs in the corner. A few meters away, the white mesh hammock stretched between two cabbage palms. It had been almost a decade since I'd visited that cottage, yet it lay there before me as recognizable as though I'd been there only yesterday.

Mother was sitting in front of this scene, her back to me. The bandages on her hands had been removed and her laser-sealed cuts showed only as thin red lines. She wore a sheer silver scarf around her head, tidying the ragged braids I'd almost gotten used to.

"Isn't it amazing?" she said.

"They've done a remarkable job," I said.

"The waves barely whispering. Do you hear them?"

Yes, I thought. So soft, I almost hadn't noticed.

She inhaled deeply. "The sea salt in the air." She pointed to the flowers on the card table. "Fresh-picked." She turned to look at me. "Well, *like* fresh picked."

"Are you okay with it? I mean, the facsimile?"

"I'm fine with it. Facsimiles can be admired. Useful, even. Like your black holes."

I smiled and pulled a chair beside hers and sat down.

She pointed to her com-desk. "But it would be nice to have access to reality."

I felt reassured by her separation from the outside.

"They might as well remove it," she said.

I agreed, but there was no need to say so. "And Nelson?" she asked.

"He's tying up loose ends," I said.

I'd made a promise to myself to veto any conversation about the project and, most of all, about the graves and the Ministers. Now I wondered if I could live up to that pledge.

"The crew's on hold for now," I continued, "and Nelson's attending to those details."

"For the time being," Mother added.

"For the time being. First things, first."

"And that would be ..."

"You. Your recovery."

I didn't get the pushback I expected—the opposition I wasn't sure I could resist—yet another sign Mother wasn't quite herself.

As Dr. Hooks would verify at day's end at our meeting. "We'll need to take things one step at a time. But I'm very optimistic. She's a willing client."

"No timeline yet, I suppose," I said.

Hooks shook his head. "We've run a brain scan. Negative. So, it's nothing organic." Yet another wave of emotions: the scare of the brain scan, the relief of no finding. "Sometimes these behavioral disruptions are sublimated requests," Hooks said. "In your mother's case, it could be a request for rest."

His theory seemed plausible. I had no idea how psychiatrists verified their theories.

"I'll mention something you probably didn't notice," Hooks continued. "There are no mirrors in her room."

I hadn't noticed, but his mentioning it stirred a wave of sadness.

"Like I said," Hooks continued, "we'll take things one step at a time."

And my daily debriefings with Hooks reflected just what he'd described: a step at a time, albeit very small steps. What Hooks considered progress, I considered heart breaking. He progressed from prescribing no mirrors in Mother's room, to one small three-panel make-up mirror with panels closed. From that closed makeup mirror, to opened panels. From that opened make-up mirror to a full length three-panel mirror—panels closed. From that closed full-length mirror, to opened panels. All mirrors, safety acrylic. He seemed to be practicing desensitization therapy with an extremely phobic patient—the phobia being Mother's own reflected image.

Yet this progress meant we were getting closer to the day Mother would be discharged.

I'd made no assumptions about what would happen after she was released, and I was afraid to broach the subject with her. Each time I considered raising the question, it felt premature, as though I were rushing things.

And I didn't discuss this with Nelson either. In fact, I saw very little of him during those first several days. What I'd feared would be a required and awkward proximity, turned out to be a marked distance between us that had begun to feel less than ideal. At least for me. But he had project-related work to attend to, so there was little I could do about it. Besides, I doubted I would've been very good company.

13

"I have to admit," Mother said, "this rest has done me good."

I was already feeling optimistic that morning and now I saw the opening I'd been waiting for, my opportunity to propose a vacation for the two of us.

"But you reach a point of diminishing return," she continued. She was staring at the view on the balcony that mimicked mid-dawn daylight on a deserted beach.

"We could be looking at the real thing," I said. "The view from your actual cottage."

"A vacation? After we put the finishing touches on the project."

"We'll need to meet with Hooks, you know," I said. "He may not want you returning to the project immediately."

"No? Well, I'm not conceding that decision!"

Her implication stung me, given that it was my decision to admit her. Still, I believed it was for the best. And it appeared I'd have to continue to fight for what I believed would allow her full recovery.

The hushed lapping of waves and hint of sea salt calmed us into our own daydreams, our personal wishful thoughts, uncontested, self-assuring. Or at least that described my drift away from that hospital room when Mother's voice brought me back.

"History is heavy on my mind," she said.

I startled to attention. And recollection. "I remember you saying it's a sin to forget."

"History is a friend only if it lays bare errors of the past."

"I'm sure there'll be a way to commemorate—"

"Some chapters are ugly," she said.

"But should not be forgotten," I said.

"But we *try* to forget them. Yet the ugliness doesn't disappear with time. The ugliness goes underground. But it can still seep into consciousness. That's when we need to face the source of your nightmares."

"I vowed not to let you go on and on about the project."

"The project?" she said.

"Yes. Those graves. The slaves. Their remembrance."

"Whoa. Calm down." She tilted her head. "I'm talking about your father."

My body went numb, disappearing behind my eyes, leaving me without sensation besides the image of mother's face, her tilted head, her eyes squinting at me. Then came pounding in my chest.

"Did you say father?"

She nodded and looked away.

I tried to calm myself. I tried to convince myself it was reasonable for a woman recapturing her identify to speak of the man she once loved. But not reasonable enough for my mother. Not after all those years.

"What's this about?" I asked as neutrally as I could manage.

"The past," she said. "I've been thinking about the past."

She hadn't mentioned that part of her past for as far back as I could remember. She hadn't spoken of my father since I last asked about him as a young teen. He died before I was born. My only images of him had come from the Repository which I'd visited regularly as a child. I'd heard her stories about him, of course. At least until I'd stopped asking to hear them. Memory convinced me she wanted it that way.

"It's the job of a seed to blossom where it falls," she had told me. "And you've fallen here in your mother's arms."

When Mother spoke those words, I sensed finality. I sensed that she wanted me to recognize that she and I had each other, and it was time for me to be reconciled to that fact. At least, that's how I remembered it. Or maybe I'd had my fill of longing and I used her words as a way to escape my grieving. In any event, I stopped asking her about him after that. I also stopped asking myself about him.

"It's been so long since I called his name," Mother said, drawing my attention back to her. "Kelvin Anueche."

It was like hearing a familiar but long-forgotten melody. "What made you think of him?"

"The Gerbera."

"The what?"

"The daisies." She pointed to the quasi-bright flowers on the card table in the holograph on her balcony, a recent addition to the scene.

"What do the flowers have to do with—?"

"Dr. Hooks asked if they reminded me of happier times. He'd done some exploring in the Repository and found a recording of Kelvin and me picnicking in Queen's Park Savannah. Your father used to fling a few Gerbera on our picnic blanket. Their scent made me lightheaded. Which I'm sure your father knew."

I was only half-listening, thinking mostly about how to stop her. "But you were talking about history before. About history and ugly chapters."

"Well, those came after," she said.

"But you were talking about errors of the past."

"That came after," she repeated. "I need to remember happier times. Dr. Hooks said it was part of my treatment. To help me reclaim myself. Odd phrase, no? To reclaim yourself?"

Yes, odd. Odd enough for me to question Hooks about it later. I wasn't happy with the results of this reclaiming business and hoped we could discuss other paths to Mother's recovery.

"You see," Hooks explained later in consultation, "I'm trying to align your mother's experienced self with her remembered self."

I didn't see.

Hooks blinked rapidly, preparing to clarify. "The remembered self can by faulty and misaligned with experience, ergo, reality. This isn't abnormal, per se. Some experiences can be so absorbing that the self, as such, disappears or, at least, recedes from consciousness. Brain scans confirm this, by the way. But the point is: the remembered self is comparable to a remembered sleeping self, i.e., a remembered dream. Now, you dream, I dream, we all dream. So, we should all be able to appreciate the potential for divergence between the two selves—the remembered self and the experienced self."

I recalled an incident in college of telling a classmate I was struggling to learn Korean. His response was to speak to me in Korean for the next several minutes. As with Hooks, I didn't understand what he was saying, and I was even more perplexed as to why he continued to speak a language I couldn't understand. Narcissism, I supposed.

***

It took several moments for me to get my bearings as Lloyd's arriving image signaled on my hotel room's com-desk.

"Napping?" Lloyd said.

"As you can see. Martini aperitifs will do that."

"Ah—plural. Yes."

I rubbed my eyes to clear the fog. "Well, I've been consuming services since your last poll. Health care, specifically. Mental health care, in particular."

"A complaint, I take it."

That's when Ramsey stepped into view. At first, I couldn't reconcile the two images, Lloyd and Ramsey, confidant and foe, side by side, in the real world. But how so? My curiosity overshadowed everything, even my misgivings.

The men began speaking simultaneously.

"I know this is a surprise," they said.

They looked at each other and exchanged wilted smiles.

"I take responsibility for the intrusion," Ramsey said.

Intrusion was one way to think of it. Trespass was another. Criminal trespass. But with Lloyd's permission. I shook my head in pity for him. He'd been used to gain easy access to me. And this wasn't the first time.

I looked into Ramsey's deep-set eyes. "You got Lloyd to try to persuade me to return."

There was no need for a reply and Ramsey gave none. He simply stared back at me, a tall and lanky centenarian with the stature and visage of royalty, at least the stereotypic kind. An imperious gaze. A sunset-tinted tan. Angular cheekbones and jutting jaw. He should have stood taller than Lloyd, but their heights appeared equal. Staged, perhaps. The duplicity, I thought. There seemed no end to it.

"Jim sends greetings," Ramsey said.

"What do you want?" I said.

"We can't replace you," Ramsey said. "You know that."

"I know you haven't posted our findings."

"Nor will we."

I glanced at Lloyd, embarrassed for him, for his having to listen to Ramsey's admitted misconduct. And now his collusion with it.

"Nothing's changed," I said. "So again, what do you want?"

"I want you to know there's a connection," Ramsey said. "There's a connection between this … this …," and he paused to extend his arms, "this malaise you're experiencing and our project at the Institute."

"Malaise?"

"It's the one piece of information you never had."

"And now you're going to provide it. And it'll make me return to the project? And I'm supposed to believe you? How could you even imagine I'd believe you?"

"It's difficult," Ramsey said. "In fact, our prognostics indicate you won't. But I have to try. We've got nothing to lose."

"*That*, I believe."

"The truth is," Ramsey said, "you're least likely to believe our most compelling evidence. So, I'll only mention dysfunctions you've witnessed. Like the graffiti artist in the capital. The hooligans. The rogues. The road ragers. The—"

"Please, please," I interrupted. "Enough. Lawbreakers all. And you, too, a lawbreaker. That's the commonality."

"*Dans les champs de l'observation le hasard ne favorise que les esprits prépare,*" Ramsey said.

I thought instantly of Hooks' psychobabble and my classmate's Korean. "I don't speak French."

"In essence," Ramsey said, "foresight favors the prepared mind."

"So, I'm the one at fault?" I said. "My mind isn't prepared to accept your point of view?"

"I'm trying to help you connect the dots," Ramsey said. "You may not believe me now, but you will eventually."

"According to your prognosticator?"

Ramsey nodded. "I only wish they offered a timeline."

"They're fuzzy on the eventually?"

"Exactly," Ramsey said. "Or inexactly, I'm afraid."

"And when I achieve enlightenment?"

"Contact us," Ramsey said. "Don't hesitate. I want you to know we'll welcome you with open arms."

"And what about your secrecy. Our hidden data. Any new dots to connect there?"

"I've tried to explain," Ramsey said. "Extraordinary science calls for extraordinary safeguards. We've learned at least that much from our nuclear scientist predecessors. We can't simply turn over our results to mere politicians."

It was easy for me to connect the dots of Ramsey's logic. Mere politicians ultimately led to mere citizens. He reserved the top of his hierarchy for himself. Everyone else was relegated to being mere.

I walked to the com-desk, knowing this disconnection would be my last. It wasn't nostalgia that tugged at my heart, but deep disappointment. Grief, actually. Over losing Lloyd who I'd known since childhood. Who I'd loved since childhood. And grief, even, over disassociating from Ramsey, who'd given me my first professional job, and yet who had, in the end, betrayed my trust. A goodbye would not have been genuine, so I said nothing as I flipped the switch and their images evaporated above the desk.

14

That evening, I summoned Nelson to dinner. I demanded he meet me at the hospital cafeteria rather than the hotel's restaurant. The hotel restaurant felt too intimate. I dictated the time. I felt guilty immediately afterward, however. I wished I'd been more courteous. Unfortunately, my desperation had overwhelmed decorum.

I was somewhat surprised when he actually showed up. I thanked him profusely, in part to make up for my summons which he thankfully didn't mention. And, of course, because I was truly thankful he came.

I did my best to translate Hooks' jargon about Mother's illness and his treatment, and I recounted Lloyd's and Ramsey's intrusion. Nelson stopped me after I related Ramsey's plea for me to return to the project.

"I mean no disrespect," he said, "and I know you're a talented scientist and all, but what makes you so—"

"Indispensable?"

"I was going to say special. You upped the ante. Okay, *indispensable*. What makes you so indispensable?"

"I guess it does sound arrogant. But I was indispensable to his team."

"But everybody's replaceable," Nelson said.

"Of course. But not necessarily with the same outcome. I was indispensable to Ramsey's team because together, we were more than the sum of our parts. We achieved a kind of synergy. Each of us was indispensable to the project as a whole. Any one of us could be replaced, but the team wouldn't achieve the same productivity."

"I understand why you quit," Nelson said.

"Well, I—"

"But I also understand why they'd conceal your results."

"You do?"

"Sending information back in time? I mean, assuming it were possible. Think of the potential for mischief. The money you could make. The power you could grab."

"You sound like my mother," I said.

"I like the company," he said. "But secrets are like rocks under water. Sooner or later, they're both revealed."

"Ancient Chinese proverb?"

"Not so ancient. But what I don't understand is why all the secrecy when it's not possible. I mean, it's not possible to send anything back in time."

"But it might be," I said.

"Fitima, if philosophers and physicists agree on anything, it's that the past is irreversible."

"Perhaps it's time for a new philosophy and a new physics. Listen, we, you and I, understand time on a human scale. We know what it means to be on time. To be late, to be early. We understand daytime, nighttime. The seasons. But we don't understand time beyond our experiences, beyond our consciousness. We don't understand time on a subatomic scale. Or on a cosmic scale."

"Come on! I look at a recording and point at the image and say this or that has happened. In the past. And that past, that recording, is unchangeable."

"Is it?"

"Of course it is."

"I've seen it change." I glanced up at the camera in the light fixture. "Okay, we're being recorded right now. And let's say we look at this recording a week from now and then two weeks from now and we see something on our second viewing of the recording that wasn't there when we viewed it earlier?"

"Define something."

"A flash of light. Several milliseconds long. Which wasn't there during our first viewing. In fact, which wasn't there originally."

"An artifact of some kind," he said.

"What if the flash was sent intentionally?"

He shook his head.

I remembered how the wonder of it left me speechless, how it made my skin crawl.

"What are you talking, a few photons?" he said. "Some hocus pocus quantum experiment in a particle collider? That's not what I'd call information."

"The size of a key doesn't matter. All it needs to do is unlock the door. And once that door's unlocked ..."

Nelson shook his head in disbelief while I nodded the affirmative.

"Insight favors the prepared mind," I said. "And you're not yet prepared."

"Wait a minute," Nelson said. "Isn't that what Ramsey told you?"

"I hate to quote the enemy," I said, "but in this case, it definitely applies."

We shared a laugh and, perhaps, a truce—to agree to disagree. I was used to such truces. I'd had so many with Mother.

"You never did say what the man wrote," Nelson said.

"The man? Wrote?"

"The graffiti," Nelson said. "In the capital."

"Oh, yes. Let me see." And it dawned on me that I'd reduced his crime to a single act of vandalism when, in fact, his message was as perplexing as the behavior.

"Actually, he wrote two sentences. First, *only the guilty have reason to fear.*"

"Wow, that takes me back. Historically speaking, that is. I'm not that old."

"It takes me back, too. To the actual incident. Creepy doesn't begin to describe it."

"But his behavior doesn't make sense. To proclaim a rationale for surveillance while breaking the law? I don't get it."

"That's because when he finished the first sentence, he went back to the beginning and wrote, *Not only the guilty have reason to fear.*"

Nelson nodded. "That makes sense. Not the sentence. The act. He's a privacy rights anarchist."

"You say that as though it's a trademark."

"A *registered* trademark! The P-R-A."

"How does a civil engineer come by this knowledge?"

"*Civil* is a wider-ranging adjective than most people realize."

At that moment, I decided it was time to learn more about this Nelson Woon Sam. The mystery of the man had become more intriguing than I could bear and if my own self-disclosure was the price for knowing more about him, I was prepared to pay it.

Static crackled from speakers somewhere above us.

"Attention, please," a male voice announced. "Attention please."

Startled, Nelson and I stared at each other.

"We ask that all visitors please leave the hospital at this time," the announcement continued. "We apologize for the inconvenience. Your cooperation is greatly appreciated. Once again, would all visitors please proceed to the front entrance at this time."

"What do you think?" I said. He shrugged.

We looked around the cafeteria, me for the first time. The room was nearly empty, most visitors probably preferring to dine at the hotel-hospital's restaurant next door.

"I don't want to leave," I said, hoping to continue our conversation.

"He did say at this time."

"Okay," I said. "But I'm not leaving without checking on Mother."

"Well ... we can leave at this time by way of checking on her," Nelson said.

I laughed. "Proving once again that time is relative."

Nelson groaned.

We left the cafeteria and hurried down several corridors and saw the lift just ahead of us when Nelson stopped suddenly and led me back around the corner.

"What's wrong?" I asked.

"That's a cop," Nelson whispered, peeking around the wall.

"He's an attendant," I said.

Nelson pointed to his waist and then to the man standing at the lift. That's when I noticed the two stun-guns holstered at his hip.

"Guarding the lift?" I asked.

"We'll take the stairs."

We reversed direction and entered the first stairwell we came to and, for an instant, I had a strange sense of observing myself, from outside my body, watching myself playing the part of a spy in some classic motion picture, skulking up the stairs, breathing shallow, peering into shadows. An instant later, reality replaced reverie.

"What's happening?" I whispered.

"An emergency of some kind?" Nelson said.

Which made me even more eager to reach Mother, and I quickened my pace, along with Nelson's, as we mounted the steps two at a time. When we reached the fifth floor, breathing heavily now, Nelson eased the stairwell door open and looked through the gap.

"My Lord," he whispered.

"What? What?"

I pushed him aside and gasped at what I saw. Several staff members were slowly advancing down the hall, holding mattresses, shielding themselves from flying objects flung at them by patients backing toward us. My mind screamed *stop it*, and my body almost followed by stepping into the hall and demanding order, but self-preservation prevailed. All I could think of was thank God it wasn't Mother's hall. Then an even greater panic struck me. I was terrified to think what we'd find there. "Which way?" I said.

Nelson took my hand and we bolted into the hall behind the retreating patients and advancing staff, running toward Mother's hallway.

"You two," a man shouted from behind us, loud enough above the din to effect command.

We stopped but didn't turn around.

"Visitors were asked to leave," he boomed.

Nelson and I glanced at each other and something in Nelson's eyes dictated my next move—our next move. We ran.

"Stop," the man commanded. "Stop, I said!"

His next command thundered from right behind me, but I continued into Mother's room.

She wasn't there. I turned to face the man who'd followed us.

"My God," he panted. "When I say stop, I mean stop!"

I realized he, too, was a cop with two stun-guns belted at his waist. His hand rested on one of them.

"You must have heard the announcement," he continued. "I know you heard me."

"Of course," I said. "But my mother'—"

"We're clearing the hospital of visitors." He gave Nelson a sidelong glance. "All visitors."

As if on cue, the loudspeaker crackled once more. "Attention, please," the male announcer said. "May I please have your attention. The West Stone Avenue exit is closed. Please use the main exit onto San Rafael Boulevard. Our attendants will assist you. We apologize for this inconvenience, and we thank you for your cooperation."

The officer bared a triumphant glare and pointed toward the lift.

"But I need to know where my mother—"

"Ask in the lobby, ma'am. On your way out."

He gestured for us to follow him down the hall. A muffled cry from one of the rooms stopped me cold. The officer turned and sighed his impatience, more concerned with me than with whatever was happening inside the room I was now pointing to.

"Did you hear that?" I said.

"Ma'am," the officer urged.

A loud wail came from the room, followed by a slap, and a woman's exclamation, "Bitch."

"What's going on?" I shouted, moving toward the room. "Ma'am!" the officer said, his hand returning to his stun gun.

I stopped, speechless, bewildered. I glanced at Nelson. The slightest shift of his head signaled caution. But why? Why couldn't we respond to an obvious call for help? I looked at the officer, standing stoic, hand poised. How could our leaving the hospital be more urgent than the cry we just heard?

"Please, ma'am," the officer urged.

His refusal to intervene made me all the more eager to find Mother. We continued to the lift and the officer watched Nelson and I descend away from his view.

"This is crazy," I said. "Absolutely. I've got to find Mother. I'm not leaving without ... And I've got to talk to Hooks. This is insane."

The lift opened on the first floor and the officer we'd seen earlier appeared to be waiting for us.

"Names?" he asked.

We answered and he administered cursory retina scans.

"I'm not leaving," I said without moving.

"I need to see my mother."

"Ma'am. Sir. If you would. Please follow me."

"I said I'm not leaving."

"I'll take you to answers," he said. "If you'll follow me."

He pivoted and began marching down the hall. His promise of answers was the only reason I followed. We continued past the main exit, and I slowed at the sight of a line of officers outside behind barricades blocking the hospital entrance. On the other side of the barricades, people shouted or wept or hurled rocks and bottles at the officers.

"Ma'am, please," our escort urged. "If you would—"

"Wait," I said, startling myself, recognizing an old man in the crowd. He was wearing what looked like the same khaki shirt he wore when Nelson and I ran into him in the forest.

"Isn't that …?" I asked Nelson.

"King Juba," he replied.

King Juba was shouting at an officer pulling him from the rest of the crowd. He was barefooted and wore the same clothes as before, but he no longer carried a machete at his waist.

"Wickedness a-gwan in there," he shouted.

"What's he saying?" I asked.

"People are sinned against," Juba ranted. "Their bodies are sinned against to correctify their minds!"

"What's he doing here?" I asked.

"I've got my orders, ma'am," our escort said. "And you do want answers, right?"

I shook my head, confused, although I did want answers and followed the officer down the hall and through a maze of transparent rooms, several of them containing security officers and civilians who seemed to be under guard.

We finally entered a large room with several jell chairs facing a tidy desk adorned with a brass nameplate which read: Patrick Warren, M.P.H., M.D., Community Relations.

"Dr. Warren will be right with you," the officer said and watched us take our seats before leaving.

I looked at Nelson, hoping to reflect the obvious. That I was dumbfounded and frightened to death. The nameplate suggested we were about to get our questions answered, my fear of knowing those answers seemed almost equal to my fear of not knowing.

"Ma'am Anueche, Mr. Woon-Sam," Dr. Warren said, sweeping into the room. "Please, don't get up."

Which never crossed my mind. I'm not sure I could've gotten up.

He maneuvered himself behind the desk and sat down. I didn't like the look on his face – the feebly camouflaged frown, the creases fanning from his eyes, foretelling his deep concern.

"I can't tell you how sorry we are," he began.

"About what?" I said. "Where's my mother?"

"She's perfectly fine," he said. "Our data confirm that."

"Your data?" I glanced at Nelson. "What data?"

He pressed a button on the wall behind him and pixels sparkled above his desk. A holograph appeared in the shape of a globe—a bird's-eye view of a vehicle racing erratically on an automated highway, apparently free of vehicular speed control.

I recognized the surrounding terrain. "That's the road to Mother's camp." I turned to Dr. Warren. "What's this have to do with Mother?"

He pointed to the alphanumeric symbols on the vehicle's roof. "That's Dr. Hooks' vehicle. Your mother's with him."

15

Panic struck, but I fought back against the fog, thinking … thinking, surely there's an explanation—just one I couldn't imagine. "Why? Why are they leaving the hospital?"

Dr. Warren shook his head. "I'm not sure. But I promise, we'll get answers."

"How could you *not* know?" I said.

"For God's sake, contact Hooks," Nelson said.

Warren looked at Nelson. "He hasn't answered. Malfunction, probably. We're checking."

His words, his statements made sense individually, but spoken together they were incomprehensible.

"Review the record," Nelson said. "What did Hooks say before they left?"

Warren never broke eye contact with Nelson, but I sensed doubt, disquiet. "Hooks' office is private."

"Private?" I said. "Private as in what?"

"Private as in they don't have a record," Nelson said. He turned back to Warren. "You didn't record his sessions with Madame Anueche, did you?"

"Not an independent record," Warren said. "Hooks kept his own."

"Voluntarily?" Nelson interrupted.

Warren looked back and forth between us, clearly unnerved. "We believe in surveillance, Mr. Woon-Sam," he said. "It's just some staff—

"Stop it!" I said. "I haven't heard anything that makes sense. Start … making … sense!"

"I assume you're following them," Nelson said. "I assume somebody's following them."

"We've got a hovercraft en route," Warren said.

"And I assume they plan to stop them," Nelson said as though speaking to a child.

"Of course," Warren said. "Listen, I need to say—"

"*Now* you want to get authoritative? The time for that has passed." No, no, no, no, no, Dr. Warren," Nelson said.

I noticed occupants in an adjacent room staring at us, security and civilians alike. Perhaps they, too, were hoping to hear answers. "I do have one concern," Warren said.

I tried to brace myself. Given all that had fallen apart around this man, I feared the one concern he'd confess would be dreadful.

"I'm not sure the hovercraft will reach them before they reach the forest," Warren said. He took a long breath as though he wished he didn't have to continue. "That's why we need your help."

"Because the forest has no surveillance," Nelson said.

"We'd like to know," Warren continued, "are there any specific locations your mother might go? I mean, besides her base camp. That's where we'd start to look, of course."

"Just follow the car," I said. "My God, what is wrong with you people?"

"But if they abandoned the car," Nelson said.

I glared at him as though he, too, were losing his mind. "Then track their signatures, for God's sake. But why would they...?"

"We're brainstorming here," Warren said. "Accounting for all possibilities."

"Where Mother might go?" I said, repeating Warren's question. It never occurred to me that she would be in the lead. "Hooks is driving."

"But he doesn't know the forest," Warren said.

"I do," Nelson said. "And I know Madam Anueche. If they make it to the forest before your hovercraft catches up with them, plan to get me on board."

"That's out of the question," Warren said. "Civilians aren't—"

"Stop!" Nelson said. "You're asking us to guess where her mother might direct Hooks? I'm offering to help. And you're ... what? Objecting?"

"Regulations are involved here, sir," Warren said.

"My mother, your patient, is AWOL with one of your doctors, and you've got the nerve to speak of regulations?"

I grabbed his nameplate and slammed it down on the desk. "I will crush whatever reputation you've got left after this fiasco if we don't get my mother back in good health. Quickly! And I won't promise not to crush it even after she returns."

Dr. Warren stared at his nameplate and leaned back. Another fleeting look of uncertainty told me I'd broken his resistance. I'd have to wait, however, for him to realize that fact.

"The decision isn't mine," he said.

"I don't care who's it is," I said. "As long as it's correct."

"I'll have to get back to you," he said, standing up. "When I've got something to tell you."

He stared at us, as though expecting us to leave.

"We're not going anywhere," I said.

"You only care about the decision, right?" Warren said. "Not the deliberations. So please, let me handle this my way."

I scanned the vicinity for a vacant room and saw one with a direct view of Warren's office. "We'll wait in there," I said, pointing to it. "When do you think?"

"I'm making no promises," Warren said. It was as though he needed to reclaim some semblance of authority, and this was his last gasp. "Either about the decision or how long it'll take."

"We'll be over there," I said, still pointing. "Waiting. And watching."

We left Warren's office and I collapsed into a chair in that vacant room. Nelson sat in the chair beside mine and rested his hand on my arm. "You okay?"

I shook my head. "Give me a moment."

"Should I be worried about you?" he asked.

I shook my head again.

"I know," he said. "It's utter madness. But I'll tell you one thing that might help, as crazy as it sounds. Your mother knows the forest like the back of her hand."

"But why?" I said. "Why would they go there? It's all so crazy. A riot in a hospital? Mother leaving with her doctor? Nothing makes sense."

I glanced at Warren in his office, pacing, gesticulating, speaking via his com-desk, stealing an occasional look in our direction. I couldn't read his body language. Was he receiving good news? Bad? It wasn't even clear to me what good news or bad news meant, other than receiving word Mother had been found safe and well.

"And Juba?" Nelson said.

"A recurring nightmare," I said.

Perhaps we were both thinking the same thing, the crazy accusations spilling from that madman's mouth, embodying the malaise around us. Malaise, I thought. Not a term I would use—a term planted in my mind by Ramsey.

I startled at hearing my name. Dr. Warren was standing at the door, beckoning us back to his office.

"You've got permission to join in the search," he told Nelson.

I swallowed hard. "You lost track of them."

"They've located Hooks' vehicle," Warren said.

"Abandoned," Nelson said.

Warren nodded.

"So they're on foot?" I said.

"Where?" Nelson asked. "The vehicle, where'd they find it?"

"Off the main highway," Warren said. "Near the entrance to the forest, the border of her project, that is."

My heart was pounding at the thought of Mother and Hooks alone in the forest, on foot. I needed something to dull the fear simmering inside me. Your mother knows the forest like the back of her hand. Nelson's assurance wasn't very comforting.

"The tracking team is on the way," Warren said. "They'll fill you in."

He seemed to be speaking only to Nelson, but his acknowledging my participation meant nothing to me. It would happen regardless.

Warren raised his arm as if to show us out, but I refused to move.

"What happened here today?"

He looked at me as if weighing whether I could bear what he had to say. "We're investigating," he said. "Interviewing patients, visitors."

"Staff?" Nelson asked.

"Staff," Warren said.

"No ideas?" I said. "I mean, a riot in a hospital? Surely you have guesses."

Again, Warren hesitated. "Mob psychology," Warren said finally. "That's what my advisors told me. Unofficially, that is. A guess. Rabble rousing. Contagious rabble rousing."

"But who?" Nelson asked. "Patients? Visitors?" He glanced at me. "Staff?"

"The rabble," Warren said.

"What about Hooks?" I asked.

"We all have to answer for our actions," Warren said. He glanced up at the camera. "Including Hooks."

"Including all," I said.

Warren looked down at his nameplate and I wondered if he was thinking about how long it would remain there.

"I'm truly sorry about this," he said. "I'm looking forward to receiving word of your mother's safe return."

I thought I heard sincerity in his voice, but I was too angry and frustrated to acknowledge the offering. All I could think was that Mother would not be returning to the Carlyle Hospital and Hotel.

Warren assigned an attendant to take us to the rooftop helipad. The air outside brought relief from the antiseptic staleness of the hospital, and I breathed it in hungrily. The landing pad suddenly flashed to life, radiating lines of red light from its center out to its circumference, a low hum drew nearer, coming from a sparkling globe approaching us, then floating above us, and finally descending on the landing pad with a gust of wind and dying whine.

It was a hovercraft and its clear surface shimmered with reflected crimson of the late afternoon sun, and the three figures who emerged from it seemed to be stepping out of a hole in the coppery sky. For an instant, an image from childhood occurred to me. My very own guardian angels, I thought. Trust that they are always with you, I recalled being taught. One must have faith. *Lean not on thine own understanding.*

16

Three figures stepped out of the hovercraft onto the rooftop and marched toward us. The one in the lead stopped first and removed his flight helmet. He had a youthful brown face. Too young for command, I thought at first, noticing the feathery mustache stretched across his lip.

"Ma'am Anueche?" he asked.

I nodded. His deep voice contrasted with his adolescent frame.

"I'm squadron commander D.C." He pointed to a young Asian woman. "Chik, flight lieutenant. And Shade, OPO."

The third, a Caucasian man, had large black bulging eyes as impenetrable as a shark's. Manmade and implanted, I guessed. Perhaps we'd learn why.

D.C. shifted his gaze between Nelson and me. "I'm a by-the-book officer," he said. "As long as you do as I say," he paused, seeming to let his authority take root, "everything will be fine."

I ignored his caution, grateful there'd be no debate about my accompanying his tracking team. Perhaps that was what prompted me to apologize for the uniqueness of the mission.

"I realize this is not your typical—" I began.

"No need to explain," D.C. said, replacing his helmet and lowering its glare-shield visor. "We're happy to help. Your mother's an important person. But regardless, this is our job— to serve and protect. All I ask is that you let us do it."

I nodded, finding it difficult to ignore his second preemptive caution.

"All right, then," D.C. said. "Let's fly!"

Chik and Shade whirled around and marched back toward the hovercraft which had begun to stir with life, its rotors jerking into motion, its interior lights blinking on. At the cockpit door, I leaned against its clear outer shell which gave way slightly, the spongy surface surprising me.

Chik helped Nelson and me inside while D.C. and Shade took seats in the front of the cockpit. She escorted us to seats in the fuselage and handed us gray-and-white jumpsuits like the one she and the others wore.

"Camouflage?" Nelson asked.

Yes, that described the color and pattern, but why? Why concealment? By the authorities, of all people.

"We fly as one with the sky," Chik said as we pulled on the jumpsuits over our clothes. "Like hummingbirds. Like wisps on the wind."

But undetectable, I thought. Nearly invisible. I couldn't have asked for stronger evidence that I was leaving civilian standards behind.

I put on my helmet just in time to hear D.C. announce through its speaker, "Lift off."

The hovercraft swooped skyward, and my stomach sank. I shut my eyes and heard myself gasp through the helmet-speaker.

"Everybody all right?" Chik asked.

Nelson touched my arm. "Yes."

It took a few moments before I opened my eyes and looked outside. Thin streaks of vapor drifted past us, and only the interior's reflections off the transparent walls kept me from thinking we were floating freely in space. I looked through the hovercraft's floor and watched green rolling hills pass beneath us, tinged yellowish orange by the setting sun. The hills leveled to pastures of sugar cane and changed again to groves of palm trees, their crowns waving wildly in our wake. Finally, we came to the main highway which we followed toward Mother's base camp. I blinked into the oncoming darkness, my fear for Mother's safety growing.

"Hover-hold on mark," a woman's voice announced, a voice I hadn't heard before—the hovercraft's, I assumed. "Mark!" she declared.

We stopped suddenly in mid-air, and I pressed my hand against the fuselage wall as if to keep myself from falling.

"Velocity, zero," the voice returned, a soft mezzo-soprano. "Altitude, three hundred meters and holding. Heading forty-five degrees, southeast."

My forehead beaded with sweat as I stared into the shadows below, looking for what, I didn't know.

"Ruby may have picked up a signal," Chik said.

"Ruby?" I said.

"Our hovercraft's alter ego," Chik said. "D.C. named her. You know, like the hummingbird?"

"D.C.?" Nelson asked.

"District of Columbia," D.C. said.

"A certified Yankophile," Chik said, laughing. "D.C. idolizes all things American. Including the capital, of course."

The hovercraft rotated and Ruby's voice returned over the intercom: "Velocity holding, altitude steady, heading ninety degrees east."

Chik leaned toward me. "Try to relax. You're not going to make it if you get worked up with every zone-scan."

The hovercraft rotated periodically until we'd turned full-circle and then slowly glided forward.

Nelson caught Chik's attention and motioned toward the cockpit. "Shade?" he asked, pointing to his eyes behind his visor.

"Laser-blind," Chik said. "Training accident. Don't feel sorry for him. His implants see sharper and farther than any eagle."

Shade turned around and extended us a slight nod.

I looked toward the west where the dark violet afterglow of sunset hovered on the horizon. A narrow black river wound its way through densely wooded hills which gave way to lowlands where the river webbed into a network of meandering rivulets.

"The swamp," Nelson said, motioning below. "Southwest portion of the forest."

My jaw tightened against the thought of Mother out there in those backwaters.

"Rotor thrust three-K ... on mark," Ruby said.

I tried to distract myself, to imagine Ruby's sweet voice delivering joyous news, that she sighted Mother safe beneath a banyan tree, huddled within its sheltering root-branches, waving up to us. Have faith, I told myself.

"Mark," Ruby said.

The hovercraft darted sideways at a staggering speed and, just as suddenly, stopped. I caught my breath and looked down at an islet lodged between two winding streams cutting through the marshlands.

"Pre-descent check," D.C. said.

"All clear," Ruby replied.

"We're landing?" I asked.

"Proceed to LZ," D.C. said.

We descended slowly, our wake stirring the high grass and a hidden flock of flamingos bolted sideways from their cover. The hovercraft swayed gently, just above the surface and D.C. left the cockpit to speak with Nelson and me.

"Good news," he said.

I stared at him, half-afraid to be hopeful.

"Ruby's identified your mother's signature," he said. "She's alive and well, moving vigorously."

A surge of relief rushed through me. I wanted to cry. "Now what?" I whispered.

"We're heading toward her now."

"And Hooks?" I asked.

"No sign of him," D.C. said. "Your mother should be able to help us focus our scan."

He returned to the cockpit and the hovercraft slowly glided forward, skimming along the stream's path between tall cypress trees on either side of us.

A canoe appeared from out of the shadows on the right bank, no passengers, no oars, no poles. Empty. As if the canoe had been a signal, the hovercraft landed in the stream. We drifted toward the right bank where slivers of moonlight and patches of shadow flitted along the shoreline. I didn't recognize anything in that mélange of changing shapes, but I stared blindly into it anyway.

"Madame Anueche," D.C. bellowed over an exterior loudspeaker. "Madame Anueche. We've come to rescue you. Your daughter is with us."

I couldn't see beyond a picket of gnarled trees with thick vegetation drooping from their limbs like dark, ragged curtains. A breeze blew through the tangle of foliage, and my heart jumped at the illusion of human movement.

"We need your help," Shade said to me from the cockpit. I walked over to his him, beside a portion of the flight panel that appeared to be a screen. He pointed to the green silhouette of a human figure crouched and motionless.

"That's her," he said. "Ruby's scan has filtered out all the vegetation. Your mother's about thirty meters inside that thicket of cypress."

She was hunkered down as though hiding, and the irrationality of concealing herself reminded me of her illness. A bitter taste seeped into the back of my throat.

"What do you want me to do?" I asked Shade.

He held his hand out to D.C. who placed a microphone in his palm. "She's afraid," Shade said, holding the microphone out to me. "We need you to reassure her."

I reached for the microphone, but he pulled it back. "She might suspect we're using a facsimile of your voice. She needs to know it's really you. You need to say something that'll convince her."

He handed me the microphone. I stood silent for a moment and felt their stares bearing down on me, crippling my memory, shaming me when nothing came to mind.

"Mother?" I said into the microphone, not expecting the burst of sound. Her image on the screen didn't move. "I've come to take you back. Not to the hospital. Back to your cottage."

The silhouette on the screen stood and my throat tightened with hope and sadness as I waited for her to speak. But she didn't.

"Your real cottage," I said. "Not the facsimile. It's been too long. I want to go back with you. I need to go back." My voice began to crack. "Maybe more than you do."

Shade pointed to the screen. Mother had stepped forward. "Fitima?" Her voice sounded more thin than distant. Weak.

"Yes, I'm here. We're here to …" but I couldn't finish, and I felt Chik's hand on my shoulder.

"Please don't take another step, Madame Anueche," D.C. said through the loudspeaker. "We'll come to you."

He turned to me. "I'm sorry. Her safety comes first." He handed the microphone to Chik. "Shade," he said, pointing in the direction Shade had been staring.

Shade jumped onto the hovercraft's pontoon, rocking on the water, and he eased himself toward the bulbous roots of a cypress tree. He stepped onto the tangled roots and then, hugging the trunk, advanced to the roots of the next tree. As he moved into the thicket, something seemed to grab his attention and he stopped. I followed his gaze about thirty meters to the right and my heart froze when I saw Mother circling a thick cypress tree, clinging to it desperately.

"Don't move," Shade shouted to her.

He jumped into the channel and slogged through the waist-deep water. And then he disappeared, as if something had yanked him under, leaving only moonlit eddies on the surface to mark where he'd sunk. I pressed against the hovercraft, looking frantically between Mother and that patch of water, now growing ominously smooth.

"Chik?" D.C. said.

Chik didn't answer him but began to move in Shade's direction.

Then Shade burst through the surface coughing and spitting water. I heard us all breathe a sigh of relief. Shade swam to where Mother stood, suspended, and hoisted himself onto the tree's roots. Then he helped her into the water and shouted something I couldn't hear.

"They'll stick close to the trees on the way back," Chik said, as if she'd heard him. "Shade knows better than to trust the swamp. One moment you're on solid ground, and the next you're in a pocket of swamp gas. There are fewer surprises near tree roots." Then she looked at me, a twinkle of admiration in her eyes. "Your mother's quite a trooper," she said, "to slog around out here like she has."

I wished I could have welcomed Chik's compliment, but I had too many frightening questions about why Mother was slogging out there in the first place.

It took a while for Shade and Mother to wind their way back to the hovercraft. I could only catch glimpses of them as they moved in and out of the moonlight, but Mother's steps seemed sturdy, her progress as unwavering as Shade's.

When they reached the hovercraft, Mother looked into the cockpit, and I saw her face relax when she recognized me. Her smile eased the tightness in my chest, and for the first time since she'd disappeared, I accepted that she was truly safe.

D.C. helped her onto the pontoon, and she teetered along the skid from Chik to D.C. and finally through the cockpit door where I embraced her, cold, wet, and trembling in my arms. I felt what a mother must feel when her child has been lost and finally found, alive and well, after agonizing uncertainty. Thank God, I thought.

"Fitima," she whispered.

I held her tighter, inhaling her musky scent as if it were the finest bouquet. She raised her head from my shoulders and extended a hand to Nelson.

"You had us more than a little worried," he said, clasping her hand.

"Let's get you into some dry clothes," Chik said, guiding Mother into the fuselage.

D.C., Nelson, and I followed them to the rear of the hovercraft where Chik pulled a fresh jumpsuit from beneath one of the seats and handed it to Mother.

"Madame Anueche," D.C. said. "What about Dr. Hooks?" His question, and perhaps his tone, set me on edge.

"I left him," Mother said.

"Left him?" D.C. said. "Left him where?"

"There's a small lake downstream," she said. "Off to the left."

"Thank you," D.C. said, moving back toward the cockpit. "Chik will get you something to eat to tide you over until we've finished our business here."

Chik helped Mother out of her wet clothes and into her jumpsuit and handed her a thick sheet of soybean. While Mother ate, Nelson and I talked over each other about our fears and hopes and the dangers of the swamp. But all along, something about D.C.'s questions, or perhaps how he'd asked them, nagged at me.

"I'll be right back," I told Mother and I made my way to the cockpit, easing past Shade, who was moving to the rear to change into a dry jumpsuit, and walked to D.C.'s station.

"What do think about Dr. Hooks?" I asked.

He removed his helmet but continued checking his screen. "We'll find out soon enough."

"You sounded ... I don't know. Suspicious?"

"I am."

"Of what?"

"Ruby can't find his signature, and there's no chance he's out of range." He looked up at me. "No signature, no life."

17

D.C. called Shade to the cockpit door, and they stared out at the black pools of water and tangled foliage spot lit by Ruby's arc lamps. We were circling the shore of the small lake where Mother had last seen Hooks.

"What' ya think?" D.C. asked. Shade shook his head.

D.C. addressed the rest of us. "If Shade can't see anything, our visual scan is over. We'll bivouac at Madame's basecamp and set out again at daylight."

"Good," Mother said. "There are a few things I'd like to pick up." I glanced nervously at Nelson. He must've read my concern.

"The crew emptied the trailers, Madame," he said. "There's nothing there but a few cots."

Mother frowned, but I sighed with relief. I didn't want her returning to remnants of the debate that may have triggered her breakdown. Still, I was afraid of returning to the place where this nightmare began. And, apparently, hadn't ended. I wondered when I'd be able to speak with Nelson about Hooks' missing signature.

We flew above moonlit shadows until the rusted roofs of the base camp trailers slid into view and the motion-sensitive lights flared on, illuminating the campground. We landed in the central clearing, so gently I didn't know we'd set down until the hovercraft lights switched off. Chik handed us duffle bags and we followed her out of the cockpit door. Outside, D.C. and Shade freed a slab from Ruby's underbelly and positioned it alongside the hovercraft. Chik joined them and we watched them go about their work, unfolding the slab, maneuvering its clear panels onto telescoping poles, and pulling cables until, little by little, a large crystalline tent arose — crinkled and skewed at first, but eventually symmetrical, smooth, and transparent.

Shade and D.C. walked into the woods, and Chik stepped into the tent, beckoning us to join her.

"Why not sleep in the trailers?" I asked. "There's room enough."

"We prefer God's ceiling," Chik said.

We all glanced upward. The sky was indeed impressive, the blinking stars undiminished by moonlight.

"Besides," Chik continued. "Sleeping outdoors reminds us we're organic. With all that technology draped around us, you sometimes forget."

I looked at the trailers and thought how quickly I'd adapted to their opacity. Accelerated, no doubt, by being in the forest. Especially at night.

Yet now I had a new and surprising motive to retreat to my trailer. Privacy. I hoped Nelson and I could talk just between ourselves.

"Well," I said, trying to signal Nelson, "I'm going to spend the night in my trailer."

"Me, too," Mother said.

"Stay a while," Chik said. "Relaxation. Fellowship."

"A while," Nelson said.

"I'll pass," Mother said.

"Understandable," Chik said, patting her shoulder. "After what you've been through."

Mother started toward her trailer, and I followed, expecting to accompany her to her bedside, but she turned to stop me.

"I'm all right, Fitima," she said. I couldn't ignore – yet question – her claim of full recovery.

I hugged and kissed her and watched her walk to her trailer, resisting the urge to follow her.

"She'll be fine," Nelson said.

She opened the trailer door and offered us a wave of reassurance.

Shade and D.C. returned with firewood and built a campfire in the clearing several meters from the tent. I thought this fireside gathering odd, but what did I know about police culture? It was only tolerable knowing Nelson, and I would eventually take our leave and meet in my trailer.

D.C. asked Nelson to turn off the campground lights and a few moments later we were all sitting in the orange glow of fire and pale luster of the moon. Nelson returned and sat down beside me. For a long while no one spoke as the fire hissed and popped, loud within our silence. I pulled a thermoscrim blanket from my duffle and wrapped it around me.

"So, Nelson," D.C. said. "I understand you know the forest like the back of your hand."

"I do," Nelson said.

"Good to know," D.C. said. "But ultimately, I'll depend on Ruby. On her technology and Shade's eyesight."

Chik pulled a wooden flute from her duffle and blew a few melodious notes. The oddities of police subculture seemed to be mounting, but I urged myself to relax despite the strangeness.

"When's the last time you sat by a campfire?" D.C. asked.

I shrugged. "Can't remember."

"Not in quite a while," Nelson said.

"We must take care not to lose our inheritance," D.C. said. "The bodies we've inherited have sat beside campfires eons before they flew hovercrafts."

Nelson nodded. "Maybe that's what times like these are for. To remind ourselves of what we still remember."

I glanced at Nelson, annoyed. Instead of looking for a chance to take our leave, he was engaging in conversation.

"And what do you remember?" D.C. asked Nelson.

I studied the flickering light and shadow on their faces, stopping at Chik's. She had stopped playing, the flute descending from her lips.

Nelson didn't reply to D.C. but simply stared pensively into the crackling fire. "Have you hunted?" D.C. persisted. "Do you remember anything of that?"

For a while Nelson sat quietly, staring into the fire. "One thing I remember," he said suddenly. "I remember how hard it is to stay downwind of prey at twilight."

I stared at Nelson, realizing, and regretting, how little I knew about him.

"That's when the winds shift unpredictably," he continued. "Twilight."

"What did you hunt?" D.C. asked.

As I wondered, myself. It never occurred to me I'd learn about Nelson sitting around a campfire.

"Well?" Chik asked.

"Frogs," Nelson said.

D.C. studied my face and Nelson's, as if seeking out the joke.

"Go 'head, laugh," Nelson said. "I'm used to it."

D.C. and the others burst out laughing and I found myself joining in.

"These were no ordinary frogs," Nelson said, deadpan.

Which only made D.C. laugh harder. "Okay, I'll bite," he said, catching his breath. "What kind of frogs?"

Nelson let the fire pop and hiss before answering. "Poison frogs."

Again, laughter, but somewhat more respectful.

"So, you had trouble staying downwind of poison frogs at twilight?" D.C. said.

"Not at all," Nelson said. "Wind's got nothing to do with hunting frogs."

"Then what's all this about shifting winds at twilight?" D.C. asked.

"You learn a lot hunting frogs in the forest," Nelson said. "And not only about frogs."

"When was this?" I asked.

"Oh, so ma'am didn't know?" Chik said teasingly.

"When I was a kid," Nelson said.

"A kid?" D.C. said.

"Earning a living," Nelson said.

"Is that legal?" Shade asked.

"There are no cameras in most forests," D.C. reminded us.

"The pay was great," Nelson said. "Not many people willing to climb for frogs."

"Climb?" I said.

"Inside the palm fronds," Nelson said, pointing up to the canopy outlined by firelight.

"Biologists pay quite a sum for rare species. And who knows, you might find a new species. But the pharmaceutical companies offer the steadiest income. Anesthetics from frog skins. Other drugs, too. There's a one-in-ten chance you'll hit pay dirt, but when you do … a tidy sum. Not bad for a kid's contribution to the family cookie jar."

Until that moment, I hadn't thought of Nelson as being very different from me, at least not in terms of our backgrounds. That's when I realized how wrong I was. I'd spent my childhood taking from the family cookie jar, not contributing to it. My heart warmed toward him, toward his duty to his family, toward his overcoming hardship. But that warmth worried me, as though it were an alarm. Here it comes again, I thought—my early warning system against intimacy with men. It felt almost instinctive.

Chik filled the lull with a few long breathy notes on her flute. The music seemed to summon a succession of yawns that circled the group. I took this as an omen. I stood first, and then Nelson. Chik stopped playing.

"No, no—please," Nelson said to Chik. "Don't stop on our account."

Chik resumed, but softer.

"Good night," I said.

Nelson and I walked to my trailer, stopped, and turned around at the front steps. "Don't worry about us," D.C. said. "We're all adults here."

I needed to dispel his sexual insinuation immediately. "We need to talk over a few lose ends from the Carlyle," I said.

"Whatever," D.C. said. "But like you said, they left the cots."

Nelson shook his head at D.C.'s chortling, and we hurried inside. I switched on the light, which seemed dimmer than usual.

"Utilities are on partial," Nelson explained. "While the project's on hold." I looked in the corner where my com-desk had been, vacant now.

"Mother's too, right?" I asked.

Nelson nodded.

"I'd love to hear more about those frogs sometime," I said.

"Well, okay, but it probably sounds more interesting than it was, really."

I squinted at him in the dimness, my eyelid twitching to distraction, and I rubbed my temples for relief.

"Do I need to keep asking about you?" he said. "Or can I trust you to tell me if you're about to lose it?"

"I just wanted to alert you," I said.

"Okay."

"They're not picking up Hooks' signature," I said.

"That explains Shade's visual scanning," Nelson said.

"No signature, no life," I said. "Those are D.C.'s words."

"Unless ..."

"Unless what?"

Nelson shook his head. "I doubt it, though."

"Doubt what?"

"That Hooks would be cloaking. But I doubt he'd have the capability."

"Who would?"

"You'd be surprised."

"And why would he anyway?" I said. But an answer to that question would truly be disturbing.

"Maybe he circled back," I said in desperation.

"We'll know tomorrow."

I'd hoped for an encouraging suggestion. "Let me tell you now," I said. "From the moment this nightmare began, I've been on the verge of losing it. When I do, I promise you'll know."

18

I woke the next morning to an uproar of birdsong and the blush of sunrise seeping from the tiny front window of my trailer. A short while later, we gathered around the hovercraft for bottles of breakfast Chik was handing out. My stomach tingled from the energizing brew and from the almost unbearable suspense of what lie ahead. I felt like I was nearing the finish line of an endless marathon.

We filed into the hovercraft and took our assigned seats in the back. "Good morning," Ruby greeted us through our helmet speakers.

"Good morning, Ruby," D.C. replied from the cockpit. "Pre-ascent check, please."

The hovercraft began to hum.

"Prepare for take-off," D.C. said. "Proceed to alpha waypoint."

The hovercraft shot skyward, and I grabbed Nelson's arm and waited to regain my equilibrium. We sped above the rippling tops of cypress and mangrove trees, heading back to the area we'd surveyed the night before.

"Alpha waypoint," Ruby announced. "Stations please, everybody."

The hovercraft slowed and glided over a row of cypress standing like sentinels along a narrow channel of water. Finally, we arrived at the lake Mother had mentioned.

Chik walked into the cockpit and took a seat with the others, dividing her attention between the view outside and the panel of lights blinking in front of her.

"The two of you traveled this far, correct?" D.C. asked Mother through helmet speaker.

"Yes," she said.

I tried not to stare at her, to study every blink and curl of her lip. I had a sense she knew more about Hooks than she'd admitted, and I thought I might glimpse a sign of that knowledge on her face.

The hovercraft descended and I spotted a canoe ensnared in underbrush on the left bank. Did Mother and Hooks arrive at this place by canoe? Why didn't D.C. ask?

"Deploy the raft," D.C. ordered.

Ruby quivered for a moment and a crystalline cube dropped from her fuselage, hit the water, and inflated like a balloon. The crystalline raft slowly spun beneath the wake of Ruby's downdraft.

D.C. rose from his seat and joined Shade at the cockpit's door. "Anchor Ruby mid-stream once we get underway," he told Chik, still seated at the controls.

Ruby settled down gently on the water and the two men walked onto the pontoons. Shade reached for the raft and held it steady while D.C. stepped inside and motioned for us to join him. Shade stepped in last, after Nelson, and took a seat in the rear and joined D.C. in paddling toward the channel.

"Where to now, Madame Anueche?" D.C. asked.

Mother raised a hand over her eyes and squinted toward the sun. "There's a field of wildflowers coming up," she said. "I can almost smell them from here."

The air was moist and tinged with the smell of wet leaves.

"Keep to the right," she said.

"This is where Hooks brought you?" D.C. asked. "Or did you bring him?"

"We came together," Mother said.

"So, you trusted him, I gather," D.C. said.

I looked at Mother and shook my head. We were searching for Hooks, not inquiring about her relationship with him.

"There was a method to his madness," Mother said.

"And what method was that?" D.C. asked.

"What's going on here?" I said. "What does any of this have to do with finding Hooks?"

"Oh, it's a puzzle, ma'am," D.C. said. "With a million pieces. Not all of them physical."

"Like Hooks," Mother said. "He believed in illusion. He believed illusion could cure delusion. He called it cognitive conditioning. If a patient thought she had a snake in her belly and Hooks couldn't convince her otherwise, he would pretend to remove it. If the patient believes she's cured, she's cured."

"Hooks told you that?" I said.

Mother nodded. "My problem was I didn't believe the image I saw in the mirror was truly me. I figured if Hooks could convince a patient to believe an illusion, why couldn't he convince me to believe reality?"

"She makes Hooks sound reasonable," D.C. said.

D.C.'s sarcasm convinced me he knew more about Hooks than I'd assumed, and that he was disapproving of the doctor. But who could've communicated this to him? It had to have been Dr. Warren.

"Look!" Mother said. "There. The wildflowers."

She was pointing to the right, beyond the marsh grass on the edge of the lake, to a field of yellow, red, and violet wildflowers on a hill that sloped upward about one hundred meters to a grove of moss-draped pine.

"Where to now, Madame Anueche?" D.C. asked.

"The dam just ahead."

We floated toward a wall of bark-stripped logs, bleached, and worn to a dull-white patina. When we reached the bank, Shade maneuvered the raft between the shoreline and the logs. D.C. jumped into the ankle-deep water and tied our line to a stump. He then helped Mother and me onto the muddy bank and we climbed to firmer ground, each footstep more solid than the last.

When we reached the edge of the tall grass, D.C. walked over to Mother and she pointed westward without saying a word, and we all headed in that direction. We proceeded through intermittent clouds of gnats and mosquitoes, and I wondered what could have possibly brought Mother and Hooks to such an unforgiving place.

"You say you trusted Hooks," D.C. said, swiping insects from his face. "No one can blame you for that. After all, what choice did you have?"

"I never said I trusted him," Mother said. "I understood what he was trying to do."

I stumbled and braced myself against falling.

"You weren't the only one to doubt him," D.C. said. "He'd deceived others, too."

"Deceived?" I said. "What do you mean?"

"I don't condemn you for seeking your revenge," D.C. said to Mother, ignoring my question. "Who am I to judge? My trust has never been violated like yours was. Seeking revenge is only human."

The heat, the bugs—those swarming around us, those screeching in the distance—D.C.'s crazy questions and Mother's crazier answers, made my head pound with confusion.

"What, what, what are you talking about?" I put my arm around Mother's shoulders, as much for receiving as for offering support.

D.C.'s gaze never strayed from her face. "Why did you come here, Madame Anueche?" he asked, his tone as sweet and sentimental as if only he and Mother were standing in that field.

"We came here for healing," Mother said softly.

"Healing?" he asked.

"Wounded souls need healing."

"Tell me more about healing, Madame Anueche."

Mother cast her eyes upward and I held her tighter. "In order to be healed," she said, "you must want it with all your heart."

D.C. remained focused on her. "Where is the place for healing, Madame Anueche?"

Mother pointed to the crest of the hill and D.C. extended his hand toward hers and she held it, allowing him to guide her as they headed for the summit, leaving the rest of us to follow. The back side of the hill was flowerless stubble and when we reached the bottom, D.C. held up his hand.

"Nobody move!" He stared at the brown decaying field ahead of us. "Did you lead him here, Madame Anueche?" D.C. took a slow and cautious step forward, his hand still raised for the rest of us to stay motionless. The tip of his boot disappeared in a brown sludge that I had assumed was as solid as the ground I was standing on. "Madame Anueche, did he call for help?"

"No, he didn't," Mother said. "I told you, he needed healing. He needed to make amends. He knew that."

D.C. took another step forward and his boot sank deeper into the sludge. "So you led him here?"

"I allowed him to find whatever salvation he could."

Shade walked up behind D.C. and unwound two long cords of rope and handed one to D.C. "It's not very quick," Shade said. "Not quick enough to drown a man, not if he wanted to save himself." Then he pointed to two dead leaves on top of the quicksand a few meters ahead of them. "You see what I see?"

D.C. nodded, staring at the two leaves that resembled footprints. Shade tied a cord around D.C.'s chest and under his armpits then took a few steps back, tugging on the rope to make sure it was secure. D.C. took a step and sank to his waist and stopped. He leaned forward and submerged his cord below the surface and appeared to be tying something under the leaves. Then he yanked on the cord and backed up.

The sludge swirled slightly, and the edges of the leaves darkened, then transformed into two shoe soles breaking the surface, followed by a pair of boots, then two muck-slimed pant legs rising from the mire, and finally—when I looked away—the bloated torso of Hooks' corpse.

19

I gasped at the sight and thought of Hooks drowned in quicksand. At the thought of Mother having been with him. At the pitilessness of it.

Nelson put his arm around my shoulder and walked me over to Mother and the three of us backed away from that ghastly scene.

Shade traded places with D.C., who clambered, dripping, out of the muck and spoke into the transceiver on his collar. "You have our coordinates?" D.C. asked Chik in the hovercraft. "Get over here right away."

He walked over to the three us. "Move back a few more meters, please. Ruby's on her way and she'll document the scene. I want everything as undisturbed as possible."

He sounded so businesslike, in contrast with Shade's grunting in the background, and the rhythmic sloshing of Hooks' body being pulled from the quicksand.

"Before we start," he said, "let's get the rules straight."

"Start?" I said, thinking of nothing but ending this nightmare. "Start what?"

D.C. spoke only to Mother. "First and foremost," he said, "I can't make you say anything you don't want to say. Even if you decide to talk to me, you still have the right not to answer any question I ask, understand?"

"No, no, no," I said, grabbing Mother's arm and pulling her away from D.C. "This is not going to happen."

"Just keep in mind," D.C. continued, "everything's on the record here." He glanced at me. "Everything." He returned to Mother. "And anything you say can be used against you in court."

"Will I need a lawyer?" Mother asked.

"Don't say anything," I insisted.

"I think you need to tell the truth," D.C. said.

"And she will," I said. "But not without a lawyer." The words sounded absurd, a ridiculous cliché like *we have not yet begun to fight*. It was as though we'd been trapped in a sensational melodrama.

D.C. craned his neck toward me. "Whether she speaks to me or not is her decision," he said. "Not yours."

"I think I know where you're trying to go with this," Nelson said, moving between D.C. and Mother. "But she wasn't obliged to rescue Hooks. Even assuming she could. Nothing criminal happened here. It was an accident."

A gust of wind swirled up around us. We looked up at the approaching hovercraft, a crinkled patch of white, blue, and gray, fading in and out of view amidst the wispy clouds.

D.C. bowed his head to speak into his transceiver. "Scan for everything," he said. He glanced up at the hovercraft, holding steady above us. "Footprints, fibers, bodily fluids." He turned around and I followed his gaze to Shade standing beside Hooks' body, lying face up and splayed at Shade's feet. "And scan the body before Shade sacks him."

D.C. then sidestepped Nelson and returned to Mother. "Now, Madame Anueche; you don't have to speak to me. And you can stop talking anytime you'd like. You can answer questions with your attorney present if you'd like."

I walked up to D.C., wondering if my assumptions were reasonable or fanciful. "Don't you think she's been through enough? Take us to your headquarters if you must. Question her there. I assume they can provide some comforts. And, of course, we can call in a lawyer."

"Yes, yes, of course," D.C. said. "If needs be, we can do as you say. But the context is right here — fresh and immediate. Available to memory and motive. Distance distorts."

He turned back to Mother. "So, Hooks didn't call for help? Did he say anything? Did the two of you talk?"

I was about to step between him and Mother if she seemed about to speak. But she only shook her head — first at me, then at D.C.

"So he, what...?" D.C. asked. "He walked into the quicksand on his own?"

Mother nodded.

"Did you have any physical contact with him?" D.C. asked.

"Enough!" Nelson said. "You're way out of line. Whether she waives her rights or not, I won't let this continue. Given what she's been through she may not even be capable of understanding her rights.'

"If you're so keen on the law," D.C. said to Nelson. "I'd think you'd be familiar with obstruction of justice."

"Justice?" Nelson said. "Justice would be for you to take her home. Now."

"I have every right," D.C. said, "I have a responsibility to question the last person who saw the deceased alive. And to arrest anyone who tries to stop me."

He glanced up at the hovercraft and spoke into his transceiver. "You about finished?" He paused, listening to Chik through his earpiece. "Good, good. Pick up Shade and the body bag. We'll walk back to the raft, and you can pick us up there. Over."

He turned to the three of us. "You convinced me. We don't have to continue this here. We can do this as easily at her base camp. Please try to relax. All of you. Remember, only the guilty have reason to fear."

I shuddered to hear those words; the slogan scrawled by the anarchist back in the capital. Nelson turned to me, also recognizing the phrase I'd told him about. The cruel irony was not the slogan but its bastardization: Not only the guilty have reason to fear. That threat seemed to be looming as real as the scene and people around us. I reached for Nelson's hand and then for Mother's and we left for the lake's shoreline.

After we landed at base camp, Shade and Chik busied themselves reattaching the raft to Ruby's undercarriage, beside the body bag Shade had secured earlier. D.C. accompanied us toward the trailers, offering more platitudes about his adherence to the law which he may have supposed were reassuring. But his insistence had the opposite effect.

"You can wait inside," D.C. said, gesturing toward the trailer in front of us.

That trailer happened to be Nelson's, but its position was no mere happenstance. Nelson had been redirecting us away from Mother's trailer and toward his own despite my modest resistance and Mother's and D.C.'s indifference. It occurred to me, thinking back on our concealed confab the previous night in my trailer, that he and I had entered a new world, a world of deception, for which we were not prepared. Or, for which I was not prepared. As we stepped into his trailer, I couldn't shake the frightening image of his machete hidden there.

"I won't be long," D.C. said. "I've got to retrieve the protocol. By the book, you know." Mother sat wearily on the cot while Nelson and I settled on the floor, leaning against the wall.

"Why here?" I asked Nelson.

He shrugged. "Maybe they're rewarded for completing their investigations in the field."

"No, no – I mean why did you lead us to your trailer?"

"Why not?" he said. "We're being held. That's what's important."

I stared at him, wondering if he would attempt to deceive me as quickly as he'd deceive D.C. But there was no defense against lies and deceit in this new world of deception. Trust was the word I was searching for. It had been superfluous in our world of transparency. Now, it was a lens through which to view each other's behavior — like Nelson's looking away from me as I stared at him. Still, I believed I could trust him. But it was only belief.

I turned to Mother. "Don't say anything," I said. "Not until we get an attorney."

"But that makes me look guilty," she said.

"To who?" I said. And as dismissively as I could, I answered, "D.C.?"

"To myself," she said. "It makes me feel guilty."

"But that's how it's played," Nelson said. "Your first spoken words should be, Get me my lawyer!"

He then turned to me. "I'm beginning to sympathize with your anarchist," he said. "I mean, his revision: *not* only the guilty have reason to fear. Seems he was onto something."

20

A sharp knock rattled the door and D.C. stepped inside. He'd changed out of his muck-soaked pantsuit into a clean one, but he appeared different in addition to his clothing. He stood more erect, his chest expanded, and he leaned forward on his toes. He seemed to be displaying a more commanding version of himself.

"*To be continued* has arrived," he said.

Nelson and I stood.

"We've advised her not to answer your questions," I said.

"Please, please," D.C. said. "That's her right." Regardless, he went about installing an omni-focal recorder on the floor in the center of the room. "I need to record that decision. From your mother."

I walked over to D.C., clutched his arm, and guided him toward the door. "You do realize," I said softly, "she was hospitalized for neuro-medical problems. Whatever she tells you here will surely be inadmissible."

D.C. freed himself from my grasp and walked over to Mother. "It's my understanding, Madame Anueche, that your daughter offered to take you to your cottage, correct?"

"Yes," Mother said.

D.C. turned back to me. "I'd say, if she's well enough to go home, she's well enough to make a statement. But, of course, if she chooses not to—"

"I want to tell what happened," Mother said. "At least, *my* version of things. You see, the ax and the tree remember wood-chopping differently."

I gnashed my teeth, infuriated by Mother's stubbornness.

"Ax, tree—I'll record it all. Whatever you choose to share, Madame Anueche."

"I have my story and I'm sure Hooks had his. We'll never know his version, though. Of course, you want the truth. But there's no surveillance in the forest so you'll have to look for truth where you're most likely find it: in your heart. The problem is, that's also where you'll find delusion." She smiled, but not sympathetically. "So maybe you'll never find what you're looking for."

"Perhaps," D.C. said. "But you're the only witness we got. I'll take what I can get."

I sat on the cot beside Mother, prepared to stop her from incriminating herself.

"So," D.C. continued, "you came to the forest. You leading him, right?"

Before I could stop her, Mother nodded. She was staring now, blankly, into the center of the room. "The forest promises healing."

"Mother please."

"So, you brought him to the forest to heal," D.C. said. "To the quicksand?"

"To the edge," Mother said.

I stiffened.

"I pointed to the quicksand," she continued. "I told him here was the healing he'd been searching for."

"Healing for what?" D.C. asked.

"For his sins," she said.

"Sins?" D.C. said.

"His promises were false," she said. "He tempted me with my own memories. He said he could help me reclaim myself. He said I'd lost myself as a woman. That I'd lost myself as a lover."

I found myself trapped inside her story.

She blinked away her blank stare and turned to me. "He said I'd lost myself as the lover I'd been in your father's arms."

Panic pounded in my ears at her mention of my father. I shook my head, unable to think clearly about what she was saying.

"Hooks took me back to the grief I felt when I lost your father," she continued. "That's when I lost myself, Hooks explained. He said he could help me reclaim myself. If only I would allow myself to be caressed and loved by a lover."

I was standing now, resisting what Mother was trying to say.

"That's how I came to feel your father's presence," she continued. "Right there in Hooks' office. Behind me. I flinched at first at the touch on my shoulders. It had been so long. But the scent, so delicate, so familiar — a hint of orange with a touch of cinnamon. The scent of Gerbera. I became so relaxed my soul floated from my body. Like an angel. I saw myself reclined on the couch, beneath my lover. I couldn't see his face, but I knew it was Kelvin's. His eyes were Kelvin's eyes and his lips on mine were Kelvin's too, soft and full and hard against my mouth."

A groan worked its way from my gut and past fingers bitten and bleeding in my mouth. I collapsed beside her, squeezing her, trying to absorb her pain. Her violation. To make it my own. To add it to my guilt. How could I have failed her so horribly?

"You can give too much," she whispered. "You become empty. You forget how to take. But I got another chance in Kelvin's arms, and his love filled me to bursting. And it had been so, so long."

She pushed me back to look at D.C.

"But Hooks snatched all that away from me. His spell conjured Kelvin and then he stole him away. Again. I looked down at that couch, at the lovers making love and saw skin too old to be Kelvin's. I closed my eyes and tried to wish the lovers away, but I couldn't. That's when I knew a sin had been committed. A sin had been committed and would have to be paid for."

"And so you took him—" D.C. started.

"But to simply punish a sin and not offer hope for atonement is itself a sin," Mother said. "That's why I took him to the forest. I told him it was a place for him to make amends."

"So you—" D.C. began.

"I led him to the quicksand. I told him to seek atonement for his sins. He waded in. Up to his knees. To his waist. He seemed surprised to be sinking. To his shoulders. His neck. He didn't struggle. He didn't cry out. He didn't speak. I waited to hear his confession, but he held onto it. I told him he could take it with him. So he did."

21

My insides roiled with rage, sadness, and guilt. Under my care, the woman I should have protected had been violated. The doctor I'd trusted had proven unworthy. That doctor, who I would now destroy, was already dead. I wanted to strike out, but I had no blameworthy target. I wanted to scream, but I had no voice. I had no words. I had only fury that churned wordless, trapped inside me. And, of course, I had the woman I held even tighter in my arms.

D.C. cleared his throat. "It can't be denied," he said. "We now have a motive."

I glared at him. He'd shrunk back to his pseudo-adult posture. Perhaps he'd been humbled by Mother's testimony. .

"You're right," D.C. continued, staring now at Nelson. "She wasn't required to save Hooks. But if she led him to his death … purposefully. Anyway, we now have a motive."

"The only one guilty of a crime," I raged, "is out there in that body bag."

"That's for others to determine," D.C. said. "I simply connect the dots. When the design spells suspect, my job is done. Looks like we'll be heading back to headquarters just as you requested."

Chik knocked on the door and hurried to D.C. to whisper in his ear while the rest of us watched his face twist and turn until he abruptly raised his arm.

"Okay, okay," he said. "Tell Shade I'll be there shortly."

The trailer door slammed with Chik's exit and D.C. hesitated, reluctant to reveal what he'd learned.

"There's been a slight complication," he said finally. "Ruby's picked up the signature of a drifter running loose." He gestured vaguely toward outside.

"And?" I said. "So what?"

"So, we have to apprehend him."

"Now? How could that be a priority?"

D.C. shrugged as though in agreement with me.

"The sooner we get to headquarters, the sooner—"

"Of course," he said. "But this guy's crimes have been, well …"

"What about us?" Nelson said.

"What about you?" D.C. said. "You wait. Not long. This guy's crazy. The nut who started the riot at the hospital. King Juba. We'll bag him and—"

"Not kill him," Mother cried.

I jumped at her alarm, startled and confused.

"Of course not, Madame," D.C. said. "We don't intend to harm, anyway. Just secure him."

"I can't imagine your superiors agreeing to this," I said. I looked at Mother. "No matter who he is."

"They're the ones issuing the order," D.C. scoffed.

I shook my head in disbelief. True disbelief. The disbelief of nightmares.

Chik cracked the door and poked her head inside. "Ready when you are." And just as quickly withdrew.

"Well," D.C. said, "duty calls." He glanced around the trailer. "Ruby scanned these trailers, by the way. They're weaponless, thank goodness. You know, *lead us not into temptation.* They're holding pens without guards. But we won't be long. You can grade us by how long we take. We're aiming for high honors."

With that, D.C. left the trailer, the door banging closed behind him. I held Mother's hand. "Are you okay?"

She nodded.

"Do you want to lie down?" I asked.

She didn't answer but let go of my hand and settled back on the cot.

"Are *you* okay," Nelson asked.

There was no point admitting to how awful I felt. For the first time in my life, I'd reached a limit to my capabilities.

A chorus of cicadas filled the silence and the time it took to reign in our emotions, gather our thoughts. Mother's eyes were closed but she was not asleep.

"You care about this King Juba?" I asked her.

"I care about his life," she said without opening her eyes. "Anyone's life."

"We saw him at the hospital," I said. "You didn't see him there, did you?"

She didn't answer. Nelson touched my arm and slightly shook his head. He was right, of course. It was the wrong question at the wrong time.

"We should be thinking about a lawyer," I whispered to him.

"Or why we need one," he said.

He watched me as though gauging my reaction.

"I don't mean technically," he explained. "I mean ...," he rubbed his hands together nervously, "a victim shouldn't need a lawyer."

"Of course not," I said, "but practically speaking —"

"Some victims are self-made," Mother said.

I stared at her, surprised. Her eyes were opened now.

"Mother, you shouldn't blame yourself for—"

"I'm not talking about Hooks," she said. "I'm talking about us!"

"Us?" I said. "Self-made victims? I don't understand."

"I'm not sure I do either," she said. "I'm not even sure …. Listen, if you can't recognize your own face in a mirror, perhaps you shouldn't expect to see the world for what it is. But I don't trust the world I see."

Again, that question of trust. I understood her misgivings. But we still had to make our way in that untrustworthy world.

"I think I understand what she's saying," Nelson said.

I turned to him, confused.

"At least," he continued, "I have my interpretation of what she's saying."

"I'm listening," I said.

"I don't know if you're in the mood to—"

"I'm just exhausted," I said, rubbing my temples. "Please, go on."

"It's a cautionary tale," he said. "Well, more like a proposal in the guise of a tale."

"Can't you fast-forward to the proposal?"

"It needs the story."

I sighed. "Okay."

"My first job as a civil engineer was to—"

I sighed more loudly. "Really?"

"Yes, really," he said. "My first job as a civil engineer was to develop computer models for evacuating buildings. I worked with architects to design, you know, exits, corridors and stairwells for various evacuation scenarios. Fires, mostly. The width, length, and number of ways to leave a building. Safely."

"I'm hoping for a connection," I said.

"Me, too," he said. "Given what's at stake."

"Please. I'm sorry."

"The challenge to developing these models is inputting correct assumptions about people's behavior. Predicting the behavior of fire and smoke is easy. Predicting human behavior … well, that's the hard part. I mean, you have your obvious variables. Age. Abilities. Are they asleep or awake? Which occupants are able to detect the warning signs? How fast can they evacuate? But then you have your intangibles. Who's willing to believe the warnings?"

"Willing to believe?" I said.

"You'd be surprised. Pre-evacuation delay, we call it. Those delays can be surprisingly long. And some people never leave."

"So, what are you saying?" I asked. "Are we missing warning signs?"

"Warning signs are learned, Fitima," he said. "We learn them from experience. But if no one's ever told us there are people in the world who mean to do you harm—"

"People?"

"Hooks. D.C."

"Two people?"

"It's not always the number of warning signs," he said. "Sometimes it's their nature. I've listened to survivor interviews from the Age of Memorials. They explained how there'd be an explosion in a building and some occupants would think, this can't be happening. The warning signals would sound but some would refuse to leave. You can't blame them. Their minds weren't prepared for the emergency they faced."

"But where's this leading? What are you suggesting we do?"

"Like I said, I'm not sure you're gonna like my proposal."

"Please!"

"Evacuate."

"Evacuate? What does that mean?"

"Run away," Mother said.

I jerked my head around to confront her. "Are you crazy?"

The word slipped from me, but I wouldn't take it back. It was exactly what I meant. "You couldn't look more guilty," I said.

Nelson stood and walked to the door's peephole. He peered outside, then turned to me. "Or we could trust D.C. like we trusted Hooks."

I shut my eyes against the blow. Anger and shame kept them shut. "That's not fair," I whispered.

"I'm sorry," Nelson said. "I truly am. But we all need a good shake. A wakeup shake. We need to question who to trust, not just blindly believe. We can't blame ourselves for what happened. But now that we've seen … now that we've felt … this …"

The term malaise came to mind, but it was inadequate. I opened my eyes and studied Nelson through the blur of tears.

"Would you trust her attorney?" he asked. "Would you trust the courts?"

"What choice do we have?" I said. "We have no choice."

"You always have choice," Mother said. "Fugitives understand that."

"Mother please! These aren't slavery days. They'll track us down."

"That's what they want you to think," she said. "That's what they want you to believe."

I glowered at Nelson as though he were the enemy. "See what you started?"

"No, no, Fatima," Mother said. "I started it. Self-made victims, remember? Victims, if we allow it. If we choose to stay. If we choose to believe their power is limitless, their reach without bounds. A very believable lie. The same one told by slave owners. Some captives create their own prisons. Ones without walls. Without guards."

I tried to untangle the threads of her demise. Her failure to recognize her own image. Her failure to protect the slaves' graves. Her rape by a monstrous doctor, their flight into the forest, her retribution, her legal liability. These were enough to drive anyone mad. I had to understand this. And I had to sympathize. But I also had to redirect her toward reason. For her sake. For all our sakes.

I leaned toward her. "You've been through so much. Too much. And I'm so, so sorry. But we need to think clearly about next steps. Objectively. We're in the middle of the forest. Held by the authorities. Waiting for their return. That's our here and now. What you're talking about has nothing to do with our situation."

"I think it does," Nelson said.

My fingernails bit into my palms. "Nelson, please. I understand her confusion, but yours? Your stories are as irrelevant as hers. You're both talking nonsense! How could we escape? Where would we go?"

"How?" Mother said. "I could just walk out that door."

"Where?" Nelson said. "I have a plan, but you may not be in the mood to hear it. But when I follow your mother, you'll have that choice."

22

I followed Mother and Nelson out of trailer and into the clearing. The air outside felt thicker, more humid, more difficult to inhale. The birds and cicadas sounded louder, their calls and screeches arrhythmic, discordant. Even the sunlight seemed brighter, as though a spotlight was shining down on us.

Motion on my right made me turn and I saw Nelson running toward a shimmering globe that I finally understood to be a hovercraft. Was it Ruby? Hadn't D.C. and his crew taken Ruby to hunt down King Juba?

Mother touched my hand and I jumped.

"Is that Ruby?" I asked, but my question sounded nonsensical, so I wasn't surprised when Mother shrugged.

Nelson returned, holding large sheets of gray fabric draped over his arms.

"Was that their hovercraft?" I asked him.

He nodded and extended the gray sheets to Mother and me.

"But I thought ...." and then I stopped to reimagine what I had, in fact, assumed. That the crew had taken Ruby to apprehend King Juba.

"They must've gone on foot," Nelson said, breathing hard.

But why, I wondered.

"Man hunting," Nelson answered my unspoken question. "The added thrill of boots on the ground."

I raised the gray sheet he'd given me and shrugged, "What?"

"Cloaking capes," he said. "Wrap it around you. Make sure your arms stay covered. Your ID implant's in your arm, right?"

I nodded, slipping my arms into the sleeves.

"Pull up the hood," he said. "Tie it tight."

I watched Mother copy my movements. The hood and cape were metallized fabric that stretched and sheathed our bodies head to ankle.

"Cloaking?" I said.

"Protection against thermal imaging," he explained. "And hiding your implant."

"But why would they hide themselves?"

"Like I said, *you'd be surprised who uses cloaking.*"

His *you'd be surprised* felt like a new mantra in my life. How much of what was true was true in my mind alone?

Nelson held my shoulders to regain my attention. His eyes were visible through a slot in the hood. "They may play hunting games with King Juba," he said, "but they're bound to use Ruby when they find us gone."

Panic returned, joining my bewilderment.

"I need one more thing," he said, drifting away from me.

"No, no," I said. "Where are you going?"

He didn't answer but raced toward one of the trailers. I stood there, stone still, but imagined my body folding in on itself—stooping, kneeling, and lying on the ground, curling into a ball. That is what I wanted to do. I didn't recognize the woman standing steadfast in that clearing holding her mother's hand, waiting for her mother's assistant to return with a plan for them to escape into the forest.

When Nelson returned, I had only his plan in mind. Where to? By way of? The laser-saw slung to his hip surprised me.

"Let's get moving," he said.

I pointed to the laser-saw.

He didn't answer but only waved for us to follow him, so I was left to invoke my own answer: You'd be surprised.

We moved westward through the forest on a narrow trail, the sunlight just beginning to slant into our faces. Nelson led, followed by Mother, so I spoke to him in a loud whisper.

"Your plan?" I said, swiping vines from my face.

"I know someone who lives off the grid," he said.

"Lives off the grid? That's not possible."

"He's an engineer," he said. "He can hide us. Contact help."

"But he's off the grid," I said.

"He's got a transmitter," Nelson said. "Undetectable. My friend's an engineer," Nelson repeated.

"Who can secret us," Mother said.

I heard their words as though in a dream—from a mindscape where speech wasn't supposed to make sense. Fleeing, secreting, sneaking— such fantasies occurred only in sleep— troubled sleep. In nightmares. Not in everyday life. Yet the fantastic had crept into our everyday lives. Reality and nightmare coincided.

And, as in a nightmare, my thoughts swung between lucid and ludicrous. So what if we continued our escape into the forest? What was the worst that could happen? We could get caught. But these weren't slavery days, after all. We wouldn't be whipped. We'd be taken back into custody and proceed from where we started. Assuming we survived our escape. And Mother and Nelson seemed so confident we would.

"How far?" I heard myself ask. "Your friend. How far from here?"

"Near St. Clemens. On the coast."

"That's pretty far."

He shrugged. "But reachable."

"Get water along the way," Mother said.

Nelson turned around to look at her. "Why, yes." He looked past Mother, at me, squinting his surprise.

"Slave narratives," Mother said. "Diaries. Speeches. From the Repository. I read as many as I could. Ever since we came upon those graves." She glanced between me and Nelson. "But who would've figured ...."

Exactly, I thought who would've figured? It all seemed so utterly fantastic. I stomped along the path to jar myself into believing it was all really happening.

We did make good progress, however. And the farther we traveled, the more I could believe what had seemed a dream was, in fact, reality, and that, with luck, we might reach Nelson's promised safety.

Suddenly, Mother stopped short in front of me and cocked her head as if to listen. Her eyes flashed wildly, surveying our surroundings.

"What?" I asked, frightened.

Nelson returned to us. "We need to get moving."

"What is it?" I asked.

But then I heard it, too. A faint sound in the distance, vaguely familiar.

"C'mon," Nelson said.

Before he could leave, Mother grabbed his arm. "Dogs!"

That was the sound. Dogs. Dogs barking. But that made no sense. There were no wild dogs in the forest. And D.C.'s crew had none. It seemed like a hallucination.

"It can't be dogs," I said.

Nelson shook his head.

"Then what?" I said.

"It's D.C."

"D.C.? But—"

"Does it frighten you?" he asked. "That's why he's doing it."

And it did frighten me. It terrorized me. The madness of a man howling like a wild animal.

"We'll need to get off this trail," Nelson said.

He pulled me into the bushes, and I glanced back and saw Mother follow. I slowed only to push her ahead of me so she could keep up with Nelson. We crawled on damp spongy ground and through dense underbrush that thickened and clawed until we spilled into a small grassy clearing.

Nelson pointed to a dark opening under a low-slung bush. "Under there."

We scurried inside the thicketed cave.

"They're not using Ruby's infrared?" I whispered.

"They still have Shade," Nelson said. "He doesn't need infrared to spot us." Nelson crouched and looked out from the mouth.

"What are you thinking?" I asked. He seemed prepared to spring forward.

"A diversion."

Before I could grab him, he darted from the thicket and disappeared into the bush.

"What's he doing?" Mother asked.

I couldn't answer. I couldn't speak.

"Listen," she said.

I tried to focus my hearing. Every sense now seemed to require purposeful direction.

The white noise of the forest slowly emerged in my consciousness.

"No barking," Mother said.

Yes, the barking had stopped. And now its absence felt even more frightening. I rubbed my eyes to clear my vision. I was right: it was a small fire flickering in the shadows to our right, about a hundred meters away. It was too distant to be an immediate threat, yet its mere presence was threatening enough. Suddenly, an explosion of dust and debris clouded over the fire, followed by a loud report.

I placed a finger over Mother's lips before she could ask a question I couldn't answer. And to keep her quiet.

"Prey-seek pistol versus laser-saw?" D.C. hollered. "Doesn't seem fair. Better hand-to-hand. But whichever you prefer."

His words were as terrifying as his bark. He was armed and we weren't. The laser-saw surely didn't count as a weapon, and D.C. said as much. I guessed Nelson had used it to start the fire—the diversion he'd mentioned, but that was about all it was good for. I wished he'd stayed hidden with us. Our cloaking apparel would shield us from the prey-seek's infrared guidance and Shade may have had enhanced vision, but he couldn't see through objects.

And then it dawned on me, unbidden, in the middle of all that danger. I'd accepted the need to hide. Accepted? I clung to it desperately. Hiding in that forest felt as reassuring as being visible had felt in the city. My feelings had reversed themselves. My new comfort in being invisible had emerged like a long-dormant instinct, and, like an instinct, I felt I had little choice but to obey it. I crawled over to Mother and drew her close to me and together we retreated deeper into our hideout.

A second explosion made Mother jump. I assumed Nelson had set another fire and D.C. had targeted it, as before. I assumed further that Nelson's plan was to start enough fires to distract them from our escape—assuming he returned.

"And so, the hunt continues," D.C. shouted from off in the distance.

Another explosion and I covered my ears against the barrage, against the thought of D.C. firing at Nelson. I nearly screamed when Nelson darted back into our thicketed cave.

"We've got to go," he said.

"Can't we just stay here?" I said.

"We could," he said. "If we trust the cloaking. Or if D.C. decides to give up." He paused for me to consider our options. "Or we could get to into that creek and follow it. Hide our trail. Stay below their line of sight."

Why did the passive option always feel more appealing? But I couldn't defend it now without feeling defeatist. So we followed Nelson out into the underbrush, dragging ourselves along the forest floor. I glanced at Mother ahead of me. Her serpentine movements, matching Nelson's, were steady, strong, and determined. Hiding, running. It all seemed so natural. Yet it was the only time in our lives we'd done either. Or so I assumed.

The explosions stopped, but D.C.'s barking and howling resumed. He sounded far away, however, and moving farther. Soon his yelping was replaced by the rush of water from the creek Nelson had mentioned. I'd imagined a shallow, lazy stream but the unseen current ahead of us sounded strong and fast. We finally reached its embankment and I looked down into swirling ribbons of white foam. I glanced at Nelson and hoped my scowl made it clear his notion of creek did not match my own.

We slid on our backsides down the muddy bank to the water's edge. Nelson stepped in, sinking to mid-thigh after several steps. He held the laser-saw to his chest which is when I first noticed he was still carrying it. He mouthed a few words I couldn't hear above the onrush of water, and then he motioned for Mother and me to follow him.

I stepped in and sank to my waist and then stumbled on a jagged stone. The water's chill surprised me, and I stood stiffly, steadying myself and adjusting to the cold.

"Stay close," Nelson said above the surging water.

The current pushed against me, and I watched Mother and Nelson ahead leaning into it, moving slowly on the rocky creek bed. Despite the current, we made progress stumbling our way forward. But when we rounded a bend, we came upon a fallen tree blocking our way. I glanced at the steep embankment on our right, closer to us.

"I'll see if there's a clear passage underneath," Nelson said.

"Can't we get out and walk past it?"

"We could, but ...."

He left the rest for me to figure out; the creek being the only route that would hide us and our tracks.

He moved toward the center of the channel, the water rising to his chest. He placed the laser-saw on the tree trunk and dove under it. He popped back up rather quickly and nodded confidently.

"There's a passage," he said. "Right here." He pointed to the middle of the fallen tree. "I'll go first. Then you, Madame Anueche. I'll be on the other side to meet you." Then he dropped below the surface.

Mother and I moved closer to where Nelson had stood, the water running colder there, and faster around our chests. Mother dove under and I followed, groping at the slimy trunk above me. When I surfaced on the other side, gasping for air, a bolt of white light flashed across my blurred vision, and I heard shouts muffled by the water in my ears.

The creek water drained from my face and a second flash sizzled on the tree trunk behind me. Nelson grabbed my arm and pulled me forward, while Mother thrashed in the water along the bank, making her way upstream.

"What's happening?" I gasped.

The splashing and my own confusion allowed me to hear only, "D.C."

Nelson yanked harder and I tried to ignore the cramp in my calf, an unyielding knot of pain that tightened and burned hotter with each step. We caught up with Mother, who'd stopped, bent forward from exhaustion. A hostile odor stung my nostrils and I glanced back at the fallen tree, a thin column of gray smoke rising above the prey-seek's strike.

"Are we safe?" I asked foolishly, knowing we weren't and only wishing it so. "We've reached Black Bottom," Mother said.

"Tar Springs," Nelson said.

The pungent smell of sulfur and ammonia further identified our location. Pitch lake. The Tar Springs. Also known as Black Bottom.

"They caught us," I said. "They're shooting at us! We've got to surrender."

Nelson grabbed my arm. "That's right, they're shooting at us."

"That's why we have to surrender."

"I can't forget Hooks," Nelson said. "Or D.C.'s madness. I can't forget ... I can't forget not only the guilty have reason to fear."

"But that's only a stupid slogan. Written by a—"

"Another madman!"

"Nelson, what choice ..."

I glanced at Mother; her eyebrows raised in apparent reply to my question. I closed my eyes against the nightmare encroaching upon us.

"We'd do better in the tar field," I heard Nelson say.

"Maybe if we separated," Mother said. "But head in the same direction."

"The tar pools should interfere with their infrared targeting," Nelson said.

Their voices drifted to me as though spoken in a dream, echoed from a canyon. "The laser-saw," Nelson said. "I left it behind."

"Too late for that now," Mother said. "We're sitting ducks if we stay here."

Or perhaps I was the phantom, the two of them speaking past me, around me, through me. Before I could find my voice to protest, my arms lurched forward as they pulled me toward the embankment, staggering, cramping, gasping air and water.

23

I scrambled up the muddy embankment, inhaling the stench of petrol. We reached the rise, and I spied an endless field of stubbled grass pitted with scattered pools of tar. Stands of stunted trees sprouted here and there, starved in that soured soil.

This is where we run? I thought.

"I can't make you," Nelson said. "Do you wanna wait for them?"

I listened for explosions and barking, but all was quiet. I scanned the primordial field in front of us and considered the horrible choice I had to make. Mother looked at me as though there were no choice, as though even in her muddled mind our only option was obvious. I had no formula to rebut her, no equation to predict the risk/reward ratio of running or surrendering.

Somewhere along the line, the rules had changed. My knowns had become unknown. Old habits seemed useless. Or worse, possibly fatal. I knew no way to calculate a next move. I had only my gut.

"If we run," Nelson said, "we head west." He pointed to a stand of skeletal trees, spindly against the dark, cloudless sky. "We fan out and then converge over there. Gotta watch for the tar pools. That's if we run."

He glanced back toward the creek. "There's no sign of them."

It sounded crazy, like so much I'd heard those past few days. "Okay," I said. "To the trees."

We crouched on the edge of the bank ready to run, when a bolt of white light blinded me. The prey-seek blast struck a gnarled tree to our right, splitting it in two—one half in flames, the other smoking.

Mother and Nelson sprinted for the tree stand, and I took a step forward, but my back foot slipped, and I slid down the embankment and back into the creek. I tried to stand, but rocks shifted underfoot, and I lost my balance and the current dragged me downstream.

I tumbled, gulping mouthfuls of water and air, and shut my eyes against the pain of my cheek scraping rock and a sharp blow to my shoulder. When I opened my eyes again, eddies of white water swirled just below my mouth. I was wedged against the tree trunk we'd swum under.

I looked back to where I'd slipped and saw another flash of light, still more prey-seek fire. I had to reach Mother and Nelson, but I was sure D.C. had come between us. The smell of burning wood caught my attention and I glanced at the tree trunk, still smoldering, with Nelson's laser-saw perched on top. Intuitively, I grabbed the saw and staggered back to the bank, bent over, and grasping the rocks in the shallower water, steadying myself. A film of oil coated my fingers, and the smell of tar was thick enough to taste.

I climbed back up the embankment and scanned the field but saw no one. I stepped onto the soft earth, around a black tar pool that reflected nothing on its surface. Not even the hint of a breeze passed over me, as if air itself had abandoned that place.

To the east, two men sprang from a thicket and sprinted toward the stand of trees Nelson had pointed out to me. It was D.C. and Shade. My heart froze as I looked for Mother and Nelson within the stand's meager cover, but I saw no one. I waited to see if Chik would follow the two men, but she didn't. Perhaps she'd been left behind with Ruby. Or maybe she was out there, hiding. Stalking.

D.C. and Shade crouched and approached the tree stand like predators, slow and steady, stopping fifty meters away.

I stood directly behind them, a similar distance. I was prepared to approach them and surrender, but I wasn't sure how without surveillance to record the event. That was how these things were done. Official acts were recorded. I would explain why we left the trailer. I would describe our state of shock, our anxiety and confusion, the adrenaline rush, the insane compulsion to run. I would defend Nelson's impulsive use of the laser-saw to distract them, given our fear of their assault.

I felt the weight of the laser-saw in my hand. I wanted to place it on the ground. But I wanted a record of my submission. My time in the forest hadn't extinguished the habit of a lifetime, my expectation of witness.

"My first hunt of the day," D.C. shouted toward the trees, "in newly fallen snow."

He seemed to be reciting.

"I sit and wait for quarry," he continued.

Yes, he was narrating. A poem?

"The air is crisp and cold, the last hunt of the year. My aim is true and bold, I finally bag my deer."

"No one hunts deer in Trinidad," Shade said in normal voice.

"Wrote that when I was seven," D.C. said.

"Cute," Shade said.

"Hey," D.C. shouted toward the tree stand. "We fired warning shots. Remember, warning shots are permissible only when deadly force would be authorized, right? If deadly force weren't authorized, we had no business firing warning shots. But we fired warning shots. So deadly force must be authorized."

D.C. seemed to be pursuing a lethal logic, preparing himself to shoot to kill, to justify murder in his own mind. Or was he trying to frighten

Nelson and Mother into thinking that was his plan? My calculus for D.C.'s thinking failed me, and I couldn't risk being wrong.

The two men marched forward toward the tree stand, moving away from me. They were silent now, searching the trees ahead of them. Then they stopped. The two men suddenly stood upright and staggered.

"Goddammit," D.C. shouted. "Damn tar!"

He and Shade teetered and flung their arms about, but they didn't move forward or backward. Only downward, ever so slightly. I had to focus on their shoulders to tell they were sinking.

"The gun!" Shade said.

"Dammit," D.C. said.

Then silence. Followed by an explosion of laughter, as though they'd just shared a joke.

I lifted out of my crouch and felt the blood flow in my limbs. An electrifying blend of fear and hope, danger and rescue made me shudder. I stepped away from behind the reeds, fingered the trigger on the laser-saw, and wondered what might happen next. Could I reason with them? Could we agree to a deal? Their rescue for our freedom. Would D.C. allow that? Could he?

I walked slowly toward the men, watching them struggle, giving myself time, afraid to arrive and have my questions answered. They had stopped laughing. They were squirming now, yet still sinking.

"Don't move," I shouted.

They turned to face me. D.C. broke into hysterical laughter. Shade looked exhausted. "Oh, look," D.C. said. "We're surrounded."

"I want to surrender," I said.

"Then surrender," he said.

"Amnesty?" I said.

"I don't bargain with fugitives," he said.

"We weren't under arrest," I said. "We had every right to leave that trailer."

"You're gonna talk rights to me?" D.C. said. "When I'm holding your mother, under suspicion of manslaughter, and she runs? And you're gonna talk to me about your rights?"

I looked at Shade. It's impossible to know a man's heart when you cannot read his eyes. "How about you?" I said. "Are you gonna keep playing follow the leader?"

He fixed his bulging, black eyes on me. "There's a reason," he said.

I had a feeling D.C. would not concede. I wasn't sure about Shade. If D.C. wouldn't trade his rescue for our freedom, would he trade our freedom for his life?

I swung the laser-saw into view and triggered its amber beam. Shade began to flutter like a fly stuck in honey. D.C.'s face hardened into a scowl.

I glanced around that barren primordial field. There were no cameras. No surveillance. A person could do whatever she wanted — absolutely anything. She just had to be able to live with herself afterward. A bitter taste bubbled up from the back of my throat. If I surrendered and trusted the system and was wrong, again, could I live with myself?

"I only want you to let us go," I said. "We'll return to your headquarters."

"But that's my job," D.C. said. "To return you."

"I beg you," I said. "Both of you. Either of you. Someone please make sense!"

"I'll show you what makes sense," D.C. said, reaching for the prey-seek pistol stuck in the tar. I lowered the laser-saw's beam to the black oily surface. A bright orange flame flared up, sputtered, and then died down.

D.C. howled with laughter, still reaching. He tried to speak, but hysterics choked his words. His fingers tugged at the pistol, gummed with tar.

A shout startled the three of us and we looked in its direction. It was Nelson. He and Mother were running back toward the creek. "Go to the water, " he shouted. "The water!"

I glanced back at D.C. He was staring now at a rippling carpet of blue flame spreading slowly from where the laser beam hit the surface. He began to high-step in slow motion, pumping his arms double time, a pathetic mark time march, going nowhere. Shade twisted and turned in place, but only seemed to be screwing himself deeper into the tar pool. The flame reached D.C. first and his jumpsuit flared orange. He jerked violently and let out a high-pitched squeal, like a band saw biting through metal. Shade stopped twisting and opened his mouth to lose a long, low moan that came from deep inside him.

The blue flame was now approaching me, and I dropped the laser-saw and ran toward the creek as fast as I could, dodging tar pools and clumps of dead grass. I ran as though D.C.'s screams might catch me, as though his flaming body was right behind me. I reached the creek and stumbled down the bank and tumbled into the water. I gained my balance and backpedaled into Mother and Nelson and stared at the bank as a flaming figure staggered to the edge and then toppled backward out of view. It was D.C. The shrieking stopped. Wisps of smoke curled upward from behind the edge. A smoldering arm reached over the rim, quivered, then fell motionless.

I bent over and threw up. Mother held me around the waist, but I couldn't stop retching. The stink of burnt flesh mingled with scorched tar sickened me. The thought of what I'd done sickened me. I couldn't disgorge that sickness no matter how hard I tried.

"Chik will be coming," Nelson said.

But I couldn't move. It was as though I were paralyzed as punishment for what I'd done.

"I know how you feel," Mother whispered. "Believe me, I know. You hope they'll find salvation. But it's not up to you. It's up to them. And then you discover they can't. They can't save themselves." She lifted me up by the shoulder. "It's hard to watch, though. I know it's hard to watch."

I gazed at her, realizing the horror we now shared—both of us witnessing a man's death.

Causing it.

24

"We gotta go," Nelson said.

I wiped my mouth with my sleeve.

"I mean now," he said, heading for the bank.

"Not here," I said, pointing to the smoke fading above the embankment. "Upstream."

He nodded and we trudged against the current, away from the sight and stench of that place, until distance and a bend in the creek allowed me to step out of the water without being sick.

"The wet capes should hide our signatures," Nelson said.

We continued westward toward the setting sun, each step bringing a spasm of hope or despair. Suddenly, a hum and heavy downdraft crushed us into crouches in the open field. I looked up at the shimmering half-hidden hovercraft and waited for Ruby's command to surrender.

But there was no command, only the whir of wind and rotors as my legs cramped, the pain deepening inside my thigh until I was forced to stand. I looked into the whirlwind, waiting, but waiting differently now, for something other than Ruby's command, because it seemed the time for that had passed. A red object dropped from a slit in the sky, and I ducked and held my breath, waiting for catastrophe. The object hit the ground behind me, and I jumped. But nothing happened. It was the size of a hand and made of fabric. It was a silk purse.

I looked at Nelson, standing now also, a dozen meters from the purse. He shook his head—a warning for Mother and me to stay back. He walked to it and picked it up.

With a sudden gust, Ruby vanished, leaving an ensuing calm as jarring as when she'd appeared. Mother and I approached Nelson; our gazes fixed on the purse in his hand. He ran his finger along the embroidered Chinese characters tufting the fabric. The yellow needlework on red silk made me think of Chik's flute playing, her notes so elegant and graceful.

"What do you think?" I said.

"A prayer pouch," he said, loosening its drawstring and pulling out a strip of polypro paper with more Chinese characters on it.

I'd never heard of a prayer pouch. "Can you read Chinese?"

Nelson nodded. "Mandarin."

"What's it say?" I asked eagerly.

He shrugged. "I don't know. It's Cantonese."

Mother and I looked at each other.

"Damon can translate it," Nelson said.

"Your friend?" I said. "He's Chinese?"

Nelson shook his head. "But he reads Cantonese."

"Why'd she let us go?" I asked, moving from one puzzle to another.

"I can't figure people in the best of times," Nelson said. "And these sure ain't those."

I shook my head. "Why'd we even think we could hide from her?"

"All prey make an effort to hide," Nelson said. "Hide or run. It's only natural."

I stared at him. He accepted hiding. He accepted running. As though Transparency was simply an option he could take or leave as the situation warranted. And I realized, without saying so, I'd also come to believe this.

***

By nightfall, we'd reached an old forest of cohune and cypress trees and we hiked several kilometers inside. The thickly clustered hardwoods provided ideal cover and we crawled into a thicket of dew-covered fern, staving off the outside world except for a few slivers of moonlight.

From within that cocoon, I prayed for sleep to rescue me from the memory of Shade and D.C.'s screams, from images of the men ablaze. Exhausted, I finally did fall asleep only to gasp myself awake to the shrieks of birds and sunlight blazing through the foliage, the ghosts of Shade and D.C. waking with me.

I looked around our makeshift shelter. Mother and Nelson had left. Tangled underbrush drooped above me—knotted vines and spore-spotted leaves threaded with hairy filaments. Before last night, I would have thought that place suitable only for vermin. How quickly circumstance can change.

We left that place and walked along an overgrown creek bed that seemed to double back on itself, if my reading of the glints of sunlight above the canopy could be trusted. Hiding may have become necessary, but I wasn't keen on the gloom of the forest. But we rested often and had our fill of fresh water from sporadic rivulets, and Nelson promised food at our journey's end which was incentive enough to keep moving. That and the sea breeze wafting toward us as we neared the coast.

The forest ended in a flash of bright sunlight and our wooded trail gave way to fine white sand in only a few meters. Seabirds squealed our arrival, and the distant, arrhythmic beat of waves foretold the unseen ocean.

Nelson sat us down in the shade of a cluster of royal palms. It seemed too soon after our last stop and there was no fresh water there. More importantly, my hunger was greater now that we'd reached the sea which I'd come to associate with the location of his friend and the end of our journey. And with food.

"One thing I need to tell you," he said.

"How much further?" I asked.

"Not much," he said.

I looked at Mother who was holding up remarkably well. Better than me, I was embarrassed to admit. She'd taken to our trek as though it were a nature hike, naming assorted flora and fauna along the way despite the concerns that kept us silent. It was a reasonable defense mechanism, I thought. Self-distraction. Dissociation. I wished I had her resilience.

"My friend?" Nelson said, interrupting my thoughts. "He'll take getting used to."

"This isn't a warning, is it?" I said.

He shook his head. "Advanced notice, that's all."

"Well, thanks," I said, "but I figured he had to be somewhat different. He's living off the grid, after all."

"No matter," Mother said. "We come with our own issues, no?"

Hard swallows followed and we gathered ourselves and headed north along the beach. The shoreline soon became rocky and gradually rose above the sea until we were circling the ridge of a small bay. Except for the seagulls, the place was as deserted as you'd expect of a retreat accessible only by foot. Below us, small waves slapped the hull of a weathered dinghy that thumped against the pole it was tied to. Nelson pointed to an opening in a granite cliff a half kilometer ahead of us. The smell of charred meat merged with the salty breeze and made my stomach groan with hunger.

Nelson pointed and I followed his direction to a dashiki-shrouded Black man sitting lotus-style at the mouth of a cave. Black Buddha was the first thought that came to mind.

As we approached, he stared at us, unconcerned. I couldn't imagine he could identify Nelson from that distance. Trusting, I thought. But why? We were untold kilometers from any form of surveillance.

He shielded his eyes as we got nearer, and finally, as we stood before him, spot lit by the morning sun. "Nelson?"

"In the flesh," Nelson said. "With friends."

"With what?"

"With *who*," Nelson said. "Friends."

Damon was silent, as though translating Nelson's speech. "Yes, of course," he said finally.

He looked past us, in the direction from which we'd arrived, then turned toward the mouth of the cave. He suddenly turned back to us as though he'd forgotten something. He extended his hand to Mother.

"Damon Early, Madame."

"Zola Anueche," Mother said, shaking his hand, then guiding it to mine. "And my daughter, Fitima." His palm was large and plump, his skin rough, but his grip gentle.

He then turned to Nelson. They didn't shake hands. Or embrace. In fact, they seemed more distant than I'd expected of good friends.

"You're in need of my services," Damon said.

Nelson sniffed the air. "Something to eat perhaps?"

"No perhaps," he said without emotion, and we followed him into the cave.

The entrance, about ten meters high, rose to four times that height at the center of the vaulted chamber. The electric light inside surprised me. A dozen or so glow globes hung from cables that disappeared into the darkness above, attached, no doubt, to photovoltaic panels. The back of the cave was higher than its mouth and a low ledge ran three-quarters around of the perimeter, a natural shelf for an array of unrecognizable objects. A lumpy cloth-covered mound that looked like bedding lay in one back corner, and glints of glass and steel in the other. Apparatus of some kind. Perhaps a transmitter.

We sat on the cool, sandy floor in the center, beside a smoldering peat fire, its thin column of gray smoke rising and dissipating in the upper regions of the cave. Damon knelt beside the fire and pulled a charred bundle of palm leaves from the ashes. He unwrapped the sheaf gingerly, revealing several whole red snapper intermixed with seaweed. With a bone-knife from his pocket, he sliced chunks of steaming filet and passed the morsels around. The fish melted in my mouth, and I almost groaned with satisfaction. I forced myself to chew slowly, thankful for the silence that followed.

"How long's it been?" Nelson said finally.

Damon glanced at Nelson then faced the glow of the fire. "I'm no good at measuring time," he said. "Which may or may not be true. The truth is, I don't measure time."

"I'm sorry, my friend," Nelson said, "but I do. Habit. Ritual."

"Don't apologize for your world," Damon said. "As for mine, let's just say it's been less than a lifetime."

Nelson turned to Mother and me. "In our world," he said, "I'd guess about a half-dozen years."

"You remind me of someone I knew a long, long time ago," Mother said. "What's it like—living off the grid?"

"I don't think about what I'm off," Damon said, still staring into the fire. "I think about what I'm on."

Mother surveyed the cave. "A very solitary place. A place to rest your spirit."

"Quite the opposite," Damon said. "A place to stimulate the spirit." He grabbed a handful of sand and let it spill through his fingers. "The rhythms of the natural world are both fast and fleeting and difficult to keep up with."

"And privacy?" Mother said. "What's it like living in complete privacy?"

"Private," Damon said. "Between me and my maker."

Mother turned to Nelson. "He's perfect. I can't think of anyone better to entrust with our secrets."

"I can keep a secret forever," Damon said.

"For at least a lifetime," Nelson said.

25

I glanced into the shadows at the glinting steel and glass. "Nelson said you had a transmitter?"

"So, you didn't drop by just for fish and conversation," Damon said. We ignored his quip and stared at him, waiting for his answer.

Damon cleared his throat. "I do."

"Undetectable?" Nelson probed.

Damon shrugged. "So to speak. My transmissions appear multi-locational. Ubiquitous! In fact, any one of them is like a byte of straw in a digital haystack. They tend not to want to pick through the hay."

Nelson looked at me reassuringly. "Undetectable."

The confidence on their faces conflicted with Damon's incredible explanation. And yet our escape up to that point had been perhaps even more incredible. What was one more fantastic step in this incredible journey?

There was only one person I could contact, after all. My so-called friends back in the States were acquaintances, mostly associates who shared little more familiarity than our given names. And none of them had expertise or experience with the problems we faced. But that was also true of Jim, my former colleague. My mentor. But at least he had age on his side. Maybe even wisdom.

"There are rules, of course," Damon said.

"Excuse me?" I said.

"Rules," Damon said. "To keep me undetected. Do's and don'ts. Like no names. No references to time or place. At least not from you. Whoever you contact can babble on about these parameters as much as they'd like. But not you. I'll be with you, of course. Right by your side, but off camera. It'll be like a movie. For me, at least. A true-to-life movie. A break in my routine. Before I return to more primeval acts of creation and destruction. You know … nature."

I refused to contact Jim at the Institute, so we spent the afternoon waiting for him to return home at the end of the workday. In the meantime, Nelson and Damon exchanged puzzling banter which only prolonged the wait. Apparently, they'd worked together after graduation, a challenging project at a challenging site, Malabrigo — pronounced with exaggerated Spanish accents. An island off Peru's Pacific coast. Malabrigo, meaning inhospitable. Uninhabited.

Covered in mist. Many credits earned, though. Laying lifelines. Infrastructure. Transportation, communication, surveillance. For an artists' colony. Or so they were told.

As dusk approached, Damon began making arrangements for my transmission. His transmitter jutted out from the cave's stone wall, a striking contrast between technology and nature, much like the man himself. He set up two stools dragged from the rear of the cave which made me wonder what other trappings of civilization he had hidden back there. One stool lined up directly with a transmitting monitor and camera and the second was placed a few meters away. I discovered Damon could direct the interior lights by pulling hemp ropes latched to the walls. One beam of light fell upon a row of small brown heads along a stone ledge, their facial features chiseled and inlaid with iridescent seashells.

"Avocado pits," Damon said.

The spotlighted heads shimmered with sinister expressions.

"My confidants," he said.

"Oh?" I said, giving Nelson a sidelong glance. If his friend were speaking truthfully, I couldn't imagine more pitiful loneliness. And if speaking in jest, anyone more tiresome.

I pointed to the transmitter. "Can we get this thing up and running?"

Damon activated the system, but it took several false starts before I reached Jim. When I did, my heart stopped for one long speechless moment. Our connection seemed to have the same effect on Jim. He stared at his monitor as though he'd seen a ghost.

"Where are you?" he said.

Only afterward did Jim's question seem cold and calculating given the months we'd been apart.

"Is your mother with you?" he continued.

I nodded.

"And Nelson Woon Sam?"

Again, I nodded. He'd been following me closely. Perhaps he knew our predicament.

"Are you safe?"

"I'm safe. But I ... I have a problem. A big problem. I had no one else to turn to."

"I know, I know," he said. "Hold on a moment."

He disappeared from the monitor, and I glanced at Damon. Jim's arranging to trace the transmission, I thought. Into a labyrinth of false leads if Damon's scheme could be trusted. When Jim finally did return, he marked time even further, pacing his home office.

The hum of his joints sounded even more pronounced in the silence between us. Why did he suddenly seem so old? I wondered. How had I managed to ignore his aging while we worked together? It seemed so obvious just then that he was showing every one of his ninety-eight years—his stride more dependent on implanted servomotors, his hair completely white, even if he had more of it than most men his age. And he'd gotten broader around the middle, adding even more strain on his retrofitted legs.

"You told me I could call if—"

He returned to the monitor. "Of course," he said. "I'm glad you called."

"You can't trace me, Jim."

He narrowed his eyes, trying to digest that improbability. "Where are you? It's just that when the three of you dropped out of sight .... We've been searching—"

"*We?*" I said.

"Never mind that," he said.

"To help?" I asked.

"Of course to help! To get you back safely. But we can't if you—"

"At what price, Jim ... at what price?"

"Don't be ridiculous. Safe and free. That's what we want for you. For the three of you. To be safe and free to choose whatever path you want. But we can't help if we don't know where you are!"

"I'll call you back," I said, flipping the off switch on the console.

"No, no, no!" Jim's voice faded with his image.

I sat numb, staring at the blank monitor.

"Excellent," Damon proclaimed. "Riveting! A genuine manhunt. An offer to rescue. From his accent, I'd say New Yorker. But not by birth. A transplant. But longtime resident. And he can get you back to New York? The confidence! Despite the travel restrictions? Good Lord, Nelson—the company you keep."

"What are you talking about?" Nelson said. "What travel restrictions?"

"Not sure where you've been, my friend, but they've cinched another notch in your collar. International travel has become a lot harder. And this affects me how? Apparently not you, either."

"Since when?" I asked.

"Recently," Damon said. "I don't keep track of precise time."

The three of us looked at each other, amazed at what we'd missed.

"But Jim has it figured," Damon said. "Not to worry. You're not worried, are you?"

"This isn't a game," Nelson said through clenched teeth.

"Of course not. Like Malabrigo. Artist colony indeed! Beware trickeration, right, brother? I've become more adept at resistance since then."

The men fixed their gazes on each other, sharing an unspoken bond—a secret.

"Let me tell you what we'll do," Damon said, turning from Nelson. "This Jim sounds resourceful. I know a village. Coastal. I'll take you there. That much I'll concede. Trinidad is a big haystack of an island, so it's not a major concession. Get back in touch with Jim and see he can rescue you from there. A true test of his confidence."

"That makes you a conductor," Mother said.

"Conductor of what?" Damon said.

"Of us," Mother said.

Damon glanced at Nelson who shook his head slightly, a polite dismissal of Mother's reference to the Underground Railroad. I didn't appreciate his condescension, but I regretted Mother's return to the topic of slavery. Still, she hadn't mentioned anything about returning to her project and I was thankful for that reprieve and did everything I could to prevent her relapse.

"What's the name of that village?" I asked Damon. "I want to call Jim back now."

***

Indigo Sound. Two streets, three shops, one pier. Eight hours from St. Clemens by motored transportation, and readily reachable by boat, according to Jim's plan. It took the rest of that day and a good portion of the next to work out the details, but we were to leave for the Indigo Sound as soon as possible and wait in the village's General Store for a Peter Conrad to meet us. He would escort us to a boat scheduled to pick us up in a day or so.

Damon was duly impressed with Jim's apparent authority. Mostly, he was impressed by Jim's arranging for us to skirt the international travel restrictions on our sea voyage to the Florida coast. And to continue by aerotrain to New York City. That was the plan.

By then, I realized there were powers far greater than Jim's orchestrating our escape. The same powers that allowed Ramsey to keep our research findings secret. The same powers that persuaded Lloyd to try to convince me to return to the Institute. I didn't know who they were but I was pretty sure why they were: to get me back on the project. But I was willing to accept their help, regardless of the price, if they could free us from the quagmire we'd stumbled into.

Damon led us to the back of the cave where the scant light in the rear silhouetted a storehouse of equipment and supplies that appeared to have been picked up and dropped by a windstorm. We made our way through the shadows, past spools of cable, boxes of clothing and firearms of various shapes and sizes. I noticed an assortment of boots, visored helmets, an acoustic guitar, a soccer ball, picks and shovels, and even several framed paintings. Finally, we stopped in front of the objective of our journey.

"Our escape vehicle," Damon said, kicking past a large red can labeled Gasoline.

The metal-covered craft looked like a cross between a bubble cab and a boat, except it had three spheres instead of four tires—one sphere in what appeared to be the front and two in the rear. From what little I could see inside, it looked like it could seat four at most.

"Beach crawler," Damon said. "Scavenged like everything else you see here."

"In operating order, I hope," Nelson said, surveying the hardware scattered near the wall.

Damon chuckled. "Not to worry. She's tuned to perfection. She can buck eight-foot waves like ripples on a pond. Her floatation orbs are that responsive! She can scale the steepest dunes or navigate ten-foot sinkholes. That is, if we were crawling on land. But that would leave tracks, so we'll be crawling the intertidal zone where sea meets sand and where the crawler leaves no trail. Nevertheless, we'll leave at dark. Till then: eat, rest. I've got grouper and cassava in the fire."

The afternoon crept along like an unyielding fog, taunting the impatient, the restless. Yet that evening, the sun set swiftly, like a quickly fading flame with no moonlight to ease the transition to darkness. When the sky was fully black, Damon drove the beach crawler from the cave to the surf where the three of us stepped inside the stabilized vehicle. Our ride was as comfortable as he'd promised, though our silence contrasted awkwardly against the lapping sea.

And that's when I remembered Chik's silk purse, a necessary cause for us to speak. Nelson had given the purse to me for safekeeping, and I removed it from my jumpsuit pocket. I held it up to Damon to read, with no intention of letting it to go.

He squinted at the characters on the strip of polypro paper, then glanced at the silk purse in my other hand. "Prayer pouch," he said. "Cantonese. Nelson couldn't help you here."

"What's it say?" I asked.

We were all now focused on Damon's face, his expression, but he didn't reveal if it were good news or bad.

"*During times of great adversity*," he read, "*lives the potential for great good.*"

I waited for more. "That's it?"

"A Buddhist proverb," Damon said. "For you."

"Me?" I said.

"To Fitima from Chik," Damon read.

"Someone contacted Chik," Mother said. "While she was flying Ruby."

"We know they were looking for us," Nelson said.

"I bet it was Jim," Mother said.

"But what does it mean?" Damon said.

They were staring at me now, waiting for my interpretation. I could only shake my head as though I didn't understand. But I understood. Mother was right. They had gotten to Chik.

Jim. Ramsey. Someone. And Chik's message was intended to get to me. And it did. Ramsey was relentless. And now I was heading right back to him.

26

I awoke to Mother's slumbering breaths beside me and the quiet whispers of Damon and Nelson up front. The beach crawler's gentle sloshing swallowed up their words, but I watched the men with half-closed eyes—Damon, a rotund Buddha of a man, and Nelson, sleek and broad- shouldered. Yet so close in spirit. Cantonese versus Mandarin, I thought. Civil engineers. Classmates. Malabrigo. I knew little else about them as a pair. "Excuse me," I whispered, glancing cautiously at Mother.

"Sorry," Nelson whispered back. "We'll keep it down."

"Down any further and you'd be reading each other's lips." The men shrugged. "After Malagrigo?" I asked quietly.

"You mean us?" Nelson gestured to Damon. I nodded. They looked at each other.

"You," Nelson said to Damon.

"After Malabrigo," Damon said. "It could be a title."

"Great," I said. "I'm all ears."

"Malabrigo," Damon said softly. "Art colony." He seemed to be looking right through me and I wondered if he'd continue. "It has the ring of contradiction," he said finally. "Art colony. Not that the two can't coexist. Art and colony. But the risk is obvious. The risk of losing control. The risk of being colonized. Colonized artists. Not a pretty picture, so to speak."

"Is that what Malabrigo became?" I asked.

"That's what it was designed to be from the very beginning," Damon said.

"Of course, we didn't know that," Nelson said.

"We chose not to know," Damon said.

Again, that look on his face, the difficulty of remembering.

"Education has lots of prefixes I respect," Damon continued. "Self. Higher. Continuing. But there's one prefix we didn't pay enough attention to that defined Malabrigo. Re as in *re*-education."

"A *re*-education center?" I said. "And an art colony?"

"For artists who needed supplementary instruction," Damon said. "For those who forgot that *transparency is the essence of democracy.*"

"Only the guilty have reason to fear," Mother said sleepily, pulling herself up to view Nelson and Damon. "Are you reviewing the Principles of Transparency?"

"No, no," Nelson whispered. "Idle chitchat. You should go back to sleep."

"Sure, sure," Mother said. "Sleep."

We gave her a few moments to resettle herself, for her easy breathing to return.

I tapped Damon's wrist for us to continue. "So you discovered this … this rehabilitation center after your project was finished?"

"Rehabilitation center?" Damon repeated, looking at Nelson. "Does she know who she's talking to?"

Nelson shook his head.

Damon extended his right forearm to me, the inner side, where a thickened, light, and shiny cord of overgrown scar tissue lined the brown flesh. Right where his ID implant would be.

"Nelson cut it out for me," Damon said.

I gagged and covered my mouth.

"Ah, you, too," Damon said. "The curse of squeamishness." He turned to Nelson. "Not so my brother here."

"He insisted," Nelson said.

"And he agreed," Damon replied. "He understood. He understood how I had to quit." Damon withdrew his arm. "People are different," he continued. "For me, once I lost faith, I gave it all up. And I mean *all*. I couldn't pretend. But I held no grudge against those who could. Or against those who actually believed in the system."

"I'm a pretender," Nelson said.

"And we'd be friends even if you were a true believer," Damon said. He patted my hand gently. "Now you know who you're talking to."

The men returned to the controls of the beach crawler as though realizing I'd had my fill of their revelations. They were right. I eased back into my seat and glanced around the vehicle's opaque interior. I imagined it slinking along the tide in the dark, avoiding notice, rejecting openness, truthfulness. And there I was, with Mother, with Nelson, and Damon—sneaking to a hideout, a safe house, and thankful to be doing so. I felt as though I'd joined an outlaw sect without even realizing it. With no rite of passage. A sect without a name. With no list of members. An anonymous group of individuals who defied universal visibility, and who seemed to get away with it. Who were grateful to get away with it. A group that included Nelson, who I admired so, and his dear friend Damon. That included Jim, to whom I was so indebted. That included Ramsey, who I'd come to despise. And Hooks, who paid the price I would've wished on him, but nevertheless, regretted. And now, me and Mother.

***

"Land ho," Damon called out, loud enough to wake the rest of us.

"What?" Mother said, glancing around the beach crawler, trying to orient herself.

"We never left sight of land," Nelson drawled through a yawn.

The beach crawler's sway had been soothing enough to lull the three of us to sleep. "Indigo Sound," Damon said. "Just up ahead."

I rubbed my eyes and pulled myself up to look through the windshield. A pair of seabirds squawked across a dim but blushing sky and, to my left, gentle waves rolled calmly onto the shore. The beach crawler was still traversing the intertidal zone, passing, at the moment, the skeletons of several abandoned shanties scattered along the coast. The shanties soon gave way to a row of tidy cottages with clothes lines, children's toys, and small fishing boats in their yards. The picturesque scene seemed to require a charming name like Indigo Sound.

Damon maneuvered the beach crawler onshore and steered it into a grove of orange trees, their scent stirring my early morning hunger. Nelson helped Damon unroll a swath of forest-camouflage fabric from the rear of the vehicle to the front, providing what seemed only slight concealment.

"These aren't city folk," Damon explained. "They won't pry. For these villagers, the intent to conceal is concealment enough."

Still, he had us scuff away tracks the crawler had left in the sand.

The road into town was empty, but I could smell morning meal-taking wafting from the cottages we passed. As we approached the village's second road, perpendicular to ours, Damon pointed to a large colonial house at the roads' intersection.

"The General Store," he said.

It was the location he'd told Jim to send his emissary. It was the place we'd meet this Peter Conrad.

We walked to the front of the house and hesitated in the doorway. A middle-aged woman stood behind a counter and beckoned us to enter. She looked Ethiopian, with smooth mahogany skin and kinky black hair pulled back tightly into a bun.

"May I help you?" she asked.

"We're supposed to meet someone here," Damon said. "We were told you wouldn't mind letting us stay until he arrives."

"No problem," she said. "Especially if you buy something."

I surveyed the rows of shelving stocked with canned goods, jars, bottles, and all manner of merchandise. A stack of burlap sacks was piled to the right of the counter. That's when I noticed the young man who, until then, had blended into the store's cornucopia. He was sitting, leaning back leisurely, on a brown sack marked RICE in large red letters.

"How about a soft drink?" he said, apparently noting my quandary.

"Sure," I said, and the others agreed.

He got up and walked behind the counter to an old cooler with tiny cracks in its glass casing. Its engraved logo labeled it a castoff of the *Lunar Mining Corporation*. He took out four sipping bottles and handed one to each of us.

"On me," he said.

I protested instinctively despite not having any way to pay for the drinks.

"Don't worry," he said. He gestured to the woman behind the counter. "She'll be happy to take my credits."

With no further mention of payment, he retrieved and handed out protein biscuits, then left for the basement to get chairs for our wait. He returned with four folding chairs which he handed out before flopping on the sack of rice, tossing his long, locked braids over his shoulders. I wondered if he and the woman would remain present when Peter Conrad arrived. I'd become so accustomed to secrecy, I fretted now over the possibility of exposing our plan.

The young man began playing with a hand-held device that triggered music throughout the store, long mournful groans, and the bluesy chords of an acoustic guitar. He turned his attention back to us, seemingly very pleased with himself. It seemed as though he and the woman would be staying, at least until Conrad arrived.

"You wouldn't have access to the Repository?" Mother asked the woman.

The woman shook her head. "Afraid not."

"Should've asked back … well, back where we came from," Mother said.

I stared at her, wondering what was on her mind. Worrying about what was on her mind.

"This music is depressing," Damon said.

"Which is why it's so popular," the young man said.

"Well, I wouldn't know about that," Damon said.

"The blues matches the mood of the times," the man said.

"I wouldn't know about that either," Damon replied.

"I just wondered what happened to Juba," Mother muttered.

"King Juba?" Damon said. "The calypso singer? What's so special about—?"

"I'd rather we just forgot about—" I began.

"You're listening to him now," the young man said.

We all stared at him. I recall thinking that his earlier generosity didn't match his threadbare clothes, almost as though he were wearing a costume. And his neat braids and perfect pearly white teeth? And now, his playing King Juba's music could not have been a coincidence. He knew there was a connection. Perhaps he knew more about that connection than I did.

"Peter Conrad?" I said.

"At your service," he said.

"What the hell is this foolishness for God's sake?"

Peter Conrad sat up straight. "Well, for one," he said, "now we all know who we're talking to."

Nelson, Damon, and I looked at each other upon hearing him repeat what Damon had said to me on the beach crawler. Perhaps it was a catchphrase among those who secreted themselves.

"Jim sent me, obviously," Conrad continued. "He debriefed me, and I flew here immediately." He nodded graciously toward the woman behind the register. "I'd like to thank Claudia, here, for her cooperation."

She nodded back. "'Long as I get paid."

"And King Juba?" Mother said.

Conrad paused to let the thick graveled groan reassert itself. "Free as a bird," he continued. "You can thank Chik for that."

His mention of Chik made me hesitate, but I couldn't hold back my frustration with Mother. "What's with it with you and this vagrant?"

She looked at me as though I were a child. Not just her child—*a* child. "Freedom, dear. A simple matter of freedom. We're running for ours. I only hoped he found his."

Compassion? I thought. Just simple compassion? For a stranger? A poacher? Or was I the crazy one? Crazy to obsess over her sympathies for the man who'd frightened me so. Crazy to allow myself to be distracted from risks we still faced.

"Chik released Juba," Conrad said. "After Jim contacted her."

"And Chik?" Nelson asked.

"What about her?" Conrad asked.

Chik didn't deserve the silence that followed. I vowed to find out what happened to her the first chance I got. I recalled the message she left. *During times of great adversity lives the potential for great good.* She was channeling Jim, of course, but in her own way. It was her rephrasing of the advice he'd given me before I left the project.

"You sure this is Juba?" Damon asked Conrad. "This is furthest from calypso I ever heard."

"True, that," Conrad said, a sly grin baring white teeth. "But it's Juba. A new path, though."

A moaning guitar harmonized with the singer's guttural groans producing the saddest sounds I'd ever heard. I was about to beg Conrad to turn it off until the snarled lyrics became distinct enough to discern and ominous enough to remember.

"There's a cold wind blowin', And she sing an omen song. Said there's a cold wind blowin', And she sing an omen song. She'll dry up all your oceans, Correctify all your wrongs."

27

Peter Conrad turned off Juba's blues, but it was too late. The music's sorrow had already taken hold and the small talk that followed didn't distract us from its residual sadness.

I concentrated on the sounds drifting into the store—the calls of birds and fishermen preparing for the mourning's catch. The distant clang of metal and thud of wood, the footsteps and murmured conversations of people passing by. Now and then a customer would enter, and Claudia would leave to serve them, thankfully, I imagined. For the rest of us, time and purpose had been put on hold.

In the midst of waiting, a child's squeal startled us, but the cry was one of thrilled surprise. The squeal got louder as it drew nearer, fever-pitched to overflowing, until a young girl rushed through the door and ran up to Peter Conrad. "They're here," she gasped.

I looked at Conrad for a sign—whether the child brought good news or bad.

"So much for keeping secrets," Conrad said, patting the girl on the head. "But I'm not good at that either. Who woulda thought we'd need to be?"

"The boat?" I asked.

Conrad nodded, then looked at Damon. "It's time to say your goodbyes."

We stood and Nelson walked over to Damon and the men embraced.

"Thanks for all your help," he said. "And try to stay out of trouble."

"I try to stay out of everything!" Damon said.

"Of course," Nelson said.

Conrad led us out of the store and Damon followed, but slowly, falling farther and farther behind, his way, I imagined, of acknowledging our departure.

When we reached the shore, I saw a boat racing toward the pier, only a couple minutes distance up the beach.

Peter Conrad chuckled. "It's nothing short of a miracle," he said as we trudged across the sand. "And me, a party to it all. Escorting you people through travel restrictions."

We reached the pier as the boat arrived; a sea-skimmer designed for sport fishing. Rods and landing nets lined the cabin's tinted glass walls. Life vests and snorkels hung from its ceiling. *Coral Run* gleamed in gold on the boat's white bow.

The engine revved and seawater sprayed up on us as the boat maneuvered alongside the pier. A gangplank descended at a sharp angle from the deck and Conrad tied the base to the pier. He waited, impatient for us to proceed.

I hesitated, realizing I didn't know when I'd be coming back to Trinidad. Although returning had always been stressful, navigating between two worlds, I always felt as ambivalent about leaving as I had about coming home. But leaving now was much worse. I was leaving with Mother and had no idea when we'd be welcomed back. If we'd be welcomed back.

"Please," Conrad implored. "Let's not become a spectacle. Or any more of one, I should say."

Of course, I thought. Our new watchword was concealment.

I clambered up the gangplank behind Mother and Nelson while Conrad rushed past us and hopped on deck. Nelson, just ahead of me, stumbled slightly, looking back on the shore, troubled by something he saw there.

"Watch your step," Conrad said, helping Mother onto the deck. He reached for Nelson's hand. "Please, sir."

"Wait," Nelson muttered.

Conrad leaned past Nelson, grabbed my hand and pulled me on board.

"Wait!" Nelson said.

"Are you coming or not?" Conrad yelled above the boat's revving engine.

Nelson looked at me as though unsure of his answer. In that instant, Conrad grabbed his arm and pulled him on board. Nelson tackled Conrad, knocking him down, straddling him.

"What?" I shouted, grabbing Nelson's shoulder.

He shrugged from my hand. "Who are those men?" he asked Conrad.

Conrad squirmed and Nelson got off him and rushed to stern where I joined him. As the skimmer backed from the pier, seawater sprayed upward, forming a veil between us and the shore, transparent enough to make out two men escorting Damon back to the village. Nelson leaned into the spray, extending toward his friend, yet stuck on the skimmer. He glared at me, then turned his glare on Conrad, still sprawled on the deck.

"I'll only ask one more time," he said. "Who are those men?"

Conrad shook his head. "I was just carrying out orders."

"Whose order?" Nelson demanded. "What are they going to do to him?"

"Nothing," Conrad said, scuttling backward. "Questions, that's all."

"Questions?" Nelson said.

"Answers," Conrad said, bumping against the side of the skimmer. "They want answers. But they won't hurt him."

Nelson looked at me. "And I'm supposed to trust this man," he muttered. "I'd just as soon throw him overboard."

"Don't. Don't do anything foolish," Conrad stammered. "I mean ... I mean, don't do anything you'll regret."

"I already regret trusting you," Nelson said, moving toward Conrad. "You turned him in, didn't you?"

"No, no," Conrad said, sliding up the side of the boat to stand. "Those men—they're documentarians. Damon was on their radar. Or, or ... he wasn't. They want an accounting, that's all. Fill in the gaps. His record is incomplete."

"And they're going to punish him for that," Nelson said, rushing to Conrad and grabbing him by the collar.

"No! No punishment," Conrad said, clutching Nelson's hands. "They only want missing data," he rasped. "I swear."

Nelson shoved him to the deck.

I wanted to believe Conrad. I didn't want to believe the alternatives Nelson suggested.

And yet, I never believed Damon would be abducted.

I put my hand on Nelson's shoulder. He didn't shrug it off. "I'm so sorry."

He stared down at Conrad ... through him. I hated to imagine what he was thinking. That Damon had been captured because he'd asked for his help to rescue his former boss and her daughter. And whether it was worth it.

A man whose face was smeared with blotches of green and black camouflage arrived. He must've come from the glass-walled cabin, though I hadn't noticed him. From the looks of him, he'd intended it that way.

"Is everything okay here?" he asked. The blue and whites of his eyes blinked from inside the dark patchwork of greasepaint.

"We're okay," Nelson said.

"I'm Bragg," he said. "Skimmer pilot. Honored to meet you, Ma'am Anueche."

"We need to turn around," Nelson said.

Bragg glanced between me and Nelson. "We can't do that."

"We must," Nelson said. "I need to check on the man who got us here."

Bragg sighed and shook his head. "Sorry. We're on automatic."

"You mean you can't steer this thing?" Nelson said.

"Only in an emergency," Bragg said.

"Well, this is an emergency," Nelson said.

Bragg narrowed his eyes. "No, it's not. Listen, for reasons beyond my understanding, Ma'am Anueche is under my protection. She's deliverable to my superiors like any other lost asset. Her safety's my one and only priority."

Nelson looked away, toward the receding shoreline.

"I'm sorry, Nelson," I said. I wanted to say more. I considered promising him we'd check on Damon the first chance we got but locating Damon would signify his friend's defeat. And how would we interpret not being able to reach Damon?

"Your friend's a resourceful man," Mother offered.

Nelson looked at her and nodded.

"That much I learned of him," she continued. "We'll just have to trust in that."

Nelson's look of resignation pained me, but I knew of no way to console him. I knew of no way to console myself or to ease my guilt over Damon's being caught. No way to ease my shame over the privileges Mother and I had been granted.

"I suggest you relax as best you can," Bragg said. He nodded toward the cabin. Sullenly, in single file, we took his advice.

The air and light inside the cabin were filtered and refreshing and we needed neither the lidded caps nor blankets Bragg offered us. Mother busied herself reading the polychrome maps on the monitors while Bragg seemed more fascinated with her wildly braided hair than in attending to the data on the screens.

"So, you're saying the skyposts will ignore us?" Mother asked Bragg.

"Not exactly, ma'am. One of them is tracking us right now." He glanced absentmindedly through the ceiling, toward the sky. "It's directing a beam on us and scrambling our signature. That way, we won't get unwanted attention from the Coast Guard. Of course, we're staying as far from them as possible."

I tried to understand what I was hearing—the application of technology to hide the real world. For what reason?

"Why?" I asked Bragg. "Why conceal us? Why not notify the Coast Guard to let us through?"

"The idea is for the travel restrictions to seem airtight. To everyone, even the Coast Guard."

Officials deceiving each other, I thought, clutching my stomach. I felt as though I might gag. Sickness from the roiling skimmer. Sickness from the substitution of lies for truth.

I left the cabin and moved to the bow where the wind and sea spray brought some relief.

A few moments later, Nelson joined me and despite our awkward silence, I was thankful. I breathed easier as the skimmer sped toward rows of pillars rising from the sea. Seabirds swooped and pirouetted among the columns as though dancing on the wind.

"You think that means we're approaching the coast?" I asked Nelson, pointing to the pillars.

"Bragg said they're light towers," Nelson said. "Fish farms. They harvest fish at night."

"Landfall can't be much farther," I said.

He shrugged indifferently and I winced at his coldness.

The light towers rose from platforms that weren't visible earlier. Above us now, the seabirds circled and squawked indignantly, protesting our presence, perceiving us as rivals for food denied them — the hectares of caged fish below the ocean's surface.

A warm breeze drifted over us carrying the scent of soil. I looked expectantly at Nelson, but he still seemed distant, aloof. We were approaching land, I thought, with a stir of anxiety and anticipation. And no one to share it with.

Reluctantly, I left Nelson and returned to the cabin.

"What happens now?" I asked Bragg.

He looked toward the distant shore, a blur on the horizon, then turned to the map on his monitor and pointed to a swirl of yellow and green. "There's an envoy waiting. He'll drive you to the station."

The skimmer went silent and glided over several kilometers of blue- and shape-shifting shallows before sliding onto sun-bleached sand. A pair of headlights beamed from inside the shadows of a tree stand about three hundred meters from the beach, and the sudden, faint hum of an engine arose there, scattering a flock of flamingos above the canopy. We spotted the sand-lorry before we heard it, bursting from the shadows, racing toward us, spewing a trail of grit and gravel from its tracks.

"For the old man is waiting for to carry you to freedom," Mother sang, slow and low-pitched.

"She okay?" Bragg asked.

"If you follow the Drinking Gourd."

28

Conrad bid farewell to Captain Bragg and joined the three of us aboard the sand-lorry, its driver, only a silhouette seated behind a smoked-glass partition. We harnessed ourselves into our seats and the vehicle sped away.

"Where to now?" Nelson asked Conrad.

"Substation sixty-seven. We wait there until 20:45, then take the aerotrain into Miami. From there, on to New York."

Substations above fifty were extremely remote which explained our travel by sand-lorry.

Its seclusion would allow us to board the aerotrain without much company and waiting until evening to board would further reduce the chance of our being noticed, at least by ordinary citizens. Powers that be, of course, Conrad had referred to them as documentarians, would be tracking us every step of the way.

"What's the opposite of fugitive?" Mother asked. "You know ... the antonym."

The motor revved as we ascended a dune, then whined as we pitched forward on the descent.

"I can't think of any," she continued.

"Let's think positive," Conrad said.

"Exactly," Mother said. "I was humming *Steal Away*. You know ... in my mind. The spiritual. Thinking about us and our situation. But that's not what we're doing. Stealing away. It's almost like we're doing the opposite. But I can't think of a word for it."

Conrad looked to me for clarification, but I looked away, struck by my ability to compartmentalize my life, to proceed stepwise, one task at a time. Mother's state of mind would need attention. Eventually. First, we had to get her to safety. But perhaps her tangents, her historical references to our situation, as she called it, were more appropriate than my distaste for them. Time would tell. Eventually.

We arrived at Substation sixty-seven by mid-afternoon and it was even more remote than I'd expected. It was the end of a line and totally deserted. The covered platform extended half a kilometer beside the levitation track which continued another kilometer before disappearing into a mangrove thicket. The foliage sprouting through the floor and creeping up the supports gave the impression the station hadn't been used in years.

The sand-lorry was stocked with bottled water and dried shrink-wrapped fish which assured we'd eat only enough to take the edge off our hunger. Throughout that long afternoon, we gathered and dispersed as the need for company or solitude struck us, but as the sun tempered from hazy white to red, we sought each other out and nightfall found us huddled together under the amber glow of the platform lights.

A strong breeze blew out of the forest before I saw the headlight approaching. The aerotrain glided into the station as quiet as a whisper and stopped, poised just above the tracks. The train was five chambers long, but only the doors of the last chamber slid open. There was no public address announcement of the train's destination as was customary. On the other hand, there was nothing customary about our catching that train.

We entered the last chamber and took seats along the circular couch surrounding a low round table, its grain fine enough to have been real mahogany. A map of North America filled an entire wall of the chamber, displaying a schematic of the Trans-rapid network with our precise location blinking at the end of a branch on the Eastern Seaboard Line. Pictures of food and drink on the opposite wall depicted the snacks and beverages stored behind them.

The holograph of a female conductor flashed on, faded, then flickered back on again. "Aerotrain leaving the station," she announced, her image slightly out of focus. Her presence wasn't as reassuring as the designers had hoped.

The train sprang forward and quickly plunged into the darkness of the mangrove forest before climbing the viaduct high above the canopy and, eventually, over starlit everglades.

"Travel time to Miami Central ... twelve minutes," a loudspeaker announced.

The sprawling terminus loomed like a sunrise in the dead of night, a labyrinth of dazzlingly tubes and sheltered platforms bordering endless airstrips that sprouted launching pads far off in the distance. And then our train descended and zigzagged through dark tunnels and descended further until we finally came to a stop at a dim, deserted platform.

"We change here for New York," Conrad said, leading us off. "It won't be long."

The train went down a graffiti-defaced tunnel, then disappeared, leaving an eerie silence in its wake. Dim fluorescent bulbs cast spectral light on the wall's advertisements for products I didn't recognize. I walked for the sake of walking, my footsteps echoing our seclusion. In the dimness of an alcove, I spotted a concrete staircase beside a stationary escalator. The place was more than simply unoccupied. It had the mournful air of abandonment. We didn't speak, I believe, out of respect for that loss.

The aerotrain that picked us up was as empty as the first, but there were no pretenses like the holograph conductor or public address announcements. We were as off-the-record as we could imagine.

I sought out a seat apart from the others, needing more air, more space than ever, but Nelson followed and sat across from me. I breathed deep and shut my eyes, hoping he'd do the same.

"Never been to New York," he said.

"It's not for everyone," I said without opening my eyes. "But you've traveled the world. You're adaptable."

"Always meant to, though," he said. "Besides facsimile tours." I heard him sigh. "New York, New York—*City of Glass*."

The epitome of Transparency, I thought, but I wish I hadn't. I wanted to rid my mind of thought. All seemed paradoxical. None brought peace.

"I assume we'll see the skyline," he continued. "Even from this train."

"The southern tip of Manhattan," I said, my eyes still closed.

I searched my memory for music, hoping song would subdue the onslaught of my thoughts, but Juba's blues and Mother's hymns ambushed that ploy.

"You know," Nelson said, his voice quiet, as though not to disturb my reverie, "I'm surprised we haven't become closer."

I felt my forehead furrow, my eyelids squeeze tighter.

"No, not surprised, really," Nelson continued. "Disappointed."

At that, I opened my eyes. "Where's this coming from? What's this about?"

"What's so incomprehensible? A man, a woman. Intelligent. Attractive—at least the female. Eligible. Hetero. Right?"

"Don't say any more," I said.

"I wasn't going to. I said it all. I'm disappointed."

He sat back as if, just like that, he could lob a grenade at my feet and watch me from behind a wall of self-assurance. Oh no, I thought. It won't be that easy.

"You do realize where we are," I said. "We're fugitives on a ghost train in violation of international law. You do realize the woman we're helping escape, my mother, the woman you used to work for, isn't well. That she's been raped by her doctor. That we've survived a hospital riot and hunted down by a rescue squad. You do realize the madness we've been through. And you have the nerve to ask why you and I haven't grown closer."

"I wanted to speak honestly," he said.

"That's a given."

"And it's all I wanted. To speak honestly."

"I wish I could forget this entire conversation."

"Well, I'm sorry," he said. "That obviously wasn't my intention. It didn't turn out like I expected."

"What did you expect?"

He hesitated a moment. "I expected you to listen. That's all."

"Okay," I said, "I heard you. Okay? I heard you speak honestly. Let's leave it at that."

But of course, I couldn't leave it at that. He'd ripped a scab off an old wound I assumed had healed. Maybe it had. But Nelson opened it up again, and it hurt as much then as it had years ago. Back then, I'd fend off their accusations of aloofness with my dedication to my work. It proved the perfect shield. If work was central to their lives, why shouldn't it be central to mine? We high achievers knew how to keep intimacy at bay. But now this, Nelson's casual question: why haven't we become closer?

I knew my response to him had been correct—objectively unarguable. But I also knew the roots to my response ran deeper. And I was afraid Nelson knew this, also.

I directed my attention outside, where the horizon glowed a bright bluish white, its epicenter incandescent, like a stellar body arising from the earth. New York City's business district approached from the south. Then suddenly this other-worldly brilliance turned black. Pulaski Tunnel. Under the Hudson. Our deceleration pressed me hard against my harness as the streaking tunnel lights broke into single globes and my weight lightened with our slower pace.

Grand Central Station wouldn't be much farther.

29

"It's only a short subway ride from here," Conrad said as we disembarked the aerotrain.

My heart fluttered like a caged bird about to be freed. I'd lived in a limbo of uncertainty for so long I could hardly trust the door had been opened. And to be rescued by my mentor was truly a gift. My last meeting with Jim had been clouded with recriminations and mutual disappointment and mutual defeat. The prospect of refuge and the chance to bridge the distance between us brought on dizzying joy.

"La Luz," Conrad continued. "That's where we're heading. La Luz di Ferro Hotel."

The station buzzed with polyglot chatter, canned music, and laughter from the countless travelers transported on conveyors or choosing to walk or to stand motionless, their mouths agape in wonder.

As we rode the crowded conveyor, Conrad tucked his chin to his chest, his gaze flicking from side to side. In contrast, I raised my face toward the cameras affixed overhead, toward whoever was watching over us, taking notice. Mother's touch on my shoulder drew my attention from the cameras. She shook her head gently and mimicked Conrad, burying her chin into her chest like frightened prey. And then I remembered and did the same.

We continued down the wide concourse, gliding under the Westclox holograph and past the quaint ticket counters for tourists wanting an historical experience at the station. As usual, the conveyor slowed as we approached Memorial Square, a succession of monuments commemorating those who died in the Thanksgiving Dirty Bomb Attack. No one stepped off to pay their respects this time, probably due to the lateness of the hour. It had been my habit to take this moment to look reflectively through the station's glass floors and ceilings, down as far as I could see, and pay my respects to our City of Glass and the overthrow of terror hidden behind brick and mortar.

The conveyor accelerated once past the memorial. We had to change conveyors several times before we arrived on a platform for the Parkchester train which took us to the 77th Street Station. A short walk brought us to the La Luz di Ferro Hotel, but we didn't enter the lobby.

Conrad insisted on more precautions.

We followed Conrad onto a staircase landing, but instead of walking up the stairs as I'd expected, he led us down. The staircase was well-lit, as was the tunnel that followed, but this route into the hotel was beginning to feel overly precautionary. Camera lenses blinked on as we made our way up a few steps and then down a few more and through a winding tunnel that seemed to be taking us away from the hotel. The air was cool, but hardly conditioned and the opaqueness of the corridor walls was beginning to weigh on me, as though the tunnel was narrowing.

Ahead of me, Nelson ran his fingers along the blackened wall and turned around. "Waterproofing," he said.

I stopped. We'd arrived at an intersection where another corridor branched off to our right, its walls and ceiling lined with pipes and ductwork.

"This way," Conrad said, gesturing to our left, away from the pipelined corridor.

"Where exactly are we going?" I asked.

"To meet McBride," Conrad said.

"But where? You're taking us away from the hotel."

"We're not meeting him in the hotel," Conrad said.

"But under it," Nelson said.

I stared at him, stunned by his reply and by his confidence. By his apparent belief in the absurd.

"In her lab," Conrad answered Nelson.

"That's impossible," I said.

Conrad shook his head.

"What lab are you talking about?" I asked.

"The lab that will shelter you," Conrad said. "And your mother. And Mr. Woon Sam." Nelson pointed down the pipelined corridor to our right, his finger gesturing assuredly.

"Air filtration system. Ventilation and heating ducts. Water pipes. Electric cables."

"But I worked there only a few months ago," I said. "Our lab couldn't be recreated in the blink of an eye."

"Of course not," Conrad said. "But it could in a decade."

"But why?" I said.

"Can't answer that," Conrad said. "But it's where Jim works. And Ramsey."

The shock took away my breath. My instinct was to run, but without the ability. Fingernails dug into my shoulder and Mother's face appeared before me and I heard her muffled voice calling my name. And then Conrad's, a cacophony of appeals for attention until Conrad finally broke through.

"I have no interest in deceiving you," he insisted. "My job is to deliver you."

"But where?" I whispered.

"To safety," he said. "To deliver us all to safety."

His claim seemed laughably cruel as we proceeded through retina-locked door after door, each proclaiming DANGER: DO NOT ENTER. An unoccupied tram sat at the end of a track that disappeared downward after Conrad had retina-scanned the last Do-Not-Enter door. Even at this remote outpost, glow-globes lit the corridor and cameras blinked surveillance of our presence. Metallic cylinders affixed to girders jerked and tracked our movement toward the tram.

"Motion-lasers," Conrad explained. "Don't worry, we have invitations. The lasers are meant for the uninvited. Apparently, your colleagues are very serious about not being disturbed."

I looked down the cold, dark tube of a motion-laser, robotically deadly, and wondered what kind of world I was entering—its gateway, a foreboding fortress of security, and the construction itself, a redundant replica of my lab. All underground. Hidden. Incomprehensible.

Conrad walked us to the tram, a tubular glass and white-paneled vehicle, designed to carry exactly our number. We took our seats and waited. A faint tremor rose from the floorboards, and we lurched forward and downward, the tunnel's granite wall, speckled and damp, gliding past. It felt like the earth's rawness bearing down on us and I had to look away, only to see Mother leaning toward the window, toward the glistening bedrock I couldn't bear.

Watching her, my thoughts ran wild, uncontrollable attacks on what I'd always hoped to be true, that she and I were harmonious, different surely, but spiritually in tune. I thought then that her nature was significantly different than my own. I thought then that she was meant for another time—the age of torchlight and shadow. I wanted a world utterly bright and crystal clear, nothing dim or shaded, nothing concealed. And there we sat, Mother and me, together and apart, rolling through her darkness, heading toward what I'd hoped would be my light.

We stopped on the edge of a large circular antechamber and filed out into its dim gloom. Several unoccupied trams extended from the chamber like spokes on their respective tracks. Red biohazard waste cans circled the circumference of the chamber, each paired with a disk stamped with an outward-facing footprint. The array suggested what we were to do, but we all stood still, awaiting specific instructions.

"Please step forward," a man's robotic voice directed, "onto the footprinted pad. You will experience a simple noninvasive decontamination procedure. Please try to relax. This will take less than thirty seconds."

We stood on the designated pads and clear cylinders descended over each of us. A dry, sweet-smelling mist filled my tube and was sucked up through an air duct hose for the promised half-minute. Then the vacuuming stopped, the mist disappeared, and the cylinders rose and recessed into the ceiling. I glanced at the biohazard can to my right and awaited further instruction.

"Inside your respective biohazard cans," the voice continued, "you will find clothing to replace the clothes you have on. Please place the clothes you have on in your respective biohazard cans."

I was thoroughly familiar with unobtrusive inspection, of course. In fact, the process had devolved into namelessness as citizens entered and exited buildings since the Age of Transparency. Perhaps that was what most surprised me: the naming of the process.

Noninvasive decontamination. Having a label made it invasive. That and, of course, the implication of biological threat.

I unlatched my can and found a stack of sterile, neatly folded clothes inside. I glanced around at the others as they withdrew similar contents from their cans. They seemed as eager as I to change out of our sour clothes into the fresh clothing we'd been supplied. As I changed, I saw we each had the same bland generic apparel: black cotton undergarments and unisex pants and shirts in the baggy subcontinent style—loose along the limbs, saggy in the crotch, slack around the wrists and ankles, but snug around the waist, all composed of cool, transparent, poly-silk crepe. After we'd finished dressing, it seemed we each inhaled deeply the freshness of our new outfits.

A faint shuffling sound drew my attention to an arched hallway, the only way in or out of the chamber. I heard Jim call my name before he entered the chamber, his arms outstretched, his corpulent body shambling slowly but earnestly toward me. He was dressed in what I'd assumed by then was the uniform of the place.

"I can't tell you how good it is to see you," he said as we embraced.

A flood of emotions burst free without warning, surprising me as I found myself sobbing on Jim's shoulder. I couldn't speak. I could only squeeze him and wonder at the pent-up fear and frustration I'd suppressed for so long.

"It's okay," he whispered. "You're safe now."

And as much as I wanted to believe him, I couldn't help but glance over his shoulder toward the hallway for any sign of Ramsey. There was none.

Jim stepped back and extended his hand toward Mother. "Madame Anueche, welcome. And you, too, Mr. Woon-Sam." He nodded politely at Conrad as though that was their first meeting.

So many questions swirled in my mind I wasn't sure where to begin. "Where are we?"

He was about to answer when a pair of familiars walked into the chamber, former colleagues from what seemed like another life.

"Gordon and Misha?" I said, utterly shocked by their presence. Frightened by their presence, actually. Not so much afraid as unnerved. "What are you doing here?" They glanced at each other and then at Jim.

"We work here" Misha said. She looked imploringly at Jim.

"It's our lab," Jim said. "Our new lab."

"It was under construction for a while," Gordon said. "A dozen years or more before you ..."

"Retired," Jim said.

"Left us," Misha said. "In the lurch, so to speak."

"But this place couldn't replace our lab," I said, recalling the seeping granite and thick subterranean air.

"Excuse me," Nelson whispered through clenched teeth. "What exactly is your plan?"

"We need to get you situated," Jim said.

"No," Nelson said. "I mean what is your long-term plan. We're in an underground bunker basically. For how long?"

We looked away from one another. It was a question on all of our minds, but only Nelson dared ask it.

"I take your question seriously," Jim spoke at last. "That said, I'd like to answer you as thoroughly as possible. But I'd like to get you settled first. Then give your question, your questions, the time and attention they deserve."

"That makes sense," Conrad said. "It's been a long journey."

"Have we reached freedom?" Mother said. "Or are we buried in our graves?"

Jim turned to her and then to me.

Tears welled in my eyes. "The journey's taken its toll."

"You know," Mother said. "The song." And then she sang, *"Before I'd be a slave, I'd be buried in my grave."*

She glanced at each of us expectantly.

"And go home to my Lord and be free," she continued.

Perhaps the ensuing silence meant we all had the same question but were unable to ask.

"You've reached freedom, Madame Anueche," Jim said. "I'm your host and I say you all have reached freedom."

I left the chamber suspended between the two promises of freedom, Jim's, and the song's.

30

The hallway from the antechamber branched into several color-lit corridors, and we took the yellow route, past a succession of open portals. Nelson turned to me, his frown deepening into a scowl.

"Where are you taking us?" I asked Jim.

"We're being situated," Nelson said.

Jim glanced at him, abundant patience in his eyes. "To your residence pods," he said.

"Resting pods?" I asked.

"Residence pods," Nelson said. "As in our new home."

I turned to Jim.

"Sanctuary," he said.

New home. Sanctuary. It didn't matter. I felt dislocated regardless. I'd given so much attention to our running away, I hadn't fully considered where we'd arrive.

I ran my fingers along the wall, soft to the touch, the translucent yellow Rubber Glass paling all other colors in its reach, absorbing sound in the vicinity. The sheer intangibility of the place heightened my sense of feeling adrift.

"And this?" Nelson called out, peering into an opening along the corridor.

We gathered in front of a screened gate that fenced off a storage area extending beyond the reach of the corridor's light. Code-stamped boxes and barrels had been stacked or pyramided on either side of a concrete walkway that continued into the darkness.

"How long do you plan to stay in this sanctuary?" Nelson asked.

"There's a difference between planning and preparing," Jim said.

"But both have a projected end," Nelson said. "Do we need to rest before we hear yours?"

"Context is crucial," Jim said. "Detail without context is meaningless."

I shuddered. I wasn't used to evasion. Jim's clichés concealed more than they clarified his intention to do so was obvious.

We arrived at a second series of portals that led, Jim explained, to our individual pods.

Our living quarters, he clarified. Our cells, I imagined Nelson thinking. We could rest however we'd like, Jim continued. Or not rest. He'd return later for orientation, as he put it.

The passage into the pod narrowed and I stooped lower and lower until I entered a wider space and immediately understood Jim's terminology. The term pod was very appropriate. The small chamber looked like inside a hollowed egg: tiny, bright white, and ovular. One curvilinear wall contained shelves that held several neatly folded jumpsuits similar to what I had on. A shower and commode were squeezed into the larger end of the egg which had barely enough room to stand comfortably under the showerhead. A hassock and com-desk occupied the smaller end of the ellipsoid. A curved bed ran along the length of the other wall. The scant floorspace in the middle seemed like an afterthought.

I set my mind to rank-ordering the questions I intended to ask Jim at the orientation he'd mentioned, but the pod conspired against me—a calming shade of lavender gradually replaced the bright eggshell white walls that had greeted me, and a hint of sandalwood oil slowly spread throughout the chamber, the combination of the two soothing my sensorium. I hadn't realized sleep had snuck up on me until Nelson startled me awake.

"Seems you've adjusted nicely," he said.

"Are you accusing me of resting?" I said, irritated by the intrusion and his tone.

His face softened and he backed away, sliding onto one of the cushions in the middle of the pod. I resettled on the side of the bed, waking, and watching for an apology.

"I'm having a hard time of it," he said.

"You're not alone," I said.

He glanced around the pod. "From the frying pan into the fire?"

"Believe better," I said, reminding him of the advice he'd offered me.

He nodded. "A safe haven?"

"According to Jim."

"You know him."

"I trust him," I said. "I have to."

Nelson shrugged skeptically. "But a reconstruction of your lab? Here, underground? With residence quarters and enough supplies to last—who knows how long?"

I shook my head, hoping he'd stop.

"And we were led here like mice following a trail of seed?" he continued. "Sown by whom? Why?"

He again glanced around the pod—a tense, twitchy inspection.

"I should check on Mother," I said.

"A nurse visited her pod," he said. "I saw. I was last to get … situated."

"I need to check on her," I said.

"Please do," he said. "But these questions won't go away."

"I'm not happy about this either," I said. "It's all compared-to-what, in my mind. What's the alternative? That's how I think about it. That's how I have to think about it. She's my mother."

He took a deep breath, observing me.

"I feel used," I continued. "I'm afraid to find out the price for Mother's safety."

"They got you back," he said coldly.

I wanted to be angry with him, but I knew he was right. He had no idea how it felt to be used, to feel trapped.

"I've had this … this recurring dream," I said. I gestured toward my crumpled pillow. "Had it just now, in fact."

His eyes brightened.

"I'm standing inside a bubble," I said. "I can see people outside the bubble. I hear their voices. I call out to them, but they don't hear me. They look right at me, but they don't seem to see me."

Now I observed him, awaiting his reaction.

He nodded sympathetically.

"It's so upsetting," I said, choking back frustration rekindled in the telling.

"Someone has to do it," he said. "When there's approaching danger. Some member of the flock has to sound the alarm to ensure the others will flee."

"But no one hears me," I said. "And I don't see any danger."

"That's what makes it a nightmare."

He leaned forward, hands on his knees.

"Or," he continued, "you're crying out against loneliness."

I glared at him. "I wasn't even sure I wanted to share that dream."

"I'm glad you did. Not everyone would admit their vulnerability."

"Some people are attracted to vulnerability," I said. "For them, others' vulnerability is a magnet."

"I'm not one of those people, Fitima. I assume we all have weaknesses. Including me, of course. Personally, I've never met any super-humans. But I've met many in search of companionship."

He raised his eyebrows as if to highlight his point.

"Hello!" Jim said from the entryway. "May I come in?"

"Yes," I answered.

Upon seeing Nelson, Jim's smile broadened, beaming his false assumption about Nelson's presence. Then again, there was no record in the Repository of my relationship with Nelson, so Jim was free to assume whatever he wished, and his wish was unmistakably romantic.

"I hope you've had a chance to rest," Jim said.

"Yes," I said, dismissing his potential double entendre.

"I understand the risk of fanning your paranoia," he continued, "but—"

"Fanning it further," Nelson interrupted.

"Exactly," Jim said. "But each of you receives a personal orientation."

"Separately?" Nelson said.

"Only initially," Jim said. "Then you'll get together and share your impressions."

Nelson looked at me, his eyebrows arched as though his suspicions had been confirmed.

"As I said," Jim continued, "I understand the risk of fanning your paranoia further. But we want to customize your orientations. Which I think you'll appreciate afterward."

"Let's get on with it," I said. "No need to debate the undebatable."

Nelson squinted at me as though betrayed.

"We all want answers," I said, staring back at him. "Don't we?"

31

Jim and I walked down the corridor we'd entered earlier, but away from the residence pods which Jim explained were only one of several clusters arrayed along multiple corridors, all of which led to a central core, a hub with branching corridors. The corridor we followed away from the hub contained labs, studios, and workrooms that were vaguely familiar from my initial orientation to the lab above-ground lab. I guessed the size and strangeness of the place would only fuel Nelson's paranoia, yet I felt oddly unmoved by my prediction, as though I realized I could manage only so much of his mistrust and that I'd reached my limit.

Jim led me into a room, its walls consisting solely of viewing monitors except for the door we'd passed through. Several swivel chairs in the center of the room provided sightlines to all of the monitors and he and I sat down.

"What is this place?" I asked.

"A viewing room."

"Orientation?"

He nodded.

"Mother and Nelson?"

"Other rooms. Saves time."

"But like this one?" I asked.

"Not exactly. The presentations are customized."

Customized? I thought. I would've preferred knowing what Mother was being shown. But before I could question him, flecks of light shimmered on several screens in the middle of the front wall, the wall opposite the door. A familiar face pixelated into view, framed by a square of dark, unlit monitors.

I hadn't seen Lloyd since I'd suspected his collusion with my former boss Ramsey, a betrayal I could never forgive, and his appearance—at this time, at this place—should have provoked me yet again. But something about his troubled eyes acknowledged the recent gulf between us and seemed to lessen that gulf. Or maybe my lifetime with him outweighed our much briefer time at odds. Or maybe it was simply the trustworthy features of a face that qualified as a pollster's that allayed my anger.

I turned to Jim. "What's this about?"

Jim gestured toward Lloyd. "He was instrumental in designing your orientation."

"Designing?" I said. "As in programming?"

"It was a mistake," Lloyd said. "My biggest. Letting them persuade me to persuade you. A deplorable breach of protocol but defensible."

"You can't have it both ways, Lloyd."

"You'll see," he said. "You must see before you judge."

"Lloyd designed what you'll see," Jim said, motioning to the walls of monitors. "He knows you better than anyone. He knows what you'll allow yourself to see."

"Allow myself?"

"You were never much receptive to bad news," Lloyd said.

"Who is?" I said.

"Some more than others," Lloyd said. "You won't remember the question, but the reply may sound familiar." He glanced down and read, "I select only information that'll nourish my mind. I do my best to avoid distraction. Sensationalism. Salacious scandal and other diversions."

He stopped and waited for me to meet his gaze.

I did, but quickly turned away. It was unsettling to hear my long-forgotten words expressing an idea I still believed.

"Your thoughts about current events," Lloyd continued. "And you behaved accordingly. You preferred to personalize your news, as you put it."

"Like everyone," I said.

"Like most," Lloyd said. "Remember, I collect the data. I am the gatekeeper, you declared. Of what I let in and what I leave out."

"That's what we were taught," I said.

"Truly," Lloyd said. "And what I kept in mind assembling the evidence."

"Evidence?"

"Your orientation." Jim said, pointing to the walls of blank monitors.

I took closer notice of those walls, arrayed with monitors in rows and columns of five by five, apparently with the capacity to combine into one image, as was the case with Lloyd's face centered on the front wall. The monitors around his face blinked on now, randomly, displaying a succession of moving images on separate screens until the entire room glowed with a pale fluorescence.

"You choose which screen to focus on," Lloyd said. "As you do, the soundscape of the moving image will amplify for clarity until you look away. Your attention can also expand the image across several screens. Until you look away."

"And if I choose not to look at all?" I said.

He glanced around at the walls. "This is a viewing room, after all. I guess you could close your eyes."

"But this is your orientation," Jim said. "It's evidence for the why behind our project."

"To send data back in time," I said. "To play roulette with destiny."

"I don't believe in destiny," Jim said. "We'll soon find out what you believe."

He stood and started for the door.

"Where are you going?" I said.

"This is a private viewing," he said.

"But if I have questions?"

"You undoubtedly will," Lloyd said as scenes on the monitors replaced the image of his face. "But they will be informed questions," he continued. "Our answers will have all the more meaning."

Nine new scenes had displaced Lloyd's image and I turned to Jim, but he had left the room. I wanted to get up and leave as well. I wanted to check on Mother. Would they take what she'd been through into consideration in customizing her orientation? Was their orientation the price we had to pay for sanctuary?

My attention drifted to the top right monitor on the front wall. I didn't want to look at any of the screens. I didn't want to comply. But I didn't feel free to leave and I couldn't just sit there with my eyes closed. I didn't think anyone could sit there with their eyes closed.

A football game was on that screen. A friendly, coed game on a freshly manicured pitch. Playful squeals and calls of encouragement arose from the men and women in their street clothes, indistinguishable as teams. The whoops and chatter got louder, and the image expanded across several screens as the players crisscrossed the field. I could even make out some of their names as they called out to each other, and I tried to imagine the mic and camera placement around the pitch.

Then the game stopped, and the players gathered near the far goal, but the image zoomed large enough for me to see their sweaty faces. One of the men picked up the ball which had begun to unravel, and he pulled a loose leather strip and continued pulling and the ball got smaller and smaller until he lifted the core that remained—a human skull.

I stood and closed my eyes. The sound of cheers from the players slowly subsided and when I opened my eyes, the scene had shrunk to the original monitor, the players still gathered while applauding the skull. I looked away and ran to the door, but my arms folded into me when I pushed. The door was locked.

I stood frozen, panicked, for myself and for Mother. What had I led us into? Some form of psychological torture? But to what purpose? And for my mentor to call it orientation? Why would he do this?

I glanced at the front wall, afraid to look at any of the monitors for too long, afraid of the scene that would emerge. I closed my eyes.

Lloyd said I would have questions. Formed by witnessing horror? He also promised answers.

I hesitated then opened my eyes and returned to my seat, my gaze fixed on the floor. I glanced at the door, into the corners of the room. Finally, I turned to the monitors and saw the images there were stationary until I looked at any one of them for more than a moment and set the scene into motion. Which is when I looked away.

I thought back to Lloyd citing my teenage speech about broadcast news. I tried to remember when I'd learned to avoid *body bag* news, as we called it, but it was like trying to remember when I'd learned to eat nutritiously or practice good hygiene. It was simply what you did. You filtered out negativity that might contaminate your spirit. Doing otherwise would... well, even the thought of it made me queasy.

I looked at the front wall of monitors, reminding myself I was in control of what I saw, that I could shut my eyes at any time. As I stared blankly, the scene on the middle monitor sprang into motion. A rusted machete fell onto a dusty patch of dirt. Who or whatever threw it remained outside the frame. And then another machete fell, and another and another, accumulating a crisscrossed pile of dark wood-hewn handles and jagged blades, glinting dark splotches of ... blood?

I shut my eyes to the image, but not the thought. Bloodshed? Slaughter? So, was this to be my orientation: viewing a succession of horrors? With an underlying link, I supposed. A lesson?

I opened my eyes feeling dirty and ashamed. Yet compelled. Feeling as though I had to complete this task like any other I'd been assigned. As though it were an obligation. Which it was. I turned back to the monitors, squinting to blur the images, yet scanning intently for any sign of blood, prepared to avert my eyes.

I spotted an old man lying on a lawn beside a flowerbed. He had his arms around someone I couldn't see, whispering words I couldn't hear. He shifted to stare up at the sky and revealed not who he'd been embracing, but what: a small, white, flowered-draped coffin.

I stared at the floor and let the tears flow. I should have been grieving the child and the old man. Perhaps I was. But I mostly mourned what I'd lost with Jim. He was responsible for subjecting me to these miseries and I would never look at him the same way again. I glanced at the door and cried harder. What was Mother being forced to witness for the sake of our asylum? After all she'd been through. Hooks. D.C.

I suddenly scanned the monitors, frantically searching for a familiar face or setting, any evidence of the miseries we'd suffered. If there was any saving grace to this orientation it would be to tie these despairing images to the despair we'd suffered. A succession of sounds and motion stirred on the monitors as I scanned them, but I found nothing familiar.

Frustrated, my attention came to rest on a maze of muddy trenches, their troughs growing wider as the camera zoomed in on a cluster of cowering, mud-spattered children.

I looked away, but I still heard music. Then I realized I hadn't shut my eyes but had simply switched to another monitor where a man sat playing a piano in a public square, vacant except for the phalanx of soldiers confronting him, their faces hidden behind their helmet shields. A long-forgotten question came to mind, one so dimly remembered I could barely claim it as my own. Was there music in the worst of times? The fleeting question of a young child exploring history stored in the Repository. Was there music? Could there have been? I shut my eyes and the room went dark and quiet.

I swallowed back nausea. I understood, now, what these images reminded me of. They reminded me of the dark, opaque years before the Age of Transparency. But these scenes were current. I could tell by the architecture, either arrived or striving toward modernity. And the clothes, either stylishly clear or shyly opaque. No doubt, these were present-day scenes. But they carried an aura of yesteryear.

I swiveled around and fell upon the scene of a uniformed officer spray-painting a woman's face purple and reciting as if to a child, "No person shall write …"

I looked away to silence him. But my avoiding the scene wouldn't undo what he'd done to that woman. It wouldn't save her. I turned back to look.

"… unless the express permission of the owner has been obtained," the officer said.

The woman's lips quivered, but she didn't speak. I looked at the yellow clapboard wall behind her, inscribed with words I recognized.

Not only the guilty.

That's as far as she'd gotten. Have reason to fear, I thought. Finally, something familiar.

"You're frightening people," the officer said. "This has to stop."

The woman's lips parted, and purple paint dripped into her mouth. "But who's gonna warn them?" she said.

Who's gonna sound the alarm, I thought. Nelson's interpretation of my dream. Of me shouting to people on the other side of that transparent bubble but being ignored. Trying to warn them, Nelson had said. Warn them to flee approaching danger.

I closed my eyes to the woman, the graffiti, and the officer. What remained was a dreamscape, a conjuring of myself inside a glass high-rise, suspended mid-level. Endless transparent floors below me. Endless transparent ceilings above. A siren wailing in the distance. The smell of smoke. And Nelson's voice, reminiscent, "Pre-evacuation delay, we call it." The siren grew louder. "Those unwilling to believe the warning," he'd said. "Some people never leave."

32

I startled to find Jim standing over me.

"Relax," he said softly, patting my forehead with a cool, damp cloth.

I felt as if I'd awoken from a dream. A terrible sadness left me searching for its cause. From my chair, I glanced around the room. The rows of monitors stared back at me, blank.

"How are you feeling?" Jim asked. "Can you sit up?"

I drew myself up in the chair, weary but reviving. "What happened?"

"You'd seen enough."

I remembered the anger I'd summoned against him — so hateful it had surprised me. But my hatred had dissipated in the flood of confounding images and lingered now only as an afterthought, the memory of a feeling rather than the feeling itself.

"I need to see Mother," I said, gathering myself.

"And you will," he said. "But what will you tell her? Did you make sense of all this?" He gestured toward the monitors. "Will you be able to help her make sense of what she saw?"

"I need to make sure she's okay."

"But what will she need?"

"Where is she?" I demanded, standing, eying the open door.

"With the children," Jim said.

"Children?"

"We have a nursery," he said.

I shook my head. There seemed no end to the surprises. "And Nelson?"

"Waiting for you," he said.

"To debrief his orientation, I suppose."

"And to hear what sense you've made of yours."

I glanced again at the monitors. "This was Ramsey's doing."

Jim frowned as he had long ago when his protégé gave the wrong answer.

"Ramsey showed up during one of Lloyd's polls," I said. "He tried to convince me to return to the project. While Mother was at the hospital, no less. He said the authorities had connected the dots of the madness running rampant in the world. He said they'd given it a name. Malaise, he called it. And claimed his project promised its cure. That's when I decided he, too, was a madman and Lloyd a traitor."

"And me?" Jim said.

"A collaborator."

"That part's true."

"Tormenter, too."

"Instructor," Jim said.

He stooped and slowly lowered himself to the floor—his hip, knee, and ankle servos whining softly under his shifting weight until he'd settled there, cross-legged.

"Malaise," he intoned as if titling a poem. "It's interesting how a name gives credibility to an idea. It helps you believe you're dealing with one discrete thing."

"When in fact you've invented a scapegoat."

"I'm sure that's how it seems," he said. "And that was taken into consideration in the naming. Who's likely to be blamed? Who vindicated? Who stigmatized?"

"So who's the winner of the game you're playing?"

"No game, I'm afraid. It's real. We had to resurrect an old early warning system to realize that."

"Early warning for what?"

"Rogue behavior."

I looked around at the monitors surrounding us. "Well, that's as plain as the images you made me watch."

"It's not as simple as pointing out abnormal behavior."

"It couldn't be simpler," I said.

"I wish it were. We lost precious time."

"Time for what?"

"To understand the problem ... the scope of it. It's more widespread than a few deviants acting out."

"Sounds like you want to one-up Ramsey."

"I guess that's how it sounds. We debated how to give you the bad news. Lloyd convinced us to avoid gruesome. Some have seen a lot worse."

"Am I supposed to feel ashamed?"

Jim shook his head. "We can't always pin down where belief about an impending disaster turns into disbelief. It differs for different people. We want you on our side of belief."

I glared at him and drew a deep breath. "I want to hear more. About this ... this so-called Malaise."

Speechless for a moment, his eyes widened, then he jumped at the opportunity. "Like I said, we had to revive the old early warning system. Anomaly detection it was called. Before Transparency. When it was needed."

An era we'd all studied but never fully understood. I'd always assumed secrecy, or even its possibility had to be experienced to be fully grasped, and none of us had had that experience.

"Deviant behavior all but disappeared after Transparency," Jim continued. "When it returned, detection programs had long since been decommissioned. It took a while to recognize what was happening."

"Just look and see," I said. "You keep talking about programs. Why not simply look and see?"

"We looked. We saw. But not enough. This particular program goes beyond observing the obvious. It compares the behavior of every individual against a template of collective behavior. That's how we identify outliers—the anomalies."

"Collective behavior? As in the world population?"

"The known world," he said. "The observable world."

"Impossible," I said. "Too much data to analyze. Observe, yes. Analyze, no."

"It's a vast operation, true. But vast isn't infinite. It isn't impossible. It's simply vast."

"But all observed behavior?"

"All. Matched against models of normality. Overt misbehavior is obvious like the sort you saw here. Like you said, no difficulty there. But we can run algorithms on all recorded data. That's how we conduct analyses. Even attempted covert misbehavior becomes visible. It stands apart from routine. Speech, for example. Rogues speak differently. They use more singular pronouns. They talk of I more than we. Me more than us. Their speech reveals their betrayal of the public good."

"Lloyd told me about these people," I said. "Fanatics who crave privacy. Secrecy, even. That their misbehavior comes from frustration of that need. And for some, public defiance is a protest against Transparency. But he couldn't say if the increase was real or apparent due to better surveillance or a growing number of offenders."

"Well put. He couldn't say."

"He wasn't allowed?" I said.

"Correct. The increase was real."

"And you kept it from the public."

"Like our research," Jim said.

"For our own good, of course," I said.

I rose from the chair and offered Jim my hand. We were at the doorstep of a familiar, fruitless debate and I'd delayed seeing Mother long enough. Jim seemed resigned to my conclusion and grabbed my hand to hoist himself up.

"The nursery?" I asked, sufficient to stop an argument before it began.

We returned to the hall and retraced our steps back toward the residence pods until we reached a door I'd assumed led into yet another room.

Jim stopped and gestured toward the doorway. "Just follow the laughter," he said before continuing down the main hall. "You and I … we'll talk later."

Once past the door, the hallway shrank. Child-sized, I thought, yet high and wide enough for an adult. I'd walked only twenty meters when I could make out an echo of children's laughter. I passed several alcoves, some containing children's furniture, others lined with stuffed animals that shimmied to life as I walked by, their heat sensors detecting my presence.

The hallway ended in a kaleidoscope of contrasting colors and patterns with phosphorescent rainbows rising above an arched doorway, red-and-white striped walls, a blue-and-yellow checked floor. I entered and turned toward the laughter and discovered a large indoor playground with brightly colored swings and slides and crawling tubes and a dozen or so joyful children and a tad fewer watchful adults scattered throughout. The gathering featured a medley of flesh tones, though I heard only English—spoken with a variety of rhythms and accents.

The entire scene made no sense. The children, most of all. Childcare was one thing, but this place, Jim called it the nursery, had an air of permanence about it. I felt as though I'd entered established recreational grounds within what I'd thought of as only a laboratory. The place was clearly more than that. But how much more I couldn't say.

33

I spotted Mother crouched among a small group of children with a middle-aged man and woman standing behind her. They were all inside a soft-play model space station, as surreal a scene as I could imagine. I was reminded of Mother's breakdown back in the trailer, her not recognizing herself in the mirror, as I tried to recall her in this playful posture and speaking in the singsong lilt she offered these children. My memory of her didn't extend that far back.

She stood and faced the two adults but didn't see me approach.

The man did. "Your daughter?" he said, gesturing toward me.

Mother turned, threw up her hands, and stepped out of the soft-play enclosure. Our embrace was such a comfort since I wasn't sure what woman I'd find in my arms.

The man left the soft-play space station and joined us. "Victor Brocken," he said, shaking my hand. "Glad you could find time."

I fumbled for a way to explain my visit and glanced at the woman he'd left behind. She whispered something to the children before leaving and joining the three of us.

"Effie Burrows," she said.

"Pleased to meet you," I said. "Actually, I came to see my mother."

"Of course," Mother said. "But aren't you impressed with this place?"

"Yes, yes, very," I said, though I would've also revealed my ambivalence about it if I weren't so eager to speak with her alone.

"Your mother has a fetching way with children," Victor said.

"Really?" I said, turning to Mother. "How long have you been here?"

"Not long," she said.

"Which makes her all the more impressive," Effie said.

"You had your orientation?" I asked Mother.

She nodded.

"And she shared some of it with the children," Victor said.

"Some of what you saw?" I countered, confused, incredulous. "Of what they showed you?"

"As a proverb," Effie said. "That's what we were discussing."

"Okay," I said, meaning enough, as politely as I could manage. I turned to Mother. "I'd really like to talk with you."

"I'd love to. I just wanted—"

"I know. I know." I quickly scanned the nursery. "Impressive, yes. Later maybe." I turned to Victor and Effie. "Please excuse us, won't you?"

"No worries," Victor said. "Come back when you can. We'll be here."

***

Mother's pod looked exactly like mine and the replication unsettled me, as if I were noticing for the first time that we were buried in an underground human hive and that I might have to will the walls apart to keep them from closing in on me.

"Your orientation?" I asked. "We each saw something different."

"You remember Serita."

"Of course. Our cook. She lived with us."

"For a while," Mother said. "In the beginning."

"When I was in primary."

"Yes, your early teens. You just loved that woman. And I depended on her."

I recalled Serita's low whispering voice. It had been so long since she'd left, but not without leaving a lasting influence on me, planting a seed of confidence that grew even in her absence.

"What about her?"

"She was my orientation."

"What do you mean?"

"That's who they showed me. Serita. In a queue. By herself. In a food line."

"I don't understand. A food line? How did she look? I mean, did she look well?

Mother shot me a sidelong glance. "She was in a food line, Fitima."

Which made no sense. Serita was resourceful. She had family. She had skills.

"But did she look ill?" I asked. "Where was she?"

"I don't know. Somewhere rural. Somewhere dry. Near an old adobe fort. In a dirt field dotted with dozens of tents, appearing and disappearing in waves of dust. It was a warning, Fitima. My orientation was a warning."

I shook my head. A warning using Serita? She'd been so kind to us. To me. I remembered how she'd offered reassurance I was too young to ask for. "You're every bit as wonderful as your mother," she once told me. "You're my princess and all princesses grow up to be queens someday."

"Did she say anything?" I asked.

"Not to me. Not directly. She mumbled a mantra of some sort. But they focused on her, isolated her speech, increased the volume. They wanted to make sure I heard her. 'The right seed in the right soil in the right season.' That's all. Over and over."

"Meaning what?"

"Famine. The whole scene cried famine. The tents. The serving line. The steaming kettles. Serita's mantra. As if there'd been a failure. As if there'd been a famine. As if ... as if."

"As if? How could it not be famine?"

"I heard a chime," she said whimsically. "Over the camp's loudspeakers. Three beautiful notes. Everything, everyone, came to a stop except the wind-blown dust. A woman's voice followed. 'We proclaim liberty throughout the land,' she said. 'The hoarders have been identified. The crisis is over. You can return to your districts, your property, your kin.' That was it. Except for the wind and people murmuring back to their tents, all was quiet."

"And Serita?"

"Serita, too."

"So the famine was over, thank God. What about the scene seemed as-if to you?"

Mother offered me the kind of smile the wise often extend to the foolish. "I've spoken into similar microphones, Fitima. I've announced solutions. I've named the guilty ... the scapegoats. Declared all's-clear. Often it was true. But not always. Besides, warnings don't come with happy endings. And my orientation was a warning. As was yours, I assume. Who did you see? Who did they show you?"

I stared at her wondering which was worse: the lie she was telling me now or lies she'd told in the past. Or perhaps worst of all, her madness was returning.

"What warning?" I asked. "The famine or the deception?"

"Not or. And. The famine and the deception. But I want to know who you saw. I'd like to put my theory to the test. Who did you see?"

"I wasn't shown anyone I know. Or knew. But you could say I saw a warning if that's your theory. They even gave it a name. Malaise."

She stared into the center of the pod. "Malaise?" she said softly. "Interesting. A question and an answer at the same time. Something's amiss. That's the answer. But no one can say quite what. That's the question. Malaise."

Her pensive tone reminded me of her presence in the nursery. "Did Jim bring you to the children?"

She returned to me and smiled. "This place is more than just a lab."

Better her composure than my agitation, I thought. If only I could understand it. "The teachers said you offered them a proverb," I said. "Based on your orientation? Based on what you saw?"

"It just came to me. After meeting the children, and their teachers. After I thought about this place. *When there is no enemy within, the enemies outside cannot hurt you.*"

"Meaning?"

159

"Therein lies the lesson."

"That's what you and the children were discussing?"

"Testing," she said. "Testing the truth of it. I saw signs of truth in it, but did they? Do you? And what about Nelson? Who, or what, did he see? A warning? And this place—a refuge?"

34

I stood outside Nelson's pod, surprised I didn't know how to announce my arrival, surprised by my uneasiness. True, our last conversation had been awkward, contentious even, but he'd been such an indispensable ally it would've been foolish to brush that bond aside. Still, the matter of our feelings for each other was a topic best dispensed with, and I wasn't sure I could count on him to share that insight.

"Are you coming in?" he asked from inside, startling me.

I made my way through the entrance. "I wasn't sure ..."

"I heard you and figured, who else?"

He was perched on a cot similar to mine and pointed to an adjacent mound of throw pillows where I nestled into place.

"I just visited Mother," I said. "Did you know this place had a nursery?" He shook his head.

"And other surprises, too, I'd bet."

"We talked about her orientation. And mine."

"And now you want to hear about mine."

I nodded – of course.

"This is difficult for me, you know."

"I know. They're using us. They're trying to force my hand. It's extortion. Suggesting the horrors they're showing us could be overturned if I rejoined the project. As if their project could reshape the past."

"That's not what I mean."

His face took on the expression he'd worn hours earlier during our last conversation—a look of emotional longing that frightened me.

"We can't avoid it, Fitima."

"Avoid what?"

"That we're entangled in each other's lives. Events beyond our control have tied us together. But we can control how we're connected."

"I don't understand."

"How we connect with each other. As I see it, it's as though you're trying to solve an equation. Consider a variable here. Discard a variable there. But lives are involved. Our own. Others'. Are we supposed to look at these lives objectively? Without feeling? Like data in an equation?"

"I don't know where this is coming from, Nelson. Is this about what they showed you? Is it about you and me?"

"It's about us. All of us. In the biggest sense. Us. Including you and me."

"It feels like it's only about you and me." I'd hoped we could avoid this topic, but to his credit, Nelson had opted for transparency.

"I like you, Nelson. I really do. I'm grateful for all your help. For your support of Mother and me. But I … I just don't feel anything romantic between us if that's what you mean by connection. And there's no point in my saying things might change." A sigh escaped my lips. "I know myself too well."

"Do I hear a tinge of regret? Or is that just me trying to save face?"

"You might hear regret. But that doesn't change anything. The truth is, I think romantic love is impossible. At least for me. That might be regrettable. But it's a fact nonetheless."

"Sad," he said with a sincerity that stung.

"Perhaps. But we all have our beliefs whether others think they're sad or not. As for me, I believe when two people say they love each other, it's not necessarily the same for both. One loves more than the other. Or more desperately. More confidently maybe. The other, more fearfully. A couple can spend a lifetime together, trying to equalize their differences. Or maybe come to terms with the inequalities. A good use of their time? A good use of their lifetimes?

"Some think so. I don't."

I hadn't considered these beliefs for so long, they almost felt brand new.

"Which doesn't mean I've escaped scot-free," I continued. "I've spent my whole life fighting to prove myself. Listening to that voice inside me, telling me: Don't give in! Don't surrender! Don't concede! Because if you do, you've lost."

He pursed his lips and nodded slowly, rhythmically, as if taking in all I'd said, weighing it, considering where to go with it.

"Regrettable?" I continued. "Perhaps. Sad? Maybe. But unchangeable nonetheless."

"It's not for me to judge you," he said. "To proclaim good person, bad person. I have feelings, of course. Disappointment mostly. But I can live with that. I know that much about myself."

He leaned forward, toward me, his eyes fixed on mine, with a new concern, more serious than romance, or so it seemed to me by the intensity of his gaze.

"One thing I need to know," he said. "One thing … to determine … well, to determine how to move forward. Together or apart. Is there room in your heart for compassion? For caring, even without passion?"

I wasn't sure I fully understood what he meant, but from what I did understand, my answer had to be yes.

"Then there's something I want to show you," he said, rising from the cot and moving to his com-desk.

He tapped the console and retrieved a holograph, a satellite image of coastline with pitch-black water on the left and mottled terrain on the right.

"Peru," he said, pointing south-to-north along the land-sea border.

The aerial view zoomed toward the surface, past layers of thin cumulus clouds. Ripples on the black ocean swelled into waves. White spots dotting the land lengthened into towers, each with blades rotating on spindles like giant pinwheels. We were approaching the largest windfarm I'd ever seen. Our view veered toward a hexagonal arrangement of brick and glass buildings in the center of the farm.

"Malabrigo," Nelson said.

"The place you and Damon …. It's a windfarm. You didn't say it was a windfarm."

"It wasn't," Nelson said. "The farm was added after we left."

The view took us through an exterior door, proceeded down a sterile hall, and ended with stacked bunk beds, empty and neatly made, connected by a wooden ladder.

"Is this what they showed you?" I asked. "Your orientation?"

He nodded. "And what I assume Jim wanted me to show you. He never said so directly, but why else let me keep the recording."

Damon sauntered into the frame of the holograph, his head and hands jutting from a shimmering covering of chameleon fabric reflecting the background behind him. He sat on the bottom bunk facing us, his upper body blending with the cabin's white rear wall, his lower body blending with the bed's blue blanket.

I thought back to the last time we'd seen him on the pier in Indigo Sound being hauled away by the authorities. "Did he … did Damon say anything?"

"Yes," Nelson said. "We talked. This is the recording."

"Hello, my friend," Nelson's voice sounded off camera. Nelson at my side withdrew to his cot.

"I wondered if I'd ever see you again," Damon said. He stood up and stepped closer, still cloaked by his surroundings, the sparest of rooms. "You see what they've done with our art colony?"

The men laughed.

"Malabrigo Wind Farm they call it," Damon continued.

"And you?" Nelson said. "How are you?"

Damon turned to survey the room. "I've adjusted," he said.

I found myself searching for his carved avocado pits. His confidants, he'd called them. Pathetic, I'd thought at the time. Pitiful signs of his loneliness. Yet now I felt heartbroken over their absence.

"But are you well?" Nelson asked.

"As well as can be expected," Damon said. "Like I said, I've adjusted. To roommates. To wind farming. To reeducation. Solitary will do that to you."

There was a long pause before Nelson replied, time enough for me to recall Damon's fierce independence when I met him—so different from the submissive tone I heard now. "So you were right," Nelson said.

"Of course I was right," Damon said. "Storage crates. Ha! Unless you're talking about storing people. Isolation crates is what they are. What I knew they were."

Another long pause. "Solitary?" Nelson said finally. "As what ... a punishment? For you? Prince of hermits. Tell me, how's that supposed to work."

"Surprised me, too," Damon said. "But I learned something. There's a difference between self-imposed solitary and the authoritarian kind. I guess that was part of my reeducation."

Again, a long pause and I glanced back at Nelson on the cot, but he averted his eyes almost as if ashamed. Or perhaps it was guilt. As for me, I felt both, guilt and shame, a gnawing in the pit of my stomach. And fear. Fear over how the scene would end.

"And wind farming?" Nelson's voice returned from the recording. "Not your specialty as I recall."

Damon laughed. "We've got mostly technician types here. The artists must be housed somewhere else. Maybe a real art colony."

Again, the men laughed.

"It turns out we technicians make good wind farmers," Damon said. "Gearbox reconstruction here. Blade replacement there. Damn lightning strikes are the problem. Metal fatigue sometimes. Nothing a competent engineer can't fix. Even you."

Nelson snickered off camera.

"And Fitima?" Damon asked.

"With me here," Nelson said. "An underground—"

"Laboratory," Damon said. "Yeah, I know. I've been briefed. Is she nearby?" I turned to Nelson, only to find him staring blankly into the center of the pod.

"Remember that Buddhist proverb you had me translate?" Damon continued. "Back where ... you know."

I recalled the silk prayer pouch Chik had dropped from Ruby and the Cantonese scrawled across the strip of polypro paper.

"*During times of great adversity,*" Damon recited, "*lives the potential for great good.*"

"You memorized it?" Nelson said.

Damon shook his head. "Fitima's mom guessed it was given to the Asian woman. To pass on to her daughter. As it was told to me to pass on to Fitima."

"By?" Nelson asked.

"Fitima's bosses. Jim and Ramsey. Via teleconference. Like now. Very formal. Very no-nonsense."

"I didn't understand it then," Nelson said, "and I don't understand it now."

"These men seemed to believe Fitima would," Damon said. "Understand it, I mean. Something to do with reversing the malaise. Or *Malaise*, as they spoke it. Very spooky. But she's very important, my friend—this Fitima. Very, very important. As you well know." He leaned closer as if about to share a secret, a habit from his subversive days, no doubt. "You guys did, after all, outmaneuver international travel restrictions," he whispered.

I felt Nelson's gaze on me, and I turned to finally catch his eye, but I couldn't read his expression.

"How big's her heart?" Damon said. "That's the question. Does she have courage? Compassion for those she doesn't even know as well as for those she loves? That's what she has to be convinced of."

"I'm not sure I can convince her of anything," Nelson said.

"Ultimately she's got to convince herself," Damon said. And then, in a softer voice, "The mother's the key. Jim and Ramsey hinted as much, and I'm pretty good at reading hints. The mother. She's the key."

35

Damon's image broke up and disappeared. I backed away from the com-desk and slumped onto the pillows on the floor.

They'd raised the stakes too high to resist. They'd placed suffering right before my eyes. Anonymous suffering. And the purposely selected suffering of Serita and Damon. Nelson had asked if I had compassion. Damon asked. Chik, too, in her own way. Now I had to answer.

"I'm so sorry," I said.

"It hurt to see him like that. And that they'd take him there, of all places."

The prison they'd help build, I thought.

"I'll see what I can do," I said. "Like Damon said, I'm obviously very important. I'll make that work for me. For him. I'll make it work."

"Damon figured out what we were building," Nelson said.

It was as though he hadn't heard my resolve.

"That's why he quit," he continued. "I stayed on. Until they fired me."

"Before construction was completed?"

Nelson nodded. "I assumed the crates in the basement were for shipping artwork. But all the same size? Large enough to hold a person? Damon figured what they were for."

"Jail cells?"

"Isolation cells. Solitary confinement. Obvious enough once you looked beyond the surface. As Damon did. The rooms were actually bright and airy. Open. But too few doors in the hallways, Damon said. And the health care facilities—too well-equipped. The dental clinic, the infirmary. Completely self-contained. Why? True, the place was isolated, but he realized the entire facility was constructed so arriving and staying were easier than leaving. So he quit. It took me longer to see what Damon saw."

I wrapped my arms around myself, hurting to hear Nelson punish himself. "I figured rehab would promote Transparency, not subvert it."

Nelson narrowed his eyes. "You still believe in Transparency? After all we've been through?"

"I don't know what to believe," I said, gathering myself up from the floor. " I'm going to trade my value for Damon's freedom. And whatever other freedoms I can wring from them. And I'd like you to come with me."

***

Several white-clad technicians we met in the hallway said Jim was finishing up in the Imaging Chamber and that we might wait for him in his office.

"Imaging Chamber?" Nelson laughed after we'd left the technicians. He pulled his cotton gauze pant leg. "They need to reimage these costumes."

Our translucent jumpsuits and the technicians' white lab coats didn't bother me half as much as the facility's impenetrable walls. The lab's opacity felt as though we'd been transported back in time.

"You'll visit the Imaging Chamber soon enough," I said.

Jim's office was situated not far from the entryway that led to the nursery. The room was barely large enough to fit three soft-gel armchairs, a com-desk, and Jim's personal chair wedged in a corner. Rows of equations crawled across the walls behind the desk and a blank data-screen hung above it on a mount extending from the chair.

Nelson reached across the desk and lifted a section of rubber tubing hanging from an arm of the chair and waggled it in my direction.

"Exercise," I said. "Stationary isometrics. Seated Chi Gun. For as long as I've known him."

Nelson released the tubing and shrugged.

"He swears by it," I said.

"I'm jealous."

"Of Jim?"

"Of your relationship. Of the fact that you and he go so far back. It's very admirable."

"I always thought so."

"Until ...," Nelson prodded.

"Yes ... until."

The top row of equations froze a moment, then renewed its crawl across the walls.

"Studying black holes," Nelson said out of the blue. "What was it like, exactly? Exciting? Boring? Frustrating?"

"Scary," I said.

"Scary?"

"Very. Three years' worth of scary."

He shook his head. "Funny. I would've guessed exciting. Mind-boggling maybe."

"That, too," I said. "But mostly scary. Death on a cosmic scale. Sucking life, and most everything else, out of the universe. And into what? Into where? When? Who knows?"

His smile twisted slightly. "Okay, I can see scary. But thankfully not nearby. The center of our galaxy, I'm guessing, is few dozen light years away."

"Sag A? Two dozen actually, give or take a few light-months. But that's not what we're studying."

"Oh? Something closer?"

"Only point six of a light year away."

"Definitely closer, but, uh, could you break that down in kilometers?"

"Five to six trillion."

"Not that I can imagine—"

"The distance light travels in seven months and a week. Approximately. In other words, pretty far. But close enough to probe. Close enough for an extended exchange between us. Ignoring the seven-month pauses."

"So that's what's been going on here."

"Don't sound so suspicious. This work has been transparent for decades. It's only recently gone underground."

We swapped smirks at my unintended pun.

"Theory's one thing," I said. "Evidence is another. We had several models of black hole geometry. Elegant models. But we couldn't test them against actual data. Suddenly we could, thanks to Anansi."

"Who?"

"Not who. What. Anansi. The stellar back hole we're studying. That's the nickname I gave it and it kinda stuck. My first prerogative for being a mathematical diva."

"A favorite pet?"

"Anansi the trickster. A West African folk character. A spider. Mother read me many stories about him. Known for his pranks. The name seemed perfect for our recalcitrant black hole."

"Recalcitrant, eh? This gets curiouser and curiouser."

I smiled, thinking: if he only knew.

His gaze followed the equations winding across the walls before returning to me.

"Anything a civil engineer might understand?"

I laughed. "They positioned a space platform just beyond Anansi's gravitational pull. They've been launching probes into her for years. Sorry, but I can't help thinking of Anansi as her. Anyway, they've got a tremendous backlog of data that we've been analyzing."

"I get the we, but who's this they?"

"The agencies we thank profusely when we disseminate our results. That is, when we used to disseminate our results."

"Ah, yes, that old bugaboo. Secrecy."

I bit my lip against his mocking tone and let my irritation pass. "I've enjoyed our conversation, Nelson. It's felt so … normal. It's been a long time since I could say that about any conversation I've had."

Nelson cast his eyes downward in what looked like contrition and seemed to be about to speak when Jim appeared in the doorway.

He glanced between Nelson and me as if linking a loosely coupled pas de deux. He nodded triumphantly, then shimmied behind his desk and eased himself into his customized chair.

"Glad to see you," he said. "Together. Mutually debriefed, I assume." He leaned forward, planting his elbows on the desk. "There's this expression one of our colleagues would shout whenever we were about to launch a new experiment. An important experiment. A who-knows-what-will-happen-next experiment. He'd shout, Revelation Time. Most would laugh. I guess it eased the tension. Not with me so much."

He looked away, as if recalling what he'd described. "Anyway," he continued, returning to us. "That's where we are now. Revelation Time."

36

"I'd like some assurances," I said. "Before I promise anything."

Jim narrowed his eyes as he glanced between me and Nelson. "Excuse me?"

"Assurances," I repeated. "In exchange for rejoining the project. A friend of ours, Damon Early, is being held captive on a wind farm. I need to make sure he's released."

Jim shook his head, and my heart sank, even as I geared up for a fight.

"If your people could sneak Nelson and me past surveillance," I said. "Despite travel restrictions. International travel restrictions. Then you can—"

"No, no, no," Jim said. "I mean, yes. Of course. We can do what you ask. We will do what you ask. Damon Early. Sure." He pinched the bridge of his nose. "Revelation Time. I was talking about my having a revelation for you. We think you're ready."

Ready? I thought. We? The corners above either side of Jim's desk began to glow in kaleidoscopic colors that quickly coalesced into the images of two familiar faces. Ramsey and Lloyd. Nelson turned to me and then back the two men and nodded as if he knew who they were. I understood, their features and bearing practically identified them: arrogant director and humble pollster.

"So, now I'm ready?" I said sarcastically.

"There's no point pressing forward if you're not," Lloyd said. "Persistence in the face of resistance can cause serious psychic harm. As it is, we may have pressed too hard, too fast."

"Without apology," Ramsey said. "The stakes are too high."

"So now the revelation?" I said.

"Which has been ongoing," Ramsey said. "But you said it yourself: insight favors the prepared mind."

A third holograph emerged between the faces of the two men, superimposed over Jim who regarded it with disgust. I wasn't sure if it was Jim's reaction or my own repulsion to the thin, segmented, serpentine coil that curled and uncurled like a snake with two heads or two tails, the ends identical.

"Single-strand RNA," Nelson said calmly.

Yes, of course, I thought, suppressing my queasiness.

"Of a virus, most likely," Nelson continued. "Which explains the decon procedure when we got here."

There was no rational reason to be disgusted by a virus. It was more the idea that repulsed me ... the thought of a parasitic bundle of protein that straddled the boundary between the living and nonliving.

"A member of the Alphavirus genus," Ramsey said. "The Togaviridae family. One of its cousins was responsible for encephalitis."

"Which was stamped out long ago," I said impatiently.

A blue honeycombed shell enveloped the RNA coil until it was completely encased.

"I'm assembling the virus to show how it's put together," Ramsey said. He pointed to the blue exterior. "This protein covering surrounds the RNA."

A grey film spread over the blue shell and bristles sprouted from the surface like coarse black hair. "The lipid casing," Ramsey continued, pointing to it, "with glycoprotein spikes."

"A mutated virus?" I said.

"A mutation, yes," Ramsey said. "But not natural. Synthetic. Manufactured."

"Related to encephalitis," Nelson said.

"Yes, but with a twist," Ramsey said.

Encephalitis? A twist? Who could remember these diseases? Why remember them? Or their symptoms? Physical? Yes. Muscular. Muscle weakness. Loss of coordination. But cognitive, also. In fact, mostly cognitive. Confusion. Delusion. And a term I'd heard just recently: malaise.

Nelson's voice arrived as if from a distance. "Fitima?"

He and the others were staring at me.

"You okay?" he asked.

I shuttered at the ghastly object rotating in front of me. And at the words spoken so casually: a virus, assembled, manufactured. A chill gripped my throat and I swallowed hard.

"Bio ... biological warfare," I said. "Bioterrorism? What is this?"

"Not terrorism," Jim said.

"Why split hairs?" Ramsey said.

"Accuracy," Jim replied.

"Semantic accuracy," Ramsey countered.

"More than that," Jim said. "These people aren't asking anyone to do anything they don't want to do. They are not terrorists. They terrify, but that's not their purpose. The terror they cause is incidental."

"Who's this they?" Nelson said.

The three men looked at each other—Jim, from behind the desk, Ramsey and Lloyd from above it.

"My work here is finished," Lloyd said. He flashed that grandfatherly smile I remembered from when we'd first met. "I've presented our rationale for your measured induction, Fitima." His gaze swept among the others. "Please continue without me."

Ramsey and Jim showed little reaction as Lloyd's image fragmented and faded away.

Every electric device in the office seemed to hum conspicuously until Ramsey finally spoke. "The they."

"The they," Jim echoed softly.

"We'll hear from one of them," Ramsey said. "But he speaks for the they."

Ramsey's face shrank and lightened, but did not disappear, alighting, instead, on a front corner of Jim's desk, perched like a thin parchment ornament. A scene materialized in the space his image had vacated, a corridor with bare white walls on the left and barred cubicles on the right. Our view moved passed empty cubicles toward one with a pair of hands gripping one of the horizontal bars. We stopped at that cell, in front of an old greyish man who seemed to use the bar to hold himself steady.

"G. G. Gregory," Jim said. "Spokesman."

"Spokesman for?" I said.

"He'll explain," Jim said.

It didn't appear as though Mr. Gregory could explain much of anything. His head swayed loosely on his shoulders and his eyes switched focus randomly on his hands, the bars, and whatever he saw in front of him. His grayness was due to more than his hair, his eyes, or even his pasty complexion. His gauzy gown was uniformly gray and the light and walls in the cubicle seemed washed of all color. But I was especially drawn to his eyes.

"Is he drugged?" I asked.

His head jerked forward, and he focused squarely on my face with an intensity that startled me.

"No," Ramsey said. "Well, somewhat. He's been medicinally primed to cooperate."

His eyes twitched toward Ramsey's image before returning to me.

"Does he know who he's talking to?" I asked. "I mean, does he know—"

"Why don't you ask me?" Gregory said. "The answer is yes. I was told to expect a visitor. Astrophysicist. Mathematician. Or some combination thereof. Female. But not Caribbean. I notice the accent."

I turned to Nelson as though he might offer a sign as to where to begin.

"The virus," I said, turning back to Gregory. "I want to know about the virus."

"History is shaped by only a few people," Gregory said. "That's not original, of course. Which makes it all the more true. A few people who share a goal. And the courage to pursue it without reservation. We chose not to be figures on the landscape. We chose to shape the landscape."

I glared at Jim and flashed my annoyance, but he raised a finger as if signaling patience. I took a breath and tried to justify Gregory's digression. He was, after all, describing the *they*. But I wanted to know *the what*.

"Some reformers," Gregory continued, "they invent a new moral order then slink off to some cornfield and sink under the weight of their morality."

"But your people...?" Nelson prompted.

G. G. Gregory's focus drifted toward Nelson. "My people," he said. "My as belonging with. Not *my* as possessive."

"Okay," Nelson said. "The people with whom you belong. Presumably, you didn't slink off to a cornfield."

"No, we didn't. We decided to invent a new order—not socially negotiated, but biologically determined."

"Hence, the virus," Nelson said.

Gregory nodded sluggishly as his eyes shifted back to me. "Time to cull the herd." His words seemed to suck the air from the room. Even as metaphor culling felt ugly. Even applied to livestock. Or any animal. But the intimation that Gregory was referring to human beings made me nauseous, and I reached for the spectral bars of his cubicle and stumbled forward before steadying myself.

"I see fear," Gregory said, staring.

"You see disgust."

"But we are the chosen ones," he said. "It seems we've been spared. The virus attacks those unfit to survive, those who dominate their fellow man. It infects those who, ironically, produce fewer offspring yet rule over the rest of us with their need for power. Those who would be king, queen, autocrat, caliph, sultan, caesar, czar, overlord—over you, over me. They and their defective germ plasm who would overpower the rest of us."

I backed away from this gray ghost of a man and looked at the faces of the others for signs of the revulsion that wrenched my stomach. "This man is mad."

"There are advantages to being dismissed as mad," Gregory said. "Those responsible for watching over you do so with less interest."

"You claim the motive for power is genetically based?" Nelson said.

"Nelson, please!" I said.

Gregory blinked slowly, then shifted his attention to Nelson. "We've known this for some time. What we didn't know was the underlying structure. The brain, of course, but which part? Or parts. Well, it turns out to be the amygdala."

"How much more of this?" I said.

"Till the whole story's told," Nelson shot back. He gestured toward Gregory. "At least his version."

I struggled to control my anger at Nelson and struggled to regain my composure. I was at war with myself, caught between wanting and not wanting to hear more.

"And the virus?" Nelson prodded Gregory.

"The crucial element is its covering," Gregory said. "It's the key that fits the lock."

"And the lock would be the amygdala," I whispered.

"More precisely," Gregory said, "the basolateral nuclei of the amygdala."

"But not everyone's," Nelson said.

"That's right," Gregory said. "Not everyone's. Our virus locks onto the receptors of dominants. And only dominants. It's not a matter of locking and unlocking, really. It's more a matter of binding. And once our virus binds with their amygdala, entropy begins."

I turned to Jim, struggling to catch my breath. "And the cure?"

Jim glanced at me, then returned to stare at his hands.

"You don't understand," Ramsey said.

"But this doesn't add up," Nelson said.

I prayed he'd reasoned a way out of this nightmare.

He got up and stood beside me, facing Gregory. "Time to cull the herd, you said. But you've said nothing about the virus being lethal."

Gregory's lips parted as though he were about to speak, but then his expression froze, nearly inanimate, as a drop of spit dribbled from a corner of his mouth.

Nelson reached toward Gregory. "You don't eliminate flaws from the gene pool unless the virus is lethal."

I grabbed Nelson's arm, stunned by what I'd heard.

Ramsey's image expanded from the corner of Jim's desk, overlapping Gregory's before replacing it.

"But we haven't heard the whole story," Nelson objected, freeing his arm from my grip.

"There'll be time enough for that," Ramsey said. "As for now, his testimony has run its course."

"You believe him?" I asked Nelson. "You believe what these ... what these people—"

"Besides," Ramsey continued, "you've heard a great deal already, enough for you to process on your own."

37

I didn't want to hear from Nelson any more than I wanted to hear from G.G. Gregory, Ramsey, or Jim, yet there we were, the two of us, alone in my pod, wrapped in awkward silence within walls that seemed to shrink each time I entered.

"I'm sorry," Nelson said finally.

I was too angry to look at him.

"I was trying ...," he continued, "... trying to make sense of —"

"Nonsense," I blurted.

"Yes," he said. "It certainly sounded that way."

"You don't have to believe them to make sense of what they're saying."

And then I had to look at him so he could see my utter disgust.

"They want to deflect responsibility for chaos away from the authorities," I said. "A virus? Please. The vulgarity of it makes me sick."

Nelson averted his eyes. "I see your point, of course. As old as ... *The serpent beguiled me.*"

"In this case, the virus is the demon called on to explain evil. But to think they'd go to such lengths."

"That's what I don't understand," Nelson said. "That's why I was trying to make sense of Gregory's story. Theoretically, a thought experiment."

And surely you can appreciate that, his gaze seemed to suggest. I took a deep breath, offering him space to continue.

"If Gregory's virus were real," he said. "*If.* And if it was designed with the intention he described. If. Then the virus would need to kill its targets in order to cull the herd."

He squinted at me as though reading the expression on my face.

"I'm trying to follow," I said.

"I have to tell you something I wish I didn't have to," he said. I raised my hand, hoping to stop him.

"I've heard," he continued, "when they slaughter sheep, they separate the butchered from the rest of the fold so they won't be terrorized by the sight."

My hand dropped to my lap.

"We've been lucky," he said. "Some would say blessed. It's been generations since we've had to think the unthinkable. Not since Transparency have we had to imagine the unimaginable. We never thought we'd ..."

His voice cracked and a choking compassion rose to my throat. "Please ..."

"I don't like that I can," he said. "Imagine the unimaginable. But I must. We must, you and I. In order to decide what to do. In order to decide what you should do."

The silence returned, as awkward as ever. The walls pressed and time seemed to stand still.

"I'll try," I said.

He lifted himself up, sitting erect. "We heard Gregory's intentions."

"Which were insane. Unthink—"

I stopped at his signal, his eyebrows raised as gentle reminder: think the unthinkable.

"We need to look at the world through Gregory's eyes, as disorienting that might be. If I understood him, he claims the point of human evolution shouldn't simply be survival. We have the ability to ask: whose survival? And we have the capacity to answer that question. Our species can rise above natural selection. He believes we can achieve a higher standard. He believes we can achieve selection by design."

"Design?" I said.

"Why allow human evolution to stumble along, propelled by chance? We don't accept this for other species. That's what he meant by culling the herd. I assume he sees our world being eroded by power-seeking dominants. They're the targets of his virus."

"So the meek shall inherit *his* earth? Is that it?"

"Well, non-dominants, anyway," Nelson said. "If," he added to lessen the sting.

I swallowed back a surge of nausea.

"Sorry," he said. "I'm thinking the unthinkable."

"The unthinkable makes me ill. The horror turns my stomach."

"It gets worse," Nelson said, closely watching my reaction. "We need to consider designs don't always go according to plan. Including Gregory's. He may have intended for the virus to be lethal for power-seeking dominants, but what if it wasn't lethal? What if it was debilitating but not deadly?"

"Or deadly for some and debilitating for others?" I said, forcing my thoughts in a direction they didn't want to go.

"Or if the virus mutated," he said. "Into lethal and nonlethal forms."

"Or benign."

"And benign," he said.

I closed my eyes against the tilt of the room. Nelson was quiet, giving me pause, but not reprieve. When I opened my eyes again, he was leaning closer.

"You can see the dilemma," he said. "No one knows who's who. Who's affected, who's not."

"Brain scans?" I said. "Brains scans could identify—"

"But would dominants volunteer?"

"Odd behavior?" I offered weakly.

"Assuming it was recognized as such," he said. *The Emperor's New Clothes*? It took a child to declare the emperor naked. The adults went along with the emperor's lie."

My fingernails dug into my palms. "It's like you want this to be true! Like you want to believe in this virus."

"Lord knows I'd rather not," he said. "I'd rather not believe the alarm to run out of the burning building. I'd rather believe the alarm false, or some inexplicable noise. Remember the pre-evacuation delay we talked about? People reluctant to leave a burning building? That some never do?"

"No, no, no," I said, shaking my head. "I won't forgive Hooks. I can't. I never will. Blame his cruelty on a virus? Forgive D.C.? Forgive the violence we've seen? It's a trick. A hoax! To avoid responsibility. Hooks was guilty! Not this fairy-tale virus."

Suddenly Nelson was seated beside me, grabbing hold of my fists pressed hard against his chest, his hands wet with my tears. He was whispering to me, consoling sounds merging with my sobs, words I felt more than heard until I finally recognized what he was saying.

"Your mother," he whispered. "Your mother."

***

Jim's assistant told us Jim had returned to the Imaging Center, but that he would locate Mother for us. He activated a map of the lab above his desk and pinpointed Mother's location.

"The garden," he said, his finger outlining her silhouette on the three-dimensional map. "She's in good spirits," he added, touching the green shading of her profile.

I glanced at the translucent sleeve of my jumpsuit. "Überwach thread?"

"Of course," he said. "All of our garments."

Reasonable, I thought—physical and emotional markers stitched into our clothing. "Garden?" I said.

"We'll show you the way." A series of red lights advanced along the floor and veered right at the door of his office.

"No," I said, shaking my head. "I mean a *garden*?"

"You'll see," he said, pointing to the lights on the floor.

Nelson beckoned for me to follow him along the red-light trail. He seemed able to proceed without looking down while I steadfastly avoided the lights, looking only at him.

"You're not surprised?" I said. "A garden?"

We continued in silence, passing several people along the way. "Nothing?" I said finally.

"Not sure what to say."

"Whatever you're thinking," I said.

We stopped alongside a waist-high bamboo partition bordering a patch of green stalks of grain. I inadvertently caught a glimpse of the red lights along the floor before I turned to Nelson.

He opened his arms to indicate the verdant plot in front of us. "In honor of our need for soil," he said. He pointed upward. "In honor of our need for sun and sky."

I looked up at the chrome parabolic fixtures directing light down on us and shrugged. "I don't follow."

He took a deep breath. "The soil is real. The sun and sky are facsimiles. As are the sounds and smells of the outdoors. But the difference is semantic. Real, reproduction. Down here, virtual is real enough."

The scent of earth hit me as if I'd just flung open a window. What had I been sensing? The taste and smell of my misery. Of my distress. My own fear-filled exhalations.

"There must be mirrors topside," Nelson said, surveying the shadows between the parabolic light fixtures. "Secondary mirrors, too, probably. Reducing infrared and ultraviolet."

He wasn't talking to me now, but mostly to himself, applying what he could see to what he could not see and reckoning the result.

"Yes, of course," he continued. "Topside mirrors following the sun across the sky like heliotropic daisies. Hidden mirrors, certainly. Fiber-optic cables channeling sunlight underground." He pointed to the green stalks. "Different wavelengths specific to the photosynthesis of different plants."

"An underground farm?" I said.

He shook his head. "No, no. A garden. Like Jim's assistant said. Not enough for significant food production. More like a diversion. A hobby. In honor of our need to work the land. In honor of our needs."

38

The route to Mother took us through several small plots growing different crops under different colored lighting, some hues nearly indistinguishable, others utterly unique, like the deep purple shadowing an assortment of mushrooms.

"It's the scale that makes me numb," I said. "The sheer size."

"I know," Nelson said. "But the intent is to soothe. Perhaps after we've been here longer it might feel less large over time."

That was no comfort, but I couldn't explain the contradiction: the sense of feeling trapped within the immensity of the place and the time frame of our stay—its uncertainty. It all made me numb inside.

We rounded a bend and I spotted Mother standing in front of a terraced tract of tall spindly stalks. A young man was kneeling beside her, squeezing water from a handful of mud. Mother and I embraced, and the man stood.

"Alex Holt," he said, raising his mud-spattered hand in lieu of a handshake. "I was explaining how little soil we use."

"Rice?" Nelson said.

Alex nodded. "Pesticide-free!"

Nelson frowned at him. "Joke?"

Alex returned a sheepish grin. "Allegedly."

Nelson pointed to the overhead lights. "LEDs. Eliminates any pests extraordinary enough to make it inside this bunker."

Alex nodded. "We have a gardening club, you know."

Nelson gave me an I-told-you-so look without pursuing the implicit invitation.

"I'll leave you folks to stroll the garden," Alex said, wiping his hand on his trousers.

"Thank you," Mother called out after him as he walked the path we'd taken.

"Everything you'd want to know about hydroponics," Mother said as we embraced again. "And then some."

She and I laughed, but only halfheartedly, perhaps out of grudging respect for Alex Holt, and out of respect for the gravity of our own situation.

My attention shifted to her appearance, her voice, her demeanor. She looked good. Her hair had grown out long enough for her to comb and shape into a curly, symmetrical, salt and pepper crown. It would soon be long enough to braid, I thought.

"How are you?" I asked, holding her at arm's length.

"I'm fine," she said, a bit too reflexively for me to believe without reservation.

"Okay, but how do feel about being here?" I pressed.

"Here?" she said, looking over my shoulder, at the terraced plot beside us. "Here in this garden? Down here in this bunker?" She nodded at Nelson, acknowledging the term he'd used.

"All of the above," I said. "Here. Where we find ourselves now. How are you feeling about being here? Is this a place where you can ... where you can ...?"

"Be close to you," she said with a mischievous grin.

"Where you can recuperate," I said.

Her grin slowly faded. "A place to recuperate. Recover? Regain something I lost?"

"A place to get better," I said desperately. "To get your strength back. After what you've been through."

She scanned the small field beside us. She stooped and scooped a dripping handful of soil. "This helps," she said, holding out her hand. "Compensation for all the technology around us. The designers must've known this. Known it in their bones."

"So it's a comfort," Nelson said. "The garden. The children?"

"Yes, yes, a comfort."

She gave both of us a sidelong glance, as if weighing our readiness.

"All in all," she continued, "I think of this place as a wilderness. Does that make sense? I realize it's an odd thought. Given all the technology surrounding us. But I like to think of it that way, as us hiding out in this wilderness. I find this a comfort. The idea that we've escaped into this wilderness and that, no matter how difficult our situation may appear, we're better off down here than topside."

Nelson and I looked at each other and perhaps we had the same thought: that Mother was comparing our situation with that of the runaway slaves whose graves we'd discovered in Trinidad. It was the way she spoke of our having escaped into the wilderness—her tone, her enunciation. Her voice had a spiritual ring to it.

But then, a subsequent question: was her comparison apt or a symptom of mental confusion?

"I want to show you something," she said. "Follow me."

We continued along the path's circuitous route, past several mini fields of wheat, soybeans, and a variety of root vegetables under subtly different shades of artificial light. Along the way Mother offset our silence with small talk—the entertaining nature of her vivid dreams, her opinion about the food as explanation as to why I'd lost weight, various examples of the uncanny intelligence of the children she'd met.

We rounded one final bend and I squinted at the rock face dead end ahead of us that turned out to be the front wall of a chamber cut from solid granite. Mother continued on while Nelson and I stopped to scan the circular structure that seemed like a cave except for the light pouring down from ceiling-high portals, dust motes dancing in branching beams.

Mother turned but allowed time for Nelson and me to get our bearings. There were a dozen or so rows of benches inside the chamber, divided by a center aisle. A platform extended the length of the front wall, and on top of it, a podium.

And then I blinked and looked again at the objects I'd identified. The objects I'd misidentified. The benches were actually pews. The platform, an altar. The podium, a pulpit.

"This is what I wanted to show you," Mother said.

We continued down the center aisle, our footsteps echoing off the granite surfaces, through the cool, dry air. Mother swept her arms outward, referring to the wall surrounding us. A succession of hollow niches midway up the wall, carved equidistant from one another, circled the chamber. Blank plaques hung above each niche and, above these, on opposite sides of the chamber, two large rectangular signs named the place we'd entered: The Temple of Heart and Mind.

Everything about the place seemed designed to promote serenity, yet I felt a vague yet growing agitation. And as my pulse pounded and my body froze to near paralysis, I realized my agitation had nothing to do with the design, yet everything to do with it. And not just the design of this temple. Nor the design of the children's nursery. Nor the garden. Or the stores of food and supplies. Or the shadow of provisions and services I had not seen but could imagine. My mounting agitation had to do with all of it—all of the designs and the designing. The idea I'd suppressed, of our prolonged stay in this place, came crashing down on me as concrete reality.

"You okay?" Mother asked.

I shook my head, summoning the strength to speak. Her hand stroked my shoulder. "Who showed you this place?" I managed.

"I showed myself," she said. "I wanted to test the boundaries. You know me, Fitima."

"But, but … do you understand?" I said.

"It was explained," she said. "I asked. People answered. Of course, I insisted. Now I can answer."

She pointed to a large, closed metal door behind the altar. Two rails of what looked like railroad tracks protruding from beneath the door.

"I understand," Nelson said.

As did I, and I shut my eyes and imagined what lay behind that door: a cinderblock tunnel, chains and pulleys, a cast iron furnace, an all-consuming inferno. And somewhere, somehow hidden from view, a venting chimney.

"Makes sense," Mother said. "Cremation is quick, space-saving, and sanitary."

She raised the hand that had scooped the wet garden soil and with her other hand brushed dried dirt onto the floor. "Topside, the dead are buried in sacred ground," she said. "There's no sacred ground down here. Unless you count the gardens."

39

"What do you mean, for the duration?" I asked Ramsey.

"Simply that," Ramsey said. "We're here for as long as it takes."

"Till thy kingdom come," Jim said.

I glared at him as if he'd lost his mind.

"Sorry," he said and looked away. "Failure has been ...." He sighed, ending too quietly to be heard.

"Until our mission is accomplished," Ramsey said.

"But I can't work like this," I said. "Not here. I'm suffocating. I can barely breathe much less think."

"We've got pharmaceuticals," Ramsey said.

"Like what he's taking?" I said, pointing at Jim.

"Drug-free," Ramsey said. "He's adjusted."

"To living in a tomb? To working next to your own gravestone? I can't adjust to that."

"So you'd rather your headstone be far away," Ramsey said. "Better yet, nonexistent. Mortality for everyone else, is that it?"

"Don't be absurd," I said. "You've built a prison down here, and you know it—designed to keep us caged in here for ... for—"

"The duration," Ramsey said.

"You caged in, and chaos locked out."

"You've shown us chaos, true," Nelson said.

His voice startled me. My tunnel vision had moved him from my view since Ramsey's hologram emerged in Jim's office. Now I could see he was as intently focused on Ramsey's image as I'd been.

"And many a disaster," Nelson continued. "But you haven't shown us disaster as inevitable."

"Correct," Ramsey said, turning toward Nelson. "We've maintained that idea with regard to all our revelations: in due time. The time for revealing our predictions has arrived."

A sphere of swirling multicolored particles hovered where Ramsey's image had been.

"Each particle is a person," Ramsey said. "A random sample. A global random sample."

"The colors?" Nelson asked.

"Each person's power index. Assessed over the years. Based on answers to polling questions about their desire for power. Red's the highest. Then orange, then yellow."

I stared into the swirling mass of colors and tried to remember those questions. There'd been so many, so often. Desire for power didn't sound familiar. But there was one possibility I recalled, mostly because of its imagery. Are you the child holding the spotlight or the one standing in its beam? I could hear Lloyd's voice posing that question to me. But I couldn't recall my answer.

"The size of each particle," Ramsey continued, "represents the amount of power each person actually wields. Fiscal authority. Power over personnel. Specialized knowledge. Data of that nature. Our aggregators comb the Repository minute by minute, harvesting reliable and weeding out unreliable info."

"How did you know to focus on power?" I asked. "I assume you hadn't captured Gregory when you noticed problems."

"That's right," Ramsey said. "Let's just say we didn't have the computing resources to conduct real-time analyses of observational data. Better visual displays helped solve that problem. Jim?"

Jim rose slowly from his chair, leaned forward toward the cloud of particles, and touched one of the larger red ones. The particle projected a two-dimensional image of a middle-aged woman above a dozen or so lines of multilingual text. Jim gripped the edge of desk and gingerly lowered himself to his chair as the woman's image and data seemed to retract into the red particle. The mass of particles faded slowly, replaced by the image of Ramsey's face.

"We became better able to link aberrant behaviors with specific individuals," he said. "A correlation between personal power and abnormal behavior began to emerge. At least among the less power-hungry analysts."

"And the brain connection?" Nelson asked.

Ramsey sighed. "We had to resort to autopsies."

"Here in the North?" Nelson said.

It was difficult to believe, autopsies having become obsolete, especially in the northern hemisphere. In fact, they'd become stigmatized. Diagnosis equaled prognosis wherever medicine considered itself advanced.

"*Virtual* autopsies," Ramsey said. "Secret virtual autopsies."

"There's secrecy again," I said.

"True," Ramsey said. "Even I thought the need for it had atrophied. But we had reputations to protect. Powerful reputations. So we had to keep our suspicions under wraps especially since they were based on our suspects' abnormal behavior. Of course, once they passed away, we had captive cases."

"But they didn't die from the virus," Nelson said.

"No, they did not," Ramsey said.

"That's how long you've been tracking this crisis?" I said.

"Long enough for your suspects to die of natural causes?" Nelson said.

"I'm afraid so," Jim replied, his cheeks flushed, his brow deeply furrowed. "I wish we'd had the time to consider this. Why it took so long? How we allowed so much time to pass without a solution. How that's still the case!"

"Jim, please" Ramsey said. "We are moving forward."

Jim looked away from Ramsey, glancing at me and then Nelson before staring into space.

"The brain connection," Nelson said, redirecting us to his earlier question.

"The virtual autopsies, yes," Ramsey said. "We installed imaging equipment in several hospital morgues. Easy enough to do secretly given the setting. Not much traffic. Imaging itself is quick and, of course, undetectable. And data storage is easy. We compared the anatomies of suspect with those of a random control group and other corpses in the morgue. Given our suspicions about behavior, we concentrated on brain structures. Still, it took a while to discover the problem was their virus-infected amygdala."

"But how was the virus spread?" Nelson asked

"All we needed to find was a common thread among them. We had the data. And the computing power. The common thread turned out to be zero degrees latitude."

"The equator," Nelson and I said together.

"Where the world is widest," Ramsey said. "All victims resided or vacationed relatively close to the equator. That may seem rather vague or not very unusual to the average observer, but the one hundred percent overlap among the victims was the safest bet compu-net could provide."

"And the jackpot?" Nelson said.

"Aedes aegypti," Ramsey said.

"The mosquito?" Nelson said.

Ramsey nodded. "Carried the dengue and Zika viruses."

"Wiped out ages ago," Nelson said.

"Mostly," Ramsey said. "Willful elimination of an entire species isn't allowed."

"So, this mosquito made a comeback?" Nelson said.

Again, Ramsey nodded. "Where the world is widest."

"Where your victims lived or traveled," Nelson said.

A mosquito, I thought. A virus. How the small can wreak havoc far beyond their size. Like subatomic particles. The difference in scale between atomic nuclei and an atomic bomb made causal connection between them inconceivable. Until connection was revealed.

"This mosquito was the vector?" I asked. "But how? How could this possibly happen?"

"How does the unthinkable become thinkable?" Ramsey said. "In our case you start with a virologist. Gregory. He designed the virus. His One-World associates bred the carriers."

"One-World what?" I said.

"A sect," Jim said. "Isn't it always a sect?"

"Never doubt that a small group of committed individuals can change the world," Ramsey said, gazing at Jim. "It's the only thing that ever has."

"A sect," Jim said.

"I don't understand," I said.

"A sect of One-Worlders," Ramsey said. "A small group of committed individuals who weren't satisfied with the movement's progress toward One World Consciousness. A group who believed they could speed things along."

"By culling the herd," Nelson said.

"Gregory's virus." Ramsey said. "Carried by swarms of Aedes aegypti. Clandestinely bred. Yes, there's that word again."

"But now you could track them," Nelson said. "Once you knew what you were looking for."

"Follow the mosquito breeding trail," Ramsey said. "Insect cages. Incubators. Larvae trays. Tuna meal. Liver powder."

"Not some poor animal's blood?" Nelson said.

Ramsey shook his head. "Researchers use a special mix."

"And off-the-grid deliveries got your attention," Nelson said.

Ramsey nodded. "Their special mix included Gregory's virus."

I stared at Nelson, amazed by his apparently detached problem-solving. Ramsey's stoicism didn't surprise me, but Nelson's cold logic did. Yet I knew he cared. He cared for Mother. He cared for his friend Damon. I believed he even cared for me. I guessed he just couldn't resist unraveling Ramsey's mystery. And I could just barely tolerate his doing so.

"But still," Nelson said. "This inevitable chaos you speak of. How did you come to that conclusion?

An assortment of two-dimensional graphs emerged in the space surrounding Ramsey's image, floating grids of horizontal and vertical x, y coordinates, some displaying ascending jagged lines, others linear step-wise progressions or plotted dots or multicolored streaks, all sloping upward. Upward, but not necessarily uplifting. Because one never knows with Cartesian coordinates, the story underlining the gradient.

"Take your pick," Ramsey said. "The horizontal axes are all the same. Time. Elapsed time of varying intervals. The difference is their vertical axes."

My hands remained on my lap, unwilling or, perhaps, unable to move. Nelson pointed to a graph with an ascending stepwise progression traced in red.

"I remember that one very well," Ramsey said. "The leading cause of injuries for children under fifteen."

"Which is …?" Nelson asked.

"Falls," Ramsey said.

"And the increase?" Nelson said.

"The increase is the increase," Ramsey said. "But more important is the consequences. From nonfatal to fatal."

I shut my eyes.

"You may choose not to look," Ramsey said. "I understand. But it gets worse. Everything depicted here gets worse. Not only did the results of injury change, but we had to change the cause of injury. From unintentional to undetermined."

"Undetermined?" Nelson said.

"The falls are from windows more recently," Ramsey said. "And it's difficult to determine if the carelessness that led to these accidents was intentional or accidental. Hence, undetermined."

"Aren't there records of …?" Nelson said.

"We record behavior," Ramsey said. "Not thoughts."

"But still—" Nelson began

"Stop it," I shouted. I couldn't take any more. All those graphs, all that data, could draw only one conclusion. Disaster. That's where we were heading. All that remained to discover was the tipping point. When would the world spiral into chaos.

"What are we supposed to believe?" I whispered. "That there's no way to protect ourselves? That Transparency is a failure and nothing more than the blind leading the blind? That's all I can figure if surveillance doesn't recognize what it's looking at. So what are we left with? A failing that requires we never feel safe? That we can never feel secure? Ever? Is that our fate?"

40

Silence.

The graphs receded into the void from which they came.

"I know how you feel," Ramsey said finally. "Your compassion for the victims. That's all well and good. But your empathy serves no purpose. I'd rather you feel indignation. Because indignation demands action. But we can't control your feelings. We control images. Data. And hope they move you to action."

"And so," Nelson said, "we're here for the duration."

"Until our mission is accomplished," Jim said.

"Or another teams'," Ramsey said.

"Another team?" I said.

"Teams plural," Ramsey said. "The vaccine team, for example. Working on an antiviral serum. There are the vector eradicators, of course. The sterile male's team—breeding and releasing sterile male aegypti. Your traps and poisons teams. Your bacterial counter-agents. Etc., etc."

"Any of these seem more promising," I said, "than sending a warning back in time. And a lot less risky."

"Too little, too late," Ramsey said. "What's done cannot be undone. Of course, the scientists on other teams believe in the viability of their projects."

"Like we believe in ours?" I said.

"Like we *have* to believe in ours," Ramsey said. "We have no choice. If you can force yourself to look at those graphs, you'll see what I mean. The random acts of arson. The robberies committed by people of means. The senseless kidnappings. Enough sex crimes to create a new category— SEPOP for sexual exploitation of the powerful over the powerless. Hoarding by the well-to-do. Vandalism. Hooliganism. You name it."

He took a deep breath as if exhausted. "Except we don't know what to call," he continued, "the disappearance of weapons-grade plutonium from power plants and research reactors around the globe."

"And ever rising," Nelson said.

"Of course, we can't be precise in our predictions," Ramsey said. "There's no way of knowing how many infected there are or their growth rate. They aren't organized, so there are no groups to track. They're geographically dispersed. We have no precedent for this kind of havoc, not even prior to Transparency."

"But the sects," I said. "The One-Worlders."

"They've done their damage," Jim said. "They've unleashed the virus so now they sit back and watch the unraveling."

"But that couldn't have been their goal," Nelson said. "Watching the unraveling isn't culling the herd."

"True," Ramsey said. "There are people trying to figure that out, their original intent. It could be a matter of their best laid plan going awry. Yet Gregory and the others we've rounded up seem smugly self-satisfied. Maybe their plan for human de-evolution was to wipe the slate clean and start from scratch. But discovering their intentions isn't a priority. Except for historians, maybe. Those who assume history's still relevant."

Again, a long silence.

"And so," Nelson said. "Here we remain. Until."

"Until our mission is accomplished," I said.

"At least until then," Ramsey said.

***

I was free to finally be alone in my pod and free to close my eyes and breathe, free to think. The irony of escaping to this sanctuary only to find myself confined inside the laboratory weighed heavy on me. As did Ramsey's remark regarding the indefinite length of our stay.

I looked around the pod and it occurred to me that people who move usually bring treasured objects with them, heirlooms and trinkets that have special meaning, that are irreplaceable. There were none of those objects for us. All we had were our memories.

I glanced at the com-desk in the vertex of my pod and considered the surveillance film I could retrieve from the Repository. That stockpile of data would provide the raw material for my memories. The finished product, however, was another matter. For me, memories were as much constructed as they were simply recalled. The settings were factual enough, as were the people and, of course, myself, even over long spans of time. But behavior, the meaning of and motivation for what was said and done, seemed open to interpretation.

I struggled to read emotions underlying tones of voice and facial expressions. The meaning behind a simple smile. Or an exclamation. Was it an expression of joy? Alarm? A bit of both? Was it me or was Mother sadder when speaking of my father? Angrier, too, it seemed.

Was single parenting the joy of her life or a burden she felt strong enough to bear? Again, perhaps both. How much more film would I need to watch to determine the truth? Was the truth retrievable? Each viewing decreased my certainty about what I was seeing. Each viewing allowed me to create my own narrative.

So, could I excuse the surveillants who misconstrued or missed entirely evidence of Gregory's plot? Were their errors understandable in light of my own uncertainties about the truth? No. Why entrust these people to protect us if they couldn't interpret the data they collected? Their failure was unforgiveable. And listening to their account after failure, heartbreaking.

And then I realized I was sobbing. Waves of grief washed over me and leaving me breathless one moment, gasping the next. My emotions pooled and engulfed me—sorrow, anger, despair—and I trembled so violently, I ached. I wanted to strike out and punish, but there was no target. There was no one to hurt as much as I hurt.

***

Guilt finally prompted my recovery—the thought of Mother being alone. I regretted having neglected her, but there was nothing to do besides make amends. A few deep breaths, a splash of cold water on my face, and the press of a warm, wet towel and I was on my way to her pod. I wouldn't let her see my true despair and I marveled at how thoroughly I'd become adept at deception. It wasn't as though I'd learned to be deceptive. It was more like a long dormant instinct had arisen in me out of necessity. Or at least that was how I explained it to myself.

Mother welcomed me inside and I sat in a chair next to hers and watched her watch the scene projected above her com-desk.

"I can almost smell it," I said, watching footage of codfish fillets simmering with cubed potatoes and thick slices of onions and peppers in a cast iron skillet.

"I can almost taste it," Mother said, nibbling on a wedge of pressed protein.

I shook my head knowing there was no comparison between her slice of protein, starch, and vitamins, and the delicious flavor of stewed cod.

"The food here could be better," I said.

"But not more plentiful," she replied, brandishing the crusted wedge. "You just need to add a pinch of imagination."

"A pinch?" I said, and we laughed. "Can you pan back?" I asked.

The scene widened to include kitchen appliances, a table and chairs, sink, cabinets, and I finally recognized the place.

"The cottage!" I said.

She didn't answer but didn't need to. The scene had been surveilled in her cottage by the sea. A hint of curry, garlic, and thyme crept into the aroma I conjured—an aroma I remembered.

"I like these recordings," she said. "The facsimile at the hospital felt so hollow. White noise for the eyes."

I glanced at her hesitantly. "I couldn't think of anything more soothing than the view of the ocean from your balcony. And maybe a wishful whim as well. I'd hoped we could return there."

She sighed. "It seems so long ago."

I wasn't sure if she was referring to her stay at Carlyle Hospital or her last visit to the cottage.

"Was I with you at the cottage?" I asked, desperate to return to the recorded past, and escape the past of bad memories.

"You couldn't have been far," she said. "I was definitely cooking for two."

She switched to a view of the sitting room. The furnishings were just as I remembered: the facing rose-colored sofas and adjacent matching armchairs, the window-wall view of the ocean, the floral area rugs scattered over the slate floor, and everything burnished in the orange glow of dusk. And there was the portrait of Mother on the wall, a painting I'd forgotten but immediately recognized.

"There I am," Mother said as her image passed through the sitting room and into the kitchen. "I don't like to leave food on the stove unattended."

She toggled back to the kitchen to watch herself cook.

"Would you go back?" I asked. "To the sitting room. Your portrait."

"Yes, yes … that portrait."

She returned our view to the sitting room from an angle focused on the painting. I wanted to ask if she recognized herself in the portrait, but the question seemed absurd. Potentially insulting, even. She appeared to have recovered from that earlier crisis. And, again, I was eager to leave bad memories behind.

I remembered receiving guests at the cottage, some who'd never met Mother, and how they'd mistake her portrait as the painting of an African goddess. She stood so statuesque, her braids down to her shoulders, coal-black back then, framing her lustrous face. Yes, she was beautiful, yet her beauty wasn't her most extraordinary feature. What I noticed most was her majesty, the boldness of her bearing, the unflinching directness of her gaze.

Then I shuddered, thinking of Ramsey's claim that Mother's very stateliness was related to her breakdown. Her power-index, as he put it, foretold her susceptibility to Gregory's virus.

Mother's hand rested on my elbow. "There, there," she said. "The past must be embraced. Then move on. Visit, but don't overstay your welcome."

She switched our view back to the kitchen stove, the simmering codfish stew.

"People don't think of stew as warm-weather food," she said, admiring her handiwork, ladling the sauce over the fillets."

"No pink or yellow blotches," I said reflexively. "Your instructions to me when I bought cod at the fish market."

"You remembered! Fresh cod, that is."

"As opposed to …?"

"Salted. Or dried."

"Fridays," I said. "That's when you'd send me to the market. Fridays or weekends. Never on weekdays."

"Cod's a rare delicacy," she said. "Overfished."

"You tried to get me to buy from the boats. Chat it up with the boys, you said. I wanted none of that."

We lingered there a few moments, each with our separated memories, I supposed, while the cod sizzled in the background. Embrace the past, I thought. Embrace the past, then move on. Because it was the present the worried me.

"How do you feel about being here?" I asked.

She drew a breath to answer.

"I mean *really*," I said. "Having escaped the insanity back home. Having survived our escape. How do you feel about our arriving here, this place? How do you feel about staying here … for who knows how long?"

"The crematorium surprised me," she said. "I mean if we're talking about how we really feel. As if we'd talk otherwise. Which is to say, you surprise me, too, Fitima. It's as though you're hiding something from me."

"I am. I'm hiding how I really feel."

"A daughter's protective instinct? Protecting your dear old mother?"

"Something like that. Without the tease."

"Oh, Fitima. Give me some credit. At least a little. I don't know the details, but I think I have a handle on the big picture. *Everyday carry bucket from the well, one day the bucket-bottom mus' drop out.*"

"Excuse me?"

"Doesn't ring a bell? You must've studied it. Entropy?"

"The second law of thermodynamics?"

"West Indian style."

"Systems wear out over time," I said. "Become disordered. Is that your handle on the big picture?"

"My best guess. Maybe it's just my age. And that crematorium. The idea of it. The fire. Purifying. Returning our elements to the material world, to the cosmos where they came from."

"Mother, please!"

"Sorry, Fitima, but think about it. Look around. The limitation of healthcare underground. Little technology to keep us on the edge of living. Shorter lives down here? Who's to say, given what's happening topside? Down here, at least we can take dying back from the technicians. Make it natural again."

Her arm embraced my shoulders and I realized I was crying, quietly, as if to soften the impression of sadness. On her. And perhaps even on myself.

"This is how we really feel," she whispered. "How could we feel otherwise? How could we have imagined we'd arrive here, at this place, not knowing for how long? But you might remember what I told you years ago: it's the seed's job to blossom where it falls. And here's where we've fallen."

"I just don't want you to—"

"Hush," she whispered. "Don't worry about me. I feel a kinship with this place. An ancient bond. I'm not sure what it means. I'm not sure if I'm simply looking to the past to make peace with the present. I feel we've escaped into this wilderness. Like runaways of old. I hear a melody, not with my ears but in my soul. *If you want to find peace, go in the wilderness, Go in the wilderness, go in the wilderness. If you want to find peace, go in the wilderness, and wait upon the Lord.*"

I examined her closely as she removed her arm from my shoulders to turn off the image of her younger self dusting the simmering cod with paprika. The backdrop of her pod returned to fill the space above her com-desk. Then it was her turn to examine me.

"You wonder, don't you," she said, "why someone would leave their home, no matter how dreadful, leave family and friends and run into a wasteland to lie on the bare ground at night, eat roots and insects, crawl among snakes and all the while being hunted by bloodhounds, liable to being shot like a beast."

She raised her eyebrows in expectation of my response, but I hardly knew what to say.

Her thoughts had returned to the graves of slaves she'd discovered on the project she'd left behind, but were such thoughts normal, I asked myself. Should they be encouraged? Redirected? And then I wondered if she were normal And that surely the laboratory would have some way to find out. That they might not have technologies for treatment, but they would have technology for diagnosis for a condition they claimed was threatening the world.

"You wonder, no?" she said, still examining my face.

I wiped at the drying tears on my cheek. "Yes, yes, you wonder. Unimaginable."

"But it should be," she said. "Imaginable. That's the problem with memories. They become buried over time. They, too, suffer entropy. No orchestrated campaign. No conspiracy. Just a slow seepage down a black hole of neglect. I hoped to offer those memories the courtesy of recollection."

"I know, Mother. I realize you had the—"

"And I'd like you to do the same. If you see our predicament as I do. There's a story to be told. Our story. Time may drain the life from it, reduce it to an abstraction. It's happened before. But if there's no trace of it, no trace of our story …"

41

The chief physician's office was down the hall from Jim's, confirming my guess that the laboratory's primary administrators were proximate to one another. The office was empty when I arrived and I sat on one of the five chairs, three along one wall and two perpendicular, adjoined by an end table. A three-paneled woodland photograph decorated the wall above the chairs while the other walls displayed dozens of monitors scrolling text, numbers, and alphanumeric symbols horizontally across their screens. Recessed lights in the ceiling defused the flicker from the monitors, balancing the room's illumination. A large com-desk filled one corner. If there were any sound, the room was bare enough to create an echo. But there was no sound.

A middle-aged woman whirled into the room, startling me, shook my hand and was standing at attention behind the com-desk before I'd fully risen from my chair.

"Fitima Anueche," she said. "Very pleased to meet you. No one's arrived here with more fanfare. All our services are at your disposal."

In that instant, she'd answered my major question, but I wanted to understand the underlying details. And I wanted to understand the woman who's provide them.

"Doctor Keller," I said. "Sage-Keller?"

"Lauren, please. Sage-Keller is for the directory. And please, have a seat."

"Lauren," I continued, sitting, noting she remained standing. "Thank you for taking the time."

"Happy to," she said.

Even fully erect, Lauren Sage-Keller was relatively short. She was brown-skinned of ambiguous ethnicity and wore a sheer linen blouse with a golden-gauze skirt, remarkable for its novelty given the standard jumpsuits or lab coats worn by everyone else. The tattoo of a bluish-black rod entwined by a snake extended down the middle of her chest, a symbol I'd always associated with medicine. It seemed appropriate, of course, even if a bit superfluous.

"I'm here about my mother," I said. "She's my major concern."

"Yes, yes," Lauren said. "And I'm here to allay your concerns."

She moved from behind her com-desk and circled the office, indicating the banks of monitors on the walls.

"Ambient Health-Assist Monitors," she said. "Please, come look." I got up and joined her in a tour of the flickering screens.

"Our network of sensors in residents' pods monitors everyone's health data. Non- invasive, of course. Blood pressure, body temperature, heart rate, exhalation analysis, gait and sleep behavior anomalies."

She turned to me, and I replied both truthfully and as she seemed to expect. "Impressive."

"We look for changes over time to prevent anyone from moving to an unhealthy state," she said. "Some more closely than others, of course. Based on risk factors. Your mother's only risk factor is her age. Still, she'll get our continuous attention. You, on the other hand —"

"Do you have diagnostic equipment?" I asked. "Scanning devices, for example."

"Yes. For all vital organs plus joints, bones, circulation, etc., etc. Treatment is another matter, however. We have limitations down here. Except for palliative care."

She turned too soon to see me recoil as she stepped behind her com-desk. She activated its surface which lit up into what appeared to be a schematic of the entire laboratory.

"Plus, we have telehealth redundancy," Lauren said, sweeping a hand over the graphic. "Cameras record health data in addition to our sensors in the pods."

The backlit blueprint displayed rows of residential pods, administrative offices, labs, studios, workrooms, several auditoriums, the nursery, the gardens, the Temple of Heart and Mind, and the Imaging Chamber. The sheer breadth of the facility amazed me.

She pointed to several blinking red lights on the schematic. "Cameras." She touched a control on the edge of the schematic and extinguished the blinking lights everywhere except the rows of resident pods and a square-shaped unit on the end of an isolated hallway.

"We're not particularly interested in visual images," she said. "We focus on biometric data. We can toggle back and forth, however. Like here, for instance."

She touched the graphic of a residence pod and a holograph of Mother sitting at her com-desk projected above the blueprint.

"And now her biometrics," Lauren said eagerly.

Several graphs replaced Mother's image, each featuring jagged multicolored lines running along horizontal coordinates.

"Everything normal," Lauren said. "ECG, EEG, GSR, EMG, EGG, NIRS." She turned to see my reaction. "Oh, my apologies! Of course. Heart, brain function … normal, normal," she said, pointing to two of the graphs. "Sweat production, digestive system, oxygen consumption are all normal."

"Impressive," I said.

"Happily so," Lauren added.

"And you also have scanning equipment," I said. "For more detailed diagnoses."

"Are you concerned about something in particular?" Lauren asked.

"No, no, I just ... I just wanted some idea of your capabilities. Just to know."

"Because like I said, all our services are at your disposal. We can take a look at that equipment if you'd like."

"No, that's not necessary," I said. "I just wanted to know."

Then my gaze drifted along that isolated corridor, to the lone square schematic at its end.

Lauren followed my gaze and flinched, or so it seemed, and slid her hand to the controls and extinguished the schematic's backlit illumination. We looked at each other for a moment, a few seconds that felt awkward. Did I spot something I wasn't supposed to see?

"And there you have it," she said. "Unless you'd like to tour diagnostics."

"No," I said. "Not now, anyway. You've been very helpful. I appreciate your taking the time."

"You're most welcome. Let me know if there's any way I can be of service. Like I say to every resident: we're all in this together."

***

In the midnight darkness of my pod I wrestled with the idea of suggesting Mother have a brain scan. But why? she'd ask. And I wasn't sure I'd be able to answer. I hated having the suspicion she'd contracted Gregory's virus. True, she'd lost her bearings for a while. The pressures of her project. The conflict with her superiors. And, of course, there was the trauma she'd suffered since. Yes, she was troubled, but who wouldn't be? Her ideas could be unsettling, but what was wrong with me that I couldn't see the merit in them?

So, what to make of her obsession with the graves of those runaway slaves? And what of my indifference? Or was it distance ... historical distance? To the point where their experience had become an abstraction. She wanted to offer them the courtesy of recollection. And wasn't that a metaphor for all storytelling? Discovering people and their predicaments. Empathizing with them.

And as she suggested, our story, also. But told by whom? Who will compose the warning sent back in time? And if me, how would I represent myself? Or Mother? Nelson? How would I explain my naiveté? How do I present the atrocities of our time to an earlier generation? Who'll receive our story? What geo-temporal coordinates will we use? Pre-Transparency, of course, but which era? Post-national? The Age of

Ethnicity? The Golden Era of Narration where our story might get lost among the countless narratives uttered, written, sung, and filmed? Will they find our story suitable? Will our plight seem worthy?

I was pacing now, surrendering myself not so much to sleeplessness but to a welcomed wakefulness. Ideas, questions, and possibilities came to me as gifts. Images, too. Like that lone pod at the end of the isolated hallway. And the look of discomfort on Doctor Lauren Sage-Keller's face when she and I realized her indiscretion in revealing that pod. And the unspoken agreement between us that we would not speak of it—a look that acknowledged Transparency had its limits.

I stepped outside my pod into the hallway's simulated night-time. I seldom felt the urge to look for cameras, but I did this time, wondering which data they might be collecting and who, if anyone, might be observing. Perhaps that small degree of doubt inspired me to continue. Or maybe it was my commitment to discover what they'd hoped to keep hidden.

I returned to the lab's central core, the hub with branching corridors, and I visualized the schematic Sage-Keller showed me. The hallway with the isolated pod burned in my memory— down the four-o'clock hall as I faced twelve, left at the end, and left again at a four-way intersection and, finally, right at the next hallway. My only surprise was the slight curve of that last hallway and its becoming narrower as I continued, neither feature apparent in the schematic. Nor, of course, the faint glow coming from around the bend.

I stepped into that glow and my heart stopped at the sight of G. G. Gregory asleep on a cot awash in pale gray light. The same bars I'd seen in the holograph when he and I had spoken separated us now. He wore the same gauzy gown over the same pasty complexion. I looked back, into the bend of the hallway, wondering what it meant that I'd come upon this man so easily. I didn't see any cameras, but they must've been recording this area. Had they allowed me to find him? Had I been prompted? Was that Sage-Keller's plan all along? Or had I arrived under my own volition?

"Well, my goodness," G.G. Gregory said, rubbing his eyes. "My, my, my. A visitor. In the flesh."

I stepped back, but not out of the light.

"You're safe, you're safe. I assure you." He sat upright and slid his legs off the side of the bed and seemed to want to stand but held himself back.

"Remind me, please," he said, "your name?"

"Fitima." My long-idle voice hoarse and sounding more fearful than I felt. "Fitima Anueche."

"Yes, yes," he said glancing up at the screen in his pod where he must've viewed my image earlier. All that appeared there now were bio-informatic graphs similar to those Sage-Keller had shown me of Mother's.

"Isn't this complex amazing?" he continued. "Terra-tecture. Earth-integrated. Terra, for earth. Plus architecture. Terra-tecture."

His speech came to me as if through water, barely audible, barely intelligible. I still couldn't believe I was able to talk with him—this man who'd wreaked so much havoc on the world. To talk freely. Independently. Only spitting distance away.

"Why?" I managed. "I mean, really, why. Without the sermon. For reward? Revenge?"

"You want insight." He stood and paced along the side of his cot. "But you want insight you can understand. I don't know if I can give you what you want."

"I want something resembling a reason. I don't expect it to make sense to me. I'd be horrified if it did. I want a reason that makes sense to you."

He walked over to the bars, grabbed two, and framed his face between them. "First, you have to assume Gaia is sick."

"Gaia?" I said, his pre-Transparency jargon puzzling.

"The earth. The earth as alive. The earth as living organism. Sick. And I don't mean slightly ill. I mean critical. If you understand that, you understand she can't be cured by half measures."

"And your virus was the cure?" I said. "A virus that attacked the best of us?"

"A virus that attached those who consumed more than their fair share of energy."

"Fair share? Who are you to judge?"

"A living organism who'd hoped to survive. Like you, actually." He pressed his cheeks against the bars. "I used to ask people this simple question. Like I'll ask you now. How much time would you spend trying to open a small, stubborn, impenetrable pistachio when you could open a larger accessible one?"

I stared at him blankly, resenting the glint in his eyes.

"The question is rhetorical," he continued. "The answer's obvious. The Parable of the Pistachios, I called it."

"Your point?"

"Living organisms, like you, like me, we calculate the cost in energy relative to the benefit of energy we gain. Energy taken in must exceed energy consumed. Otherwise, we die. An organism stays alive by taking energy from outside itself, and processing that energy to produce, within itself, the organized state of life. From the smallest creatures to the largest. Living requires us to acquire more energy than we consume in order to fend off decay."

He squinted, glaring at me now. "And what is true for organisms is also true for social systems. That is, social systems must be organized in a manner that allows them to take in more energy than they consume. The problem has been there were so many who operated systems that consumed more energy than they produced. As true for any living system, these operations were undermining Gaia's health."

"So you and your sect of true believers—"

"Exactly," he said. "Started small and stayed small. The Rule of Five. There were only so many, just a few, who could open up to a moral force that could find them, select them, to carry out what had to be done. No egos. Absolutely selfless. We had to be. Otherwise, we'd be susceptible to the virus we were creating. We surrendered to a force much larger than ourselves based on faith. And we needed every bit of that faith. You see, society provides privileges that promote the survival of the fittest, which turns out to be, typically, survival of the dominant.

"And our goal was to upend dominance. We don't know what replaces the need to dominate but we get the chance to work that out without interference from those predisposed to control others. We figured survivors would be free to create, collaborate, synthesize. Connect consciousness. Become wiser than the sum of our parts."

That glint in his eye returned. "In the end, it all boils down to addition by subtraction."

I reached through the bars and found my hands around his throat, a spray of spit sprinkling my face. His fingers grabbed mine, but he couldn't pry them from his neck as I pressed his forearm against a bar of his pod and a weak squeal seeped from his lips. All the while I envisioned Hooks. I don't know if I even looked at Gregory's face. He became Hooks to my mind as I dug my thumbs deep into the ductwork of his throat. A low moan arose. Perhaps an apology. But probably not. Such was their arrogance. The moan harmonized with a whine that seemed to come from the monitor, a wildly fluctuating wave, like an alarm, which mixed with voices that grew louder.

Then shouting. My name. Why my name? Why not the name of the monster I'd latched onto?

A sharp tug on my shoulders freed me from him.

42

Until my encounter with Gregory, I'd been reluctant to fully commit to Ramsey's mission. Even when I imagined it was possible to send information back in time, the effort felt tainted with hubris. We seemed too eager to play God, too willing to redirect the arrow of time that had flowed forward since the moment of Creation. Although I'd been tempted toward Ramsey's cause by the horrors I'd seen and the atrocities we'd experienced, I had not been fully committed. Not until I understood Gregory as the embodiment of true evil. That's when I realized if we didn't play God to counteract the Devil, who would?

Perhaps that was the trigger Ramsey and Jim had been hoping for. It didn't matter to me that I'd been manipulated to confront Gregory. All that mattered was my understanding. If our hubris was a risk, my egoism would be the greater threat. There was no room for personal vanity given the stakes.

And I felt newly energized by my resolve. Perhaps this, too, was what they'd been hoping for. Perhaps my unbridled commitment was the final ingredient for the synergy the team lacked. Regardless, I felt like a child atop a boulder looking down at the surf, at the shadows of clouds and submerged rocks dappling the water, at that clear patch of blue inviting me in. That was the thrill I brought to our work.

***

Jim had agreed to our introducing Nelson to the Imaging Chamber prior to Anansi's actual contact with a probe. It seemed there was no request Jim wouldn't grant me since I'd returned to the project. Nelson's company and his nearness to me, was my first request and despite everyone's initial surprise, including Nelson's, it was readily granted.

The Chamber was a circular room with a curved black wall and a black concave ceiling. A dozen reclined chairs formed an inner circle that radiated from the center like the spokes of a wheel, their footrests converged at the hub. A second ring of reclined chairs formed an outer circle.

"I get it," Nelson said upon entering the Chamber. "Eyes to the stars."

Jim and I exchanged puzzled looks.

"You know," Nelson continued, pointing to the chairs. "Looking up at the stars. Figuratively speaking, of course."

"Stars that govern our fate," I said, immediately regretting the cliché. "Shakespeare," I added lamely.

Jim cleared his throat. "Our fate lies not in the stars, but in ourselves," he intoned and paused dramatically. "Also Shakespeare."

"Guess Shakespeare couldn't make up his mind," Nelson said. "Well, if uncertainty was good enough for him, it's good enough for me."

"It'll have to be good enough for all of us," Jim added.

We took our seats in the inner circle, Nelson between Jim and me, and the lights slowly dimmed.

"A few words before the demo," Jim said. "I must disabuse you of a few ideas that might cloud your understanding."

"Disabuse away," Nelson said, patting my hand on the armrest.

I smiled but avoided his gaze for fear of undermining Jim's serious tone. An instant later it was too dark to see him as the Chamber turned black and the oculus above us projected a night sky speckled with flickering stars of the Milky Way.

"Our ideas about time are based on our language," Jim continued, "but our language doesn't always reflect reality. Especially on a cosmic scale. In many ways language is a crutch. A crutch that helps us maneuver through the world and share our experiences."

"Our *non-cosmic* experiences, that is," Nelson said.

Jim paused a moment, perhaps trying to interpret Nelson's attitude. "Exactly."

"Time as one-directional has been dominant in our language," I said. "Like how long we've been in the room. And how much longer before the demo. But that idea of time hasn't always been dominant. Nor universally accepted. The tides, the seasons, the motion of heavenly bodies have led many to regard time in terms of rhythms that are cyclical. Our black hole-white hole pathway relies on that idea, that time can be cyclical."

"White hole?" Nelson said.

"The probe's geo-temporal exit," Jim said.

"The where and when our probe exits the black hole," I said.

"Of course," Nelson said with a heavy dose of sarcasm. "Like exiting at O'Meara Road on the Churchill-Roosevelt Highway."

"More like a bridge than a highway," I said, usurping his sarcasm. "The Einstein-Rosen Bridge, to be precise."

"Okay, I'm listening," Nelson said. "Do I need to add it might help if we were at a pub?"

The starry sky above us lent playful truth to his comment. I let a moment's silence put whimsy to rest before continuing.

"Albert Einstein and Nathan Rosen claimed that if an entity crossed the event-horizon of a black hole—"

"An entity?" Nelson asked.

"Matter, energy," Jim said.

"Our probe, specifically," I added.

"Okay," Nelson said. "Just asking."

"As I was saying," I continued, "if an entity, our probe, crosses the event-horizon of a black hole, like Anansi, and manages to avoid the singularity at the center, it will pass through a time tunnel and emerge from a white hole at another place and time. It will have crossed the Einstein-Rosen Bridge."

"Its geo-temporal exit," Nelson said.

"Exactly," Jim said.

"I thought you were speaking metaphorically," Nelson said. "About this exiting business."

"Well …" I began.

"It sounds like you're speaking literally," Nelson said.

"But you get the picture, right?" Jim said.

"Yes," Nelson said. "Like you said, language is a crutch."

And such a necessary one, I thought, looking up at the vastness of the Milky Way, the name we've given our home in the cosmos.

"And so, to hobble on," Jim said, "our goal is to calibrate the probe's route such that it'll emerge from a white hole at a particular time and location of the past."

"We believe we can synchronize the probe's speed and angle of entry with Anansi's rotational velocity to avoid her singularity and determine where and when the probe exits. That's our conceit. Our hubris, if you will. Our faith."

"As we civilians say," Nelson said, "throw enough money at a target, you're bound to hit something."

An awkward silence followed, and, for the first time, I wondered about the wisdom of inviting Nelson into our project's inner sanctum.

"Our work frightens you?" I said finally. "That surprises me."

"It surprises me, too," he said. "I wouldn't have predicted it. I guess it'll take more effort for me to see, to think differently. About time. About human capability. About linking that capability with the forces of nature. Unfathomable forces. You two have spent professional lifetimes climbing that ladder. I'm on a low rung."

"And you may find," I said, "on each step up, the mind cries, *no*. Not possible. But the work, the data outside yourself, whispers, *maybe*. You can't shut your ears to it. At least, you shouldn't. Not if you call yourself a scientist."

My eyes had adjusted sufficiently to the night sky above us for a swirl of white cloud to separate into tiny white stars. Just then, the room was plunged into total darkness.

"Time for the demo," Jim said.

"Keep in mind," I said, "these images are schematic representations of real physical data. Matter, energy, waves, particles. All translated into images we can understand. This is a descriptive illustration of a probe we sent into Anansi a few months ago."

Thin bands of blue, pink, and purple light swirled toward a point of impenetrable blackness in the center of the oculus. The streaks branched and united in chaotic combinations of thickness and shades throughout the Chamber but shared one common feature: they vanished at the midpoint above us.

"The black hole," Nelson said, probably pointing up, though I couldn't see him.

"Yes," Jim said. "The bands represent different physical phenomena. Gravitation waves, of course. Various forms of light, heat, and magnetic radiation. The red dot there represents our probe moving toward it."

I had always pressed myself harder and deeper into my chair whenever we imaged Anansi sucking existence out of our world, as though I were resisting her pull. It was illogical, of course, but even logic seemed to fall within her grasp.

"Black holes are simple, really," Jim said. "They have mass, spin, and charge. But the sheer magnitude! Not to mention the turbulence. Accounting for the route of our probe is like trying to track a snowflake in a blizzard."

"Much more difficult," I said. "At least a snowflake plays by rules of physics we understand. Inside a black hole, the rules break down. Parallel lines can cross. The shortest distance between two points might not be a straight line. Circles can have more than one center. Navigating a black hole is like practicing magic. We're as much sorcerers as scientists."

"Metaphorically speaking, I assume," Nelson said.

"And a huge dose of hyperbole," Jim added.

I ignored their chuckle. "Approaching the ergosphere," I said as the probe turned from its linear course to an elliptical tack toward Anansi.

"Wait," Nelson said. "Where did the probe come from?"

Jim's detailed description of the space platform hovering beyond Anansi's reach and the personnel staffing the operation reminded me of how little attention I'd given their contribution to our project.

"Sorry," Nelson said afterward, "but I don't feel my comment about throwing money at a target was as rude as you two made it out to be."

"More ill-informed than rude," I said. "You haven't had time to complete a cost-benefit analysis of our work."

"The cost-*hoped-for*-benefit," Jim said.

The image of the probe speeded up noticeably as it bent toward Anansi while bands of colored light swirled past it, swallowed by the black hole.

"Another thing," Nelson said. "I thought black hole gravity was so strong nothing, not even light, could escape it."

"*Almost* nothing," Jim said. "They do emit some radiation. Hawking radiation, for example."

"Named for the man who discovered it, I suppose," said Nelson.

"Predicted it," Jim said. "We discovered it."

"The radiation emitted contains information," I said. "See, our probe isn't an empty vessel. It contains quantum information we analyze after radiation escapes the black hole."

"She makes it sound simple," Jim said. "It's anything but. The quantum information we need is entangled with Hawking radiation. Fitima is our detangler. Well, Fitima and her team. Together they're greater than they are individually."

"Plays well with others," Nelson said.

I'd slipped into a recollection of comments Jim offered our team when we first came together, comments that proved eerily prophetic: "The cosmos isn't only more complex than we imagine," he'd said. "It's more complex than we *can* imagine."

"Plays well with others," Jim whispered, echoing the statement I thought Nelson had spoken.

"Excuse me?" I said.

"Nelson's comment," Jim said. "How we play well with each other. How our collective synergy enhances our productivity. How we work as a team. How we depend on each other and are anything but autocratic."

"Absolutely," I said. "Why my leaving the project was such a problem."

"And why we're not vulnerable to Gregory's virus," Jim said.

Perhaps I glanced at him, or blinked, or had my eyes open without seeing, but when I looked for the probe, it had disappeared.

43

It wasn't as though the notion of our resistance to Gregory's virus hadn't occurred to me, but if it had, I'd kept it camouflaged by anger, confusion, and sadness over Mother's condition. But since Jim made the idea explicit, I could think of nothing else. I was plagued by guilt, a heavy weight of responsibility, even though logically, I'd done nothing wrong. My desire to help Mother, my obligation to help her, made my inability to help her weigh heavily on me.

Misha was the first to notice my difficulty to fully focus on our work and suggest we take a break in the flow of our problem-solving, a significant departure from our normal work cycle.

She noted that we were making good progress in disentangling Anansi's quantum flux data and that a break wouldn't hurt our momentum. In fact, she proposed, a break would probably do us good. She seemed to be speaking only to me, nodding suggested approval in my direction, ignoring grumbling from the others. I quickly supported her and left it for her and the others to negotiate the length of our break.

Once again, Jim's assistant located Mother, this time in the nursery. I found her with Victor in front of a group of ten or so children gathered in a blue-lit alcove toward the rear of the nursery. Several small groups of children and adults were arrayed along my way, all in good spirits, which eased my worries.

Mother and Victor Brocken noticed my approach and nodded greetings. "Good morning, Fitima," Mother crooned for the children.

"Good morning, Fitima," they sang back.

The alcove was bathed in a soothing blue like a cloudless sky, illuminating the dull, textured finish of the cushioned walls and assorted padded protrusions rising from the floor.

Mother knelt to meet the children's gaze. "Have you ever tried to see with your fingers?" she asked.

"Fingers don't see," one boy protested.

"Yes, they can!" a girl countered, but apparently with no notion of how to make her case.

"Fingers can get lazy if you don't use them," Mother said. "They forget how to see. I want you to close your eyes and use your fingers to see. Without peeking. Can you do that?"

"Yes," the children cried.

"I want you to call out the shapes you find," she said, giving me a knowing wink.

She asked them to spread out and they began groping the padded protrusions, squealing with delight, and calling out their answers.

As reassuring as it was to see the joy on Mother's face, a twinge of anxiety kept me from fully appreciating her delight. She seemed so different, so carefree. Which shouldn't have bothered me, by itself. It was just that she didn't seem herself. I'd never seen her act this way toward any other children. I had no memory of her ever acting this way toward me as a child.

Of course, I could've answered this question by exploring the Repository, but I never spent much time studying my past. The future had always seemed more urgent.

The children quieted and in due course flocked around Mother, their faces upturned and attentive, their expressions almost reverential. They spoke in low voices as though sharing reassurances or regards among themselves. Then a pig-tailed girl stepped away from the others, her wide eyes glistening with tears. "But we weren't singing, Miss Zola."

A wave of silence spread from those children to the other groups, out toward the confines of the nursery until everyone, children and adults, had stopped what they were doing and focused their attention on Mother and the girl.

Victor signaled for my attention, but I couldn't decipher his gestures.

Mother surveyed the faces around the nursery, finally stopping on mine. "They're not singing, are they?" she whispered.

I shook my head.

"I'll call Sage-Keller," Victor said. He spoke those words as though he'd rehearsed them or, certainly, had had occasion to think them.

"No," I said. "No, you won't."

"But—"

"She'll come with me," I said, announcing my decision to them all. "Mother," I said, extending my hand.

Mother cupped the girl's chin in her hand. "I believe you," she said. "I believe you weren't singing."

She stroked the girl's head and walked over to me. "I believe her," she said, taking my hand. "I believe you all. And that's better than before."

***

Back in Mother's pod there was a surprising disarray, a clutter of holographs floating above and beyond her com-desk, digital texts and photos, maps, musical scores, loops of moving images suspended midair, documents she'd retrieved from the Repository. The murmur of recorded voices and faint fragments of music added to the chaos.

"My latest project," Mother explained before I could ask.

"How can you even think with all this?" I said.

She sat on her bed and surveyed the dozen or so holographs. "I couldn't think without ... all this."

"But it's so distracting," I said, then caught myself. "I'm sorry. What project?"

"Truth-telling."

She smiled at my gasp.

"You saw what happened in the nursery," she said. "Telling the truth has become, well, a challenge for me. More than it's ever been."

There was nothing I could say that wouldn't sound condescending.

"Still, it's important, telling the truth," she said. "Given where we are. Given where I am. Given, you know, our circumstances."

I shook my head confused yet afraid of what I'd hear next, bearing in mind the words Victor had spoken: *I'll call Sage-Keller.*

"You know," she continued, "the warning you have to send? Maybe like a narrative. You know what it reminds me of?"

"Mother, please ..."

"A slave narrative. Except in reverse. Instead of an account from the past to the future, your message will be from the future to the past."

I slumped into the chair beside her com-desk and looked at her through pixilated images of the holographs. "You insist on confusing—"

"I don't think so," she said. "Of course, I can't be sure. Given my bouts of ... well, you know. But I don't think I'm confused."

"Mother, slavery is—"

"A parallel, my dear! A parallel. Not the same as, but similar to. Slaves and slavery there and then, we, here and now. We both share unfreedom."

The silhouette of photos and typescript scrolled across her face, and I blinked at her bewildering appearance.

"You and I," she said with the tempo of a teacher, "we're like Prometheus. You know, the myth? The Titan who defied the gods and gave fire to humans. The gift for which he was subjected to eternal punishment. A gift like your project, no? Your gift to humankind.

"Harnessing a black hole to send a message back in time. A gift for which we will be subjected to eternal unfreedom. Not a punishment, but a sentence, nevertheless. And a parallel to slavery. A parallel that requires telling. A parallel that requires a narrative."

It was as if Gregory's virus had let loose her thoughts and unleashing ideas she'd stored over a lifetime. How else to explain this tale of Prometheus? Yet there was nothing newly set free in her thoughts about slavery. She'd expressed them to me now and then in my childhood. The difference was how her thoughts registered — how loudly they resonated now.

"I've studied slave narratives," she continued, pointing to several textual holographs. "There's a basic form, a pattern. Your people don't have to follow it, of course, but there is a blueprint. A standard intro, for example. I was born in…, then specify a place. Town, village, state. No date of birth, however. Interesting, no?"

I found myself agreeing, captive. Captivated.

"I'm sure you and your people will provide dates," she said. "Moments in time are crucial in your case although, Lord knows, they'll be hard to believe. Hard for your audience, I mean. A message from the future? Please. If you expect them to admit receiving your message, they'll need to be free from any suspicion of psychosis, that's for sure."

I smiled at her and shook my head. Sorting science from magic, sanity from insanity would certainly require a special intellect. Perhaps someone on the margin of all four.

"Cruelties need to be described," Mother continued. "Cruelties suffered and cruelties resisted. But not sensationally. Believably. The challenge of all slave narratives — making the unbelievable believable."

"Too much, Mother, don't you think? Too much time thinking about these things. It can't be good for you, good for your state of mind."

"It's been essential, Fitima, essential for my state of mind. Our states of mind are so different, yours and mine. Our lives are at very different stages. I'm running short of equivocation time. The only things left for me are the essentials."

"Okay, okay. But what you're talking about will be taken care of. In due time. You don't have to—"

"Of course I don't *have* to. I *need* to. Who else will? No one down here knows what I know. No one here has studied what I've studied. Who here knows that your narrative needs a hero? All slave narratives have one. A hero. Or a heroine. Who else would ask if that heroine might be you?"

I shut my eyes and rubbed my temples which brought no relief to the dull pain that had settled there. I'd come to see Mother out of my guilt, to ease my conscience for having avoided the syndrome that afflicted her. Now all I could do was wish myself elsewhere, anywhere to escape clang of her stream of consciousness.

"If it is you, child," she continued, "As heroine, I mean, as narrator, you must be truthful. *We* must be truthful. There are no slave narrative myths. They're all true-life.

"Well … as much as a life history can be. Of course, your audience couldn't verify truth. Still, you'll need enough detail, enough truthful detail, to convince them the implausible is possible. Or will be possible.

Or will be probable, at least. Enough truthful detail to convince them the implausible will be true."

I sighed and waved dismissively at the holographs. "Would you please close these files?" I said. "And turn off the sound recordings."

"Of course, dear, of course. Some files, anyway." She rose and walked to the com-desk. "Trade places?" she said, signaling me to move to her bed and she sat at the console. One by one the holographs flickered off and the music and murmuring faded away.

"Thank you," I said, watching her from the bed, trying to think of something to divert our attention.

"What I say next will come as a shock," she said.

She stared at me as if gauging my response, but she ignored or couldn't detect my crumpling from within.

"A deep shock," she continued. "Perhaps a betrayal, even. No, no ... definitely so, a betrayal. But I'm not going to beat myself up about it. Truth trumps pride. Truth trumps conscience. At least down here. Under these circumstances. Who could've predicted things would come to this? Not me. Yet here we are. At the point of chronicling the truth."

I moistened my lips enough to part and breathe my question. "What are you talking about?"

"Your father. Your father's alive."

44

I looked away from her, afraid to see the return of her illness on her face. But there was no denying it now, I'd have to turn to Sage-Keller for help. This time, however, I'd monitor the doctor's every move, her every utterance, her every thought. I owed that much to Mother. I owed that much to myself.

"You mustn't blame yourself," Mother said.

"Blame myself?" I said, still looking away. "For what?"

"I was the one who insisted you leave the past to the past. It was all at my urging. You were a child. You wanted to please your mother."

I finally turned back to her. "What does this have to do with … what you just told me?"

"I told you your father had died before you were born. There was no reason for you not to believe me. You retrieved information about him you could as a child. His family. His friends. But at some point, I urged you to stop. I discouraged you from digging into the past."

"You demanded it."

"Yes, yes, I begged. I pleaded."

"You insisted. You threatened. Not directly. But I felt if I disobeyed you, I'd be denying you my love. That's how you made me feel."

"You were a child. Granting your mother's wish."

More like surrendering, I thought. That much I remembered. Mother made it seem like losing my father was like losing a useless organ, an appendix or wisdom tooth—initially painful, but of no long-term consequence. Except it was not like that. There had always been a faint echo, an afterglow of absence. Nearly indiscernible. Nearly.

And now she's guilty, I thought. Guilty enough to imagine my father back to life. To imagine him back into her life. Guilty enough to insinuate him into mine. Yet I sensed no emotion in her tone. She seemed to be giving me objective evidence of her delusion. Which brought me back to Gregory's virus, back to her illness.

"I remember the last time you spoke of father," I whispered. "Carlyle Hospital. Hooks."

I felt ashamed for reminding her of that place, Hooks' assault, but I had to take her back to her previous illusion about my father.

"You know," she continued, "the biggest stumbling block to discovering the truth is the belief one already knows the truth."

"You say that to say what?"

"You think you know your father is dead. You know this with certainty. But I'm telling you that you're holding onto an illusion and it's keeping you from discovering the truth. A truth that was kept hidden from you."

"Hidden? Impossible. Nothing's hidden. Why are you going on and on like this?"

"Because you'll be the narrator. I'm sure of it. And you'll need to be truthful."

I recognized the steely sincerity in her voice and her steadfast stare, but I didn't know how to respond. With compassion? Patience? Firmness? Point out the impossibilities of her claim. One by one, logically. Listen to her rebuttals. Challenge those, as well. But to what end? Or I could be silent. Become a quiet listener to the madness that was claiming her. If I could endure the sadness of it. That would be my challenge. Until her madness subsided. If her madness subsided. With my last resort, Sage-Keller.

"There's another why," she said. "Why our deception?"

"Our deception?"

"Mine and your father's. Why we deceived them?"

I shook my head for her to stop, but I knew she wouldn't.

"Because we could," she said. "That's why. Because we *could* deceive them. And because of what you just said. Nothing's hidden. To act as though that belief wasn't true. It was our final pact as a couple. And then we let it go. Like we let each other go. We got on with our lives. Separately. Until now. Now that truth is required."

I hesitated. How many times had her notion of truth seemed like a mirror held up to a world I didn't recognize?

"The Repository says Father died in a car crash," I said.

"Yes, yes," she said. "A pre-automated vehicle."

"Dead on arrival, it says."

"You remember it well, I see. I brought him to a cottage hospital. Since decommissioned."

"Regardless, records can't be destroyed! He was declared dead immediately."

"So it says on his death certificate. But a death certificate can be bought. Or can't you imagine that? So, too, can an unclaimed corpse. Can you believe it? That there could be sufficient need in the world, or felt need, at least, that some poor man's remains could be bought, renamed, and cremated? All while validated by official documents? Can you imagine that Kelvin Anueche could be declared dead, cremated, and laid to rest in a cottage hospital cemetery and yet be alive today?"

I had no interest in arguing with her to win. I only hoped we could find some common ground to lead us back to normalcy.

"You and Father did love each other," I said softly.

"Very much. You were borne of that love."

"You spoke so warmly of your time together. Your picnics in Queen's Park Savannah. The flowers he picked for you."

"Oh yes," she whispered, closing her eyes.

"So why separate?"

She opened her eyes and gave me a sidelong glance. "Inexplicable to the romantic mind."

"How about my mind? How about explaining your separation to your daughter?"

She leaned back on a throw pillow and propped herself against the pod's curved wall. "The amount of time spent together is no true measure of love," she said. "It's the quality of time together that matters."

"Who could argue with that, Mother? My question is, when did you lose love for each other? Why?"

"I'm afraid of the way you ask," she said. "The spirit surrounding your words. As if love should be eternal." She shook her head and pressed back harder against the wall. "Love isn't necessarily infinite, my dear. It can be time-bound. As your father and I loved. Until we did not."

"But why?"

"I stopped feeling at home in his world. He didn't change. I did. He couldn't change. We decided he shouldn't change. Instead, we changed. We separated."

"This all sounds logical, but ... maybe too logical. So ... so detached."

"Perhaps your father can explain it better."

My heart seized as she gestured to the holographs above her desk. I glanced at them and looked away, determined to avoid whatever they might reveal.

"Sit down," she said.

It was only then that I realized I was heading toward the portal. "I don't ...," I said, "I can't."

"You can. You will. And then you can send your message back in time—a truthful message."

She pointed to the chair beside her desk, and I sat down, still averting my eyes from the holographs. Then she got up to retrieve the controller from her desk, returned to her bed, and switched on the holographic recording.

"I depended on this man to help me," she said. "Here's his last transmission."

His East Indian accent drew me to his image. From a wooden chair wedged in the white-walled corner of a room, he was pouring milk from a rectangular carton into a glass with a grooved opening that brought to mind a screw-on lid. He had white wiry hair sprouting wildly from his head, chin, and upper lip and he sported a pair of thick, black-framed spectacles suggesting he'd never had corrective eye surgery. It took a moment for me to catch on to the melody and rhythm of his speech.

"He's a vagrant, you realize," he said, followed by a sip of milk. "No document trail."

"But you can find him?" Mother asked, her voice slightly hoarser in the holograph.

"Of course I can," he said. "Using audio search."

"Please stop it," I said. "I'm lost."

"Sure," Mother said, pausing the recording.

"Who is this man?"

"Arjuna Jayashankar," she said, carefully articulating the surname. "A.J., for short. At his insistence."

"But who—"

"Ethnomusicologist. Expert in folk music. Best in the world, he claims."

"What's he have to do with—"

"Your father's a musician."

She leaned back on the pillow and placed the controller by her side, granting me time to absorb the shock.

The description of my father I'd cobbled from data in the Repository couldn't have been further from my image of a musician. A folk musician? He'd always appeared well-dressed, gracious toward those around him, content, cheerful, actually. Yet why couldn't a musician have these traits? A folk musician, even. Still, had I ever seen him with a musical instrument? No. Neither had I seen anything about music in his profile.

"It just doesn't add up," I said finally.

"You're considering Kelvin Anueche's data," Mother said. "Post-Kelvin Anueche's bio tells a different story."

She picked up the control and restarted the recording.

"His auditory signature," Arjuna Jayashankar said. "Very unique. His warm-up routine. Singular. Not his voice. His instrument. Gibson Tomcat 220. He uses a Fuzztone compressor. Hand-built. Gives that sharp twang."

"But there must be countless sharp twangs coded in the Repository," Mother said.

"But his warm-up repertoire as whole is searchable," the musicologist said. "An open Fm chord. The capo on the fifth fret, delivering a B-flat minor chord. Upstroking the notes on the top three strings with his index finger, snapping the fourth and fifth strings with his thumb. I can duplicate his routine for enough bars to produce an audio file and search for a match."

A long silence followed, and I thought the recording had ended as Arjuna Jayashankar stared straight ahead, motionless. Then he took a sip of milk.

"I want you to search for him," Mother said in the recording. "Fix the geo-temporal parameter on present-day Trinidad. And if you're successful—"

"When, ma'am," the musicologist interrupted. "When I'm successful."

"When you're successful," Mother continued, "send me the audio search file."

"Of course," the musicologist said. "And my congratulations, ma'am. You are fortunate indeed to include King Juba among your acquaintances."

45

Nelson had done what I'd asked of him. He'd allowed me to tell him everything Mother had revealed to me without comment despite my sporadic sobbing and fits of hysteria. No questions. No opinions. He simply listened.

Not only to the facts, but to my feelings. I tried to describe the storm, the swell of conflicting emotions: confusion, anger, betrayal. But also excitement. Curiosity. I felt as though I were twisting in the wind, pieces of me flailing or flying away, bent to the point of snapping in two, only to be wrenched in the opposite direction yet bent so low, I wondered if I'd never stand upright again—if I'd ever be able to right myself.

And still Nelson listened. And after I'd exhausted myself, he waited for my jagged breathing to steady.

"I'm sorry," he said finally. "But I am glad." He leaned forward on his cot but still seemed apprehensive. "I'm glad you trusted me."

I bowed in gratitude, all the while knowing I had no one else I could've trusted. That was the gnawing predicament of my relationship with Nelson. It was the reason I'd kept him at arm's length. He was my only trustworthy ally, but forced choice felt like no choice at all.

"Of course," he continued, "you don't have to search for him."

"Of course I do," I said.

"You don't have to search right now," he said. "You can give yourself time."

"Time for what?" I asked about to burst into tears again. I understood what he'd meant.

"Time to prepare," he said. "For anything. Or nothing. You can't expect any particular outcome. You can't expect any outcome. I heard the story, but—"

"That's the horror of it. Either Mother's story is true. And King Juba is my father or her story's a figment of her sickness which is—"

"I know, I know."

"But I'd rather face either horror sooner than later."

An uneasy silence settled between us before I made my next request. "I'd like you to be with me. When I search for him"

Nelson nodded, okay.

"I'd like to search from here ... your pod."

"Okay," he repeated.

"I'd like to start now," I said.

He gave me a look that seemed as though he wanted to reach out to me, as I wanted to reach out to him, and I felt ashamed and saddened that my reservations kept us apart.

"I think what you're doing is brave," he said.

"Is it? I think of bravery as when you have a choice. I don't feel I have a choice. This is something I must do."

***

Searching for Juba became my priority. Targeting Anansi became a distraction. Jim tolerated the interference. My coworkers did also. They had no choice. We all had to live with my obsession.

Each evening Nelson entered the audio file Arjuna Jayashankar created into the Repository's search engine, calibrating our auditory search with present-day Trinidad. And each evening the static noise above his com-desk triggered a blend of relief and frustration. Frustration over the failure of our search and relief over that failure. My father's absence was the regularity I'd known. His presence would be an irregularity I wasn't sure I could accept.

So, when the space above the com-desk exploded with iridescent pixels, I froze. The readout below the emerging image flashed, TARGET FOUND, and my hand leapt toward the console to end the search. It hovered there a moment. Then I swallowed hard and switched on the two-way audio-visual connection.

The rhythmic ping of steel drums sounded before the pixels coalesced into the scene of a backyard, a camera panning left to right revealing men and women sitting on lawn chairs on a patio, a younger group lounging on a pool deck, and finally, a tent-covered bandstand occupied by a man with his back to the camera. The camera then reversed direction, showing details I'd overlooked; the people were eating and conversing, mostly in pairs, as were those by the pool, and a lone woman was cooking on a grill. The recorded steel drum music played leisurely over the hum of voices and clinking tableware, punctuated periodically by the strident strum of a guitar.

The woman at the grill threw up her hands just before leaving the camera's view, then suddenly appeared in front of me.

"Fixed focus," she commanded, and the camera stopped panning and homed in on her nut-brown face. She was middle-aged and very pretty despite her scowl.

"Can I help you?" she said.

I opened my mouth to speak, but no words came out. I heard the creak of Nelson rising from his cot and I felt his presence by my side.

"Miss, I would call you by name, but your I.D. is missing. Can I help you?"

Why was my I.D. missing on her display screen? I wondered. And how could this woman be the target of my search?

"Miss, I'm hosting a party here, so please, can I help you?"

Before I could answer, she turned. "Simone, watch the grill!" She turned back to me; her head tilted impatiently.

"King Juba," I whispered. "I'm looking for King Juba. I've got reason to believe he's … he's somewhere—"

"Oh, he's here, all right," she said. "Is this some kinda game you two are—"

"I want to speak with him."

She squinted at me. "If this is some kinda joke."

"I swear, ma'am. No joke."

She reached below my field of view and the camera jerked to the right and focused on the guitarist on the bandstand.

"There's your King Juba," she said off camera. "Still warming up. For almost an hour! And now you show up asking for him? With no identification?"

"I'm sorry, ma'am, I can't help the I.D. malfunction. My name's Fitima. Fitima Anueche. I want to talk with—"

"I paid this man to perform. Not practice. Not talk."

"I'll compensate you, ma'am," I said, feeling uneasy, not knowing exactly how I'd fulfill my promise.

"'Cause I can call the authorities, you know."

I heard reluctance underlying her threat. "If there's a way I could talk with him," I said. "Without disturbing your guests, of course. If the bandstand has a camera …"

"Of course it does," she said. "For documenting performance!"

"Well, if you could redirect me to—"

"I'm serious about compensation," she said.

"After I speak with Juba," I said.

She hesitated a moment. "Don't disconnect without getting back to me. I may not have your I.D., but—"

"I promise," I said.

She reached beneath the camera. "And get him to quit that awful racket."

Her image vanished, replaced by a grainy haze that slowly resolved into an overhead view of a man's grizzled head. As if suddenly aware of our presence, he turned and looked up at the camera.

I gasped at the recognizable face, dusty gray and pockmarked with beads of sweat. "I know you," he said.

"No, you don't," I said impulsively. "You don't know me."

"But you know me," he said.

"I know your name," I said.

"And I yours," he said. "And I recognize that man beside you."

Nelson simply glared at him.

"And we all know the woman who must've helped you find me," he said. "Who other than—"

"I'm really looking for Kelvin Anueche," I said.

"Kelvin Anueche is dead," he said. "Surely she told you."

"She did," I said. "She also told me he was alive."

"Dead and alive?" he said. "Curious. But not unheard of."

"She told me you are him," I said. "And she told me you're my father."

Nelson's hand slipped into mine and a wave of sadness brimmed up inside me ... a tide of loss and longing. And fear.

"I don't know how much time we have," I said.

He glanced toward the guests. "They're angry with me."

"I need to know if what Mother told me is true. Are you my ... are you my—"

"Father? Yes."

Nelson's gripped my hand tighter in surprise or support. "How could that be?" I said.

"Your mother married a man she stopped loving," he said. "I married a woman who deserved to be freed. We no longer needed each other. We needed to be free of each other."

I glanced at Nelson as though he might decipher what we'd heard.

"When you get married," he continued, "you can assume it's forever. That's reasonable. But no one can guarantee it."

"Of course not," I said. "But the faked death? The cover-up? The audacity. The crime. The disregard for me, your child."

"There was no you, my child, back then. The mother and father you see now were different people. I don't apologize for that. I'm simply explaining."

"I've heard no explanation," Nelson said.

Juba gazed at him and hesitated. "Her mother accepted my idleness back then," he said. "She accepted my belief that the worship of work was the gospel of slavery. She didn't share my belief, but she accepted it. Then she lost faith in my idleness. Perhaps that came with pregnancy."

I shuddered and Nelson held my hand tighter. "But why the deception?" I asked.

"We wanted a second chance," Juba said returning to me. "A new beginning for each of us. Many people wish they could start over. We could do more than wish. We made a commitment ... a vow to ourselves. I cut all ties to my past. Your mother cut all her ties to me. We were committed to being reborn. Yes, there was craziness to it, no doubt. For me, self-destruction. For her, a new life. Commitments normal people can't understand."

His insinuation struck hard. I could understand that he wasn't normal, but neither was Mother. From well before the virus. I would need to reimagine a whole new life history for her. A new life story for myself. And a life for the father I'd assumed dead.

"Step back," I said.

He squinted at me, puzzled.

"From the camera," I said. "Step back."

He hesitated a moment, then took a few steps back. I could see his full figure now, his torso covered in gauzy red fabric with a broad, diagonal black stripe with white borders, suggesting Trinidad and Tobago's national flag. His pants were opaque and rope tied as we'd first seen him outside Mother's camp.

Under the dust, his complexion was sun-darkened browner than mine, but he was lean and narrow-shouldered like me. Otherwise, he seemed rather average: roundish face, moderately high cheek bones, somewhat broad nose and lips. His arms and legs were hairy like mine, and unlike Mother's. She had promised me I'd shed the hair on my limbs, but I never did.

There were stark differences, too—the long, keloid scar across his chest just above his heart, smooth and ridged beneath his shirt. And the scarred lump on his forearm where I guessed he'd cut out his electronic I.D. And the labyrinthine tattoo in the middle of his stomach.

"Have you seen what you wanted, child?" he asked.

I'd heard and seen my fill, yet I still felt unfulfilled. "Call my name," I said.

"Fitima," he said. "Fitima Anueche."

My throat tightened and I fought against sentimentality. He didn't deserve it, I thought. But what did he deserve?

"I suggest you leave this place," I said. "You've upset these people." And then I realized that was nothing new for him.

"They've paid me," he said.

"I'll take care of that," I said.

"I can't sing without crying," he said. "That's why I'm here, warming up. Alone."

"Mother and I are together," I said compulsively, and I wasn't sure why. To reassure him? To hurt him?

"I'm glad," he said.

Even that, I resented. It was as if nothing he said could engender any genuine warmth. "No location listed," he said scanning beneath the monitor. "No ID at all."

"Not my doing," I said. "But I'd just as soon have it that way."

He drew his guitar up to his chest and strummed a few mournful chords and plucked several lonesome notes that sounded more like a tune than simply practice. His pursed lips hummed guttural groans that might've been words if not for his muffled crying. He stopped playing and returned to look at me.

"I can't sing the warning," he said. "*So I'll just say the words. There's a cold wind blowin', and she sing an omen song. She'll dry up all your oceans, correctify all your wrongs.*"

"What's that supposed to mean?" I said.

"I don't know," he said.

"We heard that song before we left Trinidad," Nelson said.

Yes, I remembered, a rush of memories, Damon guiding us to Indigo Sound, Peter Conrad leading us to our escape by sea, and somewhere along that route hearing the saddest music I'd ever heard coming from a transmitter. Yes, it was King Juba. The blues, Conrad called it. Foreign to my ear. Heartbreaking. It all seemed so long ago and so incredibly distant.

"The words just came to me," Juba said. "The world seemed ripe for a warning."

He glanced toward a voice from the patio and his face signaled someone was approaching.

"Where will you go?" I asked.

He shook his head absently. And then he seemed suddenly struck by my question. "Are you ... are you concerned about me?"

"Me?" I said. Was I? "Perhaps. Yes. About anyone wandering the countryside alone. In these times."

The hostess reappeared and stood at the edge of the camera's field of vision, apparently avoiding proximity to Juba. "If you're finished here," she said facing me, "I'd like to settle the arrangement we discussed."

"Yes, of course," I said. "Just provide the particulars and I'll see that you get your money back. But you must first get him back to the capital."

I saw protest brewing in her eyes, but reason prevailed. "I expect you to live up to your promise," she said before inputting her data via our cyber-connection.

"She expects?" Juba said. "Expectation stopped working for me. I had to give it up. I now put my trust in hope."

46

A strange numbness spread through me, as if I were being emptied of all physical sensation and that my mind, too, was losing thoughts and feelings. I could only shake my head at Nelson and gesture clumsily that I needed to leave. I did feel shame, though, regret over my gracelessness in light of Nelson's grace even as I silently left his pod.

But leaving him was easier than knowing where to go. I didn't want to be alone, but I couldn't face Mother after all I'd heard from her. About Juba. Kelvin. Their muddled, mingled past. And as I drifted along the corridors, I didn't feel I had much to offer my colleagues, although that's where I found myself, inside the Imaging Chamber.

"Fitima," several coworkers called out in unison, part exclamation, part question, as if asking are you ready to join us?

Uncertain, I nodded absently.

Jim walked over to me, his knitted brow, signaling more than concern about my return.

"What's wrong?" I said.

"Evaporation," he said. "Faster than expected."

I was only mildly surprised to hear it, but more surprised to feel my body and mind stirred back to life.

"Our estimations were off," I said almost matter-of-factly, after all, estimations are simply that.

Jim nodded and gestured to the team busy analyzing data on 3D grids, their wave-function equations mingling like threads of a kinetic tapestry. We'd known Anansi would shrink as a result of our probes, but we had to theorize the rate of contraction. We now had data, apparently, proving our theorizing was off—the shrinkage of her ergosphere was occurring faster than predicted.

"Do I need to say it?" Jim asked.

No, I thought. I knew he needed me, the missing piece to our team's collective proficiency.

"I think I'm ready," I said.

"I need you to know you're ready," he said. "That's how it works."

"Can I talk—?"

"We'll be right back," Jim called out to the others who didn't seem to notice.

He escorted me out of the Imaging Chamber and down the corridor to a large closet filled with an assortment of cybernetic machines for sweeping, brushing, spraying, all manner of automated cleaning, none of which I'd seen in operation. There were also several folding chairs, apparently for persons to sit on while repairing or maintaining this mechanized brigade of housekeepers.

"I've always understood your doubts," Jim said as we unfolded chairs to face each other. "I had doubts myself."

"You never told me what they showed you," I said. "You never told me which horrors you were being recruited to undo."

Jim sighed. "They showed me things I couldn't believe, probably like they showed you. Our eyes see, but our minds tell us what we see can't be true. We only see what our minds can imagine. That's when we become convinced. That's how Ramsey tries to secure our commitment. I don't deny that he's manipulative. I deny that he's lying."

"But what did you see, Jim? What did they show you?"

He looked away from me. "He shows us what he thinks will gain our allegiance. He plays to our sympathies. And it's always painful."

"And you don't want to relive that pain," I said.

Jim nodded. "His choices don't always work. He's certainly had trouble getting you to rejoin us. But he finally got you back here."

I looked past him now, trying to recall my actions, my decisions. Each choice I'd made since leaving the lab had felt independent. My decisions were often upsetting, but I'd always felt I was making a choice. Now I had to wonder how much I'd been manipulated.

"Don't let pride get the better of you," Jim said. He was studying me carefully now, reading my expression. "Does it really matter how any of us comes to see the light? What matters is that we see it. And how we respond."

The hum of electric lighting seeped into the silence between us. "What will we send?" I asked finally. "That these are the worst of times? What more is there to say?"

"That's not our job. Our job is to find a way to send whatever message we decide."

"But do you know? Does anyone?"

He shook his head. "As much information as will prevent the horrors we've seen. And the horrors we can predict. That's the key, Fitima … prevention. Giving humankind a second chance." He stroked his chin absently. "Yet another," he whispered.

"Yet another?"

"Too many to count," he said. "With each new prophet. Each conquering army. Each new age. The rise of Democracy. The Age of Narrative. The age of Transparency. Second chances all."

"But the one we offer will be successful."

He shrugged, understanding I was asking. "We have to hope so."

"And hope we won't annihilate ourselves. You're convinced of that."

"Convinced? That word sounds so naïve." He shifted uncomfortably on his chair, and I noticed my own discomfort on the firm cushion. "The universe doesn't follow the demands of our reason," he continued. "It always finds a way to surprise us. Reason tells us time is a sequence of unrepeatable events. But the universe may manage itself quite differently than we imagine. Different than we *can* imagine. Our brains are hardwired for life on human scale. For us, time passes day by day, year to year, generation to generation.

"Science tells us the universe is expanding, moving from order to disorder, everything in sequence. But that sequence, time's arrow, is only an idea. An idea that helps us think about … well, how long to bake bread. When to send Mother a birthday card. But that's people-time. It's not cosmic time. Belief in people-time may keep us from grasping cosmic time. It may limit our imagination.

"Our work pushes us beyond the idea of linear time. It forces us to think about time as coiling back on itself." He leaned forward and smiled, a playful grin, as though he were about to tell a joke. "Bear with me," he said. He cleared his throat. Then he recited.

"Our post-scientific sigh, sent through a black hole, circles back in time—Destiny's loophole."

He leaned back and I couldn't help but laugh. "You … a poet?" He nodded, still amused with himself.

"Post-scientific?" I asked.

"If we're successful. Sending information into the past."

"Destiny's loophole? Our second chance."

"Indeed," he said. "Our get out of jail free card."

I shrugged, puzzled.

"Look it up." Then his smile straightened. "We need you, Fitima. To help us take that final step."

I took a deep breath. "It's just hard. Hard to believe in what I assumed was impossible."

"That's because you haven't had much practice," he said. "Me, I follow my mentor's advice. Try to imagine one impossible thing each day."

We eyed each other, me trying to read the man who'd been my mentor, and he, most likely, trying to read me, his protégé. How could we have been drawn to each other and yet be so different? I thought back to what he'd said when we first met, the qualities he was looking for among his apprentices. I'd expected him to say intelligence, perhaps creativity. Instead, he spoke of courage and duty. So odd, I'd thought, admirable, of course, but not the first qualities that came to my mind in describing the ideal scientist. Perhaps that's what Jim and I shared—our valuing courage and duty. It reminded me of my commitment and my duty to Mother. And the courage it would take to fulfill my obligation.

He got up, the twinkle in his eyes undiminished. "I should get back to the others. Don't want them to feel abandoned."

"I'll join in a moment," I said.

Jim nodded and left while I sat collecting my thoughts, noticing a clock on the far wall, the time blinking 7:08. The numbers flashed rhythmically, hypnotically. It would soon read 7:09, I thought. As surely as night follows day.

Except, perhaps, if we succeeded in sending data into the past. From that moment on, the future could no longer be guaranteed. If new data were inserted in the flow of time, the tide would likely change. That was the point of our intervention.

The clock blinked 7:09 and I jumped. I wondered if it were possible to live moment to moment—never certain if each moment would be the last. No, I thought, the mind couldn't sustain that degree of uncertainty. Anticipation is too ingrained in our thinking. It maintains its own momentum. The lighted numbers of a clock, the unfolding notes of a melody, the pulsing beats of a heart. Belief in the future is etched in our brains. Unless our work transforms that belief from a certainty to mere possibility.

***

Anansi's accelerated shrinkage kept me in the Imaging Chamber, away from Mother and Nelson, for two day-night cycles. The urgency and overtime grated on all of us, but my irritability was becoming a distraction for my coworkers. They demanded I take the break they'd decided I needed.

I missed Nelson terribly and owed him a visit, but I had unfinished business with Mother that was immediate and inescapable. I had to talk with her. Our last conversation had been a jumble of baffling riddles. Juba's input only made matters worse. Mother was shifting out of phase with my sense of her, my memory of her, and I had to try to set things right. Or so I'd hoped.

I sighed at the sight of her in the nursery before she saw me approaching, and my hopes seemed to pass from me with that breath. She was leaning over three girls seated at a round toddler table, speaking softly to them—my explanation for why their faces turned up to hers like flowers toward the sun. This was not the woman who'd raised me. This was not the woman who'd ruled over her fiercest rivals with such power, she became their most reviled idol.

Yet she seemed so content, her face and shoulders so free and relaxed. More content, I thought, than I had the right to hope for, given her illness. My thankfulness for her contentment mixed with my sadness over her slipping away from me. My conflicting emotions must have leaked into my appearance and speech when I asked to talk with her alone.

"You okay, dear?" she asked after we entered my pod.

"No, not really. I found Juba and—"

"Your father," she said. "King Juba. Your father. Kelvin Anueche." She sat at my com-desk, I on the bed. "For nothing is hidden that will not become manifest," she continued, "nor any secret that will not come to light."

I shook my head. "None of this makes sense. If you're so pleased about the truth being revealed, why hide it in the first place? For money? To avoid something criminal?"

"No, no, no. We weren't avoiding anything. We weren't trying to recover anything. We were simply undoing our past. Rendering it null and void. Making a new commitment to ourselves as compelling as our first. Till death do us part. The death of our marriage."

"Word games," I said.

"Your father ended all ties to his past," she said. "A kind of self-destruction, no?"

"Well …"

"But also a rebirth. He devoted himself to being reborn. A touch of madness? Perhaps. A conceit normal people might not understand. But your father and I never dedicated ourselves to being normal. I assure you; we were not."

"Lloyd mentioned people like you and … my father."

"Your pollster? He gave you information? Odd, no?"

"I asked him about a man who'd written graffiti on a wall in the capital. The night I returned from New York. In a poor neighborhood, a ways from downtown. No cameras. Unseen, except for me. And he saw me watching. Fanatics, Lloyd called people like him. People who worship secrecy."

"No worship," Mother said. "Nothing like that at all. Your father and I just accepted secrecy. It was necessary for what we'd planned. I assume we weren't the first … or the last."

I thought of Gregory's virus. And Ramsey's project. And forced myself to stop thinking.

"What did the man write?" Mother asked. "The graffiti."

I hesitated, annoyed by the distraction. Then I lingered on its meaning.

"Well," she said. "Do you remember?"

"Not only the guilty have reason to fear."

47

I wasn't allowed to visit G.G. Gregory by myself, of course. Not after our last encounter. But I did demand to see him. Jim accompanied me to Gregory's cell.

I'd begun to worry that our project's success could mean Gregory might ... what? Die? Vanish? Transform into someone else? An innocent version of himself, perhaps? I would've felt cheated if I hadn't confronted the person who'd unleashed his curse upon the world. At least one last time. Even if from behind a phalanx of newly appointed bodyguards.

Jim and I led an entourage of a half-dozen or so people down the corridors toward Gregory's cell. I'd assumed Jim would be annoyed by this distraction from our work, but he offered only mild, lip service displeasure and instead mentioned an artifact he wanted me to see, objet d'art he thought offered insight into Gregory's mind. It wasn't clear why we needed to visit Gregory's cell to view this so-called artifact, but I'd grown accustomed to opacity.

"He says he doesn't mind dying," Jim told me along the way. "He just doesn't like being told when he'll die."

"So he thinks he'll be executed," I said.

"We've denied it," Jim said, "but he doesn't believe us. Of course, there's no way of knowing what will happen to him when his time comes. If it will come. Or how it will come."

A woman walking behind us muttered something, then her footfalls and voice grew more distant, softer, as we continued.

"Personally," Jim said, "I assume his keeper will show up at his cell one day and Gregory will be gone. His sentence unseen ... at least by us. Ironic, eh? In our age of Transparency. No martyr, no villain. Simply nothing."

He slowed and stroked his chin. "Well, not so simply, actually," he added. "Unwriting history, I mean. It's proven to be anything but simple."

"What if he dies?" I asked. I had more than Gregory's fate in mind as I posed my question. "If he dies in captivity?"

"He hopes to be buried in Oxford," Jim said. "Oxford, England. He's never been there, but a British woman described it to him once. One of his accomplices. He liked the picture she painted. Springtime. Bluebells in bloom."

When we turned onto the hallway leading to Gregory's cell, Jim raised his arm to halt our procession. "Father?" he called out.

"Yes?" a husky voice replied.

I turned to see a man sheathed in semi-transparent black broadcloth walking forward. His bodysuit seemed bonded to his middle-aged body while a rainbow stole was draped over his shoulders, down to his hips.

"I asked Father Stephens to join us on our way," Jim said. "Franciscan friar from Boston."

"Gregory's Catholic?" I asked.

"No," Jim said. "At first he objected to our assigning the priest as his spiritual advisor. He eventually warmed up to the companionship, I guess. Now Father Stephens actually is his spiritual advisor. Of course, our goal was to learn as much from Gregory as we could."

"Transparency in the confessional," I thought out loud.

"Absolutely," Jim said. "Where better to find truth?"

Father Stephens and I nodded mutual greetings while Jim positioned the priest at the head of our entourage. "A friendly face in the crowd," Jim whispered.

As we approached Gregory's cell, we circled a transparent, shimmering cube that seemed to be an empty holographic stage. Finally facing Gregory, I notice he looked thinner than when I'd seen him, even under the stiff sackcloth shirt and thick fabric pants he was wearing now. His pale bare feet seemed oddly incongruous with his coarse, opaque clothing.

"To what do I owe the honor?" Gregory said, his gaze sweeping over our group, landing on me.

"Fitima wanted a follow-up visit," Jim said, "and we thought it best she have an escort." A brief silence signified everyone understood Jim's meaning.

"Oh, a follow-up," Gregory said. "Which might explain the appearance of the stage." We all glanced at the shimmering cube, still without any images.

"Thought she might want to see a side of you she hasn't seen," Jim said. "G.G. Gregory, the artist."

"Why not?" Gregory said. "You're in control, my good man. Make it happen."

Jim walked to the wall opposite Gregory's cell and swiped his hand over a small section halfway up, and an instrument panel appeared, either installed or camouflaged, I couldn't tell. He input data into the panel and the shimmering cube began to sparkle with red and blue flashes that elongated into strings that looped and twirled in space, then connected, one by one, into what appeared to be neural networks of a human body, then several bodies that morphed into bone and flesh, people, several life-size people who milled about the newly crowded space. One of these avatars walked toward me, and I found myself stepping back, making way for him, until he stopped at the invisible wall of the cube.

Gregory snickered. "Don't be fooled by images."

"I know these are holograms," I said.

Then several of the bodies met and merged and reemerged, intact, their fusion and separation unsettling, as though we were witnessing something unnatural.

"Is not all, one?" Gregory said.

"The name of this piece," Jim said.

"This piece?" I said.

"His what? Art?"

Jim nodded.

"Collective consciousness," Gregory said.

I refused to look at him, his smug tone disgusting me. "How?" I asked Jim. I didn't speak what I hoped was implied: how could this man possess the skill, the equipment, the budget, the time ... to create art in addition to unleashing evil on the world.

"We weren't interested in how," Jim said. "We were interested in what and why. And who ... who comprised his social network. That Oxford, English woman? She, among others, collected his work."

"Are these people running around free?" I said. "Have they been prosecuted? Punished?"

"What's this if not punishment?" Gregory said, his outthrust arms seizing my attention. "I'm the stand-in for my accomplices. Can you imagine the mass hysteria if they were all tried?"

"We wanted the tick-tock of his mind," Jim said. "His art helped."

"Art is illusory," Gregory said derisively. "Figments. Phantoms. Like these," he said, pointing the holograph bodies. "Sure, I wanted to express an idea. Make a statement. Leave an impression. But only nature can create what's truly real. Like our virus. Like de-evolution. Now, that's real! As an artist and as a scientist, I can only re-create. I'm satisfied with that."

By now I'd forgotten why I'd returned to see this man. To curse him? To have his image so etched in my mind, I could picture him dissolving into nothingness? Certainly not to hear more of his nonsense.

Gregory continued pointing to the bodies in the cube, merging and rematerializing like ghosts, reminding me of the death and destruction his virus had wrought, that he had wrought, but with the illusion of continuity. Yes, all illusory, I thought.

"When you see a rose," Gregory said, "you don't see petals, leaves, and thorns. You see a flower. When you watch a dancer, you don't see arms, legs, and torso. If you watch long enough, closely enough, you see a dance. Unity. A composition. That's where understanding lies: in the union of disparate elements like the oneness of disparate souls. Understanding is knowing that wholeness. The trick is to be able to see wholeness even when looking at only one piece of it."

"Their dogma," Jim said. "Their rationale for de-evolution, as they call it. Elevating those who embody interpersonal synthesis by removing those who embody interpersonal dominance. Collaboration inherits the earth."

"Which explains our presence, brothers and sisters," Gregory said. "We, the survivors. Rejoice in that. Sure, mourn the others, but rejoice in our natural proclivity to work together without dominating. Rejoice! Don't be seduced by vain survivor's guilt."

"Utter nonsense," Jim muttered.

"Oh, please," Gregory said. "My visitor here proves my point." He stared at me. "You're the catalyst for your team's synergy. You're the addition that makes the whole greater than the sum of its parts. And your team's collective consciousness suffers no evil trees, eh Father?"

Father Stephens glanced at Jim apologetically, as if to disclaim any association with Gregory. He then turned to the prisoner. "Evil trees?" he muttered.

"Evil trees," Gregory repeated. "Overbearing leaders. Evil trees bring forth evil fruit. As the Good Book says, Father, a tree that brings forth evil fruit must be cut down and cast into the fire."

The priest took several steps back, his gaze darting among us. "He's distorting it. He's misinterpreting it, Mathew 7: 17!"

"You have no right!" I said. "You have no right to decide good and evil!"

"I simply spun the wheel," Gregory said. "Set the wheel in motion. Nature decides. Nature creates."

48

The Temple of Heart and Mind was as dim, cool, and dry as I recalled from my first visit, but this time a hint of incense hung in the air. The scent added an aura of mystery that matched my reasons for returning there. I'd come to untangle what I knew to be true from what I'd imagined. I'd been surprised to realize how closely entwined the two had become. The chamber's gray shadows seemed a good place to untangle my jumbled thoughts.

I nearly leapt into the pew in front of me at the touch on my shoulder.

"Sorry," Nelson whispered. He gave me a moment to catch my breath. "I take it you want to be alone."

I shrugged, trying to decide.

"Feel free to chase me away," he continued.

I slid along the pew and patted the space beside me where he sat down.

"Lots of celebrating in the Imaging Center yesterday," he said. "I figured this would be a good time to catch up with you." I felt his gaze on me. "Right or wrong?"

"Thanks," I said. The empathy in his eyes made me truly thankful.

"Success, I take it."

"Sorry you couldn't be with us," I said. "The stakes were so high. Jim opted for solidarity—the synergy of our team. For good luck, I guess."

"So, success."

"Yes," I said. "The breakthrough we'd prayed for."

"And yet," he offered tentatively, "you look like you've drawn a penalty."

I glanced at him and rubbed my forehead, knowing he was right. "It's the strangest thing."

"Most discoveries are," he said.

"You never imagine …," I said. "You never imagine yourself making a discovery. Or maybe you imagine it, but you realize it's make-believe. A dream. Just your imagination. While you go about your work. Your workaday work. We make observations, not discoveries. We observe to find out if what we see corresponds with theory."

"And I guess you finally saw your probe disappear inside Anansi. The trickster finally showed her cards."

"My first impulse was to deny what I saw. But I couldn't deny the data. Or the applause or the hugs or the tears of joy."

"Victory!" Nelson said.

He was so eager to boost my spirits and I wanted to comply. I mustered the best smile I could.

"You also never imagine yourself marking the end of an era," I said. "History happens to other people."

"The end of an era?" Nelson said. "Not a beginning?"

"Both," I said. "We twisted the arrow of time. We now know time isn't linear, at least, not exclusively. We've shown we can send the present into the past. We've changed the very idea of making history."

"Exactly as you intended," Nelson said.

"True enough. And if a tree falls in the forest, but there's nobody around to hear it?"

Nelson laughed. "Are you playing quantum theory games with me?"

I shook my head. "Very here-and-now, actually. We're not sharing our findings. No one will learn about our discovery. We're maintaining absolute secrecy."

"Back in the days of Transparency that would've bothered you," he said.

I smiled at him. "Back in the day," I said. "It's the reason I left the Institute. Ramsey's insistence on secrecy."

I tried to read his eyes, trying to decipher how I was measuring up to his expectations. But regardless, my decision was firm, even if mysterious, all the more so to me.

"You wonder when things change," I continued. "When your ideas shift. Or maybe it's a matter of shifting so slowly you hardly notice."

"But they have shifted."

"The stakes had grown larger than I'd ever imagined. And personal. God, I hate to admit that, but it's true. Saving Mother became my tipping point for saving the world. And maybe, too, making up for my mistake for not saving her earlier."

The faintest of melodies drifted from behind the altar in front of us. Children's voices, I thought. Nelson heard it, too, but eagerly returned to me.

"And your discovery," he asked, "too dangerous to share?"

"I accepted Ramsey's principle that extraordinary science calls for extraordinary safeguards. Secrecy, even. But it still troubles me … the loss of Transparency. Our success grew from what others handed down to us. One of the joys of discovery is sharing it with others, especially those who come after. But now? Dead end."

"Is that the penalty you've drawn?" he asked. "The reason for your glum, you know…," he paused to mimic my earlier sour expression.

"I'm not sure," I said. "I'm not sure I like the person I've become. I feel wiser, but less… Or maybe it's just that humanity feels less … less trustworthy. *Is* less trustworthy. It seems like a dark cloud has shadowed the world. My world, at least."

"Our world," Nelson said. "Look around you. The devil revealed himself and you and your people plan to take him out. Erase him. Hallelujah!"

I smiled at him, revealing, as best I could, my admiration, my thankfulness for his company. "You know, I never heard about the devil except in church. As a kid, what scared me most was that the devil always hid in disguises. It made me paranoid. I mean, the very people you loved and respected and trusted could actually be the devil camouflaged. But then you grow up and come to understand Transparency guards against that kind of trickery. And now we learn Transparency was no guarantee against deception. The devil really was capable of hiding from us."

"Even his victims were capable of hiding from us," Nelson said. "Hiding from themselves, even. Cloaked in the camouflage of respectability. Their authority. Their positions of leadership granted them the benefit of the doubt."

I winced at his reminder of Mother as a victim. It was one of those tangles I wanted to untie but couldn't.

"Sorry," he said softly, watching me.

I glanced around at the chamber's bare granite walls and blinked tears down my cheek. "I've always believed in the sanctity of life," I said. "Never had to think about it, really. I guess that makes me lucky. But now I find myself on the verge of violating that belief ... on the verge of negating G.G. Gregory's life, and I've searched my soul for a sense of guilt, but I can't find any. I feel the opposite of guilt. I feel righteous. I'm so, so hopeful we'll be able to do away with him. And his virus. Even if it means upending the world as we know it." I swiped the tears from my eyes. "That's my hope, actually: to upend the world as we know it."

Once again, soft music came from behind the altar, sounding like a children's choir. The softness of their melody and a sense of piety from the incense buoyed my spirits. There were other tangled thoughts I'd been trying to unravel, abstracted, intellectualized thoughts that had nothing to do with quantum flux equations but everything to do with the man sitting beside me. I slipped my hand over his and watched as he raised his eyebrows and squinted at me curiously.

"I've been afraid," I said.

He sighed, then glanced at our coupled hands. "Reluctant, I'd call it." He looked up and smiled. "*Very* reluctant."

"No, afraid," I said. "I made it sound like reluctance, and it was to a degree. I didn't want to settle for convenience. You know, the predictable. The boss's daughter and the boss's assistant synch up. So clichéd. But mostly I was afraid."

I followed his lead and looked at our hands, an interlaced two-tone sculpture. Casual. Relaxed.

"I'm not sure where that fear came from," I said. We sat quiet a while. Comfortably quiet.

"Damon said we've been reared to fear the yes inside us," Nelson said.

"I can hear him saying that."

We offered Damon a moment of silence.

"My biggest regret is not asking Mother why she didn't remarry," I said. Nelson raised his eyebrows as if to suggest the obvious solution.

I shook my head. "No, I can't ask her now. Besides, her decision has nothing to do with my choices."

Nelson laughed. "Especially since she was so eager to play matchmaker for you!" I laughed with him and felt his gentle squeeze of my hand.

"And now?" he asked.

How do I say *I desperately want to stop the bleeding* without sounding insane?

He shifted in the pew to face me, our hands still united.

"I'm a civil engineer, Fitima. I work with stuff I know. Air. Land. Water. Even in outer space, I'm familiar with whatever is, or is not, at my disposal. But with people … with you … I'm dealing with the unknown. Trying to figure out what works, what doesn't. As an engineer, the problems I face yield to my design. With you I don't have that choice."

It felt like he was speaking for me. Using his words, but conveying my thoughts, my feelings. Except without mentioning fear.

"I think I was afraid to fail," I said. "I thought any relationship was so fraught with risk of failure. Now I'm thinking what's the worst that could happen? Obviously, I'd prefer you love me as I love you, Nelson, but would failure be so horrible? Why? Pride? Who convinced me I was above failure? I think I know the answer, but it isn't relevant. I have the freedom to take that risk. I have the freedom to declare my *yes*."

He looked at me with eyes that said he'd heard every word I'd spoken yet hoped I wouldn't speak another. I had no reason to. We smiled at each other as we stood. "We'll reach my pod before yours," he said.

I nodded and we exited the Temple, our hands still joined. A tiny laugh escaped me.

"I'm almost afraid to ask," he said.

"A funny thought," I replied. "Time to put theory into practice."

49

We fell onto his bed, me beneath him, but my sensation of falling continued as he hugged my shoulders and we kissed, and I held onto him and that sinking feeling. We undressed in the half-light of his pod, and I imagined the moon looking down on us as the camera lens glinted a pale beam from the corner of the ceiling. A greedy hunger boosted me on top of him and I floated like a seabird on gentle waves, up and down, over and over, flesh on flesh, soul on soul, riding to another place, on an actual moon-lit, star-strung night on actual flight.

He nuzzled my neck and breathed a thought too softly for me to hear. "What?" I whispered.

His lips parted to speak, but I placed a finger over them.

"Shh," I said, and glanced at the surveillance camera glowing like the moon. "Whisper it to me."

He drew me closer and sighed our secret in my ear.

***

We lay there a long while, face to face, a comfortable talking distance between us, but a comfortable quiet, also.

"I don't mean to upset you," he said, "but I have to ask."

I considered the idea of his upsetting me at that moment and was pleased that nothing came to mind. I nodded for him to continue.

"Your mother," he said. "How is she?" Before I could estimate a reply, he continued, "I wish I'd called on her more."

I lived with that regret myself.

"She's ... all right?" I replied, surprised by my intonation.

"She's changing. I think that's what's kept me away," he said.

"I understand. I used to visit three, four times a day. But I couldn't accept the changes. Not at first. I'd skip a visit. Then I'd skip a day. Then two. I wrestled with guilt.

"Then I didn't. Then I wrestled with shame for not feeling guilty. And the shame proved too awful to live with. I had to return to her. But she was slipping away. Slipping away from me. Slipping away from herself. She was losing connection to her past ... to our past.

"On each visit, I prepared myself to meet a different Mother. A potentially different Mother, anyway. A Mother whose past I might not share. On each visit, our time together would take place in the present—only in the present. I can't count on us sharing the same past, so why go there? So, we will have to share one endless present."

"Kind of ironic, no?" Nelson said. "Given our hopes to change the past."

I thought back to my conversation with Jim. "There's people-time and there's cosmic time. I live with Mother in present people-time. For me, cosmic time is mathematical. It will unfold as it will."

Nelson smiled. "You see mathematics in everything."

"In the flight of smoke rising in air," I said, recalling a forgotten professor's fanciful line. "In the swing of lovers' arms waving goodbye."

"Or waving hello," he said, reaching out to pull us closer.

***

We breathed in synch for quite a while, improbably so, as we lay side by side looking up at the dimly lit ceiling.

"You remember drinking gin and coconut water at Mother's camp?" I asked.

"Of course," he said. "I remember carving open the coconut with my machete. Trying to impress you."

"You remember your toast to Mother and me?"

He shifted onto his side, and I could feel his gaze. "Uh oh," he said.

"A Chinese proverb, you told me," I prodded.

"I hope it was gracious," he said.

"You raised your glass and toasted me and Mother: *strong hearts scare away bad luck.*"

Perhaps, like me, he needed a moment to reflect on the irony … on the misfortune that followed us since that toast. But that wasn't my point.

"You saw Mother and me as alike, as having strong hearts."

"That's how I see you," he said.

"I'm just confused," I said, rolling on my side to look at him. "Why her and not me? I mean, being susceptible to the virus."

He sighed. "I guess similar doesn't mean identical."

I shifted on my back to stare at the ceiling. He was right, of course, and I knew Mother and I were not identical. As a child, the difference between us had worried me. How often had I been reassured by adults that my princess-self would someday match Mother's queen-self?

They'd noticed the difference. Her take-charge demeanor compared to my tendency to follow and support. Her insistence on getting her way. My willingness to compromise. Her delight in issuing orders and her displeasure receiving them. True, Mother and I were not identical, and I never did grow to match her inclination toward command, but the differences between us were not mutually exclusive. Not black versus white. Surely there are shades of gray between them. And it made no sense to declare a penchant for leadership universally bad, and collaboration, universally good.

"Gregory's insane," I muttered. "Ridding the human race of leaders as if you could divide people."

"The dividing's been done," Nelson said. "The virus divides. Biology is destiny, as someone once said. At least in this instance it is. Let's just hope it's not the last."

***

Lying quietly next to Nelson called to mind how much I missed talking with him and a matter I desperately wanted to discuss. But how to trace the matter back to its beginning?

"I had a nightmare," I said.

"I've had many," he said. "Sorry. Don't mean to upstage you."

"No, that's okay. I'll tell you mine. Yours?"

"Incomprehensible. Too incoherent to remember. Except each very scary."

"Mine, too, of course. But memorable. Too much so."

"Too upsetting to tell?" he asked.

"No. That's why I mentioned it." I took a deep breath and called up the sights and sounds that had haunted me since that night. "It started with smoke. Layers and layers of it. Thick. I thought they were clouds at first, or fog, except for the crackling fire. Didn't see flames, though. Just heard the snapping and popping. And hissing. Rain falling on fire. But there were breaks in the smoke, clear patches that showed what was burning. Mother's villa."

My voice cracked with those words, over that image, still vivid, over the believability of the fantasy.

"Very upsetting," Nelson said. "The villa facsimile we saw at the hospital, right?"

I nodded. "We saw the seaside view. In my dream, the entire villa was engulfed in smoke. I watched, paralyzed. I sensed I was dreaming and tried to wake up, but I couldn't. And then I heard a scream. A woman's. But I saw no one." I paused to catch my breath. "That's when I woke up."

Nelson's breathing was slow and steady, contemplative, it seemed to me, but no longer synched with my own.

"Longing," he said finally. "Sorry, I guess that's obvious."

"I visited via the Repository," I said. "I had to see it."

"See it's still standing," he said.

"And then some," I said.

"Excuse me?" he said.

"It's still standing," I said. "And lived in."

"What? Not ... not ..."

"Chik!" I said quickly, before he could say King Juba, the name I didn't want to hear spoken and the idea I didn't want to consider. "Chik's taken up residence there. Squatting, actually. Alone."

"You talked to her," he said.

"I wanted to tell you, but there's been so much on my mind. I've been so muddled. When I needed to be clear. For the project. Then there was, you know ... you. You and me."

"Okay," he said in a tone that suggested he was still weighing what I'd said. "Well, you spoke to her. What did she say?"

"The first thing is she didn't have to acknowledge being there. She didn't have to answer my call. But she did. And she did so without fear of reprisal. Despite trespassing. Despite being AWOL."

"So she's ...," he began and tapped his forehead.

"No, she's quite sane. Can't say the same for her superiors, though. Basically, Chik deserted, and the senior officers were lost in their own personal insanities. So she ran, hid out, but got the sense she wasn't being pursued. Given the chaos she left behind, this irrationality seemed rational. She knew we were fugitives so she looked up Mother's residencies, found the villa, and figured it would be vacant. At least, officially. She wasn't sure about possible intruders like herself. Once she saw the villa had been abandoned, she moved in."

"And disabled surveillance?"

"No," I said. "She didn't. Given what she'd seen at headquarters, she assumed no one would be watching. She decided to test her assumption. Turned out she was right. At least she believes so."

"So accountability has all gone to hell?" Nelson said, half-question, half-assertion.

"Seems our highest officials have been excused of their incompetency," I said.

"You have to imagine Chik telling me this as she polishes off the last pint of gelato in our fridge."

"I liked Chik," Nelson said as though he were imagining just what I'd suggested.

"If by like you mean she was the least scary of the bunch," I said.

"Sorry," he said. "Go on."

"She told me our legislature has repealed statutes that provide for removing incompetent leaders. Nationally and locally. The term *incompetent official* has been labeled contradictory. Paradoxical. Essentially, there's no such thing. Officials now serve at the pleasure of ... well, at the pleasure of themselves."

"Making Trinidad a pariah nation," Nelson whispered.

"Not really. Our homeland's following a trend. The U.S. led the way with its repeal of their Twenty-Fifth Amendment, or some such amendment in the twenties. Chik wasn't sure and I didn't pursue it. In any event, that amendment laid out procedures for replacing a disabled president. Their legislature decided the amendment was too political and its application too partisan. Potentially too messy. At least according to Chik."

Nelson took several deep, nearly mournful breaths. "And you were too … what, too muddled to tell me this?"

Shame welled up like a knot in my throat and it took a few moments to untangle it and confess. "I know I was wrong. Not to tell you, I mean. Not to tell you sooner. I knew it all along. From first hearing it. I don't know what stopped me. Or maybe I do. At some point my reluctance turned to refusal. I decided Chik's story was one torment too many."

"You spared me," he said.

"And myself, too, I guess."

"And like you said, there was the question of us … you and me."

"Yes, yes, there was that, too."

His hand slid into mine and I flinched, surprised.

"Self-imposed quarantine," he said.

"You and me both." I turned to look at him as he stared at the ceiling.

"I'm not innocent," he said.

"What do you mean?"

"I'm talking about Damon," he said.

I held my breath, afraid to hear my worst fear. "Can't say how he is," Nelson said. "I don't know."

"But you know something," I said.

"He sent a message. Don't know how he accessed my com-desk."

"But only a message? He didn't try two-way?"

Nelson shook his head. "Deliberately."

"He didn't want to talk to you? Afraid?"

"No. Not afraid. Not under surveillance. Not on the windfarm." He shifted to look at me.

"Seems Chik's onto something. Don't know what, though. Anarchy loosed upon the world? Something."

"You saved it? The message?"

"Of course," he said.

He got up from the bed and activated his com-desk. Multihued brown pixels coalesced above its surface into Damon's placid face, his peaceful smile once again reminding me of a Black Buddha that came to mind when I first met him. The blur of greenery behind him appeared more forest-like than windfarm and I immediately suspected he had every intention of keeping his whereabouts unknown. Nelson paused the image and slid back into bed beside me.

"I watched it several times," he said. "I won't watch it again after this." He activated the recording and leaned against me, shoulder to shoulder.

"My dear Nelson," Damon said.

"Like a letter?" I interjected, surprised.

"Shhh," Nelson said.

"We had such fun together," Damon continued. "I have no other friend, really. It was either me, or me and you, actually or in spirit. Our bond has been in thinking we were different. I mean, we thought of ourselves as similar, but different from other people. When all's said and done, though, I'm more different than you. You're much more like other people. You believe in the ups and the downs of life. You believe good times will follow bad. You carry optimism.

"But I now believe, deep down in my soul, good times won't follow bad times. And if one truly believes this, one's view changes. And given this certainty, you come to figure you're better off choosing utter recklessness. Because in never-ending bad times, recklessness allows at least a modicum of splendor. A touch of grandeur. A small scrap of glory. So that's my choice to go out in a blaze. I can see you now shaking your head, tsk-tsking. That's how we're different. I hope you can accept that fact. I hope you understand."

I wasn't prepared for the blank space that replaced Damon's image. "That's all?"

Nelson didn't answer.

"I'm sorry," I said, not in apology but with sadness.

"Almost like a suicide note," Nelson said. "I don't understand it."

Because you believe in optimism, I thought. Gratefully. "He escaped the windfarm," I said.

"Fugitive," Nelson said. "Like Chik."

"You received this a while ago?" I said. "You spared me?"

Nelson gazed into the center of the pod. "Anarchy loosed upon the world," he muttered. "Makes you wonder if it's better to be down here in this bunker."

50

Mother was sitting at her com-desk watching a young woman twirl in front of a full-length mirror, her dress swirling around her like a cyclonic stream. The woman stopped to admire herself in the mirror, her figure bronzed and statuesque beneath the transparent dress that fit her like shimmering second skin. It was a holograph of Mother's younger self.

"We create our own miracles," she said as I stepped closer.

I stared at the dress, its design, when it dawned on me. "Is that a … "

"Bridal gown," she said.

I searched the holograph for a time stamp but saw none. "When was this?"

"We can make a moment like this last forever," she said, turning to me while her younger image stood frozen behind her. "Memory is like that, too." She closed her eyes. "Voilà – there it is, a vision, for as long as you can recall."

"Your wedding day?" I asked. Why hadn't I seen it before? Why hadn't I sought it out? "Or before?" I continued. "After? Whichever, you look beautiful. And happy."

"Thank you, dear. I was. I *am* happy! Reaching back into the past." She turned and pointed to the holograph. "That's why I live in the Repository."

I stepped back to observe the woman Mother had become on this visit. "Have you eaten lately?" I asked.

She turned to flash her annoyance. "Hand me that protein wafer in my top drawer."

I grabbed the sealed wafer and handed it to her, noticing, even from behind her, the slouch of her shoulder. "And sleep? Sleep, Mother?"

"I miss being able to touch it, though," she said. Her finger traced the ethereal contours of the dress in the holograph. "I miss the feel of the fabric. On my skin. In my hands." She pulled her finger back into a fist. "It's like a pressed flower you'll never hold."

"You have to take care of yourself, Mother," I said.

"Truly," she said. "I am. Taking care." She turned to me. "Do you ever wake up and say to yourself: What I wouldn't give to slip into a lovely crystal organza suit today? Sheer. Striped. Off-white." She smoothed the translucent fabric of her jumpsuit against her thighs. "I'm not very fond of these standard issue clothes," she continued. "Uniforms, really. As if we were warehoused. Like in an asylum. Or worse, a prison."

"Mother, I'm concerned about how much time you're spending …."

I rested my hands on her shoulders, aching to help her find some measure of peace, but not knowing how. I watched the frozen image of her youthful self in the shimmering transparent bridal gown and wondered if a source for serenity wasn't displayed right there in front of us. Reminiscence. Had I ever seen Mother dance? I'd never viewed her as a child. I'd hardly ever viewed myself as one. And I'd not visited Grandma in the Repository as I'd promised myself.

"Perhaps we can explore together," I offered. "You and me. There's so much there I've … I've missed. So much I've paid little attention to, to be honest. And you said so yourself, faces fade away. Places lose their features. Special occasions become … well, fragments of recollection. Come with me, Mother. Into the Repository. It's something we can do together."

"You would do that?" she asked. "Spend time with me visiting the Repository?"

My heart sank at her astonishment as though my offer was far beyond her expectation. "Yes," I said. "Yes, I would. I want to."

She turned back to the holograph. "This gown's probably out of style."

I shrugged, weighing whether to mention that we wouldn't neglect eating and sleeping.

"The fabric still shimmers," she said. "I may not be able to feel it, but it doesn't fade. That's one benefit of holographs in the Repository. They don't age and die." She turned and offered me a sly wink.

Then she cleared her throat with a flourish. "The past gives meaning to the present," she said. She smiled at me knowingly, as though she'd solved a riddle. "That's the value of the Repository. If you take advantage."

"An accusation?" I whispered.

"An invitation," she said.

She returned to the holograph and activated the image in slow motion, her youthful self twirling dreamily in front of the mirror, as though dancing under water. The image, Mother observing the image, the juxtaposition of past and present, mesmerized me.

"I wonder if that applies to the future," I whispered.

"If what applies to the future?" Mother asked.

"If the future can give meaning to the present. That's what we're hoping with our message to the past. I'm not sure, though. Prophecy can be easily dismissed."

"So can the past," she said. "Easily dismissed, I mean."

She turned and grabbed my wrist. Our gazes locked and I'm sure she saw my surprise but only held me tighter.

"If you were to lose your hand," she said, "you would surely know it."

I pulled back for an instant, then surrendered to her grip.

"But if you lose an ancestor …," she continued, dangling her question, "what then?" She released my wrist. "You won't change your mind, will you?" she asked. "About exploring the Repository?"

I shook my head and heard myself ask a question even though I thought I knew the answer. "Where are you going with this, Mother?"

"I haven't forgotten them, Fitima. The ghosted bodies. Their remains. Erased history."

"The ancestors," I said. "The slaves' graves."

"Still no record in the Repository," she said. "I read his name. Block letters carved deep and scorched black on the stump of a cedar. Where the bark had been stripped. EZEKIEL ELIAS JOHNSON. REST IN PEACE."

"What you wanted to preserve," I said softly, hesitantly, uncertain about her return to the beginning of her breakdown. "The gravesite. A miracle to have found it."

"You had to know to look," she said. "A single cedar cut down in the swamp? A single stump? You had to know to sweep away the muck and moss on the surface. You had to see with your body. You had to see with your mind. You had to know where to look. You had to know *to* look."

I found myself concentrating on her every gesture, facial expression, change in her tone of voice. Searching for signs of madness. Hearing her only vaguely yet following her logic.

"I wish we knew his story," she said. "That's the sadness of it. We know someone cared enough to bury him. We know he had courage. He'd rather hide in the swamp than serve as a slave. But anything more has been lost with whoever last spoke his name."

I remembered the lead she wanted her superiors to follow: to declare the slave's grave holy ground. To strengthen the ties between the living and the dead. That's what she wanted the grave markers to do. That's what her superiors were reluctant to embrace. I felt ashamed now of my own previous reluctance.

"The Ministers back home are ignoring me," she said. "I've been trying to reach them but nothing. And me, a fugitive! You'd think I'd get their attention. They must have bigger fish to fry."

I stared blankly through her younger self, her image pirouetting slowly in the holograph. "As for you and me," I said, "we'll retrieve family gatherings. Birthdays. Anniversaries. Graduations."

"Weddings," she added.

Neither of us mentioned funerals, but it did cross my mind. "Storytelling," I said.

"Yes," she said. "I'd like that."

***

Chilled and wet from sweat, I shivered against Nelson's body. "You okay?" he asked as he held me.

"Yes, yes," I stammered. But I was not okay.

"Bad dream," he said.

Was it? Yes, he was right. I pulled from his hold while stroking his arms. He was not the problem. I simply needed space.

"Yes," I managed. "Bad dream." As he must've known, because he didn't ask, he recognized it. I waited for him to add: again? Or another. He didn't.

My breathing slowed, but my chill returned, and I reached out to him this time. "Can you go back to sleep?" he asked.

I took a deep breath and tried to gather my thoughts. "Can we talk?"

He propped himself up and I followed, our adjacent arms entwined. "I'm afraid to sleep," I said.

"Dreams," he said.

"That's what I've been telling you, but it's not true." I took note of how comfortable I'd become with deception. "It'll sound crazy."

"If it does, I'll say so," he said, adding a gentle nudge.

"I'm afraid there'll be no tomorrow."

He breathed in what I assumed was a calming breath. "A little crazy," he said finally, emphasizing *little*. "Given that each morning proves you wrong."

"The problem is it doesn't. Prove me wrong, I mean. Not deep down. It's like, well, just because I was wrong that evening doesn't mean I'll be wrong the next. That's the only way I can explain it. Because each night the uncertainty returns."

"Maybe because you're afraid of the future."

"Not exactly," I said. "Sure, I'm worried about Mother. And the breakdown topside. But there's something even more frightening."

"I'm afraid to ask what that could be," he said.

"That's why I tell you they're bad dreams. Nightmares are more easily understood."

"Than what? More easily understood than ...?"

"Than no future at all. Than not waking up."

"That's been haunting you from the outset," Nelson said. "That sending a message to the past would disrupt the flow of time. But your message won't reach the black hole for months. I'd think—"

"From the moment we launched it ...," I took a deep breath, "from the moment we launched our probe, present time and our future slipped from certainty to probability. The probability of our success. The probability we can change the past. The future had always been a time of hope, an imagined time when past mistakes could be offset, made right. That future may have disappeared. From now on, the past will have to be the time that sets things right."

"And we'll have to learn to live with that," Nelson said. "Each moment as probability. From moment to moment. Embracing each as it arrives."

I sighed at thoughts I'd tried to bury. "We're no different than our ancestors," I said. "They, too, relied on contrivances to protect themselves. Watchtowers. Border walls. Radar. Laser defenses. We thought we'd surpassed them all, masterminding Transparency, a detection system so advanced, it would serve as a deterrent. But I guess we weren't much different from those who came before us, and like them, we weren't as successful as we'd imagined. Nor as invincible as we'd assumed. Perhaps our inventions will never entirely protect us from one another."

"And yet your invention may save us," Nelson said.

"Perhaps," I said.

"There's that *perhaps* again," Nelson said. "I guess that's the only way for us to imagine our future. As possibility."

***

I watched you sleep," Nelson said. "Happy to see you at peace."

I stretched and glanced around his pod. Dawn was about to break. "I think I prayed," I said.

"You *think* you prayed," he said. "A dream?"

"Yes. But it felt so real."

"Do you remember it?"

"Mostly."

"Share?" he asked.

"My dream?"

"Your prayer."

"It seems odd."

"It's not like a birthday wish. There's no taboo against sharing."

"No, but well ... it still seems odd."

"Odd as in abnormal? Or as in exceptional?"

"Why do I bother resisting?"

He shrugged playfully.

"I prayed for forgiveness," I said.

"Forgiveness for ...," he prodded.

"Did we do the right thing? Was it right morally? Practically, even."

"Such questions in a dream? Come on."

"I know. But there they were. Coming from me. In my sleep. Thinking even if we're successful and the source of evil destroyed, will success destroy us? Have we overreached?"

"I don't think of you as a prayer. Not while awake, anyway."

"I'm not. I even admitted that in my dream. I confessed to it."

"So, why pray now – even in a dream?"

"Because I feel so alone. Not lonely. Alone." I reached for his hand and squeezed it. "Even with you by my side. It's not you. It's what we've done."

"But even if you, *we*, did overreach," he said, "it was to reduce suffering in the world."

"But the arrogance of it. The conceit! That we could change history. Improve it. Oh Lord, please forgive us our vanity. Our ambition. To seize a second chance. A chance to watch over each other. Protect each other. To realize Transparency was not enough. It was just not enough."

51

I visited Mother's pod later that morning and found her at her com-desk facing the fixed focus camera in the corner above.

"Did I laugh a lot?" she said, addressing the camera. "Did I laugh a lot?" she repeated impersonally.

Motionless, I panicked. I panicked every time I couldn't understand her behavior. Who was she speaking to? I would panic and then calm myself, prepared to meet whichever embodiment of the Mother I loved.

"Did I laugh a lot," she repeated yet again. Then she noticed me. "Here, here," she said, patting the corner of her cot, "sit and help me."

I took a deep breath and sat. I glanced at the holograph atop entitled *Because you Have Lived*.

"Well, did I?" she asked me. "Did I laugh a lot? I mean back in the day as you were growing up. What would you say? A lot?"

"Yes, I'd say so." I pointed to the holograph. "What's this?"

"An inventory. An interview."

"And you're recording it?"

"It's allowed."

"Well, of course it's allowed, but ..."

"And would you say I earned respect?" she interrupted. "That question came up just before this one. Did I earn the respect of others? Over time, sum totaled. That's how I'm answering these questions. The subjective cumulative."

"Answering for whom?" I asked.

"Good question. Answering for whom? When I'm finished, we can go back and consider it. But for now, what would you say? Was I respected?"

"I certainly think so."

"By my critics? Did I earn their respect?"

I took a deep breath, recognizing I'd arrived at yet another moment I had to confess my confusion to her.

"It's an accounting, dear," she said. "As simple as that. An accounting. The subjective cumulative. Did I leave the world a better place?"

I swallowed another wave of panic. "Leave the world?"

"Yes, dear, the world. This world." She reached across the com-desk and paused the staged recording. The camera switched to normal surveillance mode.

"I guess you've been too busy to wonder about our dying down here," she said.

"Dying? Who's dying?"

"Too busy and too young," she said with a laugh. "That's not a rebuke. Just a fact. Anyway, it's good to know this place can accommodate us. Our dying, I mean." Her eyes widened at my unrestrained alarm. "Natural causes," she continued. "Nothing dramatic. Natural over time."

It wasn't as though she were revealing something I hadn't thought about. I had thought about it, and as quickly as I could, I'd drowned the idea. Now she'd revived it and brought me to the edge of where I'd refused to go, refused to see. My heart and mind were bringing into focus what had been, until that moment, a void: the idea that we would reside in that facility for the duration. That thought now repeated like an echo, resenting its forced silence: for the duration.

"This place ... your lab, whatever," she said, "it can accommodate our deaths. This place and personnel, too, I assume. I try to pick out who might be a coroner. Guessing's more fun than knowing, so I don't ask."

I had to ask, but I was terrified of her answer. "What have you seen?"

"The crematorium. Behind the altar in the Temple. It's fully automated. AI. But I imagine there's some labor involved. Minimal, probably. There's a rehearsal room back there, too. At least that's how I've used it. I've taken the children there. Those who want to sing, that is. You know, a children's choir. There'll be cause for performing at some point. A children's choir promises, well, at least *offers* the probability of longevity. The conductor not as much."

She laughed self-consciously. "Have you heard them, the children? I thought I saw you and Nelson at the Temple when we were rehearsing."

I nodded absently as leaden images flooded my mind, images I'd seen long ago in the Repository—a vault door, a cinderblock tunnel, sagging chains and pulleys. Shadows of pre-Transparency buried in memory. A huge cast iron oven. Its all-consuming fire. A horrific venting chimney.

"They'll lay us to rest in sacred space," she continued. "Like they do topside. I've seen them. The crematoriums topside, I mean. You?"

I shook my head.

"Too busy. Too young. Not a rebuke. Just a fact."

She leaned toward me and whispered. "I know I said that earlier."

"I wasn't judging."

"It's okay, it's okay," she said. "It doesn't matter, given the big picture. You know, the *ashes-to-ashes* picture."

"Please, Mother."

"It's okay," she said softly. "I only want to describe it. Or imagine it, anyway. That they'll put the ashes in glass urns. There are scores of them down here, you know. Urns, I mean. Empty, of course. On shelves along the walls of the … well, I've come to think of it as the prayer room. It's in between the crematorium and the rehearsal room. There's a marble table in the center that looks like an altar. Or it could be. They need to add a few pews, though. Just a few. The shelves holding the urns go halfway up the wall. There's a console near the entrance. All you need to do to locate and retrieve an urn is input a name into the console. If it works down here like it does topside, the urn will activate a digital display of the deceased. Perhaps even holographic. This is northern hemisphere, after all. I expect holographic. Maybe even the deceased reciting a memorial. A recording. That's what I'm hoping. That's why I'm answering questions about the life I lived. For posterity. That's what you asked. Answering for whom? For posterity. At least the posterity down here. Anyone who wants to visit me." She signaled my inclusion with her eyes.

"I'd love to include your story," she said. "Bits of it anyway. I won't steal your glory. But I'd have to mention the most important part. Even if everyone down here knows. Of how you delivered the present to the past to help save the future. That just has to be said and I'm proud to say it."

***

Mother returned to her cyber-questionnaire and begged me to help her, and I discovered I'd rather work with her than confront the truth she'd uncovered. During our discussion, I learned from the Repository that she and I were working with Ralph Waldo Emerson's criteria for having lived a successful life. Surprisingly enough, I found our conversation soothing. But even more importantly, Mother appeared to also. My only shudder came when she shifted the focus to me and that flinch was short-lived.

I acknowledged that she'd been correct about the project's selecting my story to be sent bank in time and conceded that my story was in fact the mirror image of a slave narrative. I would, in fact, represent our sense of security as bondage. And yes, I would be offering up our story to a prospective liberator, but one from our past, not our future. I had to admit these mirror imaged reversals of the slave narrative, as much because she was correct, but also to redirect her from an obsession of hers that I feared. It was an easy concession.

"I'd love to hear more about your story's destination," she said. "Time and space, I mean. Or spacetime if you don't mind me getting cosmological."

"No dates," I said. "But I can say it's back when everyone seemed to have a story to tell. Everyone!"

"Ah," she said. "Before universal surveillance decreased the urge to self-display."

"We think our story will stand out, but—"

"Lots of competition. Cyberspace brimming with postings about me, we, and our. Everybody, a memoirist. Everybody every day! But you're not sending it *to whom it may concern*. You've got specific addressees, no?"

"We have a target. Other senders have their targets."

"Other senders?"

I nodded.

"But the cost?" she said.

"The cost not to," I said.

"But no coordination?"

"Each tub on its own bottom."

She breathed a sigh of recognition. "And yours? Your target?"

"Again, I won't speak his name. Rules."

"Surely your story includes names," she said.

"The fewer proper nouns, the better. And like I said, no dates. And absolutely no technology."

She chuckled. "What's so funny?"

"Your project's version of the prime directive."

I shrugged.

"Pre-Transparency sci-fi," she said.

"Time travel?"

She shook her head. "Travel-travel. Space travel. Treks to alien worlds. The protags of these stories pledged not to interfere with alien societies. They called it their Prime Directive. To prevent the transfer of their culture and technology to extraterrestrials. They wanted to avoid intrusions like what European explorers did to native peoples of the New World."

"How quaint! Except in our case, we're *trying* to intrude. With history, no less! You can't get more intrusive than that."

"Well, yes, I see your point," she said. "I take it, *after* your intervention, you want the past to evolve its own future. Good for their self-esteem, I guess. So, no names. No dates. No technology. Nothing?"

"I can tell you our story will be delivered to a remote location. The white hole exit from the wormhole will be too powerful to risk directing it to dense populations."

"And your target? The person? No name, of course. Can you say anything?"

"His psychohistory predicts receptivity to our story."

"Psychohistory?"

"Personality traits gleaned from the Repository," I said.

"So ... we know he's a he and alive post-Transparency."

Oh, how I loved her overbroad smile of gotcha. It felt refreshingly familiar. "And that's all you get to know."

***

To Whom It May Concern:

Beyond belief, no? Of course it's beyond belief. Beyond comprehension. It would've been beyond mine if I'd received a message from the future, prefaced with instructions to "Open Me First," followed by a salutation, "To Whom It May Concern."

I'd wonder if I'd been slipped a hallucinogen. Or if I'd suddenly lost my mind. I'd pinch myself to see if I were dreaming. Perhaps look for a familiar object to determine if it appeared normal. I know Antarctica doesn't offer many familiar objects, but what about your apparatus? Does it appear normal? Perhaps I'd see if you could fly. Be cautious, because … I want to assure you: you are *not* dreaming. What you're experiencing is real. It's real for you and, unfortunately, it's real for me.

I know you don't believe the human brain is limitless in its understanding of the cosmos. You've said as much to your colleagues. You've argued with them about this. At length. I've heard you argue that, as when the first of our species first eyed the heavens, we too should drop to our knees and acknowledge that some phenomena lay beyond our reach. I've heard you express almost these exact words. I've heard you go toe to toe with some of your colleagues who've assumed otherwise. Colleagues who assumed that nothing lay beyond human understanding. I've heard you proclaim that we are not gods to your superiors and risk your professional standing. It took courage to contradict them. And you've shown that courage throughout your career.

Yes, I know this and so much more about you. After you read my story, you'll learn how and why I know. I have confidence you'll read and re-read my story. Yet I'm not sure you'll do as we ask: kill a man you've never met and have no reason to wish dead other than our testimony herein. And even then … we cannot be sure.

So I'll ask you the question I've often asked myself: do you believe God has made everything in the cosmos to His purpose—even the wicked? Do you believe the wicked predestined to commit wickedness? Or do you believe human wisdom and action have the power to save us from wickedness? Are these either/or questions?

We believe … we hope, individuals are placed in strategic points in time and space to exercise free will to choose good over evil. We believe individuals can overcome personal misgivings and choose to overcome evil experienced by persons other than themselves. We pray this is also your belief.

Epilogue

Ah, where to begin? Beginnings have lost meaning for me. But I understand prevailing perceptions of time. So, if pressed, I'd say my journey began in Antarctica with a flash of light and clap of thunder that brought me to my knees. Fog or smoke or both spread across the top of the hill where the lightning had struck—or what I imagined was lightning. Chunks of ice rained down on me while wild ideas as to what had happened raced through my mind. An approaching thunderstorm? No, not on that frozen wasteland where none had ever been recorded. An aircraft suddenly arrived, crashed, and just as suddenly disappeared? And any number of similar ideas so wild they hardly qualified as such. All quickly dismissed. All except one.

And the Lord sent thunder, hail, and lightning to the ground.

Exodus 20. A biblical passage had recently taken root in my mind. A passage I couldn't dismiss as explanation for a sudden and miraculous eruption of hail and light.

That's one place I could begin. Or I might go back earlier and say my journey began that winter in New England when I flew south to summer in Antarctica. I was returning to my research project at Ice Station AMANDA. I was a member of a team of scientists awarded a grant to observe and record neutrinos at the Antarctic Muon and Neutrino Detector Array, hence, AMANDA.

My colleagues and I, we hunt ghosts. The ghosts of massive stars. Massive, as in double-digits times the size of our sun. Stars this large live scores of millions of years of furious thermonuclear life and they don't die quietly. Their visible death-rattle may last only a few months, but their last gasp of neutrinos can continue for several thousand years. Millennia, maybe. And that's what we hunt. Neutrinos. A supernova's final exhalation.

We were delirious upon locating the dying breath from supernova SN2 987B. We knew it would yield a plethora of data. Detailed spectral, temporal, and flavor evolution of this neutrino signal couldn't help but crack the supernova mystery. Among astronomers, that is. The nature of convection, rotation, mass and a hundred other features we wouldn't have dreamed of analyzing earlier. To those of us who work in supernova theory, the anticipation of discovery was palpable.

Yet, to look upon AMANDA, the uninitiated would be anything but impressed. Her vision, if one could call it that, was utterly counterintuitive. Unlike optical telescopes built high above the earth's obstructing atmosphere, AMANDA was designed to view her target *through* our planet. Earth serves as her lens. This is necessary because AMANDA's target emits neutrinos that pass through almost anything. We need high concentrations of matter in order to detect them. The best neutrino detector on earth actually is the earth—all 8000 miles of its diameter.

When a neutrino passes through the planet, there's a chance it will collide with Antarctica's polar ice and produce a burst of muon particles that emit photons ... or light, in layman's terms. Light that AMANDA's sensors can detect. It's the qualities of those light signals that provide details of supernova SN2 987B's death. And, ironically, the supernova's life.

And so, I flew south from New England in late December, as I had every winter for the last five years. My hopscotch itinerary brought me first to Langley Air Force Base, then to King George Island, Antarctica, and then to Palmer Station, a U.S. base on Anvers Island off the west coast of the Antarctic Peninsula. I spotted Anvers from the turbo chopper only two hours south of King George. The slab of barren rock and snow arose in a sea of pack ice, narrowly separated from the mainland's glacial plateau. Palmer Station near the coast is a miniature version of the station on King George with only a couple storage hangars, a cinder block main building, and a copter platform. AMANDA itself was a couple copter-hours' flight inland.

Immediately after we landed, a short roly-poly man wrapped in a blue hooded parka came waddling toward us. That was Bradford, Simon Bradford, the American station manager, and a veteran on the ice. He'd spent the last two winters at Palmer but was planning to return to the States with me at the end of the summer. The three of us walked to the main building where I met my tech teammates for that summer, three rookies from Toronto, two male technicians, and a female physician. The Canadian government was intent on providing their citizens with opportunities to participate on research projects like ours.

Project protocol required us to check and re-check the equipment and provisions we'd bring to Ice Station AMANDA, but we weren't scheduled to leave until the next day, weather permitting, so we spent most of our remaining time becoming acquainted with each other.

Bradford confided what we all quickly figured out: he was eager to leave the ice. Strangely enough, it was summer on the Ice that depressed him most. He'd grown weary of the season's promise going unfulfilled. He fretted that the air never smelled fertile like in Iowa. For him, the relative warmth of summer simply meant snow crust melted just enough to reveal outcroppings of windswept rock that might as well have remained hidden. He was mystified that I found the landscape so alluring.

I invited him to join me on a walk to the edge of the island to visit the pack ice separating us from the mainland. We re-bundled ourselves and left the copter pilot and the Canadians to debate the cross-border politics they'd seemed eager to hash out since their first meeting.

Our short stroll to the coast reminded me of the peculiarity of our surroundings as I struggled to keep up with Bradford and he tried to slow his pace to match mine as I adjusted once again to breathing while walking on The Ice. We came to a rock edge that overlooked the channel and watched large shards of ice glide past, their borders etched by black sea, thuds and groans of their collisions accompanying their passage. A small iceberg floated by, its glazed surface sparkling in the sunlight, followed by an even smaller, spiky berg, spinning slowly, pirouetting like a snowbird. I turned to Bradford, hoping the scene might charm him as it did me, but he was looking off in the distance lost in thought.

That evening, the night before our flight to AMANDA, I lay on my bunk, unable to sleep, anticipating the start of my work, kept awake by the perpetual dusk seeping through our unshaded windows. I now had second thoughts about turning down medication for insomnia. At some point, drifting between dozing and dreaming, a low rumble wound its way from outside our bunkhouse into my consciousness and I rose up on my elbows, annoyed by the ill-timed intrusion. I glanced around the room waiting for someone else to awaken, but no one stirred.

Nor did the noise of my wrapping myself for a look outside have the desired effect of waking any of them.

The frigid air stung my nostrils and I squinted through watering eyes and the low hanging fog but saw nothing to explain the noise I'd heard. I walked through the mist to the shore I'd visited earlier, and I can't say what bewildered me most. A low-pitched groan came from out of the haze above the pack ice. Then two huge icebergs floated into view, each over a hundred feet tall. But it was their shape that shook me: two vertical rectangles with a fissure down their midpoint, each with slightly rounded tops and illegible inscriptions on their surfaces. A halo crowned each slab and a white mist hovered at their base.

Now, I'd had similar religious training as your average citizen … as your average scientist. I was taught who in our congregation would most likely go to heaven, and who'd most likely burn in hell. Which creeds to follow, which to shun. Which symbols and texts to revere for what they signified. The myriad disguises the devil could take to work evil upon the world.

So the sight making its way past me echoed images as old as my childhood. It matched exactly my memory of the Tablets of the Ten Commandments Moses brought down from Mount Sinai. I understood my pounding heart and breathlessness were symptoms of self-induced hysteria, but I still believed I was witnessing something sacred. Or that I was witnessing a sign that something miraculous was about to happen. I didn't know where or when that miracle would occur, but those details didn't matter. What mattered was the feeling that had lodged in my heart. What mattered was the miracle that would take place—sometime, somewhere.

I'd calmed down considerably by morning. Perhaps sleep deprivation helped. I coaxed Bradford into a third cup of coffee at a table for just the two of us. I knew I'd eventually have to spend considerable time with this crew at Ice Station AMANDA and I couldn't risk them thinking me crazy before we'd even arrived. So, I rehearsed as casual a way to ask Bradford to explain what I'd seen that night.

Tabular iceberg, he said.

I'd never heard the term. And their joining together?

They must've calved as a pair, he said. Not that unusual.

I sipped coffee, trying to register nonchalance. I wondered aloud about the inscriptions on their surface, immediately regretting my use of *inscriptions*.

"Striations," he said, as though correcting me. Layers of snow from different snowfalls.

He stroked his beard. "They do kinda look like writing, don't they?"

I nodded, blowing a puff of steam from my cup. "And the halo?" I asked. I wish I'd had my camera."

"Iceblink," he said. "The sun reflecting off the ice. Reflecting off the clouds. And the fog. And through air of different temperatures. And densities." He laughed. "Lots going on there, eh? At least near sea ice. We're not likely to see anything like that at AMANDA. Nothing but white wasteland there." He sighed. "Yeah, too bad you didn't have your camera."

Recorded or not, the image of the tablets had been planted in my mind and a sense of wondrous anticipation arose inside me that the crew noticed and commented on. A welcomed optimism, they claimed, contrasting my enthusiasm against Bradford's stoic obligation, though he and I did our best to avoid any rivalry.

We took off for Ice Station AMANDA at dawn into the perpetual pinkish blue sky, traveling further south along the coast. After about an hour, we veered inland for thirty minutes or so before the domed rectangles of three Quonset huts appeared on the snow-covered plain.

Being inland, the AMANDA compound seemed more secluded than any of the other stations we'd visited. The coasts of those stations afforded a fanciful connection to home. At AMANDA, that imagined connection was lost.

The copter settled down on a flat patch of snowpack, the Quonset huts, only a hundred meters away, perched above the snow on four-foot-high stilts. White patches of ice dotted the huts' red walls of five-inch-thick fiberglass and the rusted oil drums and rotten timber strewn on the ground. Bradford led the way up the steps of the largest hut, kicking snow as he climbed, and yanked open its heavy, freezer-door entrance. We entered the gloom, the hut's only light coming from two nearly opaque blizzard-proof windows, while Bradford retreated back down the steps to the utility hut to start the generator and propane heater.

Our copter pilot flopped down on the nearest cot, obliged to stay until we got settled. The rest of us with more at stake inspected our mattresses and the half-stocked shelves. I was the first to test the water-free toilet and waterless shower ensconced in the tiny lavatory at the far end of the hut, our only private space. The others soon followed. The kitchen and dining area consisted of a sink, stove, fridge—for anything not requiring freezing—and two card-tables-and- chairs, all located opposite the cots and near the front door. A communication nook was installed in the hut's fourth corner.

The electric lights blinked on, and the temperature rose high enough for us to unzip our parkas and get to work storing the supplies we'd brought in the main hut. We warehoused surplus supplies in the hut housing the snowmobiles, tractors, and plows that had been delivered previously. I left for the third hut to bench-test AMANDA's apparatus, leaving the others to gas up and road-test the vehicles. Afterward, I gave the team a quick tour of AMANDA's equipment although there was little to see besides burnished chrome and digitalized baseline displays. I promised a better show after I'd turned on AMANDA's neutrino detection functions.

By evening, the furnace provided enough heat for us to finish the last of our unpacking without our parkas. Bradford declared us officially settled and we bid a melodramatic farewell to our impatient copter pilot. For our first meal at the station, Bradford broiled Atlantic cod, and we lit several candles to celebrate the occasion. After dinner, I felt the full weight of my fatigue, and one glass of brandy later, I fell into the first eight-hour sleep cycle I'd had in weeks.

So, what's the point? What's the point of recounting these details? Perhaps to differentiate between the believable and the unbelievable. Or maybe to juxtapose the two, so closely, they blend together. At least on the edge.

The next morning, we met in AMANDA's hut, and I delivered on my promise to demonstrate her brilliance, visual and conceptual, her alphanumeric reckonings scrolling across dozens of monitors on the shelving behind three Plexiglas walls, and me orchestrating her display from my central workstation. It was enough to remind them that our isolation for a month on the ice was worth the results. To a few select audiences, at least.

What they didn't know was that AMANDA's echo-map of her sub-ice sensors revealed slight anomalies I'd have to check. I logged the results of my initial tests as protocol required and, after checking the weather, whiteouts being my greatest fear, I snowmobiled several kilometers to the network of sub-surface sensors and began taking soundings of their alignments.

To my right, not in my direct line of sight, the rose-tinted sky flashed candescent, followed by the deepest rumble I'd ever heard, or felt, actually, which dropped me to my knees. I looked to where the flash had come from. A thick mist was rising on a hill about a kilometer away.

Scattered flashes sparked inside the mist—flashes that looked like lightning. I glanced back at the huts, yet another kilometer behind me, and wondered if they might've seen or heard this eruption. Nothing stirred back there, and I realized they wouldn't have detected anything from that distance given the hut's compact windows and thickly insulated walls.

I startled as snow and ice suddenly fell down on me, a shower that stopped almost as abruptly as it had started. I turned back to the hill where the mist had begun to dissipate, slowly revealing its snow-covered crest. I straddled the snowmobile and sat, wild ideas running through my mind, absurdities competing for consideration, including one I couldn't dismiss. Of course, there was no logical connection between the floating Decalogue I'd seen the night before, and the eruption I'd just witnessed. That's what my brain told me. Yet I couldn't help but feel they were somehow connected.

And the Lord sent thunder, hail, and lightning to the ground. .

I revved the snowmobile and headed for the crest. When I arrived in the vicinity, there was no mistaking the source of the blast— swirl of dust and vapor hung above a small crater in the hillside.

The mystery of it took my breath—the difference between its size and the power of its eruption. The crater was no larger than a … a door. Not perfectly rectangular, but about that size. A steady wind blew along the slope, whistling a fitful melody as I climbed toward the crater, panting, and feeling strangely hollow inside. I reminded myself that I was too far and hidden from the others to collapse at this point.

And how to describe what I discovered? An object, an idea, a mission. Madness and sanity become one. Of all people, I recalled my advisor in grad school. Who's to say what's possible and impossible? he lectured.

Cosmologically speaking, he meant. Sub-atomically speaking, too. In a universe of unpredictable particles, ghostly antimatter, super-cluster galaxies beyond comprehension. He confided to me that when a scientist says something is possible, he or she is almost certainly correct. And when a scientist says something is impossible, he or she is almost certainly incorrect. That damned almost, I replied. That damned almost.

And so, an imagined possibility became real for me that day. That is what I found. And so much more. But first, the imagined possibility: a white hole. Spewed from a snow-covered hillside in Antarctica. Yes, a white hole. Heretofore a theoretical thing. A calculated creation. A solution to one of Einstein's field equations. An abstraction. Now, a smoldering crater the size of a door. A skewed, four-sided portal. With an object nestled inside.

But first the portal—the white hole. The theoretical opposite of a black hole. As in a white hole is to a black hole as ... personally, I think of waterfalls. A waterfall. A waterfall with a high point and a low point. Its high point: a black hole. Its low point: a white hole. The waterfall's channel: the enchanted banks of spacetime. Its contents, not water, but time itself and all the occasions, events, and incidences embedded therein.

And the object inside?

Fitima's story. Her reminder: We see the world by force of habit. Learning to see it differently is our greatest challenge. Her story, the seed of my recurring nightmare: I'm somewhere, anywhere, outside, standing at the bottom of a spiraling staircase that ascends skyward. I look up. I can't help but look up. Children stand on the steps ... alone, in pairs, all silent and motionless. Boys, girls, black, white, tall, short, younger, or older. But all children. They wear white gowns that hang like vestments on frozen figurines. I feel sick with gnawing grief—an actual pain that remains even after I awake. I'm saddened by the children's penetrating stare, virtually through me. My sorrow grows until the sadness becomes unbearable, and I'm about to cry out. I *try* to cry out, and I awaken.

I awakened one morning, months after my last nightmare—months after I'd left Antarctica and had retired from my professional world. I awakened one morning to yet another beginning. I decided to meet this G.G. Gregory—this young budding virologist—and determine if I could persuade him to redirect his work. Of course, there was the risk he could mislead me. But I had to try. My conscience demanded it. I had to pursue a peaceful approach before I could consider Fitima's expectation. Before I could commit the sin she and her cohort had entrusted me to commit.

***

I found Gregory with the information Fitima forwarded. He was living off-campus in a neighborhood heavily populated by students in a mid-sized midwestern city. He'd recently withdrawn from the state-supported doctoral program in virology. No need to name the university. Or the city. I'm following Fitima's request to avoid revealing proper nouns. She argued that revealing names would serve no useful purpose and could do irreparable harm.

She convinced me. I accepted her request and avoided identifiers. Except for mine, of course. And Gregory's.

I discovered it was easy to rise above my mistrust of anonymity and to loosen my devotion to Transparency. And I discovered I could circumvent my aversion to deception and devise a convincing pretext for meeting Gregory. He'd dropped out of his doctoral program only a few months before he was scheduled to defend his dissertation. This much was known from the Repository. But there was no recorded data as to why he'd withdrawn. After he left the university, he steered clear of academic institutions. He passed up independent research centers, private foundations, and government agencies that might have supported his research. Instead, he went underground.

My plan was to meet him before he was known to have disappeared. I'd be able to try and convince him to … to what? Redirect his fate? Redirect my own.

My plan was to pose as a freelance writer working on a critical essay on doctoral study in the sciences. No one quits a doctoral program only months before receiving the final prize without fundamental misgivings about the enterprise. Gregory had made continual progress toward his degree until he suddenly quit. As a recent and early retiree, I could claim my own bona fides as a disgruntled scientist.

"I'm no activist," Gregory told me when I first approached him about my project. "I have no ax to grind against my adviser or my committee. Or the department or university, for that matter. I'm sure you've heard the expression *it is what it is*? That's all there is to my story."

"Great," I replied. "That's exactly where I'd like to start. Excavating the *it*."

Eventually, the idea caught on. I believe my scholarly approach intrigued him. Also, I think his being my first interviewee pleased him. And if I'm a reasonable judge of these things, I believe he liked me. Or perhaps he just liked my story. My disgruntled scientist story. That I, also not an activist, was willing to walk away from my profession prior to eligibility for retirement and launch an investigation of what was wrong with our profession. He believed his contribution to my project wouldn't be a waste of his time, and I was eager to accept his subdued approval.

We scheduled our first and only meeting at his apartment, a one-bedroom walk-up that reminded me of my life as a grad student. Three black leather armchairs were spaced symmetrically around a low coffee table that held a paradoxically elegant cubic sculpture. He'd divided the apartment into three zones by hanging gauzy white curtains at entrances to the kitchen, bedroom, and parlor. Several fix-focused cameras blinked in the corners of his ceilings and a state-of-the-art com-desk faced a blank wall in the parlor.

He had no patience for small talk and introduced me immediately to the supervisors of his work, concluding with his adviser.

"She wanted me to think newer," he said. "More innovative. Cutting-edge. Novel, even."

"I never thought of novelty as essential in your field." I didn't know how to gauge his deadpan expression. "But what do I know?" I added.

"Let me translate," he said. "Novelty is code for bigger budget grant proposals."

"After all, there are bills to be paid," I said.

He offered the faintest hint of a smile or, perhaps, a smirk.

"You know what I'm talking about," he said. "You worked with the highest tech of all."

"I know funding's essential," I said. "You can't get anywhere without it. Were you able to attract what you needed?"

"For my work? Yes. To bankroll their overhead, no."

"You're too young to be that jaded."

"Old enough to know how to do more with less," he said. "And there are advantages to self-reliance."

"Like?"

"Less oversight. Low-tech is less threatening. Less interesting to bad actors."

"Anarchists?"

"*Hostes humani generis.* Enemies of humanity. Use your imagination." He stared at me as if waiting for another guess from me.

"I was," I said. "Using my imagination. Best I could do."

He shrugged, disappointed.

"Even so, you quit," I said. "Right before the big payoff … your degree. Was there a tipping point? A final straw?"

He took a deep breath, and I sensed his summoning a deeply personal belief. At least that was my hope.

"At some point you realize you don't need their degree," he said. "You realize you can do what you want to do without it. On your own. It's so … so liberating."

"I understand. That's fine. But the degree doesn't take that freedom away from you."

"No, not materially. But the degree itself is demeaning. Spiritually. It stands as stark proof of your obedience to authority. I didn't want that.

And I didn't want them to have it." He leaned forward and I forced myself not to tilt back from him.

"I assumed I'd be preaching to the choir," he said. "A fellow dissident."

"Standard questions," I said. "Routine, actually. But I have to say you're unique. You haven't worked long enough to be overworked. That's the complaint I expect to hear. Being overworked and underpaid. And over-surveilled."

"I have no quarrel with security. We're studying viruses, after all. In our field you better get used to surveillance."

"Let Transparency reveal," I said. "Reveal something, in any event."

I was fishing, admittedly, and caught a hint of derision in his tone. "Something?"

"There's the thing," he said. "And then there's the image of the thing."

He rose suddenly from his chair, surprising me, and walked into the kitchen. He stood behind the gauze curtain between the kitchen and the parlor and turned off the kitchen lights. His silhouette picked up a knife and ran it across his throat."

"Pardon the melodrama," he said from the kitchen. "But I'm trying to make a point. Images don't always reveal reality. Yet sometimes image is all we have."

The knife clanged loudly in the kitchen sink. "Can I get you a beer?"

I swallowed my no-thank-you, emitting only a grunt.

He returned with two bottles, unscrewed the caps, and slid one bottle in front of me. "The thing and the image of the thing," Gregory continued. "Truth depends on understanding. On how we see the world. And how we see the world depends on how our associates see the world."

"Friends. Family."

"Accomplices, if you will."

He leaned forward and narrowed his eyes on mine. "My goal was never to collect grant money. And it wasn't to pass anybody's inspection. Or even to get a degree. My goal was to discover a mission larger than myself. Much larger."

He settled back and grinned widely.

"And you found it," I said.

He swiped a hand over the cube on the coffee table.

"A stunning piece," I said.

"Flawless optical glass," he said. "Yet not its finest quality."

The cube, measuring about two to three hundred millimeters laterally, began to shimmer from within.

"It's personalized," he said. "Attuned to my biometrics. Better than a monogram."

The object's sides seemed to expand, the cube growing in volume, and I glanced around the room for the apparatus that would account for the mirage.

Gregory cleared his throat to recapture my attention. "When you see a rose," he said, "you don't see petals, leaves, and stem."

I turned back to him but quickly returned to the cube. It was still growing larger.

"You see these things, of course," he continued, "but what you really *see* is a flower. A rose."

I glanced between Gregory and the expanding cube and shook my head. "I don't see it."

"Don't think literally," he said. "Think metaphorically. Think metaphorically about watching a dancer. You don't see arms, legs, and torso. Again, you see these things, but what you actually see is a dancer. You see the dancer's movement. And if you watch long enough, closely enough, you see unity among those movements."

Again, I shook my head, staring at the cube which had stopped expanding. Now it seemed to transform from within, dividing and subdividing into smaller and smaller cubes of variegated hues, each turning slowly, yet revealing nothing as figurative as Gregory had mentioned—no flower, no dancer.

"I'm sorry," I began, "but I don't—"

"That's what seeing is," he said. "We must create unity to truly see. We must discover union among disparate elements. Seeing is believing wholeness is out there. The trick is finding it."

The smaller cubes inside the expanded one began to blend and become abstract patterns and then shapes I recognized, but nothing similar to what Gregory had spoken of. Instead, a landscape began to form ... a grassy meadow with tree-like flora in the background traversed by a narrow stream spanned by a footbridge. Shapes that appeared human emerged in the scene, becoming, unmistakably, images of men and women and children, in groups and solitary, walking side by side, in single file, or past each other, and then suddenly, shockingly, passing through each other like ghosts melding and separating in a slow macabre dance.

"And this is what, exactly?" I said.

"A vision of an alternative reality. Brian Lazzara's reality," he said pointing to the cube. "The artist who composed this diorama—this electrodynamic diorama. He considers people as separate *and* connected. Not either-or. Both-and."

"Are you talking about collective consciousness?" I asked, thinking about the survivors of the virus this man might design.

"Exactly," Gregory said. "Units of consciousness—individual and united. The next stage, dare I say *final*, of human evolution."

One of the figures in the expanded cube, a middle-aged man, stepped free of the frame and strode toward me, through me, and I shuddered at the sinking sensation in my chest. A sudden, fleeting shock of falling, and I turned to look behind me in time to see him disappear.

Gregory chuckled softly. "Lazzara wants to blur the distinction between you, the observer, and whoever you observe. He wants us to think of human consciousness," he paused to fix his eyes on mine, "as singular and plural."

It took a moment to catch my breath. "Do you have other works of his?"

Gregory shook his head. "Doctoral fellowships don't pay much. Besides, Lazzara didn't create many pieces. He probably recognized there are limits as to how much he could urge one-world consciousness onto a world that glorifies one-upmanship."

I let his accusation linger, hoping to hear him elaborate his point. "What do *you* see?" I asked. "What do you see in his work?"

"Is not all one?" he said with the devilish lift of an eyebrow.

"That depends on who you mean by all. Do you mean everyone? Or only a select few?"

He leaned back and studied me. "Good intuition, sir."

I shook my head, thinking only of Fitima's story. "There are among us," I said, "self-proclaimed angels prepared to cull the alleged evil from the professed righteous."

"Great intuition," he said.

I glanced up at the blinking camera in the corner of the ceiling. Gregory understood my meaning.

"I *want* our observers to see and hear us," he said. "Keeping in mind what you and I have discussed. That the truth of what they see is limited by their understanding. They can know this and yet still not overcome their deficiency."

I hadn't heard Gregory's plans for his designer virus, but I'd heard all I needed to hear. His words, his tone, his confidence. His commitment. They told me all I needed to know to see the path I needed to follow.

And so, as he expanded on the limitations of Transparency, I imagined I was listening to a ghost—a ghost who'd yet to discover his own demise. Because at that very moment he convinced me he was capable of hatching the disaster Fitima had described even as he revealed his blindness to the fate that awaited him.

***

Of course, conceiving Gregory's assassination was not the same as performing it. Could I actually commit murder? My memory of the iceberg floating past me like the Tablets of Stone returned again and again. An omen? A reminder? Thou shall not kill. Who was I to question a commandment? Thou shall not kill. Why not? In order to preserve life. But what if killing would preserve life? Killing, not for revenge, or material gain, or catharsis. But killing in the service of life.

I tried to convince myself that killing Gregory would be a noble act. But I was not well-practiced at lying. Especially to myself. Murder had been the tool of a thousand scoundrels. False prophets. Psychotics. I tried to believe that the end I sought justified the means. But there were no guarantees. I didn't believe in them. I believed in hope. Some hopes are fulfilled, some fail. Some succeed and fail. They achieve their goal along with a myriad of unintended consequences. Some good, some bad.

In the end, however, I had to act simply because I couldn't not-act. I couldn't live with myself and do nothing about what I'd learned. For me, there'd be no searching for support from others. No soliciting accomplices. I would do my best on my own. As I'd been implored.

***

I insisted on taking the stand. Why wouldn't I? Wasn't I presumed innocent unless proven guilty? And if I was innocent, shouldn't I stand up for my innocence? That's what any jury would expect. Besides, I wished for that jury a story less dreadful than the DA's. He chose vehicular homicide as the story. I chose tragic accident. I believed the jury, the community, deserved to hear my narrative.

So I testified. I told the jury I didn't see Gregory in the crosswalk. I didn't know what I'd hit until I stopped the car and walked back to see. As was clearly captured on camera.

Earlier, my lawyer reminded them of that corner's notorious history. Cars parked there obstruct drivers' view. Especially in the morning before work. That's why the city installed traffic cameras. To detect traffic problems. To determine ways to correct those problems ... and, unavoidably, to record any and all activity there. Like my passage through that intersection at legal speed. My stopping and returning to the victim. My kneeling, leaning over him, whispering to him. I wanted to see if he was alive, I told the jury. And no, I didn't consider returning to my car to call for help. I assumed help would arrive too late. So I prayed for him. I prayed for both of us. It turned out I was right. He died as I held him.

Yes, I knew him, I told the jury. That was the basis for the DA's charge. That I knew him and had every intention of doing him harm. Killing him, in fact.

So, I admitted knowing him from the time I moved into his building. Even before I'd moved there. There was ample evidence of our encounters, in his apartment, in mine. That was my truest confession: that I continued to meet Gregory after our bogus interview in my vain effort to redirect his ambitions. So yes, I had to admit his name appeared in my com-desk files. And yes, often … very often. I followed his work, I told them. I followed him. Scientists do that—follow each other's work. Even those in very different fields … him a virologist and me an astronomer. Our former work, in any event.

So, yes, we had a history. A history of hostility, as one tenant testified. Loud quarrels, she said, from both of our apartments. The D.A.'s initial interviews with her triggered his suspicions.

I reminded the jury that Dr. Gregory and I had worked in different fields. There was little for us to fight over professionally. Besides, one observer's hostility is another's minor dispute.

There are lots of disputes in this world, I said.

"But few people are murdered over them," the DA shot back.

"Thank God for that," I said.

The courtroom went silent. In the lull, I glanced at my lawyer, thankful to have her. You need an unwavering ally when your adversary is convinced he's right and you're wrong. Worse: when he's convinced he's righteous and you're corrupt.

Revenge, the DA barked while cross-examining me. You sought revenge against Gregory.

He was wrong about that, of course. Revenge never entered my mind. And he had no proof that it had. True, he had evidence of Gregory's presence in my life. He pointed out the repeated appearance of Gregory's name in my files. He presented the tenant's testimony of our frequent quarrels. He displayed my tracing of Gregory's early morning jogging route which he'd discovered on my com-desk. He played and replayed the recording of my voiceless vigil over Gregory's dying body.

All circumstantial, of course. Sufficient to charge me with vehicular homicide, perhaps, but not sufficient to convict. None of it as believable as my story. The infamously dangerous intersection. The blinding angle of the sun that time of morning. My impeccable record: drug-free, crime-free. And if not the DA's notion of my seeking revenge, what could possibly have been my motive?

Of course, no one would've believed me if I had confessed. That a cry for help from the future could prompt a man to commit murder. That I could kill a man because I believed prevention is better than cure. That prevention is better than grief—a world of it, an age of it.

Would you assassinate Hitler, Pol Pot, Stalin was more than a carefree parlor debate for me. I mean, a recreational question a host might ask dinner guests. Would you have killed Vasili Blokhin before his war crimes, assuming you'd heard of him, if you could get away with it?

Well, that was a hypothetical I had to consider. Could I get away with assassinating a mass murderer? I realized I could. I learned that one failed prosecution would render me immune from a second prosecution for the same alleged offense. Furthermore, statutes of limitation and limits against self-incrimination would allow me to tell my story in due time. So, I could delete humanity's future archenemy and deliver Fitima's story... and the role she prayed I'd play in it. My belief in Transparency still had that much of a hold on me.

After my acquittal, the jury declined to speak with the media. My attorney made up for their silence. While we're happy for our client, she announced, there are no unharmed victors in this case. Mr. Gregory has passed on and so has his potential contribution to science... to .... Her assistant whispered in her ear. She took a breath and continued ... Dr. Gregory's potential contributions to virology have died with him. Throughout this trial my hope was to achieve justice for the defendant and the deceased. Today our legal system has exonerated my client and ... and this is important, it has not dishonored Dr. Gregory's legacy by issuing a false conviction.

Later, a young reporter asked me to fill in the gaps my attorney left blank. For human interest purposes, she claimed. I thanked my lawyer, of course. Eternally grateful was how I described myself. I also thanked the jury. I suggested that local citizens do something about that dangerous intersection. A small legacy I could admit to.

The reporter asked if I felt the ordeal had changed me. Again, for human interest purposes. Yes, I told her. The ordeal had changed me. I'd have to live with the incident, the accident, for the rest of my life. Absently, I mentioned I'd had several life-changing experiences.

She asked if I'd care to elaborate.

"Human interest?" I asked.

"Background," she replied.

I wondered what she'd make of Fitima's story. Of my receiving that story on an isolated snowbank while hunting neutrinos in Antarctica.

I shook my head. I didn't care to elaborate, I told her.

"Any response to the DA's promise?" she asked. "The vow he made at his press conference?"

"I hadn't heard his promise. I'd parted ways with my adversary as soon as the verdict was announced."

"His declaration of all-out war on crime," she said. "His newfound duty, he called it. His duty to deploy all legal means at law enforcement's disposal against lawlessness."

An accelerant to global surveillance? I thought.

"Your acquittal really riled him," the reporter continued. "He told us he liked the sound of *The Honorable* in front of his surname. All he had to do now," he said, "was earn that title. He vowed he would."

I asked if she believed he'd have much support. She shrugged.

I can't say, even now, why her shrug brought on my sobs. She put her arms around my shoulder, trying to console me, expressing her regrets over the trial's toll on me, until I, too, assumed the weight of the trial had finally come crashing down on me.

But that wasn't why I wept. I wept because I knew it was impossible to take advantage of a second chance if you don't know you've been offered one. Was human history redeemable? I'd been reminded by the reporter's shrug that despite my maniacal hope that humanity could be saved, fanatical enough for me to commit murder, I was, in fact, unsure. I had drifted from a world of hope to one filled with doubt, and I'd remain stranded there for the rest of my days. After which, the Executor of my Will is charged to make public Fitima's story and mine.

I'll suggest the title "Tomorrow Turns to Yesterday." Or, perhaps, "Cities of Glass."

About the Author

Roger Collins is an African American clinical psychologist and received his B.A. in psychology at Yale College and his PhD in clinical psychology at Harvard University. He is a Professor Emeritus at the University of Cincinnati where he received the university's Cohen Award for Excellence in Teaching. Recognized for integrating fiction into his psychology courses, he moved from assigning fiction to writing fiction; short stories at first, and eventually stage plays, and finally a novel. His short stories and short dramas have been published in a variety of literary journals and his stage plays have been produced in Cincinnati and Dayton, Ohio, Fort Thomas, Kentucky, Brooklyn, NY, and San Francisco, CA. "Cities of Glass" is his debut novel. He currently lives in Cincinnati, Ohio with his spouse, Patricia, when they not visiting their daughter, Valerie and her family in Colorado.

ALL THINGS THAT MATTER PRESS

FOR MORE INFORMATION ON TITLES AVAILABLE FROM

ALL THINGS THAT MATTER PRESS, GO TO

http://allthingsthatmatterpress.com

or contact us at

allthingsthatmatterpress@gmail.com

If you enjoyed this book, please post a review on Amazon.com

and your favorite social media sites.

Thank you!

Made in the USA
Monee, IL
18 July 2022

99941683R00154